A NECESSARY
EVIL

ALEX KAVA

A NECESSARY EVIL

MIRA®

MIRA

ISBN 0-7783-2274-2

A NECESSARY EVIL

Printed in U.S.A.

ACKNOWLEDGMENTS

Once again, many thanks to all the professionals who generously gave of their time and expertise. If I've gotten any of the facts wrong or have creatively manipulated a fact or two, it's my doing and not theirs. Also special thanks to my family and friends who continue to support me despite my long absences.

My appreciation and special thanks go to:

Deborah Groh Carlin for your love and support, but also for your constant help in researching, brainstorming and making sense of the puzzle pieces along the way, not to mention putting up with my annoying "writer quirks." You are a true friend and partner in crime.

Amy Moore-Benson, my agent and friend, for being my advocate and being there time after time no matter how small the question or how difficult the problem.

Feroze Mohammed, my editor, for challenging me to make this my best book yet.

Patricia Kava, my good Catholic mother, who allows me to tackle tough subjects in my novels, all the while lighting candles for me.

Emilie Carlin for your love and support, but also for sharing your own wonderful stories and making them such a delight to listen to.

Leigh Ann Retelsdorf, Deputy County Attorney and friend, for being my go-to person whenever I have a "killer-of-a-question."

Detective Sergeant Bill Jadlowski of the Omaha Police Department for inspiring the creation of Detective Tommy Pakula.

Christopher Kava, my nephew, for helping me understand teenage boys and their computer obsessions…er, I mean…computer skills.

Mary Means for taking such good care of my kids while I'm on the road.

Sharon Car, fellow writer and friend, for being there no matter how much time passes between our lunch dates.

Marlene Haney and Sandy Rockwood for your unconditional love, support and friendship.

Patti El-Kachouti for always being there.

Patti Bremmer, fellow writer, and her husband, Martin, for your friendship and inspiration.

Patricia Sierra and her mother, Kay, for cheering up and cheering on and always at just the right times.

Father Dave Korth for exemplifying the very best of your profession and being a constant reminder of good.

A special thank-you to my new friends and neighbors in the Florida Panhandle for showing me what true strength and perseverance look like while we picked up the pieces after Hurricane Ivan and then did it all over again after Hurricane Dennis.

And last, but certainly not least, thank you to all the librarians, bookstore owners and managers, book buyers and sellers around the country and around the world for recommending my books.

This book is dedicated to all you faithful readers who insisted on the return of Father Keller.

From San Mateo, California, to Pittsburgh, Pennsylvania, from McCook, Nebraska, to Milan, Italy—it didn't matter where I went or which of my five books I was promoting—readers always asked the same question: "When are you going to take care of Father Keller?"

I must confess that five years ago when I wrote *A Perfect Evil*, I never dreamed it would make such an impact on so many of you. And so this book, *A Necessary Evil*, is dedicated to all of you who have patiently waited for this long-overdue sequel.

Please consider this book my thank-you for an invaluable lesson that as writers and storytellers we do have the ability to breathe life into characters—characters who otherwise live only in our imaginations. And with that ability comes, perhaps, a certain responsibility to allow those characters to continue to breathe, to speak, to grow and even to be brought to justice.

A NECESSARY
EVIL

It is necessary only for the good to do nothing for evil to triumph.
—Edmund Burke

CHAPTER 1

Friday, July 2
Eppley Airport
Omaha, Nebraska

Monsignor William O'Sullivan was certain no one had recognized him. So why was his forehead damp? He hadn't gone through the security checkpoint yet. Instead, he had decided to wait until it got closer to his flight time. Just in case someone did recognize him. On this side, he could still pretend to be picking up a colleague rather than admit he was leaving.

He fidgeted in the plastic chair, clutching the leather portfolio closer to his chest. So close, so tight it seemed to crush his lungs, causing that pain again, a pain he may have dismissed too quickly as heartburn. But of course, it was only heartburn. He simply wasn't used to eating such a large meal for lunch, but he knew the flight to New York and the later one to Rome would include cardboard renditions of food, causing much more damage to his overly sensitive stomach than Sophia's leftover meat loaf and mashed potatoes did.

Yes, surely the leftovers were responsible for his discomfort, he told himself, and yet his eyes darted around the busy airport terminal, looking for a bathroom. He remained seated, not wanting to move until he examined and found an acceptable path. He shoved a thumb and index finger up under his wire-rim glasses to dig the fatigue out of his eyes, and then he began his search again.

He'd avoid the shortest route, not wanting to pass the exotic black woman handing out "reading material"—as she called it—to anyone too polite to say no. She wore colorful beads in her hair, what looked like her Sunday best dress with splashes of purple that made her hips even larger, but sensible shoes. Her smooth, deep voice almost made it a song when she asked, "Can I offer you some reading material?" And to everyone—including those who huffed their responses and rushed by—she greeted them with yet another melodic, polite stanza, "You have a most pleasant day."

Monsignor O'Sullivan knew what her reading material was without seeing it. He supposed she was a sort of present-day missionary, in her own right. If he passed her, would she sense their connection? Both of them ministers, distributors of God's word. One in sensible shoes, another with a portfolio stuffed with secrets.

Better to avoid her.

He checked the Krispy Kreme counter. A long line of zombies waited patiently for their afternoon dose of energy, like drug addicts getting one more shot before their flight. To his right he watched the bookstore entrance, quickly glancing away when a young man in a baseball cap looked in his direction. Had the youth recognized him, despite his street clothes? His stomach churned while his eyes studied his shoes. His cotton-knit polo—a gift from his sister—was now sticking to his wet back. Over the loudspeakers came the repetitive message, warning travelers not to leave their luggage unattended. He clutched the portfolio, only now discovering that his palms were also slick with sweat. How in the world had he believed he could just leave without being noticed? That he could just get on a plane and be free, be absolved of all his indiscretions.

But when Monsignor O'Sullivan dared to look again, the young man was gone. Passengers rushed by without a glance. Even the black woman greeting and passing out her reading material seemed totally unaware of his presence.

Paranoid. He was just being paranoid. *Thirty-seven years of dedication to the church and what did he get for it?* Accusations and finger-pointing when he deserved accolades of respect and gratitude. When he tried to explain his predicament to his sister, the anger had overwhelmed him, and all he had managed to tell her in their brief conversation was to have the title of the family's estate changed to her name only. "I won't let those bastards take our home."

He wished he were there now. It was nothing extravagant— a two-story split-timber on three acres in the middle of Connecticut, with walking trails surrounded by trees and mountains and sky. It was the only place he felt closest to God, and the irony made him smile. The irony that beautiful cathedrals and huge congregations had led him further and further away from God.

A squawk coming from near the escalator startled him back to reality. It sounded like a tropical bird, but was instead a toddler in full temper tantrum, his mother pulling him along, unfazed, as if she couldn't hear the screech. It grated on Monsignor O'Sullivan's nerves, scratching them raw and resetting the tension so tight in his jaw that he feared he'd start grinding his teeth. It was enough to get him to his feet. He no longer cared about accessible paths, and he made his way to the restroom.

Thankfully, it was empty, yet he glanced under every stall to make certain. He set the portfolio at his feet, leaning it against his left leg, as if needing to maintain some contact. He removed his glasses and placed them on the corner of the sink. Then, avoiding his own blurred reflection, he waved his hands under the faucet, his frustration fueled by the lack of response. He swiped his hands back and forth, finally eliciting a short burst of water, barely wetting his fingertips. He swiped again. Another short burst. This time he closed his eyes and splashed as much as he could on his face, the cool dampness beginning to calm his nausea, beginning to quiet the sudden throbbing in his temples.

His hands groped for the paper-towel dispenser, ripping off more than he needed and gently dabbing, disgusted by the smell and harsh feel of the recycled paper. He hadn't even heard the bathroom door open. When he glanced in the mirror, Monsignor O'Sullivan was startled to see a blurred figure standing behind him.

"I'm almost finished," he said, thinking he might be in the way, though there were other sinks. Why did he need to use this one? He noticed a faint metallic odor. Perhaps it was a member of the cleaning crew. An impatient one at that. He reached for his glasses, accidentally knocking them to the floor. Before he could bend down to retrieve them, an arm came around his waist. All he saw was a glint of silver. Then he felt the burn, the streak of pain, shooting up through his chest.

At the same time there was a whisper in his right ear—soft and gentle. "You're already finished, Monsignor O'Sullivan."

CHAPTER 2

Washington, D.C.

There was no easy way to pick up a human head.

At least that's what Special Agent Maggie O'Dell had decided. She watched the scene below and sympathized with the young crime lab technician. Maggie wondered if that was exactly what he was thinking as he squatted in the mud, looking at it from yet another angle. Even Detective Julia Racine remained quiet, standing over him, but unable to offer any of her regular advice. It was the quietest Maggie had ever seen the detective.

Stan Wenhoff, chief medical examiner for the District, yelled down an instruction or two, but stayed beside Maggie on top of the embankment, not making any attempt to find a way down. Actually Maggie was surprised to see Stan on a Friday afternoon, especially at the beginning of a holiday weekend. Normally he would have sent one of his deputies, except that he wouldn't want to miss out on making headlines. And this case would certainly start making headlines now.

Maggie looked beyond the riverbank, out at the water and

the city on the other side. Despite the usual terror alerts, the District was preparing for the weekend festivities, expecting sunny skies and cooler-than-average temperatures. Not that she had any big plans beyond lounging in the backyard with Harvey. She'd throw a couple of steaks on the grill, read the latest Jeffery Deaver.

She tucked a strand of hair behind her ear though the breeze immediately tugged another one free. Yes, it was an absolutely beautiful summer day, except for the decapitated head some-one had discarded on the muddy riverbank. What level of evil did it take to slice another person's head completely off and leave it like a piece of trash? Her friend, Gwen Patterson, ac-cused her of having an obsession with evil. Maggie didn't look at it so much as an obsession as an age-old quest. She had de-cided long ago that it was part of her job to root out evil and destroy it.

"Finish going through the surrounding surface," Stan called down. "Then just scoop it up into a bag."

Maggie glanced at Stan. Scoop it up? Easy for him to say from up here where his polished shoes were safe and the waft of death hadn't yet arrived. But even from above, Maggie could see it was a daunting task. The riverbank was littered with cans and discarded take-out containers and wrappers. She knew the area—this stretch under the overpass—well enough to know there were also cigarette butts, condoms and a needle or two. The killer had taken a risk, discarding the head in such a well-trafficked area.

Ordinarily Maggie would find herself assessing that risk as the killer's apparent disorganization. Taking risks could amount to simple panic. But since this was the third head to show up in the District in three weeks, Maggie knew this had little to do with panic and everything to do with the killer's twisted strategy.

"You mind if I come down and take a closer look?" Mag-gie called down.

Racine shrugged. "Help yourself," she said, but she came

to the bottom of the embankment and offered her arm for leverage. Maggie waved her off.

She searched instead for anything—branches, rocks, roots—to hang on to. There was nothing but river mud and tall grass. She didn't have much choice but to slip and slide. Like a skier without poles, she tried to keep her balance, managing to stay on her feet, skidding past Racine, but stopping within inches of ending up in the Potomac.

Racine shook her head, a slight smirk on her lips, but thankfully didn't say anything. Maggie didn't need to be reminded that perhaps she went a bit overboard when it came to Racine, not wanting to accept any favors, or worse, feel she needed to repay a debt. She and Racine had had enough challenges and obstacles in the last several years. And more importantly, they were even. That's where Maggie wanted to leave it.

Maggie tried to clean her shoes of the clumps of mud, rubbing them against the tall grass, not wanting to bring any more foreign particles to the scene. Her leather flats would be ruined. She was careless about shoes, often forgetting her slip-on boots. Gwen constantly warned her that her treatment of shoes bordered on irreverence. It reminded Maggie of Stan's shiny, polished ones, and she glanced back up the embankment, noticing that he had backed away from the edge. Was he worried she may have started a mud slide, or did he want to make sure no one expected him to follow her path? Either way, she knew he wouldn't be coming down.

Julia Racine caught Maggie looking up.

"Heaven forbid he gets his shoes dirty," Racine said under her breath as if reading Maggie's thoughts. But her eyes and attention quickly returned to the decapitated head as she added, "It's got to be the same killer. But we may have gotten lucky this time."

Maggie had only recently seen pieces of the case files on the other two heads. This was her first invitation to the crime scene, now that Racine and Chief Henderson suspected they might have a serial killer on their hands.

"Why lucky?" Maggie finally asked when it became obvious that's what Racine was waiting for. Some things never changed, like Racine demanding everyone's attention before she announced her brilliant theories.

"Getting that tip allowed us to get here before the critters finished their snack. The other two were down to the bone. We still haven't been able to identify them."

Maggie swiped her shoes against the grass one last time and came closer. Then the smell hit her like a blast of hot air. The mixture of scents that accompanied death was difficult for Maggie to describe, always the same and yet always different, depending on the surroundings. There was the faint metallic smell of blood, but this time overpowered by that of rotting flesh and the muck of river mud. She hesitated, but only for a second or two, focusing instead on the grisly scene less than three feet in front of her.

From above on the embankment she had thought there was a tangle of algae and muddy grass holding the head in place. Now she could see it was actually the victim's long hair, twisted and wrapped around the back of the head, allowing the face to stare up at the clear blue sky. A little closer still, and Maggie could see that *stare* was not the correct word. The eyelids seemed to flutter as dozens of milky-white maggots pushed and shoved their way into the eye sockets. Even the victim's lips appeared to be moving as if allowing one last whisper, but it was rather the slow-moving masses of maggots. They were pouring from the woman's nostrils too, unrelenting, determined and focused on their task of devouring their prize from the inside out.

Maggie waved at the lingering blowflies and squatted opposite the crime lab tech to get an almost eye-level view. Beyond the buzzing flies, this close she could hear the squishing sound as the maggots pushed and shoved at each other to squeeze inside the various orifices. There was a sort of sucking sound, too.

God, she hated maggots.

During her early days as an FBI newbie when she had no fear and much to prove, at the request—or rather the dare—of a medical examiner, she had put her hand into a corpse's maggot-filled mouth to retrieve the victim's driver's license. It had been the killer's trademark and not an unusual one, allowing his victims their identities even though he stuffed them down their throats. Ever since then it was still difficult for her, whenever she saw maggots up close and personal, to not feel that sticky trail of slime they had left all over her hands and up her arms as they quickly grasped at self-preservation and began sucking at her own flesh.

But now, sitting back on muddy heels, she knew what Racine meant about getting lucky this time. Despite all the movement, Maggie could see clumps of yellow-white eggs stuffed in the victim's ears and at the corners of her lips and eyes. Not all of the maggots had hatched yet and those that had were in their first stage, which meant the head couldn't have been here more than a day or two.

In the July heat, Maggie knew the process moved quickly. As disgusted by them as she was, she had learned to also have a healthy respect. She knew adult blowflies could sense blood from up to three miles away. They would have arrived in a matter of hours of death. As disgusting as flies on a corpse look, the flies eat very little. They're more interested in laying their eggs in the dark, moist areas of the corpse, reducing what was once a warm, living, breathing human being to a warm, moist host.

The eggs hatch within a day or two and immediately the baby maggots start to devour everything down to the bone. While working a case in Connecticut, Professor Adam Bonzado had told her that three flies could lay enough eggs and produce enough maggots to devour a body as quickly as a full-grown lion. Amazing, Maggie thought, how efficient and organized the creatures of nature were.

Yes, Racine was right. This time they had lucked out. There would be enough tissue left for DNA samples. But more importantly, there might be telltale signs embedded or bruised or hidden in the flesh, the last remains of this poor woman to tell them what had happened to her in her final hours.

Unfortunately, though, for the crime scene tech, his greatest challenge would be to contain the head and maggots. It'd be so much easier to brush them off, rinse, spray, fumigate the head and be rid of the pesky things, but cleaning away the maggots could mean washing away evidence.

Maggie looked around for footprints, tracks of any kind.

"How do you think she got here?" she asked, remembering to personalize the victim instead of falling into Stan's habit of using "it," something that could simply be "scooped up." But she knew it wasn't irreverence as much as it was a coping mechanism.

The crime scene tech followed Stan's lead. "It wasn't tossed—not from the overpass, not from the ledge of the embankment. I can't see any impact marks or skids in the mud. It looks like he simply placed it here."

"So, the killer brought her down here himself?" She glanced back at the steep embankment, but saw only her own skid marks.

"From what I can tell." The tech stood, stretched his legs and looked grateful for the distraction. "There are some footprints. I'll make a plaster cast."

"Oh, yeah, the footprints," Racine said. "You've got to see this." She stepped carefully, pointing out the remnants of the impressions in the mud.

Maggie stood up and looked to where Racine pointed, except it was almost fifteen feet from the victim's head.

"How can you be sure they're the killer's?"

"We haven't found any others," the tech replied, shrugging. "It rained pretty hard two nights ago. He had to have been out here after that."

"The prints come out of nowhere," Racine said. "And get this—they seem to lead right into the river."

"Maybe a boat?" Maggie suggested.

"Out here? And not be noticed? I don't think so."

"You said you had a tip?" Maggie examined the oversize prints. The tread marks were pronounced, but there was no recognizable logo.

"Yup," Racine said, crossing her arms as if finally feeling more in control. "An anonymous call. A woman actually. Called 911. I have no idea how the hell she found out. Maybe the killer told her. Maybe he got tired of us being so slow in finding the other two."

"Or maybe he wanted us to know the identity of this one," Maggie said.

Racine nodded, instead of coming up with a competing theory.

"So what do you suppose he does with the rest of the body?" the tech asked both women.

"I don't know." Racine shrugged and began to walk away. "Maybe our anonymous woman caller can tell us. They should have her number tracked down by the time we get back."

CHAPTER 3

Washington, D.C.

Dr. Gwen Patterson tried to see the crime scene from her office window, only she was on the wrong side of the Potomac. Even with binoculars the overpass blocked most of her view. But she could make out Maggie's red Toyota parked up on the road next to the mobile crime lab van.

There was an annoying tremor in her fingers as she ran them through her hair. Was it excitement? Nerves? It didn't matter. She knew the stress was starting to take its toll. And why wouldn't it? Three weeks, three victims. And yet today she had expected to feel a sense of relief. She expected the tension to begin to leave. Except there was no relief. Instead, the knot between her shoulder blades only seemed to tighten. Maybe it was silly to think that just because Maggie was on the case she would feel she had gained some sort of control over the situation. How did she ever let it get this far?

She was meeting Maggie later for dinner at their favorite hideaway—Old Ebbitt's Grill. She'd order the pecan-crusted chicken. Maggie would have steak. Maybe they would share a bottle of wine, depending on Maggie's mood. And her mood would depend on what she had seen down by the river, under the overpass. But it didn't matter. She could count on Maggie sharing with her what evidence had been left behind. Maggie would be her eyes and ears. Gwen would ask questions, play devil's advocate like she usually did. And hopefully Maggie wouldn't recognize that Gwen already knew some of the answers. She could make this work. What other choice did she have?

It was ironic that something like this would happen, now that she had purposely distanced herself from patients and assignments that included criminal behavior. Gwen left the window and glanced at the walls of her office. The sunlight reflected off the glass of her framed credentials, creating prisms of color. A whole wall full of certificates and degrees—and what good were they in a situation like this? Gwen rubbed at her eyes—the lack of sleep was catching up with her, too, but she smiled. Yes, it was also ironic that the older and wiser and perhaps even the more deserving she became, the less those framed credentials mattered.

She was at the top of her game, or at least that's what her colleagues kept telling her as they referenced her articles and books in their own studies and research. All of those hard-earned credentials had gained her entrance to Quantico, the White House and even the Pentagon. She had contacts with United States senators, members of congress, ambassadors and diplomats, many of them patients. Several even had her number on their speed dial. Not bad for a little girl from the Bronx. And yet, here she was, all those contacts and credentials worthless.

The notes had all been brief, the instructions simple, but the threat had been ambiguous, that is, until today. If there had been any doubt before, she knew now that he wouldn't hesitate to follow through on his threat. But finally she would have Maggie. Yes, Maggie could go where Gwen could not. Maggie would describe the crime scene, create a profile and help her figure out who the bastard was. They had done it before, together, plenty of cases where they took the evidence, examined the victims' similarities, considered all of the circumstances and then followed a trail that led them to the killer. She would simply be Maggie's guide, just like the old days when Maggie had first come to Quantico as a forensic fellow.

God, that seemed like a lifetime ago. What had it been? Ten years? Eleven?

Back then Gwen had been Assistant Director Cunningham's number-one independent consultant. She had taken Maggie under her wing, acting as the seasoned mentor, gently pushing her and coaxing her. Despite their age gap, the two of them had become friends, best friends. And yet because of the fifteen years that separated them, Gwen oftentimes found herself in a variety of roles with her best friend—sometimes mentor, sometimes psychologist, sometimes mother. Though the latter still surprised her. She had always believed she didn't have a maternal bone in her body, except when it came to Maggie. Maybe that's why this didn't seem so strange. Perhaps that's exactly why she thought she could pull this off without Maggie knowing, without anyone knowing. Why couldn't Maggie be her surrogate, going places she herself couldn't go, following this killer and yes, even capturing him? All Gwen had to do was lead her to him. She'd beat him at his own game. Could it be that simple? Could it actually work? *It had to work.*

Gwen packed her briefcase, stuffing papers and folders inside without really looking or choosing. Another sign that the fatigue was taking hold. Even her ordinarily pristine desktop looked as if a wind had blown through the office, disheveling the stacks of paper.

She grabbed the cell phone that had been left for her that morning in a plain manila envelope and dropped through the office complex's mail slot. She carefully wiped it down and while still holding it with a paper towel, she placed it in a brown paper sack. On her way home she'd find a Dumpster to toss it into, just as the note had instructed her to do.

CHAPTER 4

Omaha, Nebraska

Gibson McCutty found the back door unlocked, just as he had left it. He stumbled into the kitchen, bumping into the vegetable bin and cursing under his breath when he heard something thump to the floor. He hesitated, listening. It was difficult to hear over his gasps for air.

Why couldn't he breathe?

He had raced all the way from the airport, standing and pedaling, pumping and pushing his Ironman Huffy through red-lighted intersections, ignoring honks and slowing only to climb up the final incline. So of course he was gasping for breath. He just needed to stop for a minute. He leaned against the refrigerator, waiting to catch his breath. He was surprised to feel an immediate sense of comfort from the appliance's familiar noisy hum. He was home. He was safe. At least for now.

He could feel the stupid refrigerator magnets digging into his shoulder blades—annoying little garden creatures his mom used to tack up his brother's "artwork." Like she was even a gardener. No way would she allow dirt under her fingernails. The thought made him smile, and he forced himself to remember each of the magnets, hoping the tactic would block out the image of all that blood. He closed his eyes—bunny, squirrel, raccoon, hedgehog. Was a hedgehog a garden creature? Had anyone really seen a hedgehog?

It wasn't working.

The details had been scorched into his mind—that face all twisted in pain. Blood coming out of his mouth. And those eyes, staring without blinking. Had he recognized Gibson? Had he been able to see him? Of course not. He was dead. Wasn't he?

Gibson shook his head and pushed away from the refrigerator. He stumbled into the living room and stepped over the laundry basket left at the bottom of the staircase. Then he took the steps slowly, counting them out in his mind, stopping when he reached number eight. Using the handrail, he pulled himself up, bypassing the creaky ninth step. Once he made it past his mother's door he was home free. Sometimes she watched the five o'clock news in her room while she changed from work. He couldn't risk her hearing him. How would he explain where he had been? And she would certainly ask, especially when she saw he was one smelly, wet glob. Even his hair was plastered to his sweaty head under his baseball cap.

As he got closer, he didn't hear anything coming from behind her door. Maybe she wasn't home yet. And then he remembered. Of course she wasn't home yet. It was Friday. No work tomorrow, plus tonight was his little brother's sleepover. He remembered her telling him that she might treat herself and join the other ladies from the office for drinks after work. Was that tonight? Yeah, it was Friday night. He was sure of it. What a stroke of luck. Maybe things weren't as bad as he thought.

Still, he hurried to his own room and closed the door behind him, careful to muffle the noise. He tossed his backpack on the bed, then he pressed his entire body against the door as if the extra pressure was necessary to turn the lock. He held his breath and listened again, not trusting his good fortune on a day where none had existed. He heard nothing. He was home alone. He was safe. And yet, he was shaking, not just shivering, but shaking like some convulsing idiot.

He wrapped his arms around his chest, but jerked them away when he felt the wet front of his T-shirt. He really was a sweaty mess. He had almost wiped out on his bike several times as he jumped curbs and sped through blind intersections. Now he pulled off his ball cap and threw it on his bed, then wrestled out of the T-shirt, getting tangled in it and almost ripping it at the seams just to be free of the smell of sweat and diesel and vomit. The stink reminded him that he had upchucked his fast-food meal, leaving it somewhere just past the exit ramp from the airport parking garage.

Finally, he allowed himself to turn on the small desk lamp. Immediately, he noticed the blood caked under his fingernails. He tried to dig it out, wiping it on the T-shirt. Then he opened his closet door, wadded up the T-shirt and stuffed it into an empty Best Buy plastic bag he found on the closet floor. He slung the T-shirt and bag hard into the back of the closet, away from everything else. He knew his mom would never find it. After she discovered the moldy, half-eaten bologna sandwich tucked in his sock drawer, she had threatened that she wouldn't be responsible for any of his things except those in the laundry chute. He supposed she thought it was a way to make him more responsible for taking care of his own things, but he wondered if it was just another way for her to avoid seeing or knowing any negative stuff going on with him.

He kicked his running shoes off without untying them, leaving them in the middle of the floor. That's when he saw the icon flashing on his computer screen. He stared at it, approaching slowly. There wasn't a game scheduled, and any messages usually came through the chat room.

He lowered himself into his desk chair, continuing to stare at the skull-and-bones icon that blinked at him from the corner of the computer screen. Any other time he'd be anxious and excited and ready to play. Instead, he felt his stomach churning again. His finger hesitated, then he double clicked the icon. The screen jumped to life immediately, the words filling the space in bold type.

YOU BROKE THE RULES.

Gibson gripped the chair arms. What the hell was this? Before he could figure it out, the screen came alive with a new message.

I SAW WHAT YOU DID.

CHAPTER 5

Old Ebbitt's Grill
Washington, D.C.

Maggie waved off the busy hostess. She made her way through the crowded restaurant, trying to ignore the heavenly aromas of grilled beef and something garlic. She was starving.

She found Gwen waiting in their usual corner booth. A large goblet of what Maggie guessed was Gwen's favorite Shiraz sat untouched in front of her.

"Did you not want to start without me?" Maggie asked, pointing to the glass as she slid into the opposite side of the booth.

"Sorry, just the opposite. This is my second glass."

Maggie checked her watch. She was ten minutes late, if that. Before she could respond, Marco appeared alongside their table. "Good evening, Ms. O'Dell. May I interest you in a cocktail before dinner?"

Maggie marveled at his ability to make them feel as though they were his only concern in the crowded, noisy restaurant. Despite the crow's feet at the corners of his eyes, she thought he still had that youthful, tanned sleek look of an experienced and well-paid cabana boy. One who took pride in knowing his clientele. He sure knew Gwen and Maggie well enough that when they reserved a table he made sure it was this corner booth.

So it was without hesitation or confusion that when Maggie told him she'd have her "usual," he said, "Of course. I'll have your Diet Pepsi with a twist of lemon right out." Just like that. No further questions. No lectures, or worse, sympathetic glances. She liked that.

Marco handed her a menu, "May I suggest some fresh escargots for an appetizer?"

"No," Maggie said too quickly. "None for me," she added, hoping she hadn't already telegraphed her disgust at the very idea. After an afternoon filled with maggots, she wasn't sure she could stomach a plateful of snails.

"None for me, either," Gwen agreed.

"But perhaps we could start with an order of stuffed mushroom caps?" Maggie suggested. The scent of garlic had already primed her mouth for the delicious appetizer.

"Excellent choice," Marco said, rewarding her with a smile. "I'll have those out to you right away."

When Maggie glanced at her, Gwen was smiling, sipping her wine.

"What?" Maggie asked. "I'm starving, but I'll share."

"I wish you could have seen your face when he recommended the escargots. So it must have been one of those afternoons, I take it?"

"Maggots. Way too many maggots," she said as she pushed strands of hair off her forehead, surprised to find them still damp. She had gone back home for a quick shower, hoping also to wash away the memory and the feel of the wormy critters even though she hadn't touched a single one this time. Then she added, "The District PD finally called us in on the decapitated Jane Doe cases."

"Does that mean they believe both were killed by the same killer?"

"It looks like the same M.O. Plus—" Maggie stopped while

Marco placed a goblet of Diet Pepsi with a wedge of lemon in front of her.

"I'll be back with your appetizer. Is there anything else I can get either of you at this moment?"

"No thanks," Gwen told him. Then to Maggie, she said, "Go on," before Marco was gone.

Maggie, however, waited until he was out of earshot. She couldn't believe Gwen. Usually she wasn't so abrupt and never was she indiscreet. In fact, lately she seemed to be only humoring Maggie by listening, at times appearing bored and tired of the grisly details. Why was she so anxious? Almost overly anxious. Maggie leaned forward, wrapping her hands around the goblet and keeping her voice hushed. "A third head was found today."

"Jesus," Gwen said and Maggie watched her sit back as if the comment had shoved her against the booth's cushion.

"Oh, and Racine's first detective on this one," Maggie said, shaking her head as she took a sip. "I think she's already in over her head." Then she gulped half her glass. When she had raced back home to shower and change, Harvey convinced her they had time for a quick run. Only now did she realize how thirsty she was.

"Are you sure you're being fair?" Gwen asked. "After all, you're not Racine's biggest fan."

It wasn't the first time Gwen had reminded her that she wasn't exactly objective when it came to Detective Julia Racine. Maggie thought about it while she chewed some ice, a recent nervous habit that kept her from replacing her empty Pepsi goblet with a Scotch. Whether she liked it not, Gwen was right. She had started out years ago with very little respect for Julia Racine. The detective had advanced her career by taking advantage of too many shortcuts given to her just because she's a woman, while Maggie had always fought to be treated like any of her male FBI colleagues. The result was that sometimes Racine got careless, oftentimes even reckless. It didn't help matters that she had made a pass at Mag-

gie several years ago while they worked their first case together. Throw into the mix the fact that Racine had saved
Maggie's mother from committing suicide. But Maggie had
repaid that favor by rescuing Racine's father from a serial
killer. Theirs was, indeed, a complex relationship. Okay, so
maybe Maggie wasn't quite objective when it came to Julia
Racine, let alone her job performance.

"She's dragging her feet on identifying the other two victims," she said anyway.

"Is that her responsibility or the M.E.'s? Maybe it's him
who's dragging his feet? Sounds like you need to give Racine a break."

Maggie shrugged. She wasn't sure why Gwen wanted her
to play nice with Racine all of a sudden. How could Gwen
defend a woman she'd never met? "She doesn't play by the
rules," Maggie offered as a weak defense and realized her mistake as soon as she saw Gwen's smile.

"And you do?"

"Sometimes I bend the rules. Weren't you the one who told
me about a dozen years ago that there are no rules in bat-
tling evil?"

"There are always rules," Gwen said, serious again. "Good
is held to them, evil is not. Sort of an unfair advantage right
from the start."

Marco chose that moment to deliver the plate of steaming,
garlic-scented mushroom caps and small serving plates. "Ladies, enjoy. I'll return in a few minutes."

Both of them stared at the appetizer even though Maggie
had been starving.

"So what about Stan?" Gwen said and scooped up several
of the mushroom caps onto Maggie's plate. She served herself a couple as well, but kept her plate to the side. "Why is
he dragging his feet?"

"From what I understand there was little tissue left." Maggie glanced around the restaurant. The tall wooden booths allowed much privacy, but this was also a regular hangout for

high-level politicos. Which meant plenty of eavesdroppers, too. Satisfied that no one was trying to listen to their conversation, Maggie continued, "There were no dental records to match, either. Stan says he wasn't able to do an autopsy, but he also hasn't sent them to a forensic anthropologist."

"And you're thinking you've got just the forensic anthropologist he could send it to." There was another knowing smile, and Maggie tried to suppress a blush.

"That's not exactly what I was thinking." She knew Gwen was referring to Adam Bonzado, a professor in West Haven, Connecticut, with whom Maggie had worked the previous year. A professor of forensic anthropology who had made it quite clear he was interested in more than Maggie's bones.

"Seriously, though," Gwen continued, letting her off without what Maggie had come to expect was Gwen's regular lecture about her nonexistent love life. "What are the chances of using an outside expert like Professor Bonzado? Would Stan be offended?"

"Actually, I would hope he'd welcome it," she said, slicing off a bite of mushroom. "I've already mentioned the idea to Racine that the other two victims should be handed off to an expert. It's up to her to bring it up with Stan. As soon as I got to the site today, he reminded me that technically this wasn't even his case." Maggie gulped the remainder of her Diet Pepsi and started looking for Marco.

"What did he mean, it wasn't his case?"

"Traditionally when a body's been dismembered, or in this case decapitated, whoever has the heart has jurisdiction."

"That's ridiculous," Gwen said with enough force to make Maggie stop searching for a waiter and get her attention. Evidently she realized her mistake. Gwen sat back and in a much calmer, more controlled voice she said, "It's silly, isn't it? I don't remember such an archaic rule. I mean, what if the rest of the body is never found?"

"First, Racine needs to check the computer again and see if any torsos have shown up. The killer could be traveling to dump them somewhere else." Maggie watched her friend out of the corner of her eye as she opened the menu and pretended to be interested. What was it that seemed to have Gwen on edge? In the dim gaslight of the restaurant Maggie tried to study Gwen, only now noticing that her strawberry-blond hair was tousled, her usually manicured fingernails looked neglected, and there were dark lines under her eyes.

"That would mean he has a job that includes travel or it allows some flexibility in his schedule." Gwen's tone was back to normal, but Maggie noticed her fingers nervously curling the tips of her cocktail napkin.

"Quite possibly. But whatever the killer's doing with the torsos, Stan won't be able to just shrug off his responsibility. Right now jurisdiction is the last thing we need to worry about."

Gwen sipped her wine, and this time Maggie thought she could see a slight tremor in her hand. She wondered if Gwen was simply tired, perhaps stressed about a particular patient. Maybe it was nothing. Maybe Maggie was looking for something that wasn't there. She'd ask anyway. "Are you okay?"

"Of course."

Gwen's answer came too quickly, and she must have noticed the concern on Maggie's face.

"I'm fine," Gwen said, sounding a bit defensive, but then catching herself and adding, "Just a bit tired."

She smiled at Maggie as she pretended to be interested in her menu, closing the subject as she strategically hid her eyes. Maggie couldn't help wondering if Gwen was afraid she might reveal something more than exhaustion.

She followed Gwen's lead and reopened her own menu, but kept it slanted so she could watch her friend. What in the world was it that was Gwen wasn't telling her?

CHAPTER 6

Eppley Airport
Omaha, Nebraska

Detective Tommy Pakula hated messes. He didn't really mind the blood. After almost twenty years as a cop there wasn't much he hadn't seen. He could handle splattered brain matter or sawed-off body parts. None of that bothered him. What he absolutely hated was a contaminated crime scene.

He ran his hand over his shaved head, the bristles becoming a bit pronounced at the end of what had already been a long day. He had been home only long enough to change his shirt and socks, the latter at his wife, Clare's, insistence. They'd been married for as long as he'd been a cop, and his stinky feet still bothered her. The thought made him smile. There were a lot worse things she could complain about. He should be grateful. Things like calls interrupting dinner, forcing him to leave behind homemade lasagna and hot garlic rolls in order to take care of some dead guy in a toilet at the airport.

From the doorway he could easily see what irritated him most, at least three different sets of footprints. One set trailed blood from inside the bathroom out into the hallway, leading all the way around the cleaning cart that had been parked in front of the doorway to block the entrance. The footprint's owner had ignored the yellow plastic Out Of Order sign. From what Pakula had been told, the cart had been placed there after the stiff was found, so this set of tracks belonged to one of the sightseers. If all that wasn't bad enough, the stiff just happened to be a priest, a monsignor, according to his driver's license.

"Holy crap," Pakula said to no one in particular. "My eighty-year-old mother can't get past airport security without disrobing and being patted down, but every Tom, Dick and Harry can drop by to take a piss and see the dead guy on the bathroom floor."

"Guy who found him said he asked a janitor to pull his cart in front of the doorway while he went to get help." Pete Kasab consulted his two-by-four notebook, jotting down more chicken scratch.

Pakula tried not to roll his eyes at the wet-behind-the-ears junior detective and instead, watched the young black woman from the Douglas County Crime Lab. She hadn't reacted or responded to any of their chatter. Instead, she had already finished with the video camera and was now starting to work her grid on gloved hands and padded knees, filling specimen bags and bottles with items at the end of her forceps, items that seemed invisible from where Pakula stood. He had never worked with her before, but he knew Terese Medina by reputation. If the killer left something behind, Medina would find it. He wished he could trade Pete Kasab for Medina.

"The guy said he may have bumped into the killer," Kasab continued, reading it as if it were just another of his scribbles.

"He said what?" Pakula stopped him in midflip of his pages.

"The guy thinks he may have bumped into the perp on his way out of the bathroom."

Pakula winced at his use of the term "perp." Was this kid for real? "This guy have a name?"

"The guy he bumped into?"

"No." Pakula shook his head, biting down on the word *idiot* before it escaped his lips. "The witness. The guy who found the body."

"Oh, sure." And the pages started flipping again. "It's Scott…" Kasab squinted, trying to read his own notes. "Linquist. I've got his work phone, home phone, cell phone and home address." He tapped the page, smiling, eager to please.

"Happen to have a description?"

"Of Linquist?"

"No, damn it. Of the supposed killer."

Kasab's face looked crushed, and he flipped more pages as he mumbled, "Of course I do."

Now Pakula felt like the asshole. It was a little like stepping on a puppy. He rubbed his hand over his face, trying to get rid of the exhaustion and his impatience. Overdosing on caffeine only made him cranky.

"Linquist said he looked young, was shorter than him. I figured Linquist at about five-ten. He said he had on jeans and a baseball cap. Said the kid bumped into him, you know, in a hurry, on his way out of the bathroom just as Linquist came in. In fact, Linquist said he saw the body and the blood, turned around and raced back out to get help and the kid was nowhere in sight."

"How young a kid?" Pakula doubted this was the killer. Probably a kid in shock, not knowing what to do or not wanting to get involved. Maybe even afraid he'd get blamed for it.

"He couldn't say," Kasab said, but he continued to check his notes. "Oh, here it is. He said he never got a look at the kid's face."

"Then how'd he know he was a kid?"

Kasab looked up at him as if checking to see if the question was a test. "I guess by his demeanor or maybe his stature."

Great, Pakula thought. Now the rookie was guessing. Brilliant police work. Pakula wanted to groan, but instead turned and glanced back at Terese Medina who had meticulously made her way to the corpse. Pakula watched Medina pick at the back of the stiff's polo shirt with her forceps. Maybe they'd get lucky and there'd be some interesting transfer debris. Now, *that* would be brilliant police work. Just then Medina held up something at the end of her forceps.

"This is weird," she said, turning it around for a more thorough inspection. To Pakula it looked like a piece of white fuzz, no bigger than a dime.

"What is it?" Pakula came closer while she slipped it into a plastic bag and was picking another off the monsignor's polo shirt.

"I could be really off base," she said, holding it up to her nose this time, "but it looks like crumbs."

"Crumbs?"

"Yeah, bread crumbs."

Before Pakula could respond, his cell phone started tinkling, the sound of a million tiny little bells. He should never have let his daughter Angie—the techno nerd—program the damn thing. He had no idea how to change the tone and instead he resorted to ripping the phone off of his hip, breaking his record at two rings.

"Pakula." All he got was static. "Hold on." He turned his back and walked down the hallway, hoping for a stronger signal. "Yeah, go ahead."

"Pakula, it's Carmichael."

"Where the hell are you, Carmichael? I could use your butt down here at the airport."

"I'm still at the station."

"I've a got a sliced-up priest on the bathroom floor with idiots walking around him to take a piss and maybe even eat a sandwich over his dead body."

"What?"

"Never mind."

"Well, that all sounds like a lot of fun, but I thought you might be interested in the phone call I just got. A Brother Sebastian from the Omaha Archdiocese's office wants to know the condition of Monsignor William O'Sullivan's body."

"You've gotta be kidding. How the hell did he already find out? We just ID'd the padre less than an hour ago."

"Said he received an anonymous phone call."

"Really?"

Pakula could hear Detective Kim Carmichael crunching, a nervous habit that added to her waistline. Then the rest of them would pay, having to listen to her complain in a burst of choppy Korean expletives. But he'd trade Kasab for her, too.

"Here's the thing, Pakula, actually two items I think you'll find interesting. Brother Sebastian seemed awfully concerned about the monsignor's personal effects, particularly one leather portfolio. Second, he wanted us to know that Archbishop Armstrong would help us, so it certainly wouldn't be necessary to bring in the FBI."

"The FBI?" Pakula laughed. "Okay, Carmichael. Very funny. But it's been a long day, and I'm really not in the mood for—"

"I'm not kidding, Tommy. That's what he said. I even wrote it down."

"Why the hell would we call in the FBI for a local homicide?"

"He tried to sound nonchalant about it when he said it," Carmichael replied, "but I could hear something, you know. He was nervous and careful with his words, and yet, trying to be all like it's no big deal."

Pakula stopped, leaned against the wall, keeping out of earshot of the coffee and doughnut counter. He couldn't remember seeing a leather portfolio. From the beginning he thought this was a random hit, maybe a robbery gone badly despite the padre's wallet left behind filled with euros. Euros were worthless to a local petty thief. But what if the killer hadn't been looking for quick cash? What if he knew exactly who he had followed into the men's bathroom? Was it possible someone intended to kill the good monsignor? That made it a whole different case.

"Hey, Pakula, you fall asleep on me?"

"Do me a favor, Carmichael. Give Bob Weston a call and fill him in on the details."

"You sure you wanna do that?"

"The archbishop says he doesn't want us to bring in the FBI. Yeah, maybe I might check with the FBI to see why that is."

CHAPTER 7

Newburgh Heights
(Just outside of Washington, D.C.)

Maggie had just gotten home when her cell phone began to ring. She and Harvey were in the middle of their "welcome home" routine even though she had seen him several hours ago. Ever since she had rescued the beautiful white Lab, he treated each of her arrivals as if it was a pleasant surprise, those sad brown eyes so grateful she hadn't abandoned him like his previous owner. Rather than cut short his slobberfest, she sat down in the foyer and pulled out her phone.

"Maggie O'Dell," she answered, trying to convince Harvey to keep his licks confined to her other hand. Now on the floor with her face within his reach, Harvey decided it, too, was fair game.

"O'Dell, it's Racine. Did I catch you at a bad time?"

Maggie wondered if Racine could hear the sloppy kisses and was referring to the sound or the time of night.

"I just got home. What's up?"

"I know it's late. You sure this isn't a bad time?"

Maggie smiled. No doubt Racine could hear the wet licks.

She patted Harvey's head rather than push him away. Maybe it was time there were some scandalous rumors about her non-existent sex life.

"No, this is fine. Go ahead."

"The cell phone turned out to be a dead end."

"Stolen?" Maggie guessed, continuing to rub Harvey behind the ears.

"Yup. Reagan National. Last week. At least that's the last time the owner says he saw it. He seems to be on the level. Reported it missing to Sprint. It hadn't been used until this morning."

"Any way to track where it was when the call was made?"

"Only that it was in the D.C. area. It's probably been tossed in some Dumpster by now."

Maggie wasn't sure why Racine was calling her after midnight to tell her what they both already suspected. She couldn't be expecting a profile before the autopsy. But there was something more and Racine's sudden quiet telegraphed it. Maggie waited her out.

"I talked to Chief Henderson about the other two. Both he and Stan agree that we need a forensic anthropologist to take a look."

That was it? Racine had actually taken her advice. "That will definitely help," Maggie said, but something in Racine's voice told Maggie it wasn't quite that simple.

"Stan said he could get someone late next week, but I'm headed up to my dad's on Sunday. We're supposed to go fishing. I figured I'd leave before sunrise, maybe around five. Oh, by the way, Stan said he'd do the autopsy first thing tomorrow."

Racine paused as if expecting Maggie to complain, but instead she was trying to imagine Racine keeping still and quiet long enough to fish. The image didn't fit.

"Anyway," Racine continued, "I suggested I take the other two heads up to Professor Bonzado. He and my dad have become big buds ever since…well, you know." Racine left it there and it was just as well. Maggie did know. Ever since Professor Bonzado and Luc Racine rescued her from a madman's freezer. It wasn't your ordinary male-bonding ritual, but she wasn't surprised that the two men had continued to grow close.

"Are you sure there isn't someone in the District Stan might recommend?" Maggie found herself asking, which was ridiculous because earlier she had found herself thinking she would suggest Bonzado to Racine. No sense in letting Racine think she was anxious to see him again.

"I'm sure there is, but not on a holiday weekend." Racine paused. "Look, O'Dell, I'll be honest with you. I've got reporters chomping at my ass. Now that there are three victims I need some answers and I need them quick. I already talked to Bonzado. He promised he'd take a look Sunday afternoon and since I was driving up anyway, I'll take them with me. I know it's not exactly the ideal mode of transport, but Stan didn't seem to mind a personal escort for his precious cargo. Besides, I usually drive. I can do the trip in about four hours." Now it was almost as if Racine was rambling. Why did she feel she owed Maggie any explanation?

Maggie pushed up and sat on the first step of her staircase. Harvey lay beside her and now he rested his head on her feet.

"It'd be impossible to get a flight with it being a holiday weekend," Racine kept explaining. "Besides, can you imagine trying to get two decapitated heads through airport security?" Racine's laugh had a nervous edge to it. There was something else, something more. Maggie wanted to tell her to spit it out already. Again, she waited out the silence.

"So I was wondering if you wanted to ride along."

And there it was. Racine had been working her way up to extending an invitation.

"Adam said he might have some basic information for us before we left. It'd just be for the day. I know that makes a long day." Now Maggie noticed it was Adam instead of Professor Bonzado. "I'm sure my dad would love to see you. He asks about you all the time. Well, when he remembers. He's actually been having some good periods. Though they say you can't count on those lasting long."

"It would be good to see your dad again," Maggie said, thinking she had more connections than perhaps she had bargained for in Connecticut. In fact, she had seriously considered contacting her new stepbrother, Patrick, to suggest they get together for the holiday weekend. Then she immediately chastised herself for thinking instant family meant instant holiday get-togethers. He surely had his own plans and they wouldn't include a sister he had found out about less than a year ago. No, she had decided Patrick would need some time. She'd need to let him come to her when he was ready.

Why kid herself? Patrick wasn't the only reason for her wanting to suggest a family reunion. She did want to see Adam Bonzado again. Here Racine was handing her a perfect excuse. And yet at the same time, she couldn't help thinking that four, no, eight, hours in a car with Julia Racine might be eight hours too many.

CHAPTER 8

Venezuela

He turned up Vivaldi on his cheap boom box and swatted at yet another mosquito. This one had gotten him good, splattering more blood, his own blood, and adding one more bump, reducing his overly sensitive skin to that of a blister-riddled leper. Father Michael Keller had learned a long time ago to ignore the constant itch, just as he had learned to deal with his body being sweat-drenched even after his evening shower. Instead, he concentrated on the simple things, the few pleasures he counted on, like Vivaldi, and he closed his eyes, letting the strings stroke him and calm him. It was all mind over matter. And he had discovered that his mind could convince him of anything, if he only let it.

He continued his evening ritual. He lit several citronella candles and checked the kettle of water on his hot plate. His white shirt, made fresh and crisp by one of the village women, was already sticking to his back. He could feel the sweat trickling down his chest, but still he looked forward to his evening cup of scorching hot tea. Tonight he selected chamomile from the package his Internet friend had sent him. What a treat it had been to receive the box with a variety of loose-leaf teas, jelly-filled cookies and shortbreads. He had been saving it, rationing it, wanting to savor it as well as savor the idea that someone he had never met would send him such a wonderful gift, such a perfect gift.

He scooped just the right amount into his mesh-ball infuser then dunked it into the hot water, covering the mug and letting it steep. He lifted the cover, letting the steam rise into his face, breathing in the delicious aroma. He pulled out the infuser, tapping it against the lip of the mug, making it surrender every last drop.

A lone mosquito ignored the citronella scent and continued to buzz around his head. Outside, an evening shower added another layer of humidity to the stifling heat. But he sat back with his tea and his music and for a brief moment he felt as if he truly were in heaven.

He hadn't finished his first cup when a noise outside his door startled him. He sat up and waited for a knock, but one never came. Odd. It was unusual for him to be summoned at this time of night, and no one stopped by without an invitation. They were respectful of his privacy, apologetic even when there was an emergency.

Maybe it had been the wind. He sat back again and listened to the rain. Tonight it tapped soft and gentle on the tin roof. He listened, and he realized there was no wind.

Curiosity made him set his mug aside. He stood, but stopped suddenly, feeling a bit light-headed. Maybe it was the heat. He steadied himself, then approached the door slowly, quietly, still listening if anyone was on the other side. It was silly to be so paranoid. No, not paranoid—simply cautious. Something else he had learned long ago out of necessity.

He unlocked the door and swung it open with such force he startled the small boy and almost knocked him to the ground.

"Arturo?" he said and he reached out to steady the boy.

He recognized him as one of his faithful altar boys. He was smaller than others his age, thin and frail with sad dark eyes and always so anxious to please. He looked even more vulnerable, standing in the rain holding out the brown cardboard box.

"What are you doing here?" Then, noticing Arturo's confused look, he repeated, *"¿Arturo, qué hace usted aquí?"*

"Sí, para usted, Padre." Arturo presented the package with outstretched arms, smiling and obviously proud to have been entrusted with this mission.

"A package for me? But who? *¿Quién lo mandó?"* he said, taking the package from the boy and immediately noticing how light it felt.

*"Yo no sé. Un viejo…*old man," he added.

Father Keller squinted into the dark to see down the worn path to the church. There was no one. Whoever gave Arturo the package was gone now.

"Gracias, Arturo," Father Keller said, patting him on the head, thinking the boy had so little in his life he was glad to make him smile. Arturo reminded him of himself as a boy, wanting and needing someone to notice him and care about him. *"Hasta domingo,"* he told him with a brief stroke of the boy's cheek.

"Sí, padre."

The boy was still smiling when he ran off down the path, quickly disappearing into the black mist.

He picked up the box, finding himself a bit anxious. Perhaps it was another special package from his Internet friend in the States. More teas and cookies. Arturo said it had been an old man who had given him the package, but it could have been a substitute postman, someone Arturo didn't know. To young boys, anyone over thirty was old. But there was no mailing label this time. No postage stamp, nothing at all.

He brought the package in, noting, again, that it was light— too light to cause much harm. Yet he set it on his small wooden table and began to examine it from all sides. There were no marks, no markings anywhere on the box. It didn't even look as if a label had perhaps been removed. Sometimes packages were a bit battered by the time they reached him. After all, this was the rain forest.

Finally he gave in and reached for the fillet knife. He sliced through the packing tape and hesitated before slowly pushing back the flaps. He was still pulling out tissue paper when he saw it. And he snatched back his hand as if he had gotten burned.

What kind of a joke was this? It had to be a joke. Who would know? And how had they found him?

His hands were already shaking when he took the plastic Richard Nixon Halloween mask out of the box.

CHAPTER 9

Omaha, Nebraska

Gibson wondered where the noise was coming from. It was too dark to see, but it sounded like running water. Maybe it was the toilet bowl in the bathroom between his bedroom and his little brother's. All it took was a jiggle of the handle but Tyler always forgot.

He tossed and turned onto his side. He pulled the blanket up over his ears and tried to ignore the noise, burying his head in the pillow. It didn't work. The water kept gurgling. Louder now.

Damn it, how hard was it to jiggle the frickin' handle?

He crawled out of bed, feeling his way to the door like he usually did when he got up in the middle of the night to go to the bathroom. If he turned on a light his mom got hysterical and wanted to know what was wrong. Besides, she kept a night-light in the hallway, one of those light-sensored gizmos that turned on automatically in the dark. Only tonight there was no light. The frickin' thing must have burned out. Piece of crap.

He felt along the wall. The gurgling hadn't stopped. And he was right. It did seem to be coming from the bathroom between his and Tyler's rooms. He had a notion to go wake up Tyler and show him how to fix it. But wait, wasn't Tyler supposed to be sleeping over at his friend's? The big baby must have changed his mind.

Gibson noticed the light under the closed bathroom door. Not only did Tyler leave the toilet running, he left the light on. Geez, what a pain in the ass. He pushed open the door and froze. There on the bathroom floor was Monsignor O'Sullivan, lying on his side. The gurgling noise was blood streaming from his nose and mouth and chest. And his eyes were staring, unblinking, directly at him.

Gibson started backing away and slammed into the wall. He shook his head and looked around the small bathroom. Everything else was in place. Even the wadded-up towel he had left on the floor. He closed his eyes and opened them again.

That's when the priest's eyes blinked.

Jesus! Gibson turned to run, but the door had closed behind him. He couldn't find the doorknob. What the hell happened to the doorknob?

He glanced back over his shoulder. The monsignor jerked and turned, then started to get to his feet. Now Gibson pressed himself against the wall, too stunned to move. Paralyzed, with his heart pounding in his ears and a cold sweat sliding down his back. The last time Gibson had seen him he was lying on the bathroom floor at the airport. That's where Gibson had left him. There had been blood, lots of it. How did he get here?

Monsignor O'Sullivan looked at him and smiled as he brushed off his trousers.

"You didn't think it would be that easy, did you, Gibson? You just left me lying there."

The priest rubbed at the blood trickling down the front of his shirt, getting his fingers red and dripping all over the ceramic tile. He was alive. And there was a flash of anger in his eyes. Anger at Gibson.

"Because you thought I was dead?" The monsignor said exactly what Gibson was thinking as if he could read his mind. "Did you really think it'd be that easy to be rid of me? Gibson, Gibson, Gibson. You of all the boys should know better than that."

Monsignor O'Sullivan started walking toward him.

"My mom's just down the hall," Gibson warned him.

"No, she's not. I checked."

He kept coming, shaking his finger at Gibson and splattering blood as he did so. And he had that smile, that knowing look that sank Gibson's stomach. He hadn't heard his mom come home and now he remembered that even Tyler was at a sleep over. No one would hear him even if he yelled or screamed.

"On your knees, son. You know what you need to do," Monsignor O'Sullivan told him, and as he got closer and closer, Gibson could even smell the alcohol on his breath.

Gibson woke with a violent thrashing, fighting and swinging at the blanket he had managed to tangle around himself. He was wet and shaking, but when he finally realized it was only a dream, relief swept over him. Only then did he notice that he was still reciting the Our Father in a panicked whisper.

He made himself stop. He tried to lay still and listen.

There was no gurgling. Nothing.

He stared up at his ceiling, watching the familiar shadow of a tree branch from outside the window. Watching and still listening. Finally the panic subsided and that's when he noticed the smell. He cringed and allowed a disgusted sigh as he crawled out of bed. In the darkness he began stripping his bedsheets. Maybe he could change them and get them in the washer without his mom noticing. He didn't need her worrying about him. And he didn't want her knowing. It was too embarrassing even though it had been over a year since he had wet the bed.

CHAPTER 10

Saturday, July 3
Washington, D.C.

Gwen Patterson sat cross-legged on the floor in the middle of her living room dressed only in her robe. Her hair was still dripping from her shower. Her usual one cup of coffee had extended to three. She had pushed the coffee table out of the way and surrounded herself with newspaper articles and scattered files. To her right were the assorted handwritten notes from the killer—scraps of paper, each now in a plastic bag and lined up beside her. She treated the notes as evidence, handling them carefully, as if trying to compensate for not turning them over to the proper authorities. The proper authorities being Detective Julia Racine and company, which now included Maggie.

Outside, she could hear the early-morning thunderstorm receding, reduced to a gentle patter against the windows and a distant rumble of thunder. She had left the living-room windows open, hoping the cool breeze and the fresh scent of rain would revive her after another night of tossing and turning.

She glanced around at her mess, wondering what exactly she was looking for. And would she recognize it if she saw it? Was it possible the killer was someone she didn't even know? Maybe he had seen her photograph in a newspaper or on TV? He could have heard a radio interview or perhaps attended one of her book signings? Was it possible that he had randomly chosen her as his contact because he thought she was an expert? All he had to do was a LexusNexus search and discover plenty of information about her professional background. Enough information to sound as if he knew her without ever having met her.

She poked at one of the plastic-encased notes, reading the carefully chosen block-lettered words that gave basic instructions, and then almost as an afterthought came the subtle threat. The first one reminded her of something you'd find in a fortune cookie: DO AS YOU'RE TOLD OR SOMEONE YOU LOVE WILL SUFFER. It wasn't until this third note that she decided the killer had to be someone she knew. But how could she be certain? The warning simply read: IF YOU LOVE YOUR FATHER YOU WON'T SAY A WORD.

Gwen wondered if perhaps even this warning could still be seen as ambiguous and empty. Anyone could easily find out who her father was, and when they discovered that he also was a leading psychologist, might presume that the two of them were very close. Besides, Dr. John Patterson was over five hundred miles away in New York City, living in a high-security apartment complex and working at a research facility that required government clearance. In fact, if she were to tell him later about the threat, he would laugh and shrug it off, quick to excuse it as his little girl being overly cautious.

"His little girl." Just the phrase still infuriated her. All of her accomplishments, all of her prestigious degrees and certificates, a bestselling book and dozens of published articles in respected journals and he still didn't take her seriously. He thought she was wasting her brilliant mind and her time with what he referred to as her fascination and obsession with criminal behavior.

She picked up one of the articles she had clipped from the

Washington Post, although she knew she wouldn't find anything new. She had read it so many times she could recite the twelve paragraphs by heart. The article was worthless with only the basic information. Gwen tossed the clipping aside. Now she grabbed the stack of patient file folders she had brought home with her. It didn't take long for her to choose one. She started flipping through her notes. Could there be something here? Something she may have noticed or written down from one of her sessions with Rubin Nash?

Ordinarily she kept her notes brief, jotting down single words and abbreviations, her own archaic form of shorthand. It was best to keep it brief or else the patient became anxious, too focused on what she was writing. Gwen had learned to do it in such a nonchalant manner that even scratching out things like "ERRATIC," "11" and "DAD GONE" attracted neither attention nor alarm. To anyone else the notes might be meaningless, but one look and Gwen remembered that Rubin Nash's behavior became erratic whenever he talked about the summer of his eleventh birthday when his mother told his father to leave and he did.

This set of notes included disturbing words and phrases her patient had used during their fifty-minute session. She didn't need to rely on her awful handwriting. She remembered him explaining, or rather telling—there was too much confidence for him to feel he needed to explain—how he had the urge to strangle someone, a woman, any woman. It didn't matter whether or not he knew her. A total stranger would do. Women had taken so much away from him that he wanted to make them pay. It would be a symbolic gesture, he had said later, laughing, when he calmed himself. And yet at the same time he added, and this she had written down word for word, that he wondered what it would "feel like to twist someone's neck and hear it snap."

Gwen reminded herself that just because he said it it didn't mean Rubin Nash was capable of doing it. She had heard plenty of strange rantings from patients. Most of the time, the threats were simply a part of the process, a verbal exercise to blow off steam. It wasn't necessarily a sign of destructive or dangerous behavior when patients shared their darkest secrets, urges, or even their desire for vengeance. More often it was a sign that they felt comfortable enough and trusted her enough that they could share such things. However, Gwen had spent too many years profiling and assessing the criminal mind to let the violent comments, especially those delivered as calmly as Rubin Nash had delivered his, to go unnoticed. And perhaps out of habit, she had already started listening and watching Nash a bit closer even though he was a patient and not a suspected killer the FBI had asked her to psychoanalyze.

Maybe her father was right. Maybe it had been an obsession. At one time she had spent so much time at Quantico, consulting with the Behavioral Science Unit, Assistant Director Cunningham joked that she should have her own office. But in recent years when her District practice finally took off, she was surprised to find herself relieved, almost anxious to trade in the analyzing of rapists and murderers for listening to frustrated wives of senators and the nervous ramblings of over-ambitious members of congress. In fact, she had recently bragged to Maggie that she hadn't been in the same room as a killer since two years ago in Boston when survivalist Eric Pratt had threatened to shove a sharp lead pencil into her throat.

What a thing to brag about, her father would tease her. If he only knew. But she had always been careful not to tell him or her mother about the dangers her so-called obsession had often put her in the middle of. Would he take her seriously if he knew or would he consider her reckless?

Of course, it didn't matter now. It was no accident the FBI called on her expertise less frequently, respecting her wishes. These days she preferred to write books and articles about criminal behavior. She liked it that way. It wouldn't have bothered her in the least to never have to sit across from a killer again, coaxing and prodding his psyche to get him to trust and confide in her. And yet, despite her best efforts, she found herself being dragged into another killer's world. The bastard had decided to coax and prod her into being his accomplice. Only it wasn't a knife or pencil shoved against her throat or a gun pointed at her head. She would have almost preferred any one of those rather than the threat he had chosen. And he had chosen wisely. She couldn't risk telling the police and she wouldn't dare tell her father. That's why she was certain she must know him. She wondered if it could possibly be someone who sat across from her every week, examining and studying her all the while he paid to be examined and studied by her.

She checked the clock on her mantel. She had a couple more hours before she needed to get to the office for her Saturday-morning sessions; the first one had been rearranged to accommodate Nash's new travel schedule. Suddenly Gwen remembered what Maggie had said about the torsos of the three Jane Does being dumped somewhere else, perhaps somewhere outside the District. She couldn't help wondering if it wasn't a coincidence that Rubin Nash had suddenly started to do more traveling for his business.

Her cell phone interrupted her thoughts. She had to pull it out of her briefcase.

"This is Dr. Patterson."

"Hi, sweetie, it's Dad."

A chill came so suddenly she bolted to her feet, then realized almost as quickly how silly she was being. He sounded fine, cheerful even. It was a holiday weekend. He always called on holiday weekends.

"How are you and Mom?"

"Fine. Excellent. Your mom's playing bridge. But, sweetie, where are you? I've been waiting here at Regis for almost a half hour."

"Excuse me?"

"Your note said to meet you at eight for breakfast at Regis. Why didn't you tell me sooner that you were going to be in the city today?"

Gwen found the edge of the sofa and eased herself down. So the killer knew her well enough to know that she would have misgivings. This had to be his way of telling her how easy it would be to carry out his threat.

CHAPTER 11

Omaha Police Department

Detective Tommy Pakula took another gulp of cold coffee. Raised a Catholic, he had never doubted the existence of God, but too often he found himself not appreciating the divine creator's sense of humor. This was one of those moments. As he sat in the hardback chair listening to Special Agent Bob Weston drone on and on, Pakula decided this was God's way of punishing him. In fact, after a solid twenty minutes of the little man's lecturing and yammering, Pakula was convinced that Bob Weston was probably God's punishment for quite a few things.

"Stop for a minute or two," Pakula finally said, throwing up his hands in surrender. Weston appeared so shocked anyone would dare to interrupt him that he immediately went silent. "You've been at it for almost a half hour and I still don't see what fucking connection this Ellison guy getting knifed at an art festival in Minneapolis has with the monsignor getting stuck in a toilet at the airport?"

"Do you want me to start from the beginning?"

"No!" Pakula and Carmichael answered in unison. "Maybe

you should just tell us the punch line." Pakula almost said *please*. It had to be the exhaustion. "Come on, what's the connection?"

Now Weston grinned like a guy who knew he was the only one with the secret answer to the puzzle. "Ordinarily, most people wouldn't see any connection. At least not on the surface. But I happen to be from Minneapolis, so I tend to pay attention. I still have a brother up there. He has a family."

Pakula groaned and rubbed his eyes. Weston noticed. The grin was replaced with a lifted eyebrow. Pakula wondered if an irritated Weston was any worse than a cocky Weston. He decided he didn't care. He sat back in his chair and stared him down.

"Come on, Weston," Carmichael finally gave up and broke in. "We know you're brilliant. Just tell us the fucking connection."

"*I'm trying to tell you.* My brother and his family used to attend Saint Pat's where Daniel Ellison used to be an associate pastor for a very short time. He left the church, got married and became an advertising executive." Finished and looking pleased with himself, Weston sat down on the edge of the desk, his designer-clad butt crushing a stack of reports. He didn't seem to notice. Instead, he seemed to be waiting for his accolades.

"That's it?" Carmichael asked. "That's your secret connection? That he happened to be a priest?"

"And that he was stabbed in the chest and that it was done in a very public place. This was in the middle of the afternoon, a crowded festival." Weston was back on his feet. "Nobody saw it happen. Ellison's wife sort of remembered him bumping into someone and then suddenly slumping over and falling to the ground." He handed Pakula the folder he had brought with him. "After you get your autopsy report, just take a look at the two cases."

"What should I be looking for?"

"I don't know, but I bet there'll be some similarities."

"And if there are similarities, you think we have a priest killer on the loose?" Pakula shook his head. He wasn't convinced. "One dead monsignor and a guy who used to be a priest—sounds more like a coincidence to me."

"Hey, you called me." It was Weston's turn to put up his hands as if in surrender. "You asked me what possible reason Archbishop Armstrong would have for not wanting the FBI involved."

Pakula saw Kasab in the doorway, waving him over. Normally, he would have yelled for him to just get his butt in here, instead, he saw an opportunity for escape.

"Be right back," he told Carmichael and nodded at Weston. Before he got to the door, he couldn't help thinking Kasab looked like a guy with his own secret. He wanted to tell him he should never play poker, but after wrangling Bob Weston, Detective Pakula was too tired for more games.

"What's going on?"

"I've got good news and bad news."

"Okay," Pakula said. It took a few beats before he realized Kasab was waiting for him to say which he wanted first. "Okay, good news first." It was easier to play.

"I was able to get the monsignor's cell-phone record. The only calls he made were one to Our Lady of Sorrow rectory that lasted about a minute and another to Father Tony Gallagher's cell phone. He's the assistant pastor at the church. That one lasted just over seven minutes. It was made about an hour before his flight."

"So he was probably the last person to talk to the monsignor."

"Most likely, yes. Outside of anyone at the airport."

"Sounds like we need to talk to Father Gallagher. Can you arrange that?"

"Oh, sure."

"So what's the bad news?"

"I went back to the airport to pick up Monsignor O'Sullivan's luggage. Remember they told us they'd intercept it in New York and have it back in Omaha this morning?"

"Let me guess," Pakula interrupted him, "it's in Rome."

"No, it made it back to Omaha, but someone picked it up before I got there."

"You gotta be kidding. What numb nut gave it to someone without any authority?"

"Actually the desk clerk was told it had been authorized."

"Who the hell told him that?"

Kasab flipped his notebook pages, checking, wanting to be accurate. "It was a Brother Sebastian. Said he was with the Omaha Archdiocese office. And like the guy told me, who's not going to believe someone sent by the archbishop?"

CHAPTER 12

Washington, D.C.

It was on mornings like this that Maggie O'Dell wondered if perhaps something was wrong with her. Here it was another beautiful day, after rains had washed everything clean, the beginning of a holiday weekend and she had nothing to cancel. No plans to change. No friends or family or lover to let down. Even Harvey, who watched her leave with his head still planted on her bed pillow, let her off the hook too easily, it seemed, by allowing her to postpone their gardening and lounging in the backyard. What was worse, she actually looked forward to this autopsy. Not exactly looked forward to it in the same way someone would relish a good time. But rather, her mind had already begun plucking at the puzzle pieces, trying to place them in some order and needing more details, more pieces. So much so that she had awakened at two in the morning and pulled out the copies of the case files.

Dismemberment cases bothered even the most seasoned of veterans, and Maggie certainly wasn't immune. Dismemberment cases and ones involving dead kids usually had a way of staying with her long after the killers were arrested, tried and convicted. Sometimes she still had nightmares that included body organs stuffed in take-out containers courtesy of Albert Stucky. And then there were those with dead little boys, naked and blue-skinned, left in the mud and tall grass along the Platte River. Albert Stucky was dead and buried. She had seen to it personally. However, Father Michael Keller had gotten away scot-free, escaping to South America, and even the Catholic Church didn't seem to know where he was.

Maggie paused at the door to the autopsy suite to clear her mind and to finish her Diet Pepsi. Stan Wenhoff was known to expel anyone for as little as unwrapping a candy bar during one of his autopsies. Not a bad rule, though perhaps Stan's claim that it was out of respect for the dead might be a bit disingenuous. After all, this was the same guy who yelled things like, "Just scoop *it* up."

It felt like walking into a refrigerator. Maggie grabbed two gowns off the pile and said hello to Stan who only grunted. Julia Racine wasn't in a much better mood. She looked to be in her usual futile hunt, searching through the pile for a size smaller than the X-large that Stan stocked for his visitors.

"Why is it so fucking cold in here?" Racine complained.

"We have a choice, Detective. We either deal with the cold or we deal with the maggots crawling all over us."

Maggie couldn't remember Stan ever using the air-conditioning before this. The basement autopsy suites had recently been renovated, but the old steel ducts had not. Turning on the heat or the A/C during an autopsy could compromise evidence by adding debris. So Stan usually had it turned off for the hour or two during the autopsy. Evidently he would rather deal with the debris and the cold than with the maggots.

Racine didn't answer. Instead, she glanced at Maggie, who was putting on the second gown on top of the first. Racine followed her lead and took another off the pile. Racine needed to wrap both gowns several times around her tall, thin body almost like a mummy. Only then did Maggie notice that the usually athletic and fit detective looked as if she had lost weight since Maggie had seen her last. She had heard that Racine had been making frequent trips between the District and Connecticut to visit her deteriorating father even before Racine's late-night invitation. Maggie had met and grown attached to Luc Racine while working a case practically in his backyard. Despite Luc's early onset of Alzheimer's, he and Maggie had exchanged favors, sort of coming to each other's rescue. Her fondness and concern for the older Racine had created a connection with the younger Racine, one Maggie didn't necessarily want. Sometimes she wondered if she and Julia Racine had met and gotten to know each other under different circumstances, circumstances that didn't include an almost botched case and an unwanted sexual advance, that maybe they would have become friends.

She watched Racine check out the reflection of her spiky blond hair in a dissection tray. Behind all the cockiness and bravado, Maggie knew there had to be a vulnerable and insecure woman, walking a fine line, trying not to screw up, hiding any hint of fear or doubt. She had seen glimpses and in those few and brief fleeting moments Maggie realized that she and Julia Racine had that in common. They were both very good at hiding who they really were.

Maggie handed Racine a pair of latex gloves and Racine raised an eyebrow at their purple color.

"I have to hand it to you, Stan," Racine said as she pulled on the exotic-colored gloves. "You always have the newest and coolest toys."

He scowled at her over his shoulder as he slid the bagged head out of the wall refrigerator and onto a tray. Maggie realized Stan had taken Racine's attempt at making light of the situation as an insinuation that he spent department funds in a frivolous manner. Hadn't he realized by now that Racine's inappropriate behavior and remarks were simply her way of masking her discomfort at autopsies? Perhaps he was too used to working with the dead to notice, or to have patience with something as simple as human emotion or inane idiosyncrasies.

"Do you need any help?" Maggie offered, rolling up the double-gown sleeves and hoping to relieve the tension in the suite. But a second scowl from Stan, this one leveled in her direction, immediately telegraphed her mistake. *Silly of her— she knew better.* She stepped back, out of his way. Poor Stan. Maggie often wondered if he wished he could post a No Visitors sign on the door.

"Last time I had to rig up a device." He ignored her offer, and instead, pointed to a contraption on the autopsy table that looked like a clamping device made of PVC pipe and aluminum. "I didn't think I'd be using it again this soon," he said and he didn't sound happy about it.

He fumbled with the plastic bag, a miniature version of a body bag. Maggie stopped herself from reaching over to help. It would be so easy to start the zipper that was closer to her side. Her medical background allowed her to assist with autopsies, but common sense usually told her which M.E.'s or coroners would welcome her help and which would be insulted. She already knew Stan was in the latter category even before his earlier scowl, yet his fumbling and slow-motion pace constantly challenged her patience.

She glanced at Racine, expecting her to be just as impatient with Stan. Instead, Racine looked distracted, her eyes examining the shelves of specimen jars and containers. Maggie watched the young detective tighten her gown's belt and check out her shoe covers, then go back to the room's contents. Her focus seemed to be anywhere and everywhere except on the head Stan finally had unwrapped and was now propping up with his makeshift device.

The maggots had retreated deep inside, huddling to keep warm. As a result, the woman's eyes were now clear, staring straight ahead, her tangled hair plastered to one side of her head. Suddenly, a cloud of steam escaped from her opened mouth. And despite it being packed with the slow-churning worms, it looked almost as if the poor woman were taking one last breath.

"Jesus." Racine had noticed, despite her attempt not to look. "What the hell was that?"

"The little bastards' metabolism can keep them about ten to fifteen degrees higher than their surroundings," Stan explained. "It's similar to walking outside on a subzero day and seeing your own breath, the clash of warm with cold."

"Pretty freaky," Racine said.

Maggie noticed that this time Racine's eyes didn't leave the woman's face, as if she didn't dare look away for fear of missing the next "freaky" revelation. She couldn't help wondering how long it would be before Racine would be checking her shoe covers again. Would it be the removal of the eyeballs or that sucking sound when the brain is pulled out after the top of the skull is sawed off? She actually found herself feeling bad for Racine. She wanted to tell her to think about ocean waves and listen for the sound they make lapping against a white sandy shore. Something, anything tranquil that would calm her nerves and settle her stomach. It had worked for Maggie during her first autopsy, a gunshot blast that ripped away the victim's face, leaving behind what seemed like a cavernous hole of bloody cartilage and shredded tissue. The waves had been crashing in her head by the time the M.E. had finished.

"Let's get started," Stan said, grabbing a pair of forceps and a scalpel from his tray, "before these bastards start climbing up our arms and legs."

Maggie saw Julia Racine's face go white. That's when she realized what Racine's real problem was. So it seemed they had something else in common, because it wasn't the autopsy Racine was dreading. It was the maggots.

CHAPTER 13

Omaha, Nebraska

Gibson McCutty sat in front of his computer screen, watching the clock in the lower right corner—watching and waiting. He was exhausted and trying to find something, anything, to take his mind off last night. The game wasn't supposed to start for another twenty minutes, but some of the players checked onto the site early.

The game was by invitation only. He still remembered the day he received the e-mail. He had been depressed and angry, surfing Web sites, searching for answers, when suddenly the e-mail came through with an address he didn't recognize. He almost deleted it as spam except that the call name caught his attention: TheSinEater. It sounded like something from a game of Dungeons and Dragons, something that promised, or rather suggested, to take away his sins.

Could it be that easy? Play a game and feel better? Sorta like going to confession in cyberspace. And the message had been simple, easy, enticing:

DO YOU WANT TO PLAY A GAME?

The rules were strict, though, prohibiting players from exchanging any personal information and using only their given code names. But before each game they were allowed to chat, to discuss strategy and talk about their characters, sometimes slipping in information about themselves disguised as information about their characters.

Not everyone participated in the chats; some rambled, some threw in only a comment here and there, others just sat back and watched. Gibson was in the last category. He learned more by sitting back and watching others, taking mental notes, keeping track of what each one said outside of the game when they had their guard down.

The first time he felt like a voyeur, feeling guilty for listening in and not participating. You had to log on to participate. Actually you had to log on to have access to the chat messages as they instant-messaged back and forth. But Gibson figured out a way to watch the chat without logging on. So none of the players knew he was listening. They didn't even know he was there, until later when he really did log on to play the game.

Today was no different.

He waited and watched for them to begin. Anxious to see where the conversation would go. Ready to take notes, feeling almost safe again now in the light of day and from his comfortable hiding place. That is until a knock at his bedroom door startled him.

"Gibson, what are you doing in there? It's a beautiful day outside."

His hands immediately closed the lid of his laptop, not that she could see from behind the door.

"I'm just playing a few computer games." Without the computer keyboard, his fingers were already probing his face, looking for new targets to erupt. It was a nervous habit he couldn't seem to control.

"Don't you want to go to the pool or maybe play ball with some of your friends?"

He found a new pimple on his forehead underneath his bangs. He knew his mom was trying. He had to give her credit for that. But she still treated him like he was ten or eleven instead of fifteen. *Go play ball with his friends? And what friends?* Hadn't she noticed he didn't have any, at least, none outside his computer world? She had this perception that somehow he would be an athletic superstar just like his father. Sometimes he wondered if his parents had thought that by giving him his dad's name it would also transfer those athletic talents. How totally lame was that?

"Maybe later," he told her, throwing her the false hope she always seemed to need.

It was easier in the long haul to agree and make her believe everything was fine. If she knew the truth, she'd be spazzing out on him. He already knew that he could handle crap much better than she could. He didn't want her worrying about him.

"Okay, later. But do try. I don't like you spending so much time in your room."

"I will," he yelled back over his shoulder, though he knew he wouldn't.

He listened to her hesitate. She always did. He used to wish that she wouldn't let him off the hook so easily, that she would challenge him or even threaten to reprimand him just like his dad used to. But she never did.

He listened for her footsteps until they were down the hallway. He waited for the squeak of the staircase's telltale step. Then he wiped the blood from his fingertips onto his jeans and opened the laptop's lid.

On his computer screen in the upper left corner was another message waiting for him, staring out at him in red type. He started to shake. He wanted to erase it, but his fingers suddenly were useless. And instead, he simply sat there and stared at the words.

I KNOW YOU'RE THERE, GIBSON. AND I SAW WHAT YOU DID.

Gibson bit down on his lower lip and balled up his hands to stop the shaking, keeping them over the keyboard, trying to think, waiting for the panic to subside. Finally he took a deep breath and punched at the keys, not stopping to check his spelling and hitting Send before he could change his mind.

WHO ARE YOU?

Then he waited.

It seemed like forever. Maybe the person was already gone. Maybe he didn't expect a response. He could be bluffing. Or he didn't have the guts to—

I'M THE MASTER OF THE GAME. AND YOU BROKE THE RULES.

A shiver slid down Gibson's back. He stared at the words as if waiting and looking for more of an explanation. But he didn't need one. He knew exactly what was going on. And worse, he realized he wasn't safe even in his own home, in his own bedroom.

CHAPTER 14

Platte City, Nebraska

Nick Morrelli washed down his mother's potato salad with iced tea, wishing the tea was something stronger. Not a good sign before noon. He couldn't believe he had taken off the entire week, handed over his role as lead prosecutor on the Carlucci drug case and even given up Red Sox tickets. Okay, maybe the Red Sox tickets weren't such a big deal, but still, all for what? To come back to Nebraska, stay at his sister's house and attend events like this for a whole week?

"Why are you hiding over here?"

His older sister, Christine, startled Nick, suddenly appearing behind him, invading his corner of the backyard. He wasn't hiding. The old rattan chair happened to be quite comfortable despite needing a new cushion and a fresh coat of spray paint.

"I'm not hiding. Someone needs to keep old Ralphie quiet." He patted the dog's shaggy head, keeping his paper plate up and out of Ralphie's reach, even though the old dog was fast asleep.

"Yeah, he looks like he's enjoying your company." Christine sat down in an accompanying rattan chair, wincing when it wobbled a bit.

"You know Mom says guys never came to these things in the good ole days." He looked around their parents' large backyard, crowded with people, only a few he recognized.

"The good ole days? I think you mean back in the Dark Ages," his sister told him. "I thought this was all a part of that new leaf you were turning over. You remember, your attempt at becoming a mature responsible adult."

She offered him a zebra brownie, pristine, untouched and unlike when they were kids and her goodie offerings came with a bite removed. So how could he refuse? He broke a piece off and stuffed it into his mouth.

"I don't think being a mature responsible adult is all that much fun," he said with a mouthful as if to emphasize his point that perhaps he wasn't adult material. "There's hardly anyone here I know." But now he realized he sounded a bit pathetic. He expected his sister to say, "When has that stopped you before?" Instead, she decided to stoop to his level.

"Mom and I wanted to limit the guest list only to those… shall we say, friends who you haven't slept with. You know, out of respect for Jill. Sorry, if that left only Hal, Timmy and Father Tony."

"Ouch," he said, faking his best imitation of being sucker punched. And yet, he knew he probably deserved that. He had spent much of his bachelorhood perfecting the art of one-night stands, so perhaps he deserved a reminder now and then.

"Seriously, Nick. I don't get it." This time she waited for his eyes, and he knew the horseplay was over. "You claim this is what you want. That Jill Campbell is the best thing that's happened to you. And yet, here you are at your own engagement party hiding out in the corner of the yard with an old, sleeping dog."

He didn't know what to tell her. Of course this was what he wanted. His eyes left hers to find Jill, making the rounds from one group of guests to another. She almost glided instead of walked, her yellow dress making her look like a model instead of an attorney. She wore her blond hair loose today, letting it brush her shoulders. In court she usually pulled it back or wore it up, attempting to add years and authority to her smooth, youthful face.

He told her time and again that she had saved him from himself, never really explaining, presuming that she already knew that there had been someone else he was trying to forget. But instead of pressing him for details, she seemed to take it upon herself to be the one who would finally replace the other woman she had never met.

"There you go again," he heard Christine say and immediately he knew he had missed something. Before he could respond, she added, "You've been doing that a lot, Nicky. You never seem to be where you're at."

He rolled his eyes at her as if that was the most ridiculous, incoherent thing he had ever heard, but he knew exactly what she meant. He hadn't been able to focus in months. His friend and co-worker, Will Finley, claimed it all began the day he and Jill had set a date for the wedding. Or to hear Will tell it, the day he surrendered to Jill.

At the time Nick joked that of course he couldn't focus. "After all, wasn't that what happened when you fell in love and decided to take the plunge?"

His friend had just done the same thing, marrying Tess McGowen, the love of his life, only months before. He expected Will to understand. He expected Will, of all people, to sympathize. Instead, his friend's reaction felt like a sting. "Plunge?" Will had laughed. "You refer to marriage as a plunge and then you wonder what your problem is?"

Nick took another gulp of the iced tea as if needing to wash away the memory. What did Will Finley know anyway? People who were happy quickly forgot what misery felt like.

Misery?

What the hell was wrong with him? He wasn't miserable. Jill had saved him from his misery. Suddenly, he realized he had done it again—strayed off. He glanced at Christine, expecting to see her impatience, but she wasn't looking at him. He followed her gaze, only now seeing the black-and-white in the driveway.

"If this is one of those strip-o-grams, I know it was your idea, not Mom's."

But Christine wasn't smiling.

"I'm not sure what's going on."

Two uniformed officers were talking with Father Tony. Nick's first thought was that there had been a car accident or something awful that required a priest and last rites. He watched Tony's head bob in agreement then watched him swing around, looking for and finally finding Nick. Nick attempted to wave to him that it was okay for him to leave the party, but Tony made his way through the crowded backyard, guests parting for him like a sea of pastels.

"What's going on?" Christine asked, but Tony only shrugged, his eyes meeting and holding Nick's.

"Omaha police want me to come down to the station to answer some questions."

It took Nick by surprise. "To answer questions? About what?"

Tony shrugged again, and he reminded Nick of when they were boys. That same shrug came anytime they got into trouble and an adult asked for an explanation.

"Monsignor O'Sullivan was found dead in a restroom at the airport last night."

"Oh my God," Christine said. "And it wasn't just a heart attack or they wouldn't have questions."

Nick shot her a warning look. He could hear her shift into reporter gear, probably already taking notes in her head.

"I hate to take you away from your own party, Nick. But can you come with me?"

"Of course," Nick said without hesitation. He and Father Tony Gallagher had been friends since kindergarten when the two of them got deathly sick after eating almost a whole jar of paste. He thought he knew his good buddy pretty well, and unless it was his imagination, he didn't think Tony looked all that surprised about the monsignor being dead.

CHAPTER 15

Washington, D.C.

The number-one tool for dismemberment was the hacksaw, but from what Maggie could see, this guy must have never had one handy.

Stan Wenhoff dropped several strands of the victim's hair into a bottle of solvent, giving the liquid a swirl before capping the bottle and setting it aside. While he removed hair and tissue samples, Maggie couldn't take her eyes off the decapitation area. A hacksaw usually left a fairly clean cut through the skin, joints and bone. Oftentimes there might be some bone chattering where the blade would jump and come down on a different area of the bone. For the most part a hacksaw was quite effective. Whatever tool this guy used had left a mess. Forget a little bone chattering. After Stan had cleaned the caked blood and river mud, the gaping area looked raw and shredded. There were jagged cuts, almost hacking marks in the bone and torn flesh where it looked as if he had ripped instead of cut.

She had ruled out a disorganized killer because of the planning and discipline it had taken not just to discard the heads but to complete the grisly process three times. Not to mention that he had also been able to hide or dispose of the torsos without getting caught. Dismembering a body took time and privacy. No matter where he killed his victims, he would need to take them back someplace safe, someplace where he knew he wouldn't be interrupted, where he could make a mess and have time to clean up.

And yet, something bothered Maggie. If he was, indeed, organized and had carefully planned each murder, why hadn't he gone to the trouble of buying a hacksaw or something that would have made the job much easier?

The sound of electric hair clippers interrupted her thoughts as Stan began shaving off the victim's long hair. She looked younger than Maggie had first thought. Without the tangles of hair, she noticed small diamond studs in one of the victim's earlobes. As far as she could tell, there were no other piercings in either brow, the nose, lip or chin. She made a mental note to have Stan check the woman's tongue.

"We don't have much to go on," Stan said, as if reading her thoughts.

As soon as he finished with the clippers, however, he pointed to a wound, a circular indent smashed into the top left side of the victim's skull.

"I'm guessing ball-peen hammer," he said, running a gloved index finger over the area.

"Is that how he killed her?" Racine asked, swiping a couple of maggots to the floor before coming in for a closer look.

"He smacked her pretty good," but Stan didn't look convinced. He continued his hands-on examination. "The hair samples should tell us if she was on any drugs at the time."

Maggie nodded; she knew the hair bulbs could be read almost like a drug timeline, since substances are captured and remain locked as the hair grows.

"What if he gave her something to knock her out?" Racine wanted to know. "Would that show up?"

"Oh, sure. Hair analysis can identify the heavy-duty stuff like cocaine and heroin, but we can also identify any tranquilizers or GHB. Should even be able to tell you whether she was a smoker or on Prozac. People think we can't figure out much when we have only the head," Stan continued. "There wasn't much with the other two."

"That reminds me," Racine interrupted. "I've made arrangements to take the other two up to a forensic anthropologist in Connecticut."

"Fine, fine. I can't do much more on those because of the level of decomposition. But this one has a lot to tell." And thankfully he was still anxious to share.

He tilted the head back, readjusting his vise-grip contraption so that she stared at the ceiling. More maggots slid off, hitting the stainless-steel table with tiny plops like raindrops on a tin roof.

"Despite the head wound, I doubt that was what killed her. Take a look," he said, flinging maggots off her cheeks, "at the area around her eyes."

He took a pair of forceps and, although Maggie thought Stan was a bit clumsy and slow at times, surprised her by expertly pinching and flipping up the right eyelid.

"See what I mean?"

"Petechial hemorrhages," Maggie said.

"Petechial what?" Racine asked.

"Petechial hemorrhages are capillaries that ruptured," Stan told her and his fingers moved on down the victim's face.

Racine still looked confused.

"She was strangled," Maggie said.

"Are you sure?"

"Oh, yes," Stan said without looking up. "Petechial hemorrhages occur when air is cut off. You see, we don't need her neck to conclude that she was, in fact, strangled."

"Wait a minute," Racine said, hands on her hips. She wasn't happy with Stan's conclusions. "You're saying he drugged her—"

"No, I don't know that for certain, but we should be able to tell from her hair samples."

"Okay, so he *may* have drugged her," Racine qualified her remarks and continued. "He then hit her over the head with a ball-peen hammer. All this before he strangles her. Oh, and then just for fun he cuts off her head."

"Actually I'd say it was more like ripped," Maggie said, joining the speculations.

"Excuse me?" Racine came around the table for a better angle.

Stan turned his contraption so that Racine had a better view of the decapitation area.

"Agent O'Dell's correct," Stan confirmed.

"Jesus," Racine said. "What kind of fucking monster are we dealing with?"

CHAPTER 16

Washington, D.C.

Dr. Gwen Patterson tried not to stare at Rubin Nash's hands. He sipped from the glass of water she had offered him and set it aside, not letting it slow him down as he continued on and on about his mother's best friend taking his virginity when he was fifteen. It was one more thing he felt a woman had taken from him. First, his mother had taken away his father, now her friend had taken away his virginity. Yet, that revelation seemed secondary to him. Instead, he wanted to share the illicit details, trying to be as graphic as possible. Perhaps he wanted to shock her, or at least get some reaction from her. There were few, if any, sexual deviances and perversions, let alone words or phrases, that could shock her. Besides he sounded too proud of his teenage prowess. The incident had certainly influenced him and shaped his attitudes about sex and women. However, would it have affected him enough to make him a murderer?

His hands were large but the fingers stubby. How much strength was needed to squeeze the life out of someone? Gwen wished she had turned off the air-conditioning in her office, forcing him to roll up his shirtsleeves. Were there scratches on his arms? Why else would he wear long sleeves on a hot July day?

Gwen studied his face. The cut on his lower jaw was probably a shaving nick. His open-collared shirt allowed a censored view of his neck. A person who was being choked or strangled would fight back. She would claw and scratch and punch. Unless he caught her off guard. Rubin had wondered what it would feel like to *twist someone's neck and hear it snap.*

She would need to find out from Maggie how the victims were killed. Maybe she was way off base suspecting one of her patients as the killer.

"Isn't that right, Dr. Patterson?" she heard Rubin ask and realized she had drifted too far.

"I'm sorry. What was that?"

"Why older women fuck young boys? It's not just a control thing. It's because they want to be adored. Isn't that what they really want?"

"Did you adore her?"

He looked away before she could see the answer in his eyes. He wasn't prepared for her to turn it around on him. Was it embarrassment or guilt he was trying to hide? The question had definitely surprised him.

"A good place for us to pick up next time," he told her, reversing their roles with a glance at his wristwatch. "I'll try not to be so crude next time," he added with a smile—almost a smirk—that instead of a promise was more a revelation of how proud he was of today's performance.

"That's your choice," Gwen told him, standing at the same time he did, never allowing her patients to tower over her. "Just keep that in mind, Rubin. Everything you do is ultimately your choice."

This time his eyes met hers, dark gray eyes that reminded

Gwen of a wolf's. He held her gaze, then dropped his eyes to the front of her blouse and his smile resumed. It was a habit she was familiar with. His way of intimidating her when she dared get too close, too much on target. And to remind her that to him every woman was—what was that phrase he used—"a potential sexual conquest."

"Until next time," he said and turned to leave.

She waited for the door to close behind him before she began her frenzied note-taking, recording anything and everything she had observed whether or not she deemed it important at this time. There would eventually be some clue. Perhaps something Maggie discovered at the autopsy would shed new light on Gwen's observations. She started the sixth page on her legal pad when her assistant buzzed her with her next patient.

Gwen ripped the pages from the notepad and shoved them into a file folder, but her mind was still racing. Still preoccupied with Rubin Nash when James Campion walked in.

"Hello, Dr. Patterson."

"James." She pointed for him to take a seat, but already knew he'd wait until she sat, ever the polite gentleman, a stunning contrast to Nash. He told her early on that the nuns at Blessed Sacrament had done an excellent job of drilling into him good manners and respect despite their failing him in other ways.

Gwen sat, nodding for him to do the same. His long legs stretched out and then crossed at the ankles. It was the most he allowed himself in an attempt to relax.

Today more than ever—probably because she had been focused on Nash's physical traits—Gwen noticed the sharp contrast between the two men. Also she had never seen the two patients in back-to-back sessions until today, accommodating Rubin's new travel schedule. For as cocky and boisterous as Rubin Nash was, James Campion was the direct opposite, introverted and self-conscious. Even James's long-sleeved shirt could easily be explained away as an embarrassed attempt at hiding the hesitation marks on his wrists. She had noticed them during their very first session, long before he had confessed that sometimes he thought about suicide.

And instead of bragging about his sexual escapades or rather dysfunctions, or when discussing the sexual mistreatments of his childhood, James seemed almost shy and remorseful, especially when talking about the abuses he had suffered at the hands of a Catholic priest he had admired and trusted. Both Nash and Campion had been two teenage boys taken advantage of by adults they had trusted. But that's where the similarities ended.

Gwen sat back, feeling her shoulders relax, only now realizing how close to the edge Rubin Nash was able to put her. She watched James cross his arms, tucking his hands under his armpits before deciding to uncross them again and leave his hands in his lap. His handsome, boyish face seemed almost soulful, his eyes attentive but patient as if waiting for her permission to begin.

No matter how long it took, Gwen felt certain she could help James Campion. Rubin Nash, she wasn't sure about.

CHAPTER 17

Downtown Police Station
Omaha, Nebraska

"This is ridiculous," Nick Morrelli told the detectives who introduced themselves as Detectives Carmichael and Pakula. They were an odd pair, a short, chubby Asian woman and a middle-aged linebacker with a shaved head. Hardly Hollywood's version of the good cop/bad cop. "You're treating him like he's a suspect."

"Who exactly did you say you are?" Carmichael asked.

"His friend, Nick Morrelli."

"Who happens to be an attorney," Tony added.

Nick could see it wouldn't matter. Detective Carmichael already had that I-don't-give-a-shit look that he recognized. He had even used it himself a time or two as a deputy prosecutor when he had to convince some lowlife that the deal he was offering was final.

"Morrelli?" Pakula was scratching his shaved head. "Do I know you?"

"No, I don't think so." Nick was growing impatient. Carmichael may have noticed. She uncrossed her arms, but that was all.

"My apologies if the officers may have given you the impression that you're a suspect," she told Tony. "And that they dragged you all the way down here. We only want to ask you a few questions. Is there a reason why you wouldn't want to answer our questions?" Her voice was a little softer suddenly. Nick wondered if she wasn't used to playing the role of bad cop. Or was she simply changing her route of manipulation?

Tony looked to Nick as if he expected Nick to answer for him again. Nick gave him a nod that it was okay, but at the same time, he didn't like how nervous Tony seemed. *Did* he have something to hide?

"Go ahead," Tony told the detective. "Of course I don't mind answering your questions."

"We understand that the monsignor called you from the airport," Detective Pakula said as he started pacing the length of the room. Carmichael remained sitting, but Nick noticed her foot tapping out her nervous energy under the table.

"Yes, that's right."

"You may have been the last person to talk to him. That he knew, that is. You mind sharing the contents of that conversation?"

"We had spoken earlier in the day about the schedule. I was going to fill in for him while he was gone. He couldn't remember if he had told me about the church board meeting and where he kept his notes." Tony crossed his legs, his right ankle rested on his left knee. To Nick he looked perfectly calm and natural. Almost too much so.

"Where were you when you got the call?"

"In the rectory," Tony said without skipping a beat and Nick thought this should be easy. No big deal.

"Really?" Pakula asked.

Nick recognized that look. He had used it himself, a look that wobbled between surprise and sarcasm, but Tony didn't flinch.

"You sure you were at the rectory?"

"Yes, of course. I usually do paperwork on Fridays."

"Uh-huh. So Monsignor O'Sullivan would know this, right?" Pakula kept up his pacing, nodding.

"Of course."

"Why do you suppose he called you on your cell phone instead of the phone at the rectory?"

"I have no idea," Tony said.

It was a little like watching a tennis match, only Nick couldn't tell what Pakula would do with that lame lob.

"What a minute," Pakula said, spinning around to look at Nick and surprising them all. "Morrelli. Nick Morrelli. Now I remember you. You quarterbacked for the Huskers 1982, '83."

It took Nick a second or two to register the switch of subject. Earlier, when the detective thought he knew him, he had thought it might be from his stint as sheriff for Platte City, Nebraska, several years ago. After the media circus, it was difficult for anyone in the area to forget the murder of two little boys and the investigation that Nick almost flubbed up. Two men were serving life sentences and yet Nick wasn't convinced he had caught the killer. Now he found he was relieved that Detective Pakula recognized him, instead, from another era, a more successful time in his life.

"Yeah, that's right," Nick said.

"I knew I recognized that name." But as quickly as the detective had been distracted he returned to his questions. "So, Father Gallagher, how long have you worked with Monsignor O'Sullivan at Our Lady of Sorrow?"

"I've been the associate pastor there for almost three years."

"Do you like him?"

"Excuse me?"

"Do you like him? Did the two of you get along? Were you buddies?"

"I wouldn't use the term *buddies*. We were colleagues."

Nick noticed that Tony uncrossed his legs. Both hands were on his knees. Suddenly he didn't seem so comfortable.

"Does he travel quite a bit?"

"Depends on what you mean by 'quite a bit.'"

"Why was Monsignor O'Sullivan going to Rome?"

"I believe the archbishop asked him to go. The monsignor had never been to the Vatican."

"So he was excited about going?"

"Of course, why wouldn't he be?"

"Was he delivering anything important for the archbishop?"

"Like what?" Tony asked, and Nick wanted to grab Tony by the collar and tell him to just answer the fucking questions. But instead he shifted in his chair, trying to catch Tony's eyes, maybe give him a warning glare.

He saw Detectives Pakula and Carmichael exchange a glance. They might be pretending these were only fact-finding questions, but they were fishing for something. What exactly did they know and what did they think Tony wasn't telling them?

"We were just wondering." This time Carmichael took over while Pakula leaned against the wall as if taking a break. Carmichael braced her elbows up on the table, but she, too, looked calm, a bit too nonchalant, and Nick wondered what they were hoping to get out of this interview.

"The archbishop," she continued, "asks the monsignor to go to the Vatican. Doesn't it make sense that he'd want to make the most of the trip?"

"Yes, I suppose it does."

Tony was good at this. Nick wasn't sure why he was so surprised.

"Did Monsignor O'Sullivan carry a brown leather portfolio with him?" Carmichael moved on. Maybe he was wrong about them knowing what they were doing.

"Yes, I think I do remember a portfolio," Tony finally answered.

"Did he have it with him yesterday?"

"I didn't see him leave for the airport."

"But you saw him right before?"

"Yes."

Carmichael stared at Tony, waiting for more. Nick found himself staring and waiting, too. Tony, however, just shrugged and said, "If I didn't see him leave for the airport how would I know for sure what he took with him?"

This time there was a sigh from Carmichael. Nothing from Pakula except a slight shift in his leaning.

"Last question…for now," she emphasized. "Any idea why someone might want to kill Monsignor O'Sullivan?"

"Life is the ultimate gift from God. I can't even imagine who would do such a thing," Tony said with too much of a reverent whisper. Nick watched for Carmichael's reaction, looking to see if she had noticed that Tony had managed to not answer yet another one of her questions.

Carmichael nodded without looking up from the notes she jotted. She glanced back at Pakula, then looked directly at Nick when she said, "If we have any more questions, we'll be in touch."

And immediately Nick figured that she and Pakula probably did know more. They hadn't been interested in his presence the entire time. But now all of a sudden they were telling him they'd have more questions. They were telling Tony's friend, the attorney.

CHAPTER 18

Washington, D.C.

Gwen Patterson made the last of her notes. She needed to head home. Maybe she'd stop at Mr. Lee's World Market, pick up fresh mozzarella, some garlic and Italian sausage to make her stuffed manicotti with Bolognese sauce. Cooking had a way of relaxing her, soothing and calming her nerves. It worked twice as well if she cooked for company.

She thought about Maggie, but they had just had dinner last night. The last thing she wanted was to look too needy, especially with Maggie, especially now. She thought about R. J. Tully, Maggie's partner, but he wouldn't be back for another week. Gwen wished she didn't miss him. Two weeks of vacation with his daughter, Emma, somewhere in Florida, and already…damn, she hated to admit it, but she did miss him. Not a good sign since the two of them had decided to take it slow, to get to know each other outside the stressful confines of the FBI files that had thrown them together in the past.

Funny. She was always telling Maggie to take some chances, to throw caution to the wind and have some fun when it came to love and romance, and yet, she couldn't take her own advice. Couldn't? Or wouldn't?

A soft tap at her office door startled her.

"Come in."

Her assistant, Dena, peeked around the door. "I just finished. I'm taking off. Anything else I can do or get you?"

"No, I'm fine. Thanks for coming in today, especially on a holiday weekend."

"No problem. I needed to catch up on some things."

Gwen refrained from following up with a comment about less time spent on the phone and looking for misplaced things and perhaps she wouldn't need to come in on the weekends. But that wasn't quite fair. The girl was doing a good job. And patients liked her, felt comfortable with her. That was more important than her misplacing a file or spending an hour extracting a bracelet caught in the copy machine.

"Any plans for tomorrow?" she asked instead.

"Actually, a friend called this morning and we're thinking about trying out that new nightclub. How about you?"

"I'm hoping to catch up on some rest."

"That's probably a good idea. You've been looking kind of…well, not quite yourself. Are you okay?"

"Yes, of course. Just a bit tired. I need a day off."

"Okay. Well, I hope you have a restful day off."

"Thanks, Dena."

"I'll see you on Monday. Oh, wait, I almost forgot." She left the door open and Gwen could hear her scurry back into the reception area, probably to her desk. Seconds later she came in with a manila envelope.

"This was left for you."

Gwen watched her place the envelope on the corner of her desk. She could see there was no return address, no indication who it was from, but already she knew, and immediately she felt as if the air had been knocked out of her.

"Did you see who left it?"

"No. It must have been when I was fixing coffee or maybe when I stepped out to make copies."

"What time?"

"Excuse me?"

"What time did you notice it?"

Gwen tried to get rid of the alarm from her voice, but she may not have been as successful as she'd like to be, because Dena was looking at her with concern.

"Gosh, I'm not sure exactly. It was between Mr. Rubin's and Mr. Campion's appointments."

Gwen tried not to stare at the envelope. Of course, he must have brought it with him. But wasn't that a bit risky, or perhaps *ballsy* was a better term? Would he actually bring it with him and simply place it on her receptionist's desk? Could he have slipped this time and left his fingerprints on it? Surely he wouldn't have worn gloves in the July heat.

"Is it something important?"

Gwen had briefly forgotten about Dena and did her best not to let it show on her face. She shrugged as if it were no big deal. "I doubt it. If it was important, the person who left it wouldn't have just placed it on your desk without an explanation, right?"

"I suppose. And I really wasn't gone that long to make the coffee, although that new contraption you bought takes a little more time." She smiled as if to make sure Gwen knew she was only joking, giving her a hard time about the fancy gourmet coffeemaker Gwen had made a fuss over. "So I'll see you on Monday."

But Dena stayed in the doorway and when Gwen didn't respond, she added, "Maybe you should take off and get started on that relaxing time."

Gwen glanced up at the girl and returned her smile. She was the first one she had hired in years who seemed to have a genuine concern for her. Others had been wonderfully precise—not one of Dena's top skills—but they lacked what Gwen could only describe as warmth, something she believed essential for the person outside her office door who greeted and cared for the mentally fragile patients who sometimes came through those doors.

"I'll take that under serious consideration. Now, go get out of here and enjoy what's left of your weekend."

"Yes, ma'am."

And she left, gently closing the door behind her. For a moment Dena had almost made her forget about the envelope.

She picked it up by a corner with only her forefinger and thumb, careful in case there were fingerprints. She hadn't noticed the slight bulge at the bottom. With her other hand she reached for a letter opener and tucked it under one of the flaps, holding firm as she slit the envelope open. Then she took a deep breath and turned the envelope over, letting the contents slide to the top of her desk. This time there was no note and she even peeked inside to make sure it didn't get stuck to one of the sides. The only thing in front of her was the bulge, a plastic bag, zipped shut, the contents of which looked like a single gold earring.

CHAPTER 19

Omaha, Nebraska

Nick knew he should wait.

He grasped the steering wheel a bit too tight, took the left turn a little too wide. He wasn't even sure why he was angry, but he knew he should wait until he calmed down. It would be better if he and Tony sat down across a table from each other, over a cup of coffee or maybe even a beer. It would be better if he waited.

He glanced at Tony who was staring out the passenger window of the rental car. That was one bad thing about his trips back to Nebraska. He missed his Jeep. There was a lot of thinking a guy could do taking the long way home in his Jeep. He could let off some steam by getting off the beaten path, kicking up some dirt, feeling the challenge of some rocks and mud beneath him. It just didn't work in a rented Oldsmobile Alero.

The Jeep wasn't the only thing he missed. Over the last several years there were plenty of things that made him feel as if he was split between two homes, maybe even two worlds.

Some days his move to Boston felt like the right choice, the best thing that had happened to him. It had allowed him to get out from under his father's shadow and expectations. Besides, he liked his job as deputy prosecutor for Suffolk County. He had met some incredible people, including Jill. But on days like today, it felt as though he had never left Nebraska, that it simply wasn't possible when there were still so many connections, so many pieces of himself that had stayed behind. So much of who he used to be still floated to the surface, despite his attempt to change and to move on. His impatience—as he was certain his sister, Christine, would be happy to agree—was one of those flaws.

"What the hell's going on?" Nick blurted out, deciding he couldn't wait.

"Pretty weird, huh? That something like that could happen?"

"No, what's weird is that you think you can pull something over on me."

"Excuse me?"

Finally he had his friend's attention diverted from the passing scenery.

"Detectives Carmichael and Pakula might have let you get away with all that dancing around because they don't know you. I know you, Tony. You're not fooling me. And you know what, you didn't fool those detectives, either. They'll be bringing you in again for more questioning."

"What are you talking about? I already answered all their questions."

"Oh, yeah, you answered their questions, all right. You know what it reminded me of?" Nick tried to calm his anger down a notch. "Remember in sixth grade when we kidnapped Mrs. Wilkes's antique vase off her desk because she always made us come up with those stupid poems about it?"

"They were supposed to be haiku."

"Yeah, well, see, that's even more lame."

"I remember," Tony said, but from the look on his face Nick

could tell he had a different memory of the event, one that didn't instill shame and guilt like Nick's.

"We hated that ugly vase," Nick continued. "We wanted it gone. But we really were just going to hide it in the closet for a while. Make her sweat, then find it and be her heroes."

"Still sounds like a brilliant idea," Tony said, laughing.

"Yeah, brilliant. Only you dropped it."

"It slipped out of my hands."

"And it shattered into a thousand tiny pieces."

"It was an accident."

"Principal Kramer called us into his office," Nick said, now pleased that Tony's renewed memory was not quite as pleasant as his initial one. His sudden defensive tone was accompanied by his arms crossed over his chest, and his interest in the scenery was no longer convincing. "He asked if we stole Mrs. Wilkes's vase. You told him no. It wasn't a lie because we called it kidnapping. He asked if we broke the vase. You told him no. That wasn't a lie either because you accidentally dropped it. I felt like we were back in Principal Kramer's office again. You sidestepped all of Detectives Carmichael's and Pakula's questions."

He took a long glance at his friend, catching his eyes if only for a brief moment. "I gotta ask, Tony. What the hell are you lying about?"

Nick expected more sidestepping. He expected Tony to get angry with him. Instead, he simply said, "I can't tell you, Nick." And he looked away, to stare back out the window, closing the subject and keeping Nick completely in the dark.

CHAPTER 20

Omaha, Nebraska

Gibson didn't realize he had been sitting staring at the computer for what must have been hours. The game had come and gone and he had watched, not participating, not really even paying attention. It was the first time ever that he hadn't played.

He heard the front door slam and searched for the time in the lower right-hand corner of his computer—5:25 p.m. His mom would be pissed. She'd go on and on about how worried she was that he was cooping himself up in his room. That he'd become a recluse like Emily Dickinson and die without anyone really knowing him. This week it was good ole Emily because his mom's summer college class had been discussing dead poets. Several weeks ago she had compared him to some fourteen-year-old Palestinian boy terrorist whose tearful parents described him as always being so quiet and smart and keeping to himself until he walked into an Israeli café with enough dynamite strapped to his body to kill fifteen innocent people. There seemed to be a new comparison every other week.

His mom wasn't like this when his dad was alive. At least

Gibson didn't remember her being like this—worried all the time about the littlest of things, the stupidest things. So tense and nervous that she couldn't make a decision or stand up to even a rude grocery clerk who wouldn't give her a discounted price. And now she cried all the time. At least she did at first. Maybe not so much anymore, not since the Zoloft.

He didn't remember her ever crying when his dad was still alive. But then his dad had a way of making them all feel safe and secure. They didn't need to worry as long as he was around. He just took care of things. He had been the strongest and most confident…the best man Gibson had ever known.

For Gibson it hadn't just been about knowing that his dad could and would fix his broken bike or that he'd not be afraid to tell Mr. Fitz, the Nazi English teacher, that Gibson and the rest of his class needed more time for their assignments. It was more. It was a feeling that everything would be okay. A feeling of just plain old happiness. A feeling Gibson hadn't felt since.

But then his dad had to go and get himself killed, getting in the way of some frickin' drunk driver. And that's when Monsignor O'Sullivan started calling Gibson into his office at school, claiming to be worried about him, wanting to make sure he was okay. He'd make Gibson pray with him. They'd recite the Our Father while the monsignor told him how special he was. He'd stand behind Gibson, leaning in against him so that sometimes Gibson could even smell the alcohol on his breath. He'd rub Gibson's shoulders, his neck and then not just his shoulders and neck. The first time it happened, Gibson could hardly believe it.

He shook his head and pushed away from the computer. He didn't want to think about it. It wasn't right, no matter what the bastard said. It just wasn't right. And he knew it. Why else would he insist Gibson tell no one? Only, who would he tell? He didn't have anyone he could tell. Nobody'd believe him. Nobody, except The Sin Eater.

He heard firecrackers in the distance. Someone down the

block. Maybe Tyler and his buddies. He couldn't believe he had almost forgotten tomorrow was the Fourth of July. It used to be one of his favorite holidays. Now it was just a lot of irritating noise.

CHAPTER 21

Omaha, Nebraska

Nick smiled and waved, disguising his relief. Jill evidently didn't notice. She climbed back into the BMW packed with four of her old college girlfriends. Her high from the engagement party continued. He'd never seen her like this—almost giddy. Maybe it was just being around her old friends. Whatever it was, Nick was quickly learning that he played a small role in this week's events.

"So I guess you're stuck with me tonight," Christine said, coming out onto the porch of their parents' farmhouse. She let the screen door slam behind her and handed him one of the two longneck beers in her hands.

He took her offering, moving over and making room for her next to him on the old wooden porch swing, setting it creaking and swinging. The beer was cold, the condensation wetting his fingers. It was just what he needed. He guzzled half the bottle before Christine's sudden laughter made him stop.

"Is the prospect of spending an evening with your big sister that bad?"

"It's been a helluva day," he told her, but now he rolled the bottle between his hands, watching the amber liquid swish against the inside of the bottle. "How 'bout I take you and Timmy out for pizza? Mom, too."

"You can ask, but I think Mom's pooped. And Timmy went with a couple of his friends to a movie."

"What movie?"

"I don't know. I don't even care. It's bad enough I had to bribe him to go. He's been spending way too much time alone in his room on his computer."

Nick glanced over at his sister, seeing her frustration. He knew it had to be tough raising a teenage boy all by herself. Christine complained about many things, but Timmy was rarely one of those. After her husband, Bruce, cheated on her a second time, Christine threw him out again, but this time with little of the fanfare or emotion of the first blowout. It was almost as if Christine had expected it, had prepared herself.

Sometimes Nick wondered if the emotion would catch up with her, sort of like an aftershock knocking her off her feet long after the initial impact. Christine had a way of reacting on impulse without thinking things through, without weighing the consequences. He hoped that wasn't the case with Bruce, especially where Timmy was concerned. But then, who was he to judge? He certainly was no expert on relationships. After all, here he was an engaged guy, sitting on his parents' front porch asking his sister to go get a pizza with him on a Saturday night.

"How did things go with Father Tony?"

"Are you asking as a friend of Tony's or as a reporter?"

"Give me a break," Christine said, but he recognized that faked, hurt look. Yet she diverted her eyes and was suddenly interested in the dust she brushed from the porch-swing arm. "I heard that Monsignor O'Sullivan may have been murdered, too much blood on the bathroom floor for a heart attack."

"How did you already hear that?"

Now she gave him her eyes, only to roll them at him. "I

work for the largest newspaper in the state. How do you think I found out?"

"Which brings me back to my original question. Are you asking about Tony as a friend or a reporter?"

"As a friend, stupid. I have other ways of finding out about the case. Come on, give me a break. It's been almost four years."

Nick took another gulp, watching her out of the corner of his eye, letting her know it wasn't that easy to forget, to let bygones be bygones. Almost four years ago when he was sheriff of Platte City, she undermined a murder investigation—his investigation—using him to scoop her competition and to get front-page headlines and front-page bylines for herself.

"They just had some basic questions for Tony," he said, carefully leaving out any information.

"Basic questions like who would want O'Sullivan dead?"

"Yeah. Basic questions like that."

She shook her head at him and smiled, acknowledging that was all she was getting from him. Nick smiled back and took another swallow of beer. They knew each other too well. When had everything become a game with them? Two steps forward, three steps back—it was something his father always said, though Nick couldn't remember at the time what his dad meant by it. Antonio Morrelli was the power broker of mind games. Or rather, he had been. There weren't too many games the old man could play these days, lying in his bed, unable to move or speak, the massive stroke leaving him with eye movement his only communication tool.

"Actually I shouldn't be telling you this," Christine said, but paused, waiting for his attention. "We've been putting together a piece for the paper that involves the Omaha Archdiocese. It involves O'Sullivan."

She got his attention, just like she wanted. He couldn't help wondering if this was what Tony couldn't talk about.

"Involves the archdiocese in what exactly?" he asked, pretending it really didn't matter to him.

"What else? The same thing that's been plaguing the Catholic Church all over the country for the last several years."

"You're saying Monsignor O'Sullivan's been abusing boys?"

"Keep it down," Christine whispered, getting up from the porch swing to glance inside the house. "If Mom found out I was working on something that might go against the church, she'd be lighting candles for the salvation of my soul for weeks." Satisfied that their mother wasn't listening at the door, she leaned against the porch rail and took a sip of her beer before she continued. "A lot of what we have right now is considered speculation and rumor, because no one's willing to go on the record."

"Maybe no one's willing to go on the record because it is speculation and rumor." Nick wasn't good at hiding his disdain for the news media, despite his sister being a part of that crazy world. And right now, he hated that Christine seemed willing to point to O'Sullivan's death as proof of a bunch of rumors, some sort of way to validate a story she was trying to dig up. Hadn't she learned anything from four years ago?

"Sometimes even the most outrageous rumors have a grain of truth to them."

"And sometimes they're simply started by bitter, vengeful people," he added.

"Okay, then how about the rumor that O'Sullivan was taking secret documents with him to Rome and now all of a sudden they're missing."

Too late. The expression of surprise must have registered on his face, because she was nodding at him with that "I gotcha" look.

"What kind of documents?" he asked.

"So the police did ask about them?" Now Christine sat down next to him again on the swing, leaning in as if they were about to exchange secrets.

"They asked Tony if Monsignor O'Sullivan was delivering anything to the Vatican for Archbishop Armstrong. And they asked about a brown leather portfolio."

"Really? So the documents might be missing."

"What kind of documents, Christine?"

She hesitated as if she needed to think about what she could and couldn't tell him. Ordinarily he might have enjoyed having the tables turned for a change. She was concerned about divulging classified information to him instead of him trying to decide what pieces of an investigation or criminal indictment he could share with her.

"It hasn't just been rumors. There *have* been complaints registered against Monsignor O'Sullivan, but not with the police department. Only with the archbishop," she said in almost a whisper. Her eyes darted to the front door again as if she was still worried their mother might overhear. "Affidavits have been signed, money exchanged, promises made. But all in secret."

"If it's all so secret, how did you find out?"

"People feel less motivated to keep secrets when promises are broken. Let's just say Armstrong hasn't been holding up his end of the bargain."

"So why wouldn't he just shred any so-called documentation? Why even bother to hand deliver all of it to the Vatican?" Nick wasn't sure he was buying any of this. It sounded too sensational, too much like some conspiracy theory.

"Nicky, I'm surprised at you. Shredding such documents would be against the law," she said with a smile before she resumed her serious tone. "When the *Boston Globe* did its investigation on Cardinal Law and the Boston Archdiocese, they discovered that bishops were being told to send any documents in question to the Vatican to store. After all, the Vatican has diplomatic immunity."

"And that's what you think is happening here? In Omaha?"

She smiled again and shrugged, took another sip of her beer.

Maybe it wasn't so sensational after all, and it was exactly the kind of thing Tony would feel he couldn't talk about, couldn't tell anyone because of his loyalties to the church. Sometimes Tony could be loyal to a fault. But he also knew his friend wouldn't sit back and keep quiet if there was a chance the allegations might be true. No way would Tony allow a child abuser to get away with it even if the abuser was a priest and his boss.

"Do you think Tony knows about any of this?" Nick asked, hoping that might be the case, but from the look on his sister's face, he could tell she didn't think so.

"That's what I'd like to know," Christine said.

CHAPTER 22

Washington, D. C.

Someone was following her. Gwen glanced in her rearview mirror as she pulled into the tiny four-slot parking lot behind Mr. Lee's Market World. She had circled the block three times and so did the black SUV. Only now she didn't see it. Was it possible she was being paranoid?

The SUV's tinted windshield had been too dark to see the driver, although during the left turn at the last intersection she had gotten enough of a glimpse to know it was a man's silhouette. Traffic was crazy on a Saturday evening and it was a holiday weekend at that. Finding a parking spot in this neighborhood of small shops with a few clapboard houses tucked in between sometimes took three and four times around the block. That's probably all it was—someone trying to find a parking space. And yet, she stayed in her car, waiting, checking the mirrors and watching along the street, giving him plenty of time to catch up with her.

The killer had no reason to be following her. He had to know by now that his threat—albeit subtle—had kept her in line. She had done everything he had demanded, played along with his evil game of scavenger hunt. Why would he think she'd suddenly run to the police with his latest puzzle piece? Although this one was different from the rest. In the past he had sent her instructions, maps, information—even a cell phone—all for the purpose of directing her, leading her to find his victims. She believed it was to show her what he had done, what he was capable of doing. But why send a single earring? She couldn't help wondering if this latest victim was still alive. If that was true, was this a cruel taunt? Or was he giving her a chance to stop him?

Gwen twisted around, searching up and down the side streets in both directions. No black SUV with dark tinted windows. This was ridiculous. Her mind was playing tricks on her. She was allowing him to screw with her mind and he wasn't even here.

She glanced down at the manila envelope sitting on the passenger seat, now encased in plastic. Next to it was the water glass she had offered Rubin Nash, also in plastic. Before she left her office she had phoned Benny Hassert at Hassert Independent Labs. She had decided to drop off the items on her way home. Benny had agreed to put them on his priority list, no questions asked. After all, she was a longtime client. He was used to her bringing him anything, from human saliva for DNA testing to soil samples. He had no idea if this was for an FBI case she had been independently contracted to help on. He hadn't asked. He didn't care. He would simply have the results for her on Monday. And then she would know whether or not the fingerprints on the envelope with the earring matched those on the water glass and whether or not Rubin Nash was the killer.

And if it was Nash, she'd have something solid, something substantial. There would be enough of a reason to believe he posed a serious threat to do harm. And she would have just cause to give everything to Maggie, to disregard any and all patient/doctor confidentiality. The police would have enough to make an arrest. He couldn't possibly hurt her father or any other woman ever again once he had been arrested and became their prime suspect.

Maybe it sounded a bit arrogant to think she could catch Rubin Nash so easily. Had she suspected him sooner, she could have already put an end to his killing spree. And maybe, just maybe, if the earring's owner was still alive, she could save her.

Gwen checked both sides of the street again and finally decided the SUV must have found a parking space somewhere else. She must have been wrong about it. She convinced herself that she needed some rest. A good night's sleep would be a nice change, and once inside Mr. Lee's World Market she started to browse the wine aisle, looking for a choice chardonnay.

The scents of ginger, garlic and fresh-baked bread worked its magic, soothing her frayed nerves. Each aisle was a sort of aromatherapy. She didn't need a degree in psychology to know that she sought comfort in food, not just eating it, but preparing and sharing a meal. She had her mom to thank for that. Her Italian mother had always insisted mealtimes were to be joyful and enjoyable. Arguments were never allowed around the dinner table and everyone, including guests, participated in the preparations. Almost every important conversation she had ever had with her parents happened during this time. It was while stuffing a batch of cannoli that she convinced her father she should leave New York City to go to college. Her mother had been her silent advocate, not realizing at the time that Gwen would never return home to live and work alongside her father.

It wasn't until Gwen had her doctorate that she realized what an education in mediation and negotiation her mother's mealtimes were. Once in a while she'd recommend to her own patients—especially those who respected rituals—to share a meal as an excuse to reach out to someone they otherwise had difficulty talking to.

"Hey, Doc, how you today?" Mr. Lee nodded and waved at her from behind the meat-and-cheese counter as he sliced what looked like a chunk of corned beef.

"I'm in dire need of some buffalo mozzarella," she told him.

"Yes, yes, I have plenty. And I give you some garlic butter, too. I just made. Fresh. Lots of garlic, the way you like it."

"Sounds wonderful." Gwen smiled at him, thinking how wonderful, indeed, it was to have a man know exactly what she liked and needed. Never mind that he was eighty-one, five inches shorter than her and had a jealous wife who accused him of flirting with all his redheaded female customers.

He shuffled to the back room as he always did, as if getting her mozzarella and garlic butter came from his private stash instead of from what he kept out front. What he kept out front looked equally delicious and fresh, but what came from the back he put in special containers made of hard plastic. It was almost like taking food home from a relative or friend and feeling the need to return the container.

She glanced around the store again as she waited, looking for anything else that might help make her feel better, that might ease the tension. That's when she saw a woman turn and duck into the next aisle.

"Dena?" she called, but stayed put, not wanting to embarrass the young woman or herself if it wasn't her assistant.

It took longer than it should have for Dena to come back around the corner and when she did, her pale cheeks were flushed as though she had been caught somewhere she shouldn't be.

"Hi, Dr. Patterson. I thought that was you." She flipped her unruly dark hair out of eyes as if it may have been the reason she hadn't been able to recognize her boss.

"I didn't know you shopped here," Gwen said, noticing that Dena's handbasket was filled with a variety of cheeses, a bottle of wine and some Bavarian chocolates, an assortment one might choose for a romantic evening. But as far as Gwen could tell, it looked as though Dena was alone. Or perhaps not? There was a slight glance over her shoulder.

"I remember you raving about it," Dena said. Then as if she felt the need to explain, she added in almost a whisper, "I just started dating someone new."

"You've come to the right place." Gwen found herself glancing around, hoping for a glimpse, which only seemed to make Dena flinch.

"Yeah, I know. It's great. I'm sort of in a hurry though." And she started to back away. "I'll see you on Monday."

"Have a great weekend," she said, but Dena had already escaped around the same corner.

Was she that uncomfortable sharing a piece of her private life with her boss? But then, Gwen knew she had contributed to the discomfort. She had purposely not encouraged any kind of personal relationship with her assistant, never so much as confiding any special hangouts, habits or even where she lived.

Dena was free to shop wherever she wanted. So why would she bother to lie about Gwen telling her about Mr. Lee's World?

CHAPTER 23

Saturday evening
Columbia, Missouri

Father Gerald Kincaid excused himself from the group of chattering women. If they gave their husbands or children half the attention they gave him, they'd have less to complain to him about. A vicious circle, no doubt.

However, he enjoyed the attention. It felt good to be needed again. He knew he could take their vulnerabilities, their weaknesses, their sins, and gain energy and power from them. Perhaps he needed them as much as they needed him.

This party, though it officially celebrated All Saints Catholic Church's silver jubilee and an early Fourth of July, was also a special occasion for him, too. Today was six months since he'd arrived, having finished his required leave of absence. The time away had been good for him. Though the New Mexico air had dried out his skin, the Servants of the Paraclete had been kind and generous. Now he was ready—more than ready—to get back to work.

He walked through the crowded parking lot, greeting everyone by name. The surprise on each face at his ability to remember was worth the memorization drills he had put himself through.

The entire congregation had worked for two days to transform the parking lot and children's playground into a carnival. There were pushcarts with anything from funnel cakes and pink cotton candy to corn dogs and Sno-Kones. Game booths lined the back lot and the local hardware store had even constructed a fun house. Streamers and balloons snapped and waved in the breeze, a few of the balloons breaking free and sailing off into the cloudless sky. A barbershop quartet, made up of two church council members, a deacon and his son, found themselves with a constant audience, though Father Gerald couldn't help thinking that positioning themselves next to the altar society ladies' baked-goods stand added to their popularity.

Families had begun to lay out blankets on the grass, setting out their picnic dinners and settling into their spots for the fireworks show that would come later, just after dark. The small children already had their glow tubes ready, swirling them around, preparing for their preshow. Some of the teenagers made themselves comfortable on the hoods of the family cars that lined the far end of the parking lot.

Some of the younger boys had gathered in the back field for a game of touch football. There were a dozen things Father Gerald needed to check on, and yet that's where he found himself headed—to the field of boys. That's where he felt most at home. He still believed it was because his own childhood had been cut short. If only his mother had let him finish high school with his classmates instead of insisting he enter the seminary two years early. If only…

Being with the boys made him feel young. It seemed to make up for what he had missed as a boy. Just being around them rejuvenated him in a way the New Mexico treatment center could never accomplish. He had tried to explain it to Dr. Marik, but the old doctor didn't quite understand. Nor did he want to understand. Instead, he seemed more concerned with writing glowing reports that would please Cardinal Rose.

Two of the boys waved at Father Gerald, and he jogged the rest of the way to the field. Someone tossed him the ball, and after several runs and handoffs he found himself at the bottom of a pile of giggling and yelling boys. Sean Harris lay stretched across him with his butt up against Father Gerald's groin, and despite having an elbow in his side and Jacob Raine's foot in his face, he found himself getting excited, excited enough that he could feel an erection starting. Excited enough that he asked Sean Harris to help him clean up after the fireworks show.

He knew the boy's father had recently lost his job. The family was strapped for cash and the twenty dollars he offered Sean for an hour's work would be considered very generous. In fact, the boy's mother would probably even agree to Father Gerald's suggestion of driving Sean home.

Yes, this was turning out to be a wonderful occasion for him. He tried to make his way through the crowd, now bumping into people as they oohed and aahed, their faces turned up to watch the spectacular light show that was just getting started. The only light came from the fireworks since even the parking lot had gone dark to accommodate the show. Music blasted on four large speakers, synchronized to the flashes and pops.

He stepped over several blanket corners, trying to avoid stepping on any occupants. The flashes of light gave an odd sense of motion almost setting him off balance as he tried to adjust his eyes. He stumbled over a cooler, waving off a muffled apology from its owner and bumping into several boys who pushed to get a better view.

"Sorry, Father," one of them sang out.

The blasts were louder now, and Father Gerald could even feel the vibrations of sound. Finally he was almost through the crowd when someone ran into him again, only this time without stopping and without an apology. It knocked the air out of him. He couldn't breathe. He grabbed his chest and gulped for air. His fingers, his hand, became wet and sticky. Only in the dark he couldn't see.

The sky lit up again, and he saw the stain blooming on the front of his shirt. The pain, the sting, seemed to suddenly race through his insides. When had he fallen to his knees? He could still hear the bangs and pops, but even they became faint, fading out somewhere in the background.

The fireworks show wasn't finished, and yet, everything went black.

CHAPTER 24

Sunday, July 4
Interstate 95

They had been on the road for almost two hours when Maggie realized she and Racine were discussing the case without disagreement, with no cheap shots or competing theories. Racine had even allowed Harvey to come along, giving him the entire back seat of her Infiniti G35 without cringing or fussing about his huge paws on her immaculate leather.

At first Maggie thought it was all for show, a way to impress her, win her over. But Maggie wasn't that easily impressed, and Racine wasn't exactly patient or polite enough to ignore something that rubbed her the wrong way. And a Labrador retriever—even a sleeping one—in your forty-thousand-dollar car would be difficult to ignore.

"On your weirdo-meter, where would you say this guy falls?" Racine's voice broke into Maggie's thoughts.

"My weirdo-meter?"

"Hey, I know you've tracked down some major mother-fuckers—excuse my French. I've been trying to tone down what my dad refers to as my potty-mouth when I visit him."

Racine took a gulp of Diet Pepsi as if to wash it away. "You know what I mean. What category does this guy fall into? Is he a Simon Shelby or an Albert Stucky?"

Racine was referring to two very different serial killers Maggie had encountered in the last several years. Simon Shelby killed his victims to possess their imperfections, bottling brain tumors and sticking diseased hearts in jars to compensate for his own childhood illness. Shelby was sick, mentally, not physically. Albert Stucky, however, was simply evil, or at least that was Maggie's explanation for why any madman would steal his victims' organs, drop them into a take-out container and then leave them for someone to discover.

Despite what most people thought, profiling serial killers wasn't as simple as putting each one into some category and predicting the next move, like some twisted or elaborate chess game. Instead, it required crawling inside the killer's mind and looking into the dark corners without being sucked in.

"It's not as simple as figuring out a category," she finally told Racine.

"Oh, I know that. But try to give me an idea of what kind of brain drain strangles a woman and then chops off her head. Are we talking major loose screws or what? This goes beyond the search for the ultimate boner, doesn't it?"

"I think this guy is more about rage than sexual gratification."

"Rage, huh? So you don't think he's hanging on to the torsos for convenient boinking?"

"Boinking?"

"Yeah, you know sort of his own preserved blowup doll but without the hot air."

Maggie smiled at Racine's lingo and simplistic profile. She glanced at the detective with her hip Ray-Bans, spiky blond hair, pink Key West tank top and Ralph Lauren khakis. She couldn't remember ever looking or feeling that chic, young and carefree. Only recently had Maggie started to splurge on designer things for herself, like a pair of expensive Cole Hahn leather flats that she let Gwen talk her into buying. Even her two-story Tudor in upscale Newburgh Heights just outside of the District—which had been bought with funds from a trust her father had left her—was decorated in what might be politely called traditional and practical.

She was logical and disciplined, stubborn and determined. She attributed it to the necessity of having to grow up too soon and too fast, of losing her father and becoming a caretaker of her alcoholic suicidal mother all at the young age of twelve. Whatever carefree spirit she may have possessed had easily been squelched sometime during those dark days of fighting off her mother's drunken suitors or while trying to make sure the electric bill was paid or finding something to eat before getting herself off to school in the morning. She worked her way through college and even her ex-husband, Greg, had once been attracted to her mature and responsible sense of duty. Never mind that those were the same traits that ended up driving him away when she transferred them to her job as an FBI agent.

Racine had lost a parent as a child, too. One more thing they had in common. So it wasn't as if she had had a fairy-tale or even a carefree life. The difference, however, was Luc Racine, a loving, doting father who made sure his little girl got to be a little girl. Ironic because here Julia Racine had been trying so hard to impress and emulate Maggie and as it turned out, Maggie actually envied Racine. Funny, Maggie thought, how life threw you curveballs just when you thought you had everything figured out. Just when you thought you could trust your judgment of people.

"Hey, earth to O'Dell. Are you still with me? Do you need to get out and stretch?"

Maggie realized she had tuned out Racine for too long.

"No, I'm fine," she said, twisting around to check on Harvey. The dog was sprawled out and fast asleep.

"You sure you're okay?"

"Just a little tired, I guess."

"Another big night, huh?"

Racine gave her a look over her sunglasses and only then did Maggie remember Harvey's slobberfest that Racine had overheard on Friday evening. She started laughing.

"Hey, it's none of my business," Racine said, waving a hand at her as if to say it was no big deal. "You don't have to tell me anything."

Maggie couldn't help it. She kept laughing, harder now, and somehow she managed to say, "It was Harvey."

"What?"

"It was Harvey you heard the other night."

It took Racine a second to register. Maggie thought she saw a bit of a blush. It was difficult to tell with the sunglasses. Maggie started laughing again, and soon Racine was joining her.

CHAPTER 25

Omaha, Nebraska

Tommy Pakula knew he'd be making up for this one for months. It didn't matter that it was a holiday. His wife, Clare, was used to him working plenty of holidays. However, he and Clare had agreed long ago that Sunday mornings would be family time. He had even signed up to be an usher at Saint Stan's to prove to her how serious he was about keeping that pact. They'd all go to early Sunday mass, and then out for brunch. He actually looked forward to it every week.

There had been three times he had been called away on a Sunday morning in the last several years since the pact was made. But being called away could and had been forgiven easily. This time was a bit harder to forgive. He had tried to explain the urgency to Clare. When that didn't work, he'd tried joking that he was missing mass for a private consultation with the monsignor.

Now as he looked down at Monsignor William O'Sullivan's gray body laid out on the stainless-steel autopsy table, Pakula realized it wasn't much of a joke. This was sort of a private consultation in which Pakula hoped the monsignor would tell him what happened in that airport bathroom.

Martha Stofko, Chief Medical Examiner for Douglas County, had already taken the external measurements and samples. Before she made the Y incision, she inspected the old priest's chest, taking several pictures and now sticking a gloved finger into the wound.

"Tell me again why we're doing this on a Sunday morning," she asked, looking up at Pakula.

"You can thank Archbishop Armstrong. For some reason he's got the chief convinced expediency equals respect." Pakula wasn't sure Stofko would understand. She was a transplant from somewhere in California—not a hometown kid. It took firsthand experience to realize the politics and power of the archbishop.

"So Chief Ramsey is Catholic?"

Maybe Stofko understood better than Pakula gave her credit for.

"Supposedly the monsignor's sister wants him back home in Connecticut as soon as possible." Pakula repeated the request, or rather the demand, word for word, just as Brother Sebastian had ordered over the phone.

However, this time Martha Stofko looked up at Pakula over half glasses that sat at the end of her nose.

Pakula simply shrugged. "You know me, Martha. I just do as I'm told."

"Yeah, right. In that case, come over and take a look at this."

Pakula watched her poke at the wound, separating the flaps of skin.

"See how the wound is crisscrossed?"

"It looks like an X."

"Or a cross. You usually get a cross-shaped appearance like this when the knife is twisted as it's pulled out. It was a double-edged blade, thick in the center, but less than an inch wide. I should be able to tell you how long once I dissect and follow the path."

Stofko stuck her index finger into the wound again, this time making her finger almost disappear.

"It was an upward thrust. I can be more definitive once I see the tract."

"Right-handed or left?" Pakula asked.

"I'm not sure."

Stofko started examining the monsignor's hands, lifting each and checking all the way up the arms.

"There doesn't appear to be any defensive wounds."

"I noticed that," Pakula said. "We found him by the sink. I think the killer came up behind him. Probably took him by surprise."

"If that's the case, I'd say the killer's right-handed. He may have come up from behind on the monsignor's right side, leaned around and stuck him up and under the rib cage."

"Just lucky, or how hard is it to know where to stick so you don't hit bone?"

"It's a fifty-fifty chance," Stofko replied. "Your guy used enough force to better his odds. Take a look at the bruising below the wound." The two-inch mark was a straight, narrow purple line. "The hilt of the knife left quite an imprint, which means there was considerable force to the thrust."

"Could that tell us anything about the size of this guy?"

"Not necessarily. It has more to do with rapid movement than bulk or strength. This whole area," Stofko said, waving her gloved hand across the priest's abdomen, "is fairly vulnerable. The skin is the body's most resistant tissue. Once it's penetrated it takes almost no additional force to penetrate the other tissue or organs, especially if the weapon doesn't encounter any bones. Knowing that the hilt of the knife was pushed against the body will give me a better idea of how long it was, although with this kind of forcible thrust the depth of the wound usually exceeds the actual blade length. So I take that into consideration, too."

"Any guess on what kind of knife?"

"It's a wide hilt for such a long, narrow blade. I haven't seen anything quite like it. My initial guess would be some kind of dagger. And you see this darker, larger bruise in the center of the hilt?" She pointed it out, and Pakula was surprised he hadn't noticed it earlier.

"What the hell is it?"

"Again, it's just another guess, but I'm thinking the hilt and the handle might be decorative. Which would make sense with a dagger or perhaps a fancy letter opener."

Stofko made the Y incision on the Monsignor's chest and began pulling back the layers of skin and fat, careful not to disturb the wound's path until she was ready to dissect it.

Pakula hated the snap of cartilage, but he didn't look away as Stofko took what looked like garden clippers to the rib cage and started snipping. He had gotten the information he needed, but he'd stay and keep her company for a few minutes before heading over to the Douglas County Crime Lab. Hopefully they had found something, anything that would shed some light on who the killer was.

Brother Sebastian and the archbishop seemed content with the monsignor being a victim of unfortunate random violence. They seemed more concerned about what happened to the leather portfolio than they did the monsignor. But Pakula's gut told him there was nothing random about this murder. If that was true, then there were more secrets being kept than what was inside that missing portfolio.

"This is interesting," Martha Stofko said, getting Pakula's attention.

Stofko had been hunched over the chest cavity, but now stood back, scooping out a yellowish glob and placing it on the scale. "Fifteen hundred grams," she mumbled, jotting down the information quickly then moving the glob to a dissection tray.

"Okay, what are we looking at?" Pakula asked, coming up beside her. Try as he might, Pakula still saw just a glob of tissue where M.E.'s saw tumors or nodules.

Stofko grabbed what looked like an ordinary butter knife and began slicing into and sectioning what resembled chicken fat.

"A healthy liver usually has the texture and color of calves' livers. You've probably seen them in the supermarket."

"This sure doesn't look like a healthy liver." Pakula grimaced at what looked more like a soft, yellow mush of tissue. "So what was wrong with Monsignor O'Sullivan?"

"I'd say the good monsignor liked to throw back a few. Actually, more than a few and over a very long period."

"Oh, great, an alcoholic priest," Pakula said as he wiped his hand over his shaved head. Just one more secret to add to the mess.

CHAPTER 26

Venezuela

Father Michael Keller folded the vestments and placed them in his special wooden box alongside the newspaper clippings. He was quite pleased with himself. The Sunday-morning mass had gone better than expected, despite his nausea. He only wished he could figure out what was making him ill.

By now he had grown accustomed to the heat and humidity. He had gained control over the insects, rarely sharing his home with them anymore. And although there was no end to the mosquitoes, he thought he had developed an immunity to their venom, unless…unless he had contracted malaria or West Nile Virus. Was that possible?

He felt his forehead again, wiping the dripping sweat off, then placing his palm flat against his hot brow. Definitely a fever. Perhaps he needed to fix himself another cup of tea. It certainly had soothed him earlier and gotten him not only through the mass but the meet-and-greet afterward.

He hated the meet-and-greet, smiling and nodding, pretending he understood their crude English. He had come up with the perfect response, one they all seemed pleased with, one that sent them away smiling and nodding—"I'll keep you in my prayers." It worked every time. Poor wretches needed to be in someone's prayers. And after all, he was here to help them, to be a part of their miserable little community.

He had grown weary of picking up in the middle of the night and moving to a new location. And for that reason, this place was supposed to be different, though it wasn't much different than any of the others. In fact, they all looked the same, the same weathered shacks and huts kept together by the grace of God. And the villagers were the same, too, apparently content with their rags for clothes and gruel for food, but so desperately needy for attention and praise, especially from God, and so of course, especially from him. He was, after all, the next best thing in their minds. And to some—the dying old women and the innocent little children—he was God.

Yes, he was tired of moving. He had come to that decision, even after hours of panic over the Halloween mask, that death mask from the past. He had convinced himself that it was someone's idea of a bad joke. It had to be. There was no way anyone could have tracked him here. It was impossible. Besides, he wasn't about to let anyone scare him into the night ever again.

The tea kettle began to hiss just as the rains started, again. He tried to remember how long it had been since he had seen the sun. It was beginning to take its toll. The familiar throbbing in his head was starting again, too. Maybe it was simply sinus problems, the humidity making it impossible to feel any relief. Could that be the reason for his fever? For the nausea? For the damn throbbing.

He poured the tea, inhaling its therapeutic aroma and already feeling better. It was times like this when he felt a bit vulnerable, that the tea reminded him of his mother, his dear saintly mother. Hot tea and cookies had been her one indulgence, which she hid from her husband lest he take that away from her, too. The day she shared it with him, treating him to the whole ritual—the entire experience, including the secrecy—he felt an eternal bond. It had been their special treat, their special time with each other. Perhaps that's why it was still such a comfort to him. It had become a way to conjure up those few good memories from his past.

He checked the time and brought his cup of tea to the wooden table with the laptop computer. The computer had been an enormous splurge, beyond a guilty pleasure, but also a godsend. It had become his connection to the outside world, to civilization, oftentimes restoring his sanity with a press of a button. And always, there was someone in the village who, no matter what cost or inconvenience or magical skills, was able to get an Internet connection for him as long as there was a phone line close by. However, the dial-up speed was slow and the time frame to access it annoyingly short.

He waited patiently for the computer to boot up and then for it to go through its tedious process of trying to locate and make the Internet connection. He sipped his tea and sat back, listening to the rain. The computer prompt asked for his password and he punched it in. Then he sat back again, expecting to wait some more. The connection came up immediately.

"YOU'VE GOT MAIL," the computerized voice told him and it brought a sense of comfort almost as strong as the tea. His friend from the States, it had to be. It was the only person he had given out his e-mail address to. Although they had exchanged very little personal information about each other, they had shared some wonderful in-depth discussions on current events and moral quandaries. It was the closest to a friend that he had had in years…actually, maybe ever.

He clicked on New Mail. Yes, it was his friend, the clever e-mail tag always making him smile: TheSinEater@aol.com.

There were never greetings, a detail he appreciated, not wanting to waste time on pleasantries that were no longer necessary. This message contained two separate links that looked like news articles. It was something they did quite frequently, drawing each other's attention to particular events and starting a whole new discussion. At the end of the message his friend simply wrote: YOU MAY BE NEXT. Probably another attempt at humor; he liked his friend's dry sense of humor, their occasional exchange of playful barbs.

He clicked on the first link and again sat back to wait for the ever-slow connection. When the page finally came up, the headline startled him enough that he jolted upright, almost spilling his tea: Omaha Monsignor Knifed To Death In Airport Restroom.

CHAPTER 27

University of New Haven
New Haven, Connecticut

Maggie stood back and watched Professor Adam Bonzado turn the flesh-eaten skull around in his hands, holding it and examining it as if it were a jeweled treasure. She had never realized before how strong his hands looked. The long fingers like that of a piano player, careful and gentle yet probing the loose flesh, inquisitive without hesitating and without cringing. Gwen had given her a hard time, suggesting she had met her match with Bonzado—finally a man just as obsessed with evil as she was.

"I know there's not much to go on with either of these," Racine said, also standing back. She had placed the metal cooler on one of his classroom lab tables and let him open it. Maggie wondered if it wasn't a professional courtesy so much as Racine wasn't anxious to handle a human head with or without maggots.

"These are in much better shape than some of the ones that pass through here," Bonzado said, lifting and looking at it from all angles. "I enjoy teaching, but this is the stuff I live for. Keeps me on my toes. Besides, I get to take two attractive women out to lunch."

Maggie thought she saw Racine blush, but she looked away, pretending to be preoccupied with the contents of the room. Was it possible Racine had a crush on Bonzado? Long before Racine had hit on her, Maggie had heard rumors that Racine was bisexual. Still, it had come as a surprise. At the time, Maggie was married, obsessed with her work and naïve—or perhaps *oblivious* was a better term—to anyone's advances whether they be male or female. Actually, when she thought about it, that wasn't much different than what she was like now. Except for the married part, she was still pretty oblivious.

"And Maggie, I promise lunch will be much better than vegetable soup on one of my Bunsen burners."

He glanced up at her as if to see if she remembered or perhaps to see if she would catch this one, this advance, this attempt at flirting. Case in point. Could he read her mind? Maggie couldn't help smiling. Of course she remembered. The last time she had been to his classroom lab he had a pot of soup cooking alongside a boiling pot of human bones. It had sort of freaked her out when she saw him scooping up a bite. That was before she knew it was his lunch and not more human remains.

Bonzado laid the skull down carefully on the table in front of them and brought out a penlight, bending over to examine the inner orifices. The table was one of only two not filled with boxes of bones or lines of skeletons. Many of the skeletons looked like failed attempts at putting the pieces together, missing major sections.

Last time there had been many more pots, huge ones, boiling on the burners, filling the room with the smell of cooked flesh. Thankfully the burners were empty this time, perhaps because of the holiday weekend. Even the dryers and the sinks in the far corner looked empty, no bony hands waving up at them.

The shelves that lined the back wall, however, were just as crowded as she remembered with jars and vials, bowls and cardboard boxes, all filled with jigsaw pieces of bone, some labeled, others waiting, perhaps forever, to be identified or claimed.

A streak of sunlight came in the classroom's double-paned windows, a yellow-orange splash that cast an eerie tone over the entire room. Maggie couldn't help thinking they didn't need the added sense of drama. Bonzado already looked like an actor out of *Hamlet* with skull in hand and a soulful look. That is, of course, if you could imagine Hamlet in a purple-and-yellow Hawaiian shirt, khaki walking shorts and hiking boots.

"The one we found Friday might be identified by sight. I've got someone checking against the missing persons list. Dental's intact, too. It was in much better shape," Racine explained, and Maggie wondered if she was simply trying to fill the silence. Bonzado didn't seem to be listening. "Well, better shape if you don't count all the fucking maggots it had on it. Jesus! I haven't seen that many in a long time."

"You're lucky in this heat. The little suckers work fast," Bonzado said. So he had been listening. "Where was this one found? Was it close to the water, too?"

"Is that Jane Doe A or B?" Racine asked, looking for the toe tag Stan Wenhoff had attached to each bag. Without the tags it was difficult to tell the two skulls apart. Racine rummaged through the cooler, searching for any ID that may have been left behind.

"It's Jane Doe A," Racine finally said, pulling out the tag. "This one was found in Rock Creek Park. A wooded area down away from the running trail. A woman and her dog found it. She called it in and gave the directions. Said her dog stumbled upon it."

"It was preserved fairly well for being in the woods."

"It was covered with leaves and dirt." Racine was checking her notes from the file.

"Did you say a woman called it in?" Maggie didn't remember seeing a name in the file and now she realized it may have never been given. "She didn't take you to the site or meet you there?"

"No, she didn't even come in to file a report," Racine said. "Called it in to 911 and the dispatch operator took all the information."

"And she didn't leave a name?"

"No name." Racine looked up from her notes and met Maggie's eyes.

She could see the detective was thinking the same thing she was. Had it been the same woman caller who directed them to the bank of the Potomac on Friday? To another one of the killer's dump sites?

"Did a woman call in the other one?"

Racine pulled out another file folder and started riffling through it. "Here it is. Jane Doe B was found outside a construction site for a new parking garage. The owner, a Mr. Bradford Zahn, contacted the police. Hmm...no mysterious woman caller." She wasn't pleased and shrugged when she looked up at Maggie. "So much for our theory."

Bonzado appeared unfazed by it all. Instead, he had laid the head on its side and was examining the marks at the base of the severed skull.

"I can't be certain what he used to cut off her head, but I'm thinking it was more like he chopped it than cut."

"Chopped and ripped," Maggie added. "The last victim's neck had a lot of rips and tears."

"This reminds me of a case I had a couple of months ago," Bonzado told them. "All that was found was the right leg. It was fairly decomposed, too. Somebody fished it out of the Connecticut River. The chop marks were very similar to this. I kept trying to reproduce the marks, using just about everything I could think of. The closest match was a small hatchet, the kind you'd use for camping."

"So it was literally a hatchet job, huh?" Racine laughed at her own joke.

Bonzado didn't. But he did smile even though he went on to point out gashes on what was left of this victim's split vertebrae. "Usually when a body's dismembered, the joints and bones are sawn or cut with a blade. A sharp, blunt object like a hatchet or ax—or he could have even used a machete—leaves gashes in the bone from the attempts that didn't quite slice through. That probably explains the rips and tears you were seeing in the skin and tissues, too."

"There's one thing that bothers me," Maggie said as she watched Bonzado add some cleaning solvent to the bone. The liquid seemed to highlight the chop marks. "This guy has to be disciplined and organized enough to plan not only the murders, but the drop sites. And yet, it's almost as if he completely loses it after he's killed them. The last victim showed signs of being strangled and hit over the head with a ball-peen hammer. A hatchet or machete just contributes to this idea that he sort of loses it."

"Yeah, and what about that? Why not a saw or knife?" Racine asked. "Is it poor planning? Does he use whatever is handy?" Racine asked, but she was directing her question to Maggie, the FBI profiler, instead of Bonzado.

"He has to take them someplace safe to cut them up," Maggie said. "Where could he go that just happens to have a hatchet or machete handy?"

"My dad keeps a machete in his garden shed," Bonzado offered. "He claims it works for anything from hacking off tree branches to plucking up dandelions. As for the hatchet, someone who camps a lot might actually carry one around in his trunk with other camping supplies."

"Even if he keeps it in his car, where the hell does he take them?" Racine wanted to know. "Cutting off someone's head is a messy job. And it's not like there's a whole lot of gardening sheds in the District."

"We can't assume he kills them in the District," Maggie said. "Just because their heads are dumped there."

"Fair enough," Racine said with no argument. Maggie thought she was awfully agreeable this trip. "So he could possibly have access to a cabin or toolshed, but he probably lives in the District, right? From what I know about serial kill-

ers, they don't usually display their handiwork too far from
where they live or work."

"Excuse me, ladies." Bonzado now had forceps and was
bent over a patch of loose flesh, pulling it away from the base
of the skull. "I might have something here. Mind if I pluck
this off?"

"Whatever you need to do."

Maggie came in close over Bonzado's shoulder, but she
wasn't sure what had gotten his attention. The flesh was so decomposed it had turned gray and black in the areas where it remained attached. Even the cleaning solvent couldn't help here.

"What is it?" Maggie finally asked, thinking something
had been embedded in the flesh.

Bonzado carefully ripped off a piece of tissue about two
inches in diameter. He held it up in the sunlight, but Maggie
still couldn't tell what it was that had gotten his attention.

"The epidermis is gone and I need to clean this up." He was
grinning now and it reminded Maggie of a proud schoolboy
with a show-and-tell project. "If I'm not mistaken, I think this
may be a tattoo from the back of her neck. The killer may have
thought he removed it when it ripped off the top layer, but tattoos actually show up better deep under where the ink settles."

"You think there's enough to figure out what it is?"

"Hard to tell." And now he was holding it up under a fluo-
rescent desk light. "But if there is enough, tattoos can be
pretty unique. We've identified victims by their tattoos in
other instances."

"So maybe the killer slipped up." Racine sounded hopeful.

"Oh, yeah. I'd say he may have made a big-time boo-boo."

CHAPTER 28

Omaha, Nebraska

Tommy Pakula left Clare and the girls outside under the canopy in their backyard. They eagerly excused him so they could discuss plans for the big Fourth of July bash later at Memorial Park without him breaking into his off-key rendition of the Beach Boys, just one of the has-been entertainment lineups for the event.

He didn't mind. He had the family room to himself. Even better, he had the TV remote to himself. He clicked the TV on, switching channels, and leaving it on Fox News for background noise while he pulled out the file folders he had brought home. He didn't usually bring home files, but something about this one bugged him and Weston's taunt only made him anxious.

He pulled out crime scene and autopsy photos along with the reports he had downloaded from the Minneapolis Police Department. With no leads in their investigation they seemed to welcome his inquiries. Right now Minneapolis considered it random, but Pakula wondered if the killer knew that his victim was an ex-priest.

The Douglas County Crime Lab hadn't much for him yet. It was too early. Medina had, however, tagged and labeled some of the trace she had collected. Locard's Principle had come through for him many times in the past. No matter how careful a killer was, there was an exchange of debris that took place between the killer and the victim. It was inevitable. Unless the killer came to the scene in a sterilized suit he was bound to leave something—mud from his shoes, fibers from his shirt or if they were really lucky, hairs from his head.

Pakula looked over the plastic evidence bags Medina had included. The first one looked like bread crumbs. He held up the bag to read Medina's note on the back label:

Location: Front of victim's shirt.
Lab Test Conclusive—white unleavened bread.

Pakula scratched his head. He still couldn't figure this one out. Why the hell would there be bread crumbs on the front of the victim's shirt? No way could he have picked them up from the floor. Did one of the voyeurs who trampled in on the scene have a sandwich? Nothing had been left behind, so it wasn't like the monsignor had put aside his dinner. Or if he did, was it possible one of the assholes who came in to take a piss, decided to help himself to a half-eaten sandwich? Sounded ridiculous, but he had seen stranger things.

Pakula picked up the next plastic evidence bag. This time he started to get excited when he noticed the short strands of hair. Hair wasn't always a guarantee for DNA extraction. You needed the root or bulb or a part of it to get anything credible. Even two strands from the same person weren't always conclusive. Right now with no evidence Pakula would take a single nose hair if it proved to be the killer's. He read Medina's label and let out a disappointed sigh. He wanted to toss the bag across the room:

Location: Strands taken from back of victim's shirt.

Lab Test Conclusive—Canine hair. Breed Unknown at
this time.

All his excitement and it was a fucking dog the monsignor
had encountered, not the killer.

He glanced out the window. Clare and the girls were still
under the canopy, laughing. No serious debates or arguments
to bring one of them in, at least not for a while, so the coast
was clear. He sorted through the photos and selected several
to lay out on the cocktail table in front of him.

One from the crime scene showed Monsignor O'Sullivan
crumpled on the floor, lying on his side, his legs twisted, and
his crushed eyeglasses beside him. Pakula looked for a close-
up of the glasses and quickly found it. They hadn't broken like
that from the fall. Someone had stepped on them. Maybe the
killer. Possibly on purpose. He made a mental note to see if
Medina had been able to pull a shoe print from either the len-
ses or from somewhere beside the eyeglasses.

He flipped through Medina's notes on other traces collected: a stray French fry, a breath mint, several fibers, some
tramped in clay and a couple of blades of some kind of weed.
Could be all from the floor and have nothing to do with the
crime scene. What would you expect from a commercial restroom floor? Not much to go on. It was as if the killer walked
in, stabbed the monsignor and walked back out without even
washing his hands. There wasn't a single bloody paper towel
in the trash can. So he walked back out with a bloody knife
and no one—not even the guy who thought he bumped into
the killer—saw the knife. How was that possible?

Pakula left the photos on the table, but set aside the file
folder. Now he was ready for Minneapolis. He scanned the police report. It was just like Weston had said—an outdoor festival during Memorial Weekend. The victim was stabbed in the
chest in the middle of the crowd. No one saw it happen. No one
claimed to see anything other than ex-padre Daniel Ellison fall
to his knees, grabbing his chest. Maybe this one was random.

Pakula tossed several of the downloaded images onto the table alongside the Omaha ones. Not much here, either. He sat back, leaned his head against the soft leather of the sofa and absently watched Fox News top-of-the-hour news report, not really listening, his mind focused instead on the scant evidence.

He was tired and frustrated and mostly he dreaded telling Chief Ramsey that he had diddly-squat. He wondered if Archbishop Armstrong's only concern was to continue to keep secret the monsignor's drinking habit. Maybe they didn't even know what was in the missing leather portfolio. Or could it simply be something embarrassing but not incriminating?

Pakula remembered Armstrong several months ago expelling two students from one of the parochial high schools for accessing porn sites on a school computer, sites the kids claimed their theology instructor—a priest whose name Pakula no longer remembered—had shown them just the day before.

At the time, Pakula thought it was Armstrong's knee-jerk reaction, an attempt to ward off the slightest suggestion of impropriety in the wake of the sexual-abuse scandals rocking other archdioceses across the country. Armstrong had managed to keep a squeaky-clean record—no criminal reports filed or any civil lawsuits pending.

Just then Pakula noticed the photo of a priest being shown on the Fox News update—his black shirt and white collar grabbing Pakula's attention even before he could read the caption below. He grabbed the remote and punched up the volume in time to hear only "…was mysteriously stabbed during a fireworks display. No other information is known at the moment. Father Gerald Kincaid was the pastor at All Saints Catholic Church in Columbia, Missouri. He was fifty-two years old."

Pakula could feel the prickle at the back of his neck and the twist in the bottom of his gut. He grabbed his cell phone and without hesitation dialed the home phone number for Chief

Ramsey. No matter how much he hated to admit it, he was beginning to think Bob Weston might be right.

Somebody was killing priests.

CHAPTER 29

Meriden, Connecticut

Maggie O'Dell watched Harvey take turns racing and chasing the much smaller Jack Russell terrier. She had never seen the big dog play so hard. She could swear Harvey looked like he was smiling and laughing as hard as Luc Racine was. Luc had already told Maggie three times that he didn't know Scrapple liked to play with other dogs, and it wasn't because he was forgetting that he had already told her but because he seemed truly amazed. Amazed and pleased. Which she knew had to make his daughter, Julia, a bit more relieved. This behavior, here and now at Hubbard Park, felt better especially after the alarming greeting they had gotten earlier at Luc's front door.

Racine had called her father, talking to him several times in the hour it took them to get from West Haven to Wallingford. He sounded excited about having guests, even suggested that if Bonzado was picking up lunch and meeting them, he should stop at Vinny's Deli. He seemed perfectly fine and yet minutes later when he answered the door he didn't recognize his daughter or Maggie. He had no idea who the two women on his front porch were or what they could possibly want.

Maggie still remembered the sick feeling in the pit of her stomach when Luc's eyes met hers and she saw that empty, confused look, a look that told her not all his pistons were firing no matter how hard he tried. It had been Harvey—who Luc had never met before—who ended up pulling him out of his memory lapse. The big dog nosed his way around Maggie to greet Luc and sniff Scrapple, Luc's Jack Russell terrier. Now the two were best friends.

Luc had managed to stay with them, keeping up with the conversation throughout the sandwiches, exchanging forensics jokes with Bonzado and asking questions when Racine got into some shoptalk. Even when he wandered off to play with the two dogs, he still appeared to know where he was. Not bad, Maggie thought, for a man with early-onset Alzheimer's.

"You've got to see the way Scrapple catches this ball," Julia told Maggie and grabbed the dirty yellow tennis ball Luc had brought along, using it, Maggie suspected, as an excuse to be with her father.

"He worries about her," Bonzado said when it was obvious both father and daughter were out of earshot. "You know, whether she'll be okay without him? They're pretty close. I don't know if Julia would admit that to you or not."

"No, she probably wouldn't," Maggie said. "I really don't know her that well."

"Really?" Bonzado seemed genuinely surprised. "She talks about you quite a bit. I guess I thought you two were pretty good friends."

Maggie didn't say anything. She wondered if Racine actually had any good friends if she considered Maggie one. Chalk it up to the job and to the crazy schedule. After all, how many people, other than another cop, could you go out with for drinks and to shoot the breeze, sharing your day, when the day included maggot-riddled heads on the edge of the Potomac? Again, it struck Maggie that Racine wasn't that much unlike herself. Other than Gwen, and maybe Tully, what good friends could she claim? She noticed Adam watching her.

"What? Do I have mayo on my face somewhere?"

"No, no. Your face is fine. Actually your face is quite perfect."

It took his follow-up smile to realize he was flirting with her.

"Why do you suppose he leaves the heads?" It was better to keep it business. She wasn't sure she remembered how the flirting thing worked anymore.

"Excuse me?"

"The killer. It's probably more convenient and much easier to transport and display the heads, but is he making a statement? Is he telling us something by leaving only the heads?"

Adam shook his head. "Always on duty," he said with another smile.

"It's a habit." But she tried not to make it sound like it was an excuse. She loved her work. Anyone who knew her accepted that. Perhaps she expected that anyone who wanted to know her would also need to accept it.

"The head's about as personal as you can get. As for what kind of a message he's sending, well, that's your expertise. One thing that has been nagging at me," he said, laying his hands flat on the top of the picnic table, "is the angle. He didn't just cut straight across her neck." His fingers emphasized his point, the right hand's index finger moving along the surface in a straight line. "Instead, he cut from just below the left ear—" and he brought the same index finger to his own throat to demonstrate the angle "—went across, dipped down and back up, almost like a notch."

"Does it mean anything?"

"I have no idea."

"Could it just be a part of his rage, a glitch, a haphazard zigzag?"

"Possibly. But it's exactly the same on both. The rest of the neck is jagged and ripped in sort of a maniacal style and yet here's this very precise, squared-off notch at the base of the throat. It's just odd. It seems out of place. You might have the M.E. check to see if the third has the same thing."

"Yes, I'll do that." She let it sink in, trying to figure out what kind of symbol the killer might be leaving behind. Adam was watching her again.

"The national forensic conference is in D.C. next month. I'll be spending over a week there for the conference and also doing a little work at the Smithsonian. How about having dinner with me?"

This time his smile wasn't quite as self-assured. His soft brown eyes seemed a bit vulnerable, and Maggie wondered if it had taken some effort for him to get to this invitation. Was it possible the handsome, outspoken professor thought he was as inept at this flirting thing as she was? Before she answered, he added, "I promise I won't even try to break any of your habits."

She couldn't help smiling. "And I promise I won't ask a single severed-head question."

Maggie's cell phone started ringing.

"Excuse me a minute," she said, flipping open the phone. "This is Maggie O'Dell."

"O'Dell, glad I reached you. Sorry to interrupt your holiday."

It was her boss, Assistant Director Cunningham. She could hear papers shuffling and imagined him at his desk, multitasking as he cradled the phone between his neck and shoulder. No holiday for him. She waved an apology to Bonzado as she got up from the table and wandered away for some privacy.

"Actually, I'm working today, sir. Detective Racine and I brought the first two Jane Doe heads up to Connecticut for Professor Bonzado to take a look at."

"Is it conclusive that the three murders were done by the same killer?"

Just like Cunningham—straight to the point. She had gotten used to his abrupt, unemotional manner. There was more flipping of pages and Maggie could hear what sounded like a TV in the background. Maybe he wasn't in his office.

"It's too early to be positive," she told him, but she knew he'd still want to hear her first impressions. So she continued, "All the decapitations look very similar. We're talking rage. The guy rips and cuts in a frenzy. Bonzado thinks he uses a hatchet or machete. He's disorganized during the killings or at least he feels safe enough to go into a rage. The decapitation must happen almost immediately after he strangles them. But then he's able to compose himself and plan the dumps. I'm still not sure I have any idea what he does with the torsos."

"Sounds like you're off to a good start. I hate to pull you away from this, but I don't have another available agent, especially with Agent Tully still on vacation. Everyone else is out of town on assignment and I have another case that needs a profiler. The body's been autopsied already, but they could hold it for another day. Do you have enough to put together a profile for Detective Racine and Chief Henderson?"

"It'd be pretty sketchy, but yes, I could do a preliminary."

"Good. That'll give them a start. Hold on a minute."

This time Maggie could hear voices in the background and Cunningham answering them, telling someone he would be there in five minutes. Was this urgent enough that he would be calling from his home? Maggie couldn't even imagine it. For one thing, she couldn't imagine Cunningham at home, although she knew he had a wife. There were never any photos or personal items on his well-organized desk or anywhere in his office to suggest a life outside that office. With anyone else it would seem odd. With Cunningham it seemed quite natural that after ten years she wouldn't even know where he lived, whether he had a three-bedroom house in the suburbs or an upscale apartment in Georgetown.

"Actually I need you on a flight tomorrow morning," he said before she realized he was back talking to her.

"Where am I going, sir?"

"Omaha, Nebraska."

CHAPTER 30

Memorial Park
Omaha, Nebraska

Tommy Pakula hated everything about these events—the crowds, the noise and the heat, all served up with warm beer and entertainers from the '60s, entertainers who had become parodies of themselves. Although he had to admit Frankie Avalon still looked pretty damn good for his age, if only he'd left those silly white shoes at home.

What Pakula especially hated was the hotshot public officials slapping him on the back, pretending—when they were really hoping—that he was one of them. He didn't know how Chief Ramsey put up with it, either. But as hometown boys—Pakula a graduate of South High, Ramsey of Creighton Prep, but about five or six years before Pakula—they both had to put up with it to a certain degree. The chief more so than Pakula, because he had left Omaha for almost a decade for greener pastures before finding his way back home and working through the red tape of politics and good ole boy networks. As hometown boys they knew about the hometown politics, too. And that's exactly why they were trying to discuss police procedure, or rather protocol, out here in the middle of a crowded park rather than some quiet coffee shop clear across town. They figured no one would ever suspect they'd talk about something so important on a sunny holiday weekend, in the middle of Memorial Park where the entire northwest lawn was riddled with blankets and lawn chairs, ice chests and portable umbrellas, leaving only narrow strips of grass on which to make your way through the maze.

They had left their families somewhere in the sea of red, white and blue with the simple excuse of finding something cold to drink. Vendors lined the circular drive around the monument at the top of the park, away from the blankets and almost out of reach of the half-dozen seven-foot amplifiers Frankie and crew had brought along. Pakula ordered a kraut-dog with the works and a tall, bucket-size Coke, while the chief settled on less indigestion with a plain dog and a tall bucket of his own, only Dew instead of Coke.

"Not sure why you want to waste your money on that." Pakula nodded at Chief Ramsey's pathetic hot dog swallowed by a bun and drowning in mustard while Pakula bit into his own, piled high and wide.

"Yeah, ask me that later when you're popping the antacids."

Chief Ramsey eyed a couple of teenagers on bicycles scoping the terrain below as if they might attempt to ride down into the crowd. Pakula recognized the habit and caught himself checking out a double-parked van with its back doors left swinging open but the owner nowhere in sight. It bugged Clare and she continuously accused him of not listening to her just because he wasn't looking at her. But with two cops it wasn't unusual at all to carry on a complete, detailed conversation without ever making eye contact.

"There's something you need to know, Tommy." Chief Ramsey glanced at him, but his eyes were quickly gone, now checking out something behind Pakula, off to the right. "Vice has had an eye on O'Sullivan and Our Lady of Sorrow."

"Holy crap," Pakula said under his breath, caught with a

mouthful. He swiped at the corner of his lips with the back of his hand. "Why the hell didn't you tell me that yesterday?"

"Because it's nothing official, not even a single complaint filed. Just some reporter from the *Herald* who's been nosing around and hassling Sassco to do something. I know Sassco's been head of Vice for only six months, but you know the guy. It doesn't take much to get his nose all bent out of shape if it involves kids. If there was anything at all, he'd be all over it. Could just be a lot of gossip and rumor. Maybe this reporter's trying too hard to hunt up a story. Maybe she's thinking it's been happening all over the country, why not here? You know how the goddamn media works."

Pakula nodded, but this time kept quiet. The chief wasn't finished, and so he took another bite.

Chief Ramsey looked all the way around them, but no one was staying in one place long enough to seem interested in their conversation.

"I'm just saying that could be why the archbishop has his shorts all in a twist about this. He's pretending that it's no big deal, but it's got to be a big fucking deal for him to send his messenger boy to pick up the luggage before the monsignor's even had a chance to get cold."

"Maybe he knows about the other priests getting iced?" Pakula suggested.

"Could be. Either way, his reputation is to round up his yes-men and very quietly but powerfully discredit, damage and ruin whoever the fuck he perceives as his enemy. And we both know he can do a pretty damn good job of it."

"If some psycho is running around the country offing priests, why wouldn't the archbishop want to do everything in his power to stop him? What am I missing?" Pakula pushed up his sunglasses and tossed the wrapper from his kraut-dog, glancing back at the vendor booth, contemplating another. After all, he still had more than half of his extra-large Coke. The chief noticed.

"Go ahead. Hell, I'd have two or three of them if they didn't stay with me for the rest of the night."

"No, I'd better not. Clare brought some meatball sand-wiches."

"Look at it this way," Chief Ramsey said around a sip at his straw, "if there was some shit going on at Our Lady of Sorrow and O'Sullivan was about to smear the entire diocese, maybe the archbishop would be grateful to have his murder chalked up to a random slice and dice. If there even was a leather portfolio full of damning evidence, it's nowhere to be found. Case closed and there's nobody digging any further. I don't believe for a second O'Sullivan's poor sister in Connecticut wants him back as soon as possible for some elaborate burial. Armstrong's probably thinking the sooner he gets buried the sooner those secrets get buried with him."

"Sort of like O'Sullivan's murder was a mixed blessing from above?"

"Exactly."

"So what are we gonna do about it?"

"Well, I'll tell you one thing, I'm already tired of His High and Mighty jacking us around and thinking he can tell me what I can or can't do. He doesn't even have the balls to do it himself. He sends his pasty-faced bully, Sebastian." Chief Ramsey paused as if he needed to settle himself down. He took another sip. "I have a buddy I met years ago, Kyle Cunningham. Long story, but he owes me one. Archbishop Armstrong thinks he's almighty, so we bring in someone he can't reach, someone who doesn't give a shit about what kind of power he thinks he has. And also someone who takes the reins and the heat if this mess ends up being some fucking serial killer offing priests. That happens and you can bet we won't just have Armstrong and the *Herald* to worry about. Besides, these days nobody minds blaming the FBI."

"We're calling in the big boys and not just Weston and crew?"

"Cunningham promised me his top profiler, so not necessarily boys, but his top boy for sure. That should be enough."

"I just want to figure this one out. Shouldn't that still be our priority?" Pakula didn't mean to sound like he was second-guessing Chief Ramsey's decision. Yet at the same time, he didn't much trust the FBI to bring any answers to the case no matter who they sent. Fact was, he didn't believe bringing a profiler in would be much help at all, despite the chief's argument. When the going got tough, he knew as lead detective it'd still be his neck on the line, not some spooky flash-in-the-pan profiler, trying to simplify everything by telling him whether the killer put on his pants any differently than the rest of them. Maybe…just maybe if they were lucky, the feds would, at least, help connect the dots with the other cases. And if there was a killer murdering priests, that could be where there were some answers.

Pakula looked squarely at the chief, waiting for his eyes to meet his, expecting some sort of reprimand for his cynicism, but instead he said, "Me, too. I just wanted it figured out." Chief Ramsey took a bite of his hot dog as if he finally had an appetite. "But when we do, you'd better be prepared to watch all hell break loose."

CHAPTER 31

He sat in front of the computer screen. He was exhausted, his vision was blurred and every muscle in his body ached. It was the same every time, as if he had been drained completely of energy. Yet he waited, watching the lines of chat appear, one after another, all mundane, inane chitchat that didn't make much sense nor did it matter. He didn't participate. He never did. Instead, he waited for the game to begin.

He had left the window open despite the hot and humid air pushing its way in, breathing down his neck. Down below he could hear the traffic, too much for this time of night. The fireworks hadn't stopped either, annoying pops and bangs at varying distances. Now and again a string of them went off with a series of hissing and snapping, sometimes with a loud blast for the finale, sometimes only a sizzle and a spit.

He hated the Fourth of July and the memories it revived. It was those memories that got him into trouble. Every single time. They could come out of nowhere, unexpected, unpredictable. Sometimes they rushed in, overwhelming him.

Sometimes they were quiet, subtle…sneaky. There was no harnessing them, no matter how much he tried.

He checked the time in the lower corner of his computer screen—fifteen more minutes. He didn't know why he bothered to wait. He was so tired. He just wanted to rest his weary body. The game always calmed him even if it wasn't enough anymore. In the beginning it had quieted the rage. His invitation to play had been a sort of godsend. It was exactly what he needed. A venue, a brotherhood where he could be safe to expose his anger and eliminate his enemy. It didn't stop the memories but it redirected them.

Now he couldn't remember when the game started to not be enough. When it had gotten to the point that he needed more of a release. How could it be enough when the subject of his anger was still free to wander the earth? How could he continue to allow that?

Suddenly he realized that his fingers, his hands were still bloody. He had smeared the keyboard and riddled his desktop with droplets. The unexpected sight of it made him jump out of his chair, holding his hands up and staring at them as though they belonged to someone else. They did belong to someone else. Someone he hardly recognized anymore. It was getting worse. It was an evil penetrating through his skin, into his veins, even down into his bones. An evil that would destroy him if he didn't soon find a way to destroy its source. And he knew the source. He just needed the courage to eliminate it.

He took several deep breaths, checked the computer clock again. He had just enough time to clean up. He turned to go to the bathroom and only gave a fleeting glance to the freshly decapitated head that sat staring at him from his living-room coffee table.

CHAPTER 32

Monday, July 5
Archdiocese of Omaha Administrative Offices

Tommy Pakula shifted his weight, but there was no getting comfortable in the hardback chair. It sat low in front of the gaudy ornate desk. Lower, he was certain, on purpose. Probably so that when the archbishop sat behind the desk he would be looking down on his visitor. That was when the archbishop would finally grace his visitor with his presence. Pakula was also certain this waiting was a part of the intimidation.

He had nothing better to do than look at the huge framed portraits on the wall behind the desk, a line of past archbishops. He recognized only Curtiss and Sheehan, and Curtiss seemed to be staring him down. He shifted in the chair again, glancing around the rest of the room. *Sterile* was the word that came to mind. He wanted to run an index finger over the windowsill, maybe the top of the bookshelf, just to see if any dust dared to exist in His Holiness's presence.

He wouldn't be here if Chief Ramsey hadn't insisted on one last-ditch publicity attempt just to say they had made every effort before they announced they were calling in the feds. Pakula had never met Archbishop Armstrong. Chief Ramsey had acted surprised at that revelation. "But aren't you one of those offertory collectors or some crap like that at Saint Stan's?" the chief had asked, obviously not worried about revealing his own long-expired Catholicism.

Truth was, being a part of the church meant more to Clare than it did to him. But he had given in, wanting his daughters to grow up knowing enough of what was available to reject or accept. Clare had even pointed out to him that they must have done something right because their oldest, Angie, had decided on her own to stay in Omaha and go to Clare's alma mater, Creighton University. And she had been serious enough about it to work hard all through her final years of high school to land a soccer scholarship that would thankfully help pay for the expensive but prestige college.

He already ribbed Angie that if she wasn't leaving Omaha to go to college he wouldn't be able to bring his punching bag and all his weights in from the garage and take over her bedroom just yet. But he had to admit, he was proud of her. And he liked keeping her close, being able to watch over her for at least a few more years. Of course, he also looked forward to going to the games and watching her play on the Creighton soccer team this fall. She had bragged that they have VIP seats for all the parents. He stopped himself from telling her bleachers were still bleachers to his butt.

A door opened, startling him, and he caught himself sitting up straight almost as if he was in church and had fallen asleep during the sermon. He twisted around in the chair, not sure what was appropriate. Should he stand? Why the hell stand?

"Mr. Pakula." Archbishop Armstrong said it like an announcement, only getting the pronunciation wrong, so that it ended up being PAYkoola instead of Pa-koola.

"It's Pakula and it's detective," he said, correcting the archbishop. Getting it wrong was just another way he thought he could intimidate Pakula, make him feel he needed to explain himself. He noticed the archbishop stayed standing alongside the desk, hesitating. Was he waiting for Pakula to stand? Chief Ramsey had assured him he needed to be polite, but no sucking up was required. Pakula remained seated.

"Czech?"

"Polish."

"Ah, yes, of course," Armstrong said and glided to his chair behind his desk, finally taking his place, as if the ancestry of Pakula's name was something they needed to get out of the way, as if that might help him understand Pakula.

The chair seemed to swallow the archbishop's tall, lean body. Evidently he was aware of its effect because immediately he sat forward on the edge of the seat with his hands in front of him on the desk, clasped almost reverently as if in constant prayer mode. They were the smallest hands Pakula had seen on a man, smooth, not a callus or cuticle in sight with buffed, pearly white-tipped nails. Definitely a professional manicure. So much for that vow of poverty.

"What can I do to help you, Mr. Pakula?" he asked with a tilt of his head to show concern, but already purposely exchanging "detective" for "mister." Pakula recognized it for another maneuver or strategy in the archbishop's game of control. The detective decided to ignore it for now.

"You offered your assistance through Brother Sebastian. I wondered if you might have some thoughts, some insights…you know, on who could have killed Monsignor O'Sullivan?" No sense in beating around the bush, be it burning or camouflaged.

"Who, indeed?" Archbishop Armstrong said in a deep voice as if it were the beginning of a sermon.

He opened his clasped hands, holding them palms up before bringing them to the desk again, this time softly and slowing tapping all ten fingertips on the desk's polished surface. The gesture reminded Pakula of some ritual right before a blessing, although he doubted that it was a blessing the archbishop had in mind for him at the moment.

"Perhaps it was a drug addict? Some poor soul only looking to find money for his next fix?"

Pakula restrained himself from laughing. The archbishop was serious. His youthful face creased with concern. The fingertips continued to tap out some secret code as he added, "It was a random act of violence. Was it not?"

"It's still too early to answer that."

"So you have no suspects?"

"Not at the moment." Pakula watched to see if the archbishop looked disappointed or relieved. He couldn't tell.

"Was the monsignor having any problems at the school?" Pakula asked.

"Problems?"

"He was the principal of Our Lady of Sorrow, correct?"

"Yes, he was, and he did a fine job."

Interesting, Pakula noted. He hadn't asked what kind of a job the monsignor had done, only if there had been any problems.

"Did he voice any concerns recently?" He'd try again. "Any trouble with other instructors. Maybe a student?" He continued to watch closely, more interested in reaction than verbal responses, although this could be fun if the archbishop continued to throw in things Pakula didn't ask about.

"Students," he said, but it wasn't a question. Instead, it seemed an idea he hadn't thought of before. "He never mentioned any threats."

Pakula wanted to smile. He had asked about trouble. The archbishop had converted it to threats. What the hell was he hiding?

"We had Father Tony Gallagher down at the station on Saturday." Pakula waited to see what that did to the archbishop although he certainly already knew this. Pakula wondered if it was a sin to bluff an archbishop. He'd do it anyway. "Why did you ask the monsignor to go to Rome? Was he delivering something to the Vatican for you?"

"Is that what Father Tony told you?" He shook his head, disappointed and hesitant about confessing what he was about to say, opening his hands again as if necessary to forgive his priest, "I'm afraid there may have been a bit of jealousy. You may find that's true with Sister Kate as well. Both of them have projects that require funds—funds that we just don't have available right now." He shrugged and looked at Pakula as though surely he could understand.

"Sister Kate?"

"Sister Katherine Rosetti. She teaches history, takes the teenagers on field trips to museums and such. She gives little conferences and seminars in various places. For the most part her speaking fees cover her own travel expenses, but she seems to think such travel experiences should be available to her students. We simply can't afford the expense nor the liability. I'm afraid she can be a bit vocal when she's not pleased, and we've had to cut back on her budget recently."

"So she's not pleased right now."

"No, I imagine not. I wouldn't be surprised if she mentioned something."

"Perhaps she will. I haven't met her yet, but I'm sure we'll be talking with her soon," Pakula said, wondering if Sister Kate had been a bit vocal about the archbishop cutting her budget or if the archbishop had cut her budget because the good sister had been a bit vocal. It didn't matter. What did matter was that there had been no denial about the monsignor's mission to Rome. The archbishop's only concern appeared to be about a couple of disloyal shepherds in his flock.

"Was there something in the missing portfolio? Anything that perhaps you asked Monsignor O'Sullivan to deliver to the Vatican?"

"There seems to be no portfolio." The fingers stopped tapping and the hands clasped again.

"No, you're right. There doesn't seem to have been a portfolio with the monsignor. Of course, I have no way of knowing that it wasn't with his checked luggage since Brother Sebastian picked it up from the airport." He waited a beat, and added, "Illegally."

"I've instructed him to have all of it ready for you to take back this morning."

Never mind that it had already been ransacked, Pakula wanted to say, but let a smile at the corner of his lips do it for him.

"Hopefully, we'll be able to put all of this behind us soon," Archbishop Armstrong said with a sweep of his hands, now standing and putting an end to their meeting. "I trust you'll keep me informed."

Now Pakula couldn't resist. Chief Ramsey would be pissed, but what the hell, the archbishop would find out anyway. Certainly it would be in the news by tonight. He stood and said, "I appreciate your taking time to talk to me. I'm sure we'll have more questions especially after the FBI get here."

"The FBI?"

Pakula nodded as he turned to leave.

"Does Mayor Franklin really think that's necessary?"

Pakula stopped at the door. So Ramsey was right. Archbishop Armstrong was prepared to round up the yes-men. The power play was on and Armstrong was announcing his first move.

"Actually, it's not Mayor Franklin's decision. I'm sure you understand in a case as sensitive as this that it's simply procedure to call in other experts."

"Of course," the archbishop said and waved at him as if he understood completely. This time he turned to leave out the side door, but stopped in the doorway so that now the two of them were each in an exit, like gunslingers ready to hurl the last word at each other rather than the last bullet.

"Of course I understand. We, too, have procedures that we need to follow. Procedures, for instance, with our college scholarship allocations. I'm sure you understand. Good day, Mr. Pakula."

And he left without letting Pakula get a shot at him. It didn't matter. He wasn't sure he would have been able to hurl anything with the knot that suddenly formed in the center of his chest.

CHAPTER 33

Our Lady of Sorrow High School
Omaha, Nebraska

Gibson McCutty pretended to be bored while his eyes scanned the shelves. Secretly he loved this room. It was the most fascinating one in the high school. But he'd be a total nerd if he admitted it.

He didn't know how Sister Kate managed to do it. There was always a gob of new stuff mixed in with the old faithful. Well, not really new. Most of it was hundreds of years old. Some of the fragile or valuable pieces she kept locked in a glass case, like the hurdy-gurdy. It was a weird kind of fiddle but with a hand crank and a row of keys. It was used by street musicians and beggars in twelfth-century Europe.

Geez! He couldn't believe how many details he remembered. But Sister Kate made the classes interesting.

He watched her greet the new kids, how cool and calm she was. There was something about her that calmed Gibson just being around her. It didn't hurt that she also looked good. He heard his mom once describe Sister Kate as an ageless, natural beauty. He wasn't exactly sure what she meant by it, but he supposed it was because when she wore khakis and a T-shirt like today she looked more like one of the kids than one of the instructors. Even her usual clothes set her off from the other instructors, classy suits—sometimes jackets with skirts, sometimes jackets with pants—but in bright colors: gold, red, bright blue, even lime green. With either wardrobe Gibson thought she always looked cool, and he wasn't the only one. All the kids thought so, even the in crowd who thought history sucked.

As for the in crowd, he couldn't help thinking how geeky these kids coming through the door looked. The Summer Explorers' Program was open to qualifying students from all of the parochial high schools in the area. It was here at Our Lady of Sorrow since Sister Kate started and ran it. Gibson had the home-school advantage. For once maybe he'd be one of the cool kids simply because he had all the insider knowledge. Stuff like where the restrooms were and how to make the Pepsi machine spit out a free can if you fed it one more dime at the right time. Earlier, all of his insider knowledge hadn't mattered at all when he tried to figure out a way to get to the second-floor history room without passing Monsignor O'Sullivan's office at the bottom of the stairs. There just wasn't a route, probably why the monsignor had chosen that office.

Gibson had tried to rush by it without looking, swinging around to go up the next flight of stairs, but then he saw him. He was standing in front of the monsignor's desk, wearing a black polo shirt and black trousers, just like the monsignor. For a minute Gibson thought his imagination was playing tricks on him again. He broke out in a cold sweat, unable to move. He was beginning to believe in ghosts when suddenly the man turned. Of course, it hadn't been Monsignor O'Sullivan, but instead a tall man with a hawk nose and powder-white skin but coal-black eyes that sliced into Gibson, pinning him right where he stood.

"Is there something you need?" It was a deep voice, one Gibson thought he recognized.

"Uh, I just…I thought you were Monsignor O'Sullivan." Gibson knew it sounded stupid, but it fell out of his mouth before he could stop it.

"Monsignor O'Sullivan won't be returning," the man said and he started to close the door, but something furrowed his brow and narrowed his eyes, something he saw just over Gibson's shoulder.

The guy had given him the major creeps. Gibson had spun, readjusting his backpack on his shoulder, and raced up the flight of stairs. He thought the guy had called to him, but he didn't stop. Just kept going, not looking back until he got to Sister Kate's room.

The guy hadn't followed him, but he still felt a little sick to his stomach.

He wouldn't think about it. He needed to focus on something, anything else. Now he tried to concentrate on the kids wandering in, the so-called qualifying students. He took a deep breath and sat back, waiting for the nausea to leave. He reminded himself how much he liked this room, how comfortable it felt. He watched the faces of the kids coming in and it actually made him feel better. He realized it might not be so tough to be one of the cool kids. These kids all looked like losers.

There were supposed to be a dozen of them, three girls and nine boys. Gibson had stolen a peek at the roster on Sister Kate's desk. He already knew that he was the only one from Our Lady of Sorrow. His mom had been thrilled, like it was some big honor. There was no talking her out of it even when she discovered there was a five-hundred-dollar tuition fee to cover their field trips. She shrugged and said she'd get Grandma McCutty to pay it. Gibson complained that the three weeks would totally ruin his summer, but he knew he had already lost the argument. He overheard his mom on the phone telling Grandma McCutty what a privilege it was for Gibson to make the program, if only she could contribute the thousand-dollar tuition fee, then Gibson wouldn't have to turn down such an honor. So there was the real reason his mom was so excited—not that he had qualified. Not that he would get out of the house and do something all summer other than play computer games. No, it was just one more opportunity to scam Grandma McCutty.

"What do you suppose this is?" a small kid with freckles and reddish-blond hair asked.

Gibson hadn't even noticed the kid come up beside him. He was pointing to one of Gibson's favorites, not daring to touch what at first glance looked like some kind of primitive chalice.

"It's called a skullcup," Gibson told him and picked it up carefully, watching the kid's blue eyes widen as if Gibson had done something forbidden, but Gibson knew Sister Kate wouldn't mind. The items she left on the counters were to be handled, carefully, of course, and examined. He turned it over to show the new kid where the base adhered to the top of a human skull.

"In Tibet, priests use these for ceremonies and stuff. See, they cut a human skull in half and use the top for the cup part. They attach all this decorative crap." He pointed out the jewels and polished stones and his stomach hardly hurt anymore. "It's supposed to symbolize consuming the mind of the dead guy. Or something like that."

The kid was looking at him as if Gibson was not just cool but brilliant. Gibson pretended it was no big deal, yet he started thinking maybe this wouldn't be so bad. Maybe it wouldn't ruin his summer after all.

CHAPTER 34

Reagan National Airport
Washington, D.C.

Gwen Patterson snapped her cell phone shut and dropped it into her pocket.

"Still no answer?" Maggie asked as the two of them made their way through the Monday-morning travel crowd.

"Dena came in on Saturday, her day off, so I don't mind her coming in late today. I just wish she would have let me know."

"You don't have to stick around here with me if you need to get to the office. This place is a zoo today."

"I don't mind. How long will Harvey be okay in the car?"

"It's cool this morning. With the window cracked, he'll be fine."

They found a place to sit, not far from the security checkpoint. Maggie tucked and zipped her wallet in the side pocket of her carry-on, an oversize computer case. She stashed the airline ticket in her jacket pocket then began removing her watch and a bracelet, slipping them into another side pocket. She had already relinquished her firearm along with the side holster she wore under her jacket. All the necessary procedures of getting through security in order to fly the friendly skies.

Despite Gwen's calm exterior she felt her insides were screaming at her to tell Maggie she couldn't leave. Not now. She would be getting the results from Benny Hassert's lab sometime today. Then she could hand everything over to Maggie. But now Maggie would be hundreds of miles away in Nebraska. She wanted to tell her now. She didn't want to wait. Twice this morning she had come very close to mentioning the single gold earring he had left for her on Saturday morning. That, of course, would have opened the entire Pandora's box for her to confess about the notes, the map and the cell phone. But Maggie was leaving and Gwen needed a new plan.

"Bonzado seems to think the killer used a hatchet or machete," Maggie said out of the blue. Evidently the case still preoccupied her mind, too.

"How is the handsome professor?" she asked, perhaps overcompensating by changing the subject even though the case was exactly what she wanted and needed to hear about. Was it possible Rubin Nash had easy access to a hatchet or machete?

"He's fine."

She was pleased with Maggie's smile. She hadn't seen Maggie smile about a man since that Nebraska cowboy-turned-district attorney tripped her up. Too much chemistry and no substance was how Maggie explained the disappearance of Nick Morrelli from her life. But Adam Bonzado held some hope. He was certainly someone she could finally share her crazy career with as well as her obsession with evil. And Bonzado was someone who wouldn't flinch or run away from a woman who tracked killers for a living. Quite the contrary, it would be something that would intrigue him. Adam Bonzado also seemed like a man who knew exactly what he wanted and would be patient enough to wait until Maggie was ready. Gwen hadn't been convinced that Morrelli had any clue as to what he wanted, nor did he have such patience.

"He has a conference in the District next month," Maggie offered.

"Oh?"

"So maybe we'll get together for dinner."

"Good."

"Have you heard from Tully since he left for vacation?" Maggie asked, very matter-of-fact, as if it was the most natural progression of the conversation.

Gwen felt a sudden knot in her stomach. Had she opened a can of worms by asking Maggie about Bonzado? Now it was supposed to be her turn to share about Tully. Despite confiding in Maggie about her feelings for R. J. Tully, Gwen still wasn't sure she wanted those feelings validated or confirmed. Not just yet. Nor did she want to admit she had missed him.

"Couldn't Cunningham send Tully to Nebraska when he gets back?"

"Gwen?" Maggie laughed. "Tully's gone for another week. Besides, I thought you'd be anxious to see him."

"Of course, it'll be good to see him. That's not what I meant. It's just that I don't understand how Cunningham can send you out on another case when you only got started on the one here. And it sounds like you made some major progress yesterday."

"I faxed over my preliminary report to Cunningham this morning," Maggie said as she pulled out her watch to check the time, which Gwen knew meant that she needed to get in line for security soon.

"You were able to come up with a profile that quickly?"

"A preliminary one. When we know more about the victims I'll learn more about the killer. Racine and Stan have an ID on Jane Doe number three. That'll help."

"They know who she is?" Gwen asked.

"Dentals matched a Virginia Tech college student. Her name is Libby Hopper. She's been missing since early last week."

"Missing? How did she go missing?" Gwen tried, but couldn't remember where the university was. What would

Nash be doing cruising college campuses? But, of course, easy prey.

"She was supposed to be staying with relatives here in the District between summer sessions. Her car was found in the parking lot of a nightclub in Richmond."

"Why would he risk bringing her back here?"

"Actually he may not have brought her back here," Maggie explained.

"What do you mean? Of course he did. You found her head on the banks of the Potomac."

"He might not have killed her here," Maggie said, lowering her voice, and Gwen thought it was unnecessary. No one could overhear with the speaker system blasting every other minute about leaving unattended luggage. "He may have killed her somewhere between Richmond and here. That could explain why we haven't found any torsos. It's less of a risk to carry around the head."

"So if Racine gave you all this information about Libby Hopper, does that mean you're still on this case?" She tried to sound curious, not desperate.

"I'm sure Racine will want me to stay involved."

"Of course, she'd be crazy to not keep you involved." She wasn't sure she could guide Racine as easily as she had hoped to guide Maggie.

"I'll keep you posted," Maggie said as she stood. "Gotta go." And she opened her arms, waiting for Gwen to stand so she could give her a hug. "Thanks for taking care of Harvey."

"Harvey and I have a good time. He takes me for nice long walks in Rock Creek Park. I find so many more interesting things with him along." Gwen tried not to think of the scribbled map that had led them to the second skull on one of the park's trails. Instead, she hugged Maggie, then stepped back and smiled. "Hey, I forgot to ask what the case was about in Nebraska."

"Ironically, it's priests getting killed instead of doing the killing."

"Really?" Gwen knew Maggie well enough to recognize that this feeble attempt at morbid humor was only to disguise her own anxiety. She had been too wrapped up in her own mess to even consider what Maggie might be going through. Her friend avoided eye contact as if expecting Gwen's next question, "Are you okay about going back there?"

Maggie frowned at her like it was a silly question. Another failed disguise, because Gwen could see the lie even before Maggie said, "Of course I'm okay. That was what, four years ago?"

"Some scars take longer than four years to heal," Gwen told her, this time meeting and holding her eyes. "Especially when there's unfinished business."

Maggie just shrugged then reached out and gave Gwen's arm a gentle squeeze. "Don't worry about me. You're the one who looks tired. Get some rest. I'll call you tonight."

And then she was off, down the long ramp with that confident stride that she used to fool everyone. Almost everyone. But Gwen wasn't fooled. This time she'd let Maggie get away with it only because it allowed her to disguise her own secrets. Selfishly she was relieved that Maggie didn't seem to have a clue about the knots twisting in her stomach, or even suspect the mental time bomb wreaking havoc with her conscience.

CHAPTER 35

Our Lady of Sorrow High School
Omaha, Nebraska

Nick Morrelli hoped his sister, Christine, didn't make him sorry he had come along for the ride. It was Timmy's first day of the Summer Explorers' Program at what would be his new high school in the fall. The school was just one of the changes resulting from Christine's divorce and recent move from Platte City to Omaha.

She said Timmy was excited about the new school, although Nick couldn't help thinking that it might just be Christine putting her positive spin on it. Just the other night she had complained about Timmy spending too much time in his room on his computer and not out with his friends. Nick wasn't sure that sounded like a fourteen-almost-fifteen-year-old boy excited about much of anything.

Yet when they arrived, Timmy left them behind, racing up the steps, knowing exactly where he needed to be. Maybe he really was excited, though Nick suspected that Timmy might not want his new classmates seeing him with his mother. It didn't take long and Nick was wishing he had kept up with

Timmy. At the bottom of the stairs Christine pointed to an office door with Monsignor O'Sullivan's nameplate. He nodded and kept walking, hoping she'd follow. She didn't.

Nick was halfway up the stairs when he heard her confronting someone inside the office. She started a full-blown interrogation and by the time Nick made it to the doorway the tall, pale man dressed in black was explaining—or rather it sounded more like an announcement—that he was Brother Sebastian, assistant to Archbishop Armstrong and that he had been sent to collect monsignor's personal effects.

Christine was asking if the Omaha Police Department knew Brother Sebastian was contaminating what she insisted could be valuable evidence in an ongoing investigation. She was threatening to call the OPD just as Nick grabbed her arm and coaxed her out of the office and up the staircase. She was still ranting about the nerve of the archbishop when they found the classroom for the Explorers' Program.

It wasn't until she introduced Nick to Sister Kate Rosetti, Timmy's new history teacher, and the head of the Explorers' Program, that she seemed to forget Brother Sebastian and remember why they were there. Christine even embarrassed the nun by including in her introduction a brief résumé of Sister Kate's international and national conferences and presentations.

"We're very lucky to have her in Omaha, let alone right here at Our Lady of Sorrow," Christine had said, revealing the news reporter in her.

It didn't surprise Nick. Christine had told him the Explorers' Program cost five hundred dollars, which meant she'd researched anything and everything about the program and Sister Kate to make sure it was well worth it.

"Sounds like you're keeping busy this summer," Nick had said.

"Yes, but mostly short weekend conferences especially now that the Explorers' Program has started," Sister Kate had explained with a shrug of her shoulders as if downplaying her notoriety. "I was in Saint Louis yesterday."

Then shortly after the introductions, Christine did surprise Nick by suggesting he stay and check out Sister Kate's classroom. Not only did Christine do her research, but his sister had a good memory. She had to know that Nick would jump at such an invitation. It wasn't just those preteen summers of digging for treasure in the backyard. As a history major in college he loved studying ancient cultures, their tools and weapons, especially the kinds of stuff Sister Kate obviously enjoyed collecting. Just from the door he could see medieval swords and pieces of armor behind the locked glass cabinets. The room looked like an explorer's heaven.

So maybe he didn't mind Christine trying to get rid of him. Of course, she was trying to get rid of him. She wanted to nose around some more.

Chances were, Christine was headed back down to Monsignor O'Sullivan's office, making good on her threat and calling the OPD. Nick wondered if Christine was really concerned about justice and legalities or if she was simply frustrated the guy had gotten to the office before she could.

"Mr. Morrelli," Sister Kate said, suddenly appearing beside him. "Your sister said you might like to join the class for the first hour this morning."

"You sure I won't be in the way?"

"Not at all. I'm letting the kids get comfortable, check out the classroom and introduce themselves. We'll be ready to start in a few minutes."

"It's quite a classroom." Nick hoped he didn't sound like a starstruck fifteen-year-old.

She smiled, and Nick couldn't help thinking she didn't look like any of the nuns he'd had in grade school. For one thing, he didn't remember any of them wearing makeup, let alone lipstick. Although Sister Kate wore soft colors, she didn't really need makeup, with her short but full and silky hair, creamy smooth skin and warm blue eyes.

"If you don't mind my asking, where…or how did you get some of this stuff?"

"It's amazing the things people want to give me when they discover what I do," she said. "Many of these pieces started out as loaners and became permanent donations. Some I've found myself in out-of-the-way places, antique stores, flea markets, even on eBay, believe it or not. There are so many people who don't recognize what they have sitting in their closets, especially if it's something that was left to them by an ancestor. Take this braquemard," she told him while lifting a flat-bladed sword from the counter. "I'm going to show this to the students today. It's from the 1400s."

"You can't tell me this was sitting in someone's closet collecting dust?"

"No, I accidentally found it in a butcher's shop outside a little French village called Machecoal. Someone had given it to the owner's father, but it originally belonged to a wealthy baron, a soldier who fought alongside Joan of Arc. See the engravings?"

She held it up for him, and he ran an index finger over the worn engraved stamp above the hilt. There wasn't much left, but it was some kind of archaic symbol, no initials like one would expect. He could smell the metallic, acrid cleaner on his finger. Sister Kate took good care of her artifacts.

"Amazingly it had not traveled far in almost six hundred years," she told him.

"Joan of Arc, huh? I guess it makes sense that you'd like to collect pieces that belonged to saints and heroes."

"Oh, Gilles de Rais, the baron, was hardly either, though many believed him to be. He led what you might say was a secret double life." She set the sword down now with what Nick would call almost a reverence. She gently rubbed her fingertips over the wide flat blade that was pointed and sharp on both edges. "It's believed that he used this very horseman's sword to slice open the bellies of over a hundred and forty boys, sometimes beheading them, too. That is, after he choked and hanged them and masturbated over them. No, he was hardly a saint or a hero."

CHAPTER 36

Reagan National Airport
Washington, D.C.

Maggie had barely settled into her newly assigned first-class seat when the flight attendant named Cassy brought her the Diet Pepsi she had requested. She included a glass of ice and several bags of "premium" mixed nuts. They were giving her the royal treatment. Earlier Cassy had tapped her on the shoulder and whispered that the captain had insisted she be moved to first class, upgrading her from her coach window seat almost at the back of the plane.

Well, Maggie wasn't going to argue. Coach was full, first class half-empty. She knew it was because somewhere on the passenger docket the captain had discovered he had an FBI agent on board and wanted her close to his cockpit door. Her weapon had been confiscated for the flight, but she didn't blame them for wanting as many reinforcements as was available and close by. These unexpected upgrades had happened to her several times on other flights since 9/11. And each time she avoided telling them that she might be worthless at thirty-eight thousand feet. She hated flying. Each time was an effort just to get on the plane.

As soon as she was able to, she'd bring out anything and everything that might distract her. This time she pulled out both tray tables—since the first-class seat next to her was unoccupied—and began sorting through files and notes, including those Cunningham, her boss, had e-mailed her early that morning. One of his e-mail attachments had an assortment of crime scene and autopsy photos. She kept those in a folder even when she looked at them. No sense in tipping off anyone else about what she did for a living. The photos were not quite as disturbing as the decapitation ones. In fact, other than a single stab wound to each of the bodies there appeared to be no other injuries. No mutilation. No grotesque display of the dead bodies. No bite marks. No signs of torture.

There were supposedly three cases: two priests, one former priest, all stabbed to death in very public places. Maggie's job was to figure out if the cases were related, to determine if they were the work of one killer, or perhaps two working together, and then to come up with a profile.

She found the police report and scanned the details on the case in Omaha. Fifty-seven-year-old Monsignor William O'Sullivan had been stabbed once in the chest while using an airport restroom on a busy Friday afternoon. Not only a busy Friday afternoon, but a holiday weekend. There were no witnesses with the exception of a Scott Linquist who allegedly may have bumped into the killer on his way into the restroom. Linquist's description was brief: a young man in a baseball cap. He mentioned no weapon, no blood.

The autopsy report presented little evidence, as did the toxicology and the crime lab reports. Maggie stopped and flipped back to something that caught her attention in the autopsy report. This was interesting. The weapon, according to the M.E., was a double-edged, nine- to ten-inch blade that appeared to have been wider in the center and thin at the edges, with an unusually large hilt that may include possible engravings. The M.E. had drawn a sketch in the margin of what looked like an antique dagger.

A dagger. The last time Maggie was in Nebraska, a fillet knife had been the weapon of choice for the killer. She could still remember every detail of that case: the small white underpants, the Halloween mask, the ritualistic oil on the forehead. But mostly when she thought about it—and in recent months, she tried not to—she remembered the bitter cold, the snow and ice chunks in the Platte River. And no matter how she tried, she could never forget the image of those little blue-gray bodies abandoned along the muddy riverbanks, each one with crude, raw X carved on the chest. Only, later, they discovered it wasn't an X at all, but a cross.

Two men were serving life sentences, but Maggie had always been convinced that the real killer had gotten away. For months afterward she had tried to track him, unsuccessfully, of course. She had no jurisdiction in South America and no cooperation and no official support. Moreover, Platte City, the community he had ravaged and betrayed, seemed eager to move on, unwilling to accept that a young, charismatic Catholic priest could do such things. No one wanted to believe that evil could lurk within a man who had been ordained to do good. Yet Maggie wondered if, even in his own twisted mind, Father Michael Keller believed he had been doing the work of the Lord. Why else would he have bothered to give each of his young victims the last rites?

She had told Gwen that she was fine returning to Nebraska. After all, she was going to Omaha this time, not the small rural Platte City thirty miles to the south. She wouldn't be close to any of the crime scene sites. And instead of a small-town, inexperienced sheriff like Nick Morrelli, she'd be working with a veteran detective of a metropolitan police department. So there should be no similarities, no reasons to be reminded of or even haunted by that case that had been closed for almost four years. Now if only she could close it in her mind. It was difficult to just forget such things or even put them out of her mind when every day she had to look at the scar on her side where the killer, the real killer had cut her…with a fillet knife.

Yes, Gwen was right. Some scars took longer to heal.

The nightmare didn't come as often anymore, but when it did, it was as real and palpable as ever. She was back in that dark, damp tunnel under the cemetery. Dirt crumbled down into her hair. The smell of decay filled her nostrils. The darkness pushed against her from all sides. She could hear his steps crunch closer and closer. She could feel his breath on the back of her neck. And this time when he sliced her, he didn't stop at her side but continued to carve the sign of the cross deep into her flesh.

"Ms. O'Dell." The flight attendant startled her. "Is there anything else I can get you?"

"No, thanks. I'm fine." She smiled at the woman and waited for her to go on to the next passenger. But she wasn't fine. Her palms were slick with sweat and her stomach twisted in knots. Only this time neither was from her fear of flying. Not much consolation. Gwen had mentioned "unfinished business" and that's exactly what Father Michael Keller was to Maggie. Anyone who could kill innocent little boys and slice a cross into their chest had not stopped just because he had escaped. He may have a change of scenery, but she knew there would not be a change of heart. That wasn't the way evil worked.

And on the subject of evil, she had a hunch that these three cases were, indeed, connected, if not by the same killer, then perhaps by the victims. Maggie slid a file folder out from underneath the others. She had put it together hastily before Gwen picked her up for the airport. Now she had an opportunity to flip through the articles she had downloaded from the Internet. From Boston to Portland, from New York City to Albuquerque there had been allegations of sexual abuse by priests all over the country. Nowhere seemed to be exempt. James Porter, Paul Shanley, John Geoghan—the names read like a who's who of the few who had been convicted and punished. But from her brief research she had learned that there had been an estimated fifteen hundred American priests in the past fifteen years who had faced allegations of sexual abuse.

Of course, she needed more information. Perhaps she was jumping to conclusions, but these three cases didn't sound like a serial killer who happened to single out priests because he was trying to make some crazy religious statement. Instead, Maggie couldn't help wondering if someone had taken it upon himself to carry out his own brand of justice. Because a single stab wound to the chest and through the heart sounded more like an execution.

CHAPTER 37

Washington, D.C.

Gwen finally conceded defeat, allowing the voice-messaging service to start answering the phone and collecting the messages. Besides, after Benny Hassert's call, telling her that he couldn't match the fingerprints from the manila envelope to those on the water glass, she didn't want to talk to anyone else. Had she been wrong about Rubin Nash? Or had he simply been more careful than she anticipated? He could have delivered the envelope without getting his fingerprints on it, but it would be tricky. She was too exhausted to think about it.

Even letting the voice-messaging service answer the calls still meant the phone had to ring. It was beginning to wear on her nerves. It didn't help matters that each ring startled Harvey from his sleep. He'd get up and pace, following her even after she commanded him to stay. Well, that wasn't exactly true. He did stay once or twice, but looked absolutely miserable doing so, as if she was asking him to do something totally contrary to his nature. At the rate she was going she'd never get any of her work done, and Harvey would never get any of his required naps. It was a good thing she didn't have appointments on Mondays.

She had called and left several messages for Dena at her apartment and on her cell phone. Gwen's first thought was that she had decided to take off with her new beau. She had been irritated, but more with herself than with Dena. After all, why did she seem to have such a knack for hiring irresponsible young women? No that wasn't fair. Their chance meeting at Mr. Lee's World Market Saturday evening had been awkward. Dena had appeared...flustered, anxious, but what young woman wouldn't, running into her boss when she was in the middle of preparing for a romantic evening? And despite Dena's occasional faux pas at work, Gwen could hardly call her irresponsible.

That's why she had started to get concerned. Was the girl hurt? Had there been a family emergency? Gwen was beginning to regret not even knowing if Dena had a roommate or any family close by. If something had happened, who would she contact?

It was a recent necessity, the vow to adopt a policy of not getting involved with her hired staff. Past assistants had milked her for advice and free diagnosis as if both should be a part of every psychologist's employee benefits plan. It wasn't doling out free advice that bothered Gwen. It was, instead, the emotional drain of being dragged into the chaos of their lives.

One assistant had gotten Gwen to act as a mediator between her and her ex-husband during their custody battle, then to evaluate the children's mental and emotional capacity to testify at the trial that followed. Another had Gwen appealing to the state's parole board on her brother's behalf. Still another pleaded with Gwen to convince her elderly mother that it was time to give up her home and independence for the security of an assisted-living facility. That was the one that broke the camel's back, when Gwen discovered her assistant and the man she was living with had moved into the mother's home, instead of selling it—as they had agreed—to pay for her mother's care. It was one thing to be taken advantage of, quite another thing to be taken for a fool.

Sometimes Gwen wondered if it wasn't one of the hazards of not having a family of her own, to constantly be drawn into the lives of the people around her. She had purposely never returned to Manhattan to establish a practice, lest she forever be destined to follow in her father's footsteps and live in his shadow, as well as be judged by their professional peers under a much different standard—the standard of being John Patterson's daughter. Even at Christmas parties she was still introduced as John's little girl. She was almost fifty years old and definitely not anyone's little girl.

She saw her parents maybe a half-dozen times a year. Every Christmas she made her annual pilgrimage to New York, accepting her parents' traditions as her own. She went through the motions, never really considering if there might be an alternative. It wasn't until last Christmas when R. J. Tully had asked her to join him and his daughter for Christmas Eve that she realized she had no traditions of her own.

She missed Tully, and she didn't particularly like admitting that even to herself. She had gone for over a decade without missing anyone. She considered calling him. Just to talk. Before he and Emma left on vacation he had made sure she had his cell-phone number along with the number for their hotel and another for a friend they would be visiting. Yet he had been careful in telling her that it was no big deal if she called and no big deal if she didn't. But she had been able to read his tight smile as an indication that he really would like it if she did call. And so of course she didn't. Which was silly. That at their age they still played games like they were a couple of teenagers, not wanting to let the other know just how much they might care. When in reality they were two very independent adults, comfortable and complacent in the lives they had carved out for themselves and a bit reluctant to relinquish some of that independence. Perhaps she was also a bit reluctant to take a chance at having her heart broken again. She had gotten to a point in her life where she was happy, content with being alone. But somehow, despite how careful and calculated she had tried to be, she ended up caring for R. J. Tully. And… she missed him.

She heard the door to the reception area open and Harvey stood up again, looking at her, waiting for her direction. With no appointments scheduled, Gwen thought it would be quiet most of the day, but Dena evidently had decided Mondays would be delivery day. Gwen had already signed for a case of her beloved gourmet coffee, three boxes of supplies from Office Depot and a new patient's medical report sent via messenger service from a Dr. Kalb.

"Package for Dr. G. Patterson?" The messenger didn't look up from his electronic pad, punching in numbers. He had already set the box on the reception desk. "Just need a quick signature."

When he looked up, he jumped at the sight of Harvey. He had been so focused he hadn't noticed that the big dog had managed to sit down on the floor beside him.

"He's harmless," Gwen assured him and signed the electronic pad he held out for her.

"Not a bad idea to have extra security." He gave Harvey a pat on the head before he left.

She shoved the box aside on the reception counter, glancing for the sender's address, but not concerned when she didn't find one. She picked up the phone, tucking it under her chin, checking voice messages while she slit open the envelope that accompanied the box. But there wasn't a note inside. Instead, a single gold earring slipped out of the envelope, falling onto the counter. Gwen watched it spin like a coin on one end. For a second everything stopped, all sound, all movement other than the earring that now spun in slow motion. Even her heart seemed to stop. She didn't need to examine it closely. She knew this was the match to the one left on Saturday.

Gwen slowly put the phone back in its cradle, her eyes

never leaving the earring. The dread immediately gripped her stomach. She forced herself to look at the box. It was about a one-foot cube. Much bigger than any of his other packages. More instructions? Another map? Could it be another cell phone? What would he have sent her this time to direct her to his victim? And why the box? Certainly he wouldn't...no, he wouldn't dare. Or would he? She couldn't help thinking it was probably the right size, just big enough for a human head to fit into.

She glanced down at Harvey who sat at her feet, staring up at her. He'd be able to sense, to smell, to know if it was something...dead. Wouldn't he? There'd be blood, even dried blood. Yes, of course, he would.

She used the letter opener to carefully slit the packing tape on the sides of the box. Using the palms of her hands rather than her fingers, she lifted the flaps, trying to avoid adding her fingerprints to the many that may already be on the outside. Once the flaps were pressed back she still couldn't see beyond the white packing material. She poked at it with the letter opener and made no contact. There seemed to be nothing of substance under the crinkled white paper. Did she dare peel it back?

She stood paralyzed, staring at it. Finally she set the letter opener aside and commanded her fingers to touch, then grip a corner, to lift, to pull it back. She found herself squinting and cringing as if preparing for something to jump out at her. When had she started holding her breath? Her chest already ached. But her fingers were steady. Thank goodness, since nothing else seemed to be.

Her fingers peeled and pulled and tugged until all the white packing paper had been removed, a pile of it now on the counter. At the bottom of the box remained only a single key on top of an index card. Without removing either, she recognized his familiar block-style handwriting. And what was worse, she recognized the address he had scrawled on the card.

CHAPTER 38

Our Lady of Sorrow High School
Omaha, Nebraska

Nick couldn't find Christine. He wasn't surprised that she hadn't waited for him right outside the classroom like she'd said she would. He wandered over to the second-story windows facing the street. No police cruisers. No cops. That was a good sign.

He dug his hands into his jeans pockets. He hated waiting. He could go back in for the second half of Sister Kate's class and make Christine come get him. Yep, that's exactly what he'd do. Make her wait on him for a change. He was headed back to do just that when he noticed down the hall the door to Tony's office was open. He hesitated. He and Tony had known each other a long time. Maybe he'd been too hard on him the other day when all Tony had wanted and needed was a friend, not an attorney.

He reached in and knocked on the open door, startling Tony.

"Hey, come on in." He nodded at Nick, but his eyes returned to the computer screen and his fingers flew over the keyboard, as if he needed to close down whatever he was working on before Nick could get a glimpse. Or was Nick still just being suspicious?

"You haven't seen Christine, have you?"

"No, is she here, too?"

"We brought Timmy for the Explorers' class. I sat in on the first half. I think Christine's downstairs giving that guy in the monsignor's office a piece of her mind."

Tony looked up at the mention of the intruder. Nick tried to figure out whether that was how Tony saw the guy, as an intruder. But Tony just shook his head and reached for a coffee mug that sat on the bookshelf. Nick waited, letting him take a gulp of what he knew was chocolate milk and not coffee. He only put it in a mug to draw less attention, or at least that was his explanation. Nick had ribbed him about it, jokingly asking if he thought a chocolate-milk-drinking priest would be taken less seriously than a coffee-drinking one.

Instead of some explanation of why the guy was going through the monsignor's stuff, Tony said, "Christine should be careful."

It wasn't at all what Nick expected him to say.

"And why is that?"

Tony shrugged, took another sip. "Everyone's on edge right now. I'm sure the archbishop won't appreciate the media snooping around."

"But he doesn't mind sending some goon to snoop around?"

This time Tony smiled. "Brother Sebastian does look a bit like a goon, doesn't he?"

"Yeah, in a freaky sort of way. Who exactly is he?"

"Assistant to Archbishop Armstrong, his right-hand man."

"And his job description includes rummaging through dead priest's offices?" Nick asked.

Another shrug from Tony. "Brother Sebastian would probably do anything the archbishop asked of him."

Nick leaned against the doorjamb. Tony didn't seem too concerned. Christine had probably blown it out of proportion. Of course, someone had to go through the monsignor's stuff, box it up. He had never paid much attention to Tony's office before, but suddenly he was taking it all in with new eyes, thinking of his own office back in Boston and what someone might find if they had to clean it out for him. Tony's was a little neater, but not much. Stacks of magazines lined the far corner. Books and computer games were piled together on two shelves of the bookcase. They were an odd combination. The books were mostly English-lit stuff, poetry and Shakespeare. The computer games appeared to be about warriors and crusaders. A bulletin board had layers tacked over each other—anything from class changes and teachers' phone numbers to Nebraska football ticket stubs, dry-cleaning receipts and take-out menus. A duffel bag had been thrown under his desk, the zippers undone with a dirty towel halfway out and a pair of muddy running shoes beside it. He'd forgotten how small Tony's feet were. They looked like kids' tennis shoes.

Nick glanced out into the hall. Then he came in and sat in the recliner Tony kept in the corner. Keeping his voice low, he said, "Christine seems to think the archbishop has a few secrets he'd like to have die with Monsignor O'Sullivan. Don't worry, I know if something's going on you probably can't talk about it."

He studied Tony while he hoped for a response, but didn't expect one. There was a heavy sigh and Tony sat back, setting the wood creaking and the rollers squealing as he slid the chair so that they were facing each other. But then Tony crossed his arms over his chest and didn't say anything. It was almost as if he wanted to hear what Nick thought he knew. Okay, Nick could play that game.

"I have to tell you," Nick said, this time in almost a whisper. "I didn't even know Monsignor O'Sullivan was gay."

"What? Who told you that?"

"Nobody told me, but if he was messing with boys—"

"Pedophiles are rarely homosexuals, Nick." Tony shook his head as if he couldn't believe he needed to explain this.

"But I thought that was part of the church's solution to the mess, to screen candidates better."

"Yeah, well, it wouldn't be the first time they ignored science and professional research. I guess you haven't worked on any pedophile cases in Boston, because you'd know that if you had."

"I've been lucky. Since I left Nebraska I haven't had to work on any other cases involving kids. So how do you happen to know so much about pedophiles?"

"I was a victims' advocate when I was at Saint Stephen of the Martyr in Chicago," Tony said, but he was staring out of his window now. "It was an unofficial post, since officially the archdiocese didn't have a problem to begin with."

"That had to be tough," Nick said, watching him. "How could you work with those kids and know the guys who abused them were probably just being reassigned?"

"I didn't know that. Not at the time. You have to understand, Nick—" and for this Tony met his eyes "—we were told things were being taken care of."

"It didn't clue you in when there were no charges brought against them?"

"That's not the way it works," Tony answered, but his eyes were away from Nick's again, darting around the room, out the window and back to Nick. He scraped a hand over his jaw, as if looking for the right words. "The church didn't look to the county or the state to handle things," he said carefully, slowly, as if explaining it to a child, but there was nothing condescending in his tone. If Nick didn't know better, his friend sounded almost remorseful. "Priests are to be held to a higher standard and should be judged as such. They answer to a higher authority."

"Sure, I know," Nick said. "You mean a higher authority as in the archbishop?"

"No. I mean a higher authority as in God."

CHAPTER 39

Eppley Airport
Omaha, Nebraska

Tommy Pakula forked over five bucks for a Krispy Kreme doughnut and the grande designer coffee when he really just wanted a large, plain coffee with no cream, no sugar, no froufrou on top. Geez, for five bucks he could have gotten all the coffee he could drink plus two eggs, toast and a side of bacon down at the Radial Highway Café. Froufrou or not, it sure tasted good and he needed the blast of sugar and caffeine. Lately it seemed necessary to keep a steady injection of caffeine pumping through his system like some constant electrical charge. He wasn't sure he wanted to see what happened if and when he got unplugged.

He glanced at the flight arrival board for the thirteenth time. The D.C. flight was still scheduled to arrive on time. That was ten minutes ago. So where the hell was it?

There had already been two streams of passengers but no FBI guy, no Special Agent M. O'Dell. Pakula could spot a feebie a mile away, the same dark suit, the same distant look that took everything in with a sweep of the eyes. He was starting to think the guy missed his flight. He planted himself by the bookstore where he wouldn't miss anyone coming up the ramp from the gates. He leaned against the wall. He finished his doughnut in three bites and sipped the coffee.

He was watching another stream come up the ramp from the gates when a woman came out of the bookstore and stopped in front of him. She was young, attractive, dragging a black leather computer case.

"Excuse me, are you Detective Pakula?" She addressed him by name, even getting the pronunciation right. And this time he really looked at her instead of his routine brief once-over, trying to remember how she knew him.

"Yeah, I'm Pakula."

"I'm Special Agent Maggie O'Dell."

He almost dropped his coffee. Holy crap! He stood up straight, trying to look all nonchalant as he freed up and wiped his right hand to offer it. "Nice to meet you, Agent O'Dell. You been wandering around here long?"

"Not long."

Now that he got a good look at her—navy blue suit, eyes drifting and catching everything around her—Pakula realized he wasn't so far off. He just had the M wrong. Geez, Chief Ramsey would laugh his ass off. So would Clare. He wasn't too sure O'Dell would.

"How'd you figure out who I was?" he asked her.

"I'm a profiler. It's my job." But before he could look impressed, she smiled and added, "I could say it was because you didn't have any luggage. That you were off to the side and didn't look excited to pick up whoever you were looking for, or that it was the bulge in the back of your jacket. Truth is, the doughnut and coffee was a dead giveaway."

Pakula wanted to laugh. Here he was looking for the stereotypical FBI agent and she was doing the same thing. He pretended to look insulted. "Geez, O'Dell. You know I could be offended that you've already stereotyped me."

"Then we're even," she said, "because you were looking for a man, weren't you?"

He met her eyes, and there was no drifting this time. He could see that it actually didn't bother her, that she was used to it, instead of being offended, and that she was simply jabbing back at him.

"Okay, we're even," he said, and he decided he liked her.

He started to fill her in on the case, giving her some background that hadn't made it into the case file. But she seemed distracted as they headed toward the escalators.

"We have to get your bags downstairs," he told her. "I'm parked just across in the garage."

"Do you mind if we stop at the restroom?"

"Oh, sure. No, I don't mind. I think there's one downstairs you can use."

She stopped and smiled at him. "No, I mean the restroom where you found Monsignor O'Sullivan?"

Pakula was a bit embarrassed that he'd misunderstood. Of course, she'd want to see the crime scene. "Yeah, sure. Right back here."

He led her off to the left and down a hallway. When they got to the restroom he went in first, checking to see if there was anyone at the urinals. They lucked out. A guy was on his way out when Pakula propped open the door and invited O'Dell in.

"He was over here," Pakula indicated, walking to the area in front of the last sink on the left. "The way I figure it, he was standing, washing his hands at the sink when the killer came up behind him. We found his eyeglasses on the floor. Could be why he didn't see his attacker come up behind him. Could simply be he didn't think the guy looked like anyone he needed to worry about. From the direction and angle of the stab wound, the M.E. says the killer came in behind him. He was probably shorter. Not sure how much. But enough that he could easily reach under the monsignor's arm and shove the knife up into his heart. He pulled it out, let the monsignor drop to the floor, then stepped on the padre's glasses and simply walked out the door."

A thick middle-aged man came in the door, did a double take when he saw O'Dell and backed up to check the sign on the door.

"You can come on in. We're just visiting," Pakula told him, but the man waved an angry hand at him and left, muttering something about privacy.

"One door to enter and exit," O'Dell said, looking around. "And no one saw the killer on a busy Friday afternoon?"

"These restrooms are sort of off the beaten path. Most people would use the ones at the gate or down next to the luggage carousel. There was one guy—he's listed in the report—thought he bumped into a kid on his way out. Said the kid was in a hurry. The guy couldn't identify him other than a baseball cap, slight build. Didn't even see his face. By the time the guy saw the monsignor's body, realized what happened and ran out the door, he said the kid was nowhere in sight."

O'Dell moved to the doorway and stood, looking out. "There's nowhere to go except down the hallway to the terminal, right?"

"Not that I know of. Other than the women's restroom next door, there's a locked supply closet. We checked it that night to make sure he didn't have access to the closet to dump a weapon, his clothes, anything else."

"What about cameras?"

"No cameras except at the security checkpoints."

"I saw one in the bookstore," she told him. "It looks like it's set up to cover the entrance. It may be a stretch, but I wonder if it catches anything beyond the entrance? If it does, it might show people turning to come down this hallway to use the restrooms."

"Usually store cameras are pretty crappy, but I'll check it out."

"Speaking of cameras, what have you released to the media?" O'Dell asked.

"Released to the media?"

"Has anyone openly made the possible connection between the three murders? There are three that we know of, correct?"

Pakula nodded. "Yeah, three. The monsignor, an ex-priest

in Minneapolis and one in Columbia, Missouri. The Minneapolis one happened over the Memorial Day weekend. The Columbia murder was about twenty-four hours after Monsignor O'Sullivan. There are similarities, but I don't think anyone can say for certain that they're all connected." Pakula didn't like where this was going. Ramsey had brought in the FBI to squelch any political rhetoric and media sensationalism. What exactly did O'Dell expect them to release?

"Whether there's a connection or not is what you want me to figure out, right?"

"Yeah, I guess so. Three priests dead in a coupla months, all in the Midwest, you gotta wonder if there's a serial killer on the loose."

"Is there a reason why you haven't talked about this in public?" O'Dell asked.

"You mean like a warning?"

"Yes, partly a warning."

Pakula wondered what Ramsey had shared with his old buddy Cunningham. Evidently it hadn't been enough to convey how sensitive the power structure in a city the size of Omaha could be. Ramsey may have beat around the bush with Cunningham. Pakula wasn't about to beat around any bushes.

"How's the media breathing down my neck and screwing around with my words going to solve any of these cases?" he asked, and he let her hear his contempt.

"Ah, but you see, Detective Pakula, what you do is screw with them before they screw with you. If we take a proactive role, we might just be able to get them to do our dirty work."

She was ready to leave now, but stepped back to let two men in golf shirts come into the restroom. They stopped in midstride and midsentence when they saw her.

"Hello, gentlemen," she said as she started around them. "Welcome to Omaha."

Pakula smiled and followed her out. He still wasn't happy about her wanting them to cozy up to the media.

"I'm not buying your logic on opening the door to the

media. And I'm thinking Chief Ramsey's gonna have a massive hemorrhage."

"I'm not saying you open up the door or the case to them. But I do think if there's something that connects these three cases, the media might be able to bring a few things to the surface that would take us months to dig up."

"There's no abuse scandal in the Omaha Archdiocese, if that's where you're headed." He kept his voice down, pointing to the escalators and letting her go first.

"You sure about that?"

"A reporter from the *Omaha World Herald*'s been digging and nagging vice to nose around. Nothing so far." After this morning's exchange with Archbishop Armstrong, Pakula almost wished there was something to dig up.

She stepped onto the escalator, maneuvering the rolling computer case beside her. She turned her body toward him so they could still talk on the way down.

"And the other two cases?" she asked. "Anything to dig up there?"

"Not sure about those yet. But what do you think the media can get at that we're not gonna have access to?"

"Remember when the *Boston Globe* blew the top off Cardinal Law and the abuse throughout his diocese? There didn't seem to be enough evidence for law enforcement agencies to do anything for decades. I'm just saying if there's some dirt, who better to dig it up than professional dirt diggers?"

Pakula thought about Armstrong's smug threat. Why bother to make a threat if there wasn't something to hide? He followed her off the escalator. "Baggage claim is down to the left here."

They stayed off to the side when they realized her luggage wasn't in yet. Pakula kept his eyes moving and his voice low. "From what you saw in the files, you think there's any chance these cases might have been random?"

"You obviously don't think they are or you wouldn't have called in a profiler." She waited for his eyes to meet hers and confirm it before she added, "However, I'm not convinced they're the work of a serial killer."

"Excuse me?"

"All three of these…" She stopped short of using the word *murders* now that they were surrounded by more people. "All of them have been done in very public places with people coming and going. This guy either gets a kick from the huge risk factor or he's meticulous in his planning. I'm guessing it's the latter. But from what I know about the three, they look more like cold, calculated executions."

"Executions of priests," Pakula said in almost a whisper. He had already thought about that. It wasn't one of those ideas he necessarily liked having validated.

"You may have an assassin on your hands. Either way, it doesn't much matter, we need to find out the similarities and figure out who might be next. The media may actually be able to help us with that."

"Maybe it was just these three and that's it."

"That would be great if it was. But I'm guessing there's a list and the killer's going down it, one by one."

CHAPTER 40

Washington, D.C.

Gwen slowed the car, braking enough to send Harvey's front paws slipping and readjusting on the passenger seat next to her.

"This is crazy," she told him as she started searching the brownstones, keeping the address on the dashboard, now re-written on a Post-it; the original index card was back at her office in a plastic bag.

Her heart pounded in her ears. It hadn't stopped since she opened the box. She was trying to stay calm, trying to think instead of run on emotion, but all she had to do was look at Harvey's brown eyes watching her to know she wasn't very successful. The dog could sense the panic. He could probably smell it on her. Every once in a while he licked her hand or arm as if that was his way of comforting her.

"We make a good team, Harvey, but just between you and me I certainly wish Maggie was here, too." Even as she said it, she wondered if she would have finally given in and told Maggie if she was still here. Would she have confessed it all? She was running low on logic and professional ethics. Right now the panic and fear of what she may have allowed to happen closed in around her. The calm and logical psychologist in her was having a difficult time hearing over the screaming woman who seemed to be much closer to the surface.

"There it is," she said, braking again, only this time Harvey was prepared.

She waited for a delivery truck to leave and squeezed her car into the last parking space on the street. Then she sat there, looking up at the brownstone. She double-checked the numbers again, but she knew this was it. Earlier in the day, when she hadn't been able to reach Dena by phone, she'd pulled her file, jotting down her home address on a Post-it note just in case she decided to drop by and check on her. Why hadn't she recognized that first lone earring as Dena's when he left it for her on Saturday? Would she have been able to stop him? Could she have saved Dena? Jesus! Was he the new man in Dena's life? Had he gone that far? Maybe this was all some elaborate hoax. It was so different from the others. Could he simply be warning her, playing with her? Back at the office when she recognized the address she had actually pinched herself, hoping it was all a nightmare.

She stuck her hand in her jacket pocket and wrapped her fist around the key he had left at the bottom of the box. Of course he was Dena's new man. How else would he have a key to her apartment?

She stared at the door, then glanced around the other brownstones, across the street and down the block. Was he here someplace, watching? This was ridiculous. She should have called the police. She should have at least asked them to meet her here. Her cell phone was also in her pocket. She could still do it. She could still call.

And what would she tell them?

She took a deep breath, clutched the key and grabbed Harvey's leash. The big dog came reluctantly, almost as if he was letting her know this wasn't such a good idea. His instinct was definitely better than hers.

She rang the doorbell and waited, still glancing around, hoping to maybe rouse a neighbor. The neighborhood was quiet. She unlocked the door and it pushed open with ease.

"Hello? Dena?"

She stayed in the entrance, watching Harvey's reaction while she held tight to his leash. She watched his eyes, the pitch of his ears and tilt of his head as he listened and sniffed the air. So far there wasn't anything that made him jerk or whine like he had when they found the skull half buried in the park. Almost like a trained bloodhound, he had been able to sense the rotting flesh, or what was left. His instinct had been to show her, then get the hell away from it. He had tugged so hard she'd thought he'd break her hand. But there was none of that now. A good sign. Yes, a very good sign, and she closed the door behind them.

"Dena?"

Was it possible that he had simply left her tied up or drugged? Something to prove to her how close he could get? He had done it with her father, showing that he could get him exactly where he wanted by simply leaving a message that his daughter wanted to meet him for breakfast. Was that what he was doing with Dena? Showing her again that he could get at anyone close to her? It made sense. Maybe that's all it was. Something to scare her, just to let her know he could.

Dena's place looked lived in, but there certainly had not been a struggle. There were too many knickknacks on dusty shelves. Had one been misplaced or even knocked down, it would have been obvious. Dust doesn't lie.

Gwen tried to take in as much as possible with each slow step, all the while listening and watching Harvey. Her eyes skimmed the highest shelves, the mantel and even inside the fireplace, under chairs and the far corners. Suddenly Harvey stopped and started scratching at a cabinet door to what looked like an entertainment armoire. Immediately her heart began pounding again, and she had to force herself to breathe, to keep from holding her breath.

He scratched twice, then sat down in front of the cabinet door, staring at it. He glanced up at her as if to see if she had noticed. She could still call the police. Let them handle this. It wasn't too late. Harvey scratched at the cabinet door and looked up again.

"Okay, okay. Just wait a minute."

She pulled a clean tissue from her pocket and tried to grab the cabinet's door handle, leaning in from as far away as possible. Her hand was shaking so badly she dropped the tissue and had to pick it up. Harvey was getting more and more anxious and she had to tug him to the side. The more anxious he got the more her hand seemed to shake. Even after she had a good grip on the knob, she still hesitated. Her chest hurt from what felt like a constant time bomb banging against her rib cage.

She took a deep breath and yanked the door open. She jumped back from the skittering sound as something came spewing out of the cabinet, an avalanche of jelly beans, bright colors plopping to the floor, spilling out of an overturned decanter. And Harvey strained at the leash, lapping up several before Gwen's mind and heart started working again. She pulled and tugged and escorted him away from the mess.

"Jesus, Harvey."

She needed to sit before her knees gave way. She found the corner of the sofa. She should check the other rooms and leave. But if Harvey could smell nothing but jelly beans, then there was nothing else here. He would have sensed it by now. Wouldn't he? She needed to think about this. Maggie had rescued Harvey from his previous owner's bloodied bedroom where he had lost that owner to a serial killer in a battle that almost cost him his life. That's why he was so protective of Maggie and that instinct seemed to transfer to Gwen, too. Wouldn't it therefore be logical that he would be freaking out if there was even the scent of blood anywhere in the apartment? Wasn't that exactly how he had reacted with the skull in the park? Maybe it was ridiculous to think she could psychoanalyze him like one of her patients. She wasn't a dog shrink, but it did make sense. She didn't allow herself to feel relieved. Not just yet.

She persuaded him to check the bedroom, leading him to the closet and bathroom, looking behind the shower door and under the sink. There was nothing. With each discovery, or rather non-discovery, she felt the tension and the panic slowly subside. Her heartbeat and her breathing had started to return to normal. Until they got to the kitchen.

She checked the refrigerator and the oven, even the dishwasher, only to turn around and find Harvey pawing at yet another cabinet door under the sink. She told herself she would treat it like the other doors and cabinets, quick like a Band-Aid, no hesitating, no imagining, just get it over with.

Easier said than done.

The cold, clammy perspiration returned to her forehead and the back of her neck. The tremor in her hand, though not as pronounced, slowed her quick grab of the handle. And Harvey's side-step dance made her nervous.

She yanked open the cabinet door to find a roll-out trash bin under the sink. The smell of rotting garbage pushed her back so that it took some effort to see the apple peel and coffee grounds on top.

"Harvey, next time I need to feed you first."

She smiled down at him and patted his head, but he was still nervous, pacing, pulling against his leash. And this time she realized he no longer wanted to get at the trash bin. This time he wrenched and jerked at the leash, trying to get away from it. He twisted against his collar and his panic quickly spread to Gwen. Then there came that horrible low-pitched whine coming from the back of his throat, barely audible but hard to listen to, an uncontrollable moan that sounded as if he was in pain.

This time when she looked, Gwen saw the plastic bag. It was buried underneath the rotting fragments of vegetable peels, coffee grounds, empty boxes and cellophane—the bits and pieces of ordinary household garbage. She had been right about Harvey. He sensed blood and wanted to be as far away from it as possible. Underneath all the garbage, Gwen could see through the plastic. She could see Dena's brown eyes looking up at her.

CHAPTER 41

Downtown Omaha Police Station
Omaha, Nebraska

Maggie dreaded these introduction sessions. Usually they turned into tugs-of-war with local law enforcement officers strutting their stuff and reinforcing their jurisdiction. Other times there was blame to be ducked or screwups to be excused. But she had to admit she was impressed with Detective Tommy Pakula, mostly because he wasn't the least bit interested in impressing her or marking his territory or looking to place blame. Even when he discovered he had been waiting for a female FBI agent instead of a man, it didn't seem to faze him. In a quiet sort of way, Detective Pakula seemed only determined to do his job.

He had a group assembled and ready when they arrived at the downtown Omaha police station. Well, almost ready. There were a few in and outs to the small conference room for coffee and one last phone call before they sat down. Pakula offered to get Maggie coffee, but she declined, asking if there was a vending machine nearby. He nodded, but instead of pointing her in the direction of the machine, he asked what her "poison" was. Yet he never left the conference room. Just as Maggie decided he had forgotten about her a uniformed officer came in with two ice-cold cans of Diet Pepsi and placed them beside her.

The long table filled one side of the room. The other side had an easel-back chalkboard already filled with three columns, three lists of evidence, one list for each of the cases. A large bulletin board took up the wall. On one half were photos of the three victims along with crime scene photos. On the other half was a map of the Midwest, colored pushpins marking Omaha, Columbia and Minneapolis.

Around the table Pakula introduced his group. Maggie couldn't help thinking they looked as though they had been taken directly out of a diversity training video: Terese Medina, a black woman from the Douglas County crime lab who looked as if she belonged on the cover of Vogue; Detective Carmichael, a short, stocky Asian woman; Chief Donald Ramsey, a middle-aged guy in wrinkled khakis who was a contrast to his counterpart, young Detective Pete Kasab in a suit and tie. At the head of the table, looking like the matriarch of this eclectic family, sat Martha Stofko, the Douglas County medical examiner who managed to make a well-pressed white lab coat look chic with a royal-blue dress and pearls.

Terese Medina passed out copies of her detailed reports along with Stofko's autopsy report, a set for each. In the middle of the table she left what appeared to be evidence samples and also an assortment of digital photographs.

Detective Carmichael—whose first name Maggie noticed Pakula had never mentioned—had a pile of information stacked in front of her that, when she sat, almost towered over her. Without breaking her constant frown, she teasingly announced that somewhere in "this pile of crap" were answers that would solve the "whole damn thing."

Chief Donald Ramsey shook Maggie's hand, thanked her for coming at such short notice, then propped himself in a chair and let Pakula run the show. He looked tired, the creases in his forehead permanent worry lines. Sitting next to Kasab, the earlier contrast Maggie had noticed was even more pronounced. Chief Ramsey wore khakis and a knit polo shirt with an embroidered Omaha Police Department patch on the pocket. Detective Pete Kasab wore what looked like a tailored suit, creased trousers and starched shirt collar, perfectly knotted silk tie and salon-styled hair. Unlike Ramsey, who brought only a mug of coffee, Kasab had a bottle of water and granola bar. His small spiral notebook was open, his gold pen ready in hand.

"I've filled in Agent O'Dell and brought her up to speed," Pakula said. He remained standing. "I'm hoping there's new stuff. Anything from toxicology?" And he looked to Terese Medina.

"O'Sullivan's blood alcohol content was at point zero five, so he had a couple of drinks in the hours before. Nothing to impair him. No traces of any other chemicals in the blood. The wound, however, showed residue of ammonia and an aliphatic petroleum distillate."

"And in English that would be…" Pakula prodded her.

"Aliphatic petroleum distillate is like a Stoddard solvent found in a lot of household cleaning products. The combination with the ammonia would most likely make it a common metal polish of some sort."

"So our killer has a fetish for cleaning his knives," Carmichael said. "No wonder he didn't just toss it afterward."

"Or if the weapon is, indeed, a dagger or letter opener as I suspect," Stofko offered, "it may be valuable to him. Perhaps sentimentally, if not financially."

"Anything else new?" Pakula asked Medina.

"The canine hairs found on the back of his shirt were from a Pekingese."

"Holy crap!" Pakula said. "You can tell that?"

"In this particular case I can." Medina smiled at him.

"I already checked," Carmichael offered. "O'Sullivan didn't have a dog."

"Any chance the dog hairs were already on the floor?" Pakula asked.

"Anything's possible," Medina said. "But there weren't any on the floor around him. Just his shirt. And just the back of his shirt."

"That makes sense. Martha thinks the killer came up from behind," Pakula said, waiting for her to nod in agreement. "The dog hairs could have been on the killer's shirt and transferred to the victim. Locard's Principle," Pakula continued, leaving it for everyone to fill in the blank. Maggie looked around the table as each of them seemed to agree in some way with a nod of the head or a wave of the hand. They all knew and expected that there would definitely be some transfer of debris, just as Locard had predicted.

"So we just need to look for a guy who has a fascination with knives and Pekingese dogs," Carmichael said, picking up her own profile. "Should be a piece of cake. What the hell does a Pekingese look like?"

"Small, long-haired, no nose," Medina offered.

"You looked at the other two cases," Pakula addressed Medina. "Either mention dog hair?"

"No, but they could have easily missed it, especially since both were outdoors. Minneapolis's M.E. notes some ammonia residue in the wound. Could be the metal polish." Medina flipped the pages in front of her. "Columbia guys told me they found bread crusts, not crumbs, in Kincaid's shirt pocket."

"You're kidding," Pakula said.

"What's with the bread crumbs?" Maggie asked, speaking for the first time since the meeting started.

"Crusts," Medina corrected her. "It might not mean anything. He was at an outdoor picnic. He may have put some bread or something in his own pocket. It's just that I found bread crumbs all over the front of O'Sullivan's shirt, too."

"Dog hair on the back of his shirt and bread crumbs on the front?" Maggie wondered if the monsignor was a sloppy eater. Maybe his housekeeper owned the Pekingese. None of these things made much of an impression on her, except to note that Terese Medina was very good at her job.

Almost as if she sensed Maggie's skepticism, Martha Stofko looked at her and said, "O'Sullivan's stomach contents didn't include any bread. Looked pretty much like meat loaf and mashed potatoes."

"Yum," Pakula said and drew a few laughs. Then he turned to Carmichael. "So what goodies do you have in that pile?"

"I might just have us a suspect," Carmichael told him, pausing to finish a mouthful of peanut M&M's. "Remember our friend, Father Tony Gallagher? Seemed a bit…evasive, but oh so polite."

Carmichael reminded Maggie of a stand-up comic, her statements short punch lines all delivered with a poker face and an even tone. The pile was for show. She didn't refer to it or to notes. She didn't need to.

"I did some checking just because he kinda pissed me off. About seven years ago he was an associate pastor for a short time in Chicago at Saint Stephen of the Martyr. Just so happened he was replacing none other than a Father Gerald Kincaid who was being reassigned."

"That's interesting," Pakula said and sipped what Maggie thought had to be his third cup of coffee, not counting the airport brew.

"It gets even more interesting," Carmichael continued. "Father Gerald Kincaid recently went away for a while. The Catholic Church has a cute little term for it, 'in between assignments.' He spent six months at a treatment center in Jemez Springs, New Mexico."

"What was he being treated for?" Chief Ramsey asked. This information seemed to have caught the chief's attention. He sat forward, elbows on the table.

"A Father Quinn at the center told me they treat priests who suffer from a variety of conditions including what he referred to as 'challenges with alcohol' and, of course, any mental or emotional problems."

"And Father Kincaid's problem?" Maggie found herself sitting forward, too, anxious that her early gut reaction to this case might be true.

"That was a confidential matter," Carmichael said, but held up her hand to stop several groans. "However, I waited and called back a little later. This time I didn't ask for anyone of an official capacity. I just chitchatted with the volunteer answering the phone. She had lots to tell me."

"Gossip," Pakula said and he didn't look happy. "Inadmissible gossip."

"Yep, you're right," Carmichael said as if that was exactly what she expected him to say, but it didn't break her routine or slow her down. "So do you wanna hear the inadmissible gossip or not?"

She looked to Chief Ramsey and he nodded, waiting. Unlike Pakula, he didn't seem to have a problem with it.

"Barbara told me that Father Gerald Kincaid had a little problem with what was officially being called 'inappropriate behavior with preadolescent boys.'"

"And so he was reassigned," Maggie said. "Did the Chicago PD have anything on record?" she asked even though she thought she already knew the answer. She had discovered in her short research that up until recently most of the cases had been settled out of court and under the radar of local law enforcement.

"Nothing," Carmichael said. "Absolutely nothing. Barbara, however, told me that Chicago hadn't been the first incident. There had been dozens of allegations. And you're right," she told Maggie. "Each time Father Kincaid had simply been 're-assigned.' In fact, he was reassigned to five different parishes. This last time the parents threatened to go to the cops, but his archbishop convinced them Kincaid would be sent away for treatment."

Carmichael paused and looked around the table. "About six weeks ago he was released and assigned to All Saints Catholic Church. I talked to the church council president and the cleaning lady at the rectory—a pretty good mix in the way of gossip, by the way—and the funny thing is, nobody at All Saints in Columbia even knew Father Kincaid had been in a treatment center let alone what he was being treated for."

"Sounds familiar," Maggie couldn't help saying, and she met Pakula's eyes.

"Agent O'Dell thinks that could be the connection. That we might have an assassin on our hands."

Maggie felt all their eyes on her. Carmichael actually smiled…a little.

"What about Daniel Ellison?" Pakula wanted to know. "Agent Weston said Ellison left the priesthood to get married. Doesn't sound to me like someone who messed with little boys."

"I haven't found any allegations, but if Kincaid's case is any indication, I'd say the church is pretty good at keeping allegations under wraps. I was thinking we might ask our new friend, Father Tony Gallagher."

"Oh, really. Why is that?"

"Seems he and Ellison were in the same seminary class at Notre Dame."

"Holy crap!" Pakula said. "So Father Tony has a connection to both men?"

Maggie watched Carmichael finally grin as she seemed to relish the information she had just presented.

"Not only that," Carmichael said, looking as if she had saved the best for last, "but when our good Father Tony was in Chicago, he started and headed up an unofficial victims' rights advocacy group. I imagine he got to hear all kinds of the things—or rather the allegations—that Father Kincaid was accused of doing."

"If the church was keeping it hush-hush, how did you find out about the advocacy group?" Ramsey asked.

"One thing I should probably tell you, Chief, is that for some reason people tell me all kinds of stuff. So I guess we should probably have Kasab bring the padre back in for more questioning, huh?" she asked Ramsey and Pakula, but was looking over at Pete Kasab who sat up for the first time at the mention of his name.

"Yeah, I suppose so," Pakula said and then added, "And you might just as well have him bring his quarterback attorney." He looked over at Chief Ramsey. "Speaking of attorneys and other bottom-feeders, Agent O'Dell thinks we might be able to manipulate the media into helping us find out a thing or two."

Ramsey sat back, arms crossed. One hand strayed to rub at his jaw. His eyes met Maggie's, gentle but tired blue-gray eyes outlined with pronounced wrinkles, what were once laugh lines. "Let us know how you want to work it. We'll make it happen."

"I think it should be today. We can go over what choice information we release. Maybe we even leave out Ellison for the time being and see if anyone comes forward, connecting him," she told both Ramsey and Pakula.

Pakula gave her a nod of agreement or perhaps it was admission. To the others he said, "Sounds like we better find out what rumors there may have been about Monsignor O'Sullivan. As much as I hate it, we probably should call in that nagging reporter from the *Omaha World Herald* and find out what the hell she thinks she knows."

CHAPTER 42

Omaha, Nebraska

Gibson tried to remember the last time he had invited someone over to his house. He did it all the time when his dad was
alive. But then his dad was sort of like a magnet. Gibson could
remember inviting a friend over after school once and his dad
talked them into a game of H-O-R-S-E. Before they knew it
there had to be like half a dozen neighborhood kids playing,
taking their turns and laughing so hard nobody could hit the rim.

It was like that all the time whether they went sledding or
to a ball game or even just washed the car in the driveway.
Everyone wanted to be around his dad. Sometimes he wondered if he ever had any real friends or if they all just wanted
to be around his "cool" dad. But this kid, this Timmy Hamilton was different.

They'd figured out that Gibson would turn sixteen a month
before Timmy turned fifteen—so he was more than a whole
year older than Timmy—which allowed Gibson to call him
"kid." Timmy didn't care. He seemed in awe of Gibson and
his knowledge, and not in awe like he couldn't believe how

geeky Gibson was, but like he really was interested, like he really wanted to be Gibson's friend. Not an easy task. Gibson knew he didn't make it easy for people. He knew he was sort of odd, compared to other kids. He didn't care about the right things, or at least not the things his classmates cared about. Instead, Gibson loved playing chess. He listened to a strange combination of music, with the Stray Cats being one of his favorites. He collected old pop bottles and had every episode of *The X-Files* on DVD. He wore his hair longer than was the style and wore a baseball cap even during class until the teachers asked him to take it off. Except Sister Kate's class. He never made Sister Kate ask.

When his dad passed away, Sister Kate was the only one who wasn't all weirded out about it. Instead, she had asked for his help, wanting to know if he might be able to come in after school a couple of days a week to catalog her collection on a new computer program she had just created especially for it. He missed his dad the most those first weeks, but his afternoons with Sister Kate had been some of the best. They talked about stuff and she made him laugh. But then the project was finished. And the next week was when Monsignor O'Sullivan started asking him to come to his office so Gibson tried to spend as little of his extra time at school as possible. That was partly why he had told his mom he didn't want to ruin his summer by having to go to the Explorers' class. But he liked being around Sister Kate. And now that the monsignor was gone for good…well, maybe he could finally enjoy stuff again. Stuff like his own collection.

Back during class he had told Timmy about the medallion he bought off eBay, and now he was excited about showing it to him. He kept it in the strange little wooden box it came in even after he shined it up. He'd spent a whole Saturday afternoon working the metal cleaner into the black-crusted grooves, using Q-tips so he could be careful not to scratch or rub too hard.

"You can make out the date at the bottom if you use this

magnifying glass," Gibson told Timmy as he handed him the glass and held the medallion up to the sunlight.

"Wow! Ten ninety-six? That's old. Did it cost a lot?"

"Nah. I don't think the guy knew what it was." Truth was, Gibson wasn't sure it was the real deal, and Timmy wouldn't know the difference. He pointed to the engraving again. "This part is Latin." He ran his fingertip over the top of the medallion. "It's something about courage and honor. Only a few of these were given out by Pope Urban II. I found a picture of it on a Web site that has a bunch of stuff about the Crusades. Pope Urban II's supposedly the one who came up with the First Crusade."

"Yeah, I like reading stuff about the Crusades and the Knights Templar. Or anything about medieval times. My mom thinks it's silly and violent and stuff, but I just think it's really interesting."

Just then Gibson noticed Timmy's eyes wandering over to his computer screen. He had been checking out Gibson's room since they got here. Gibson didn't mind. It wasn't like Timmy seemed freaked out by the mess or any of Gibson's collections. But his eyes kept going back to the computer screen. Gibson did a quick panic glance when he realized there might be another crazy instant message. But there was nothing out of the ordinary. Now Timmy looked embarrassed, like he had been caught at something he shouldn't be doing.

"Sorry, I wasn't trying to be nosy or anything. It's just that…that icon." Timmy pointed to the skull and crossbones that Gibson had moved to the bottom right of the rest of his icons. Even with the others and at the bottom it still stood out.

"It's just a game," Gibson said, pretending it was no big deal, not wanting to explain. One of the rules was that you didn't tell anyone about the game. You couldn't talk about it except with other invited players. He reached over and closed the lid of the laptop.

"Sorry," Timmy said again, only now he was staring at Gibson. "I didn't mean anything—"

"It's no big deal." Gibson picked up the medallion again and put it in the box. Maybe it was time for Timmy to go.

"It's just…" The kid was still stuttering. "I play that game, too."

"What?"

"The game."

"This isn't just an ordinary game," Gibson told him, trying to figure out what Timmy meant.

"I know it's not. It's by invitation only. You got an invitation to play, right?"

Now Gibson was staring at Timmy and the kid's eyes didn't blink, didn't look away. Was it possible? Everybody who played had almost been imaginary to him, sort of like the game itself. All of a sudden it was becoming way too real.

"How'd you get an invitation?" Gibson asked, letting it sound like the test he meant it to be.

"I was surfing Web sites one day and I got an e-mail that asked me if I wanted to play a game."

"Yeah? Who was it from?"

Timmy hesitated, and Gibson thought it was because he couldn't fake his way past this question.

"It was from someone who calls himself The Sin Eater."

"Jesus," Gibson whispered. He couldn't believe it. It was true. "Did you…" He wasn't sure how to ask, but if the rules were the same for all of them… "Did you have to submit a name?"

Again, Timmy hesitated, and this time he looked away for a brief moment as if he wasn't sure he wanted to confide anything more. Finally, he said, "Yeah, I did."

"Mine got killed," Gibson blurted out as if it had been festering for too long and suddenly exploded from his mouth without warning.

"Yeah, I'm supposed to start plotting to kill mine."

"No, no," Gibson said and he could feel a sense of panic returning along with his confession. "I mean really killed. Not just playing around. Not just part of the game."

"You mean like for real? He's dead?"

"Yeah."

"Did you do it?"

Gibson didn't know how to answer that. He sort of shrugged and looked away. "I wanted him dead," he said.

"Are you sure he's dead?"

"Yeah. I saw him." This time Gibson met Timmy's stare and he could see the realization finally coming into his eyes. "I was at the airport on Friday," he explained, hoping that was enough. And it was. He could see his new friend knew exactly what he was talking about. Of course he did. It had been all over the news all weekend. Gibson remembered Timmy saying that his mom was a reporter for the *Omaha World Herald.*

They were both quiet for what seemed like a long time to Gibson. They stared at each other, glancing away as if to think and then looking back to each other with knowing, frantic eyes. With guilty eyes.

Finally Timmy broke the silence. "Do you think mine's dead?"

"I don't know," Gibson answered in almost a whisper. "But if he isn't, I bet he's gonna be."

CHAPTER 43

Washington, D.C.

Gwen Patterson accepted the glass of water Detective Julia Racine offered. Gwen sat on Dena's leather sofa, her legs still spread apart, her body bent forward and ready to resume the position of head between her legs even though the nausea had subsided. When Racine continued to stand over her, Gwen took a sip, thinking she needed to convince all of them that she would be okay, that there would be no more vomit to mess up the crime scene.

She wasn't sure who ended up cleaning the kitchen sink. She just kept telling herself, better there than in the garbage can. Racine had handed her a damp paper towel and then the glass of water. Had Gwen remembered what Maggie had said about the detective, she would have realized that, of course, Racine wasn't waiting to make sure she was okay. It wasn't until she saw Racine's foot tapping that it dawned on Gwen that the detective wanted to know what was going on.

"Tell me again why you came here."

Without looking up, Gwen gave her the same answer, hoping that instead of sounding rehearsed it would only sound as if she was growing tired of repeating the same answers. "She didn't show up for work. I left phone messages for her and she didn't return my calls. It's not like her to just not show up. I was worried." It was all true. And yet, she had no idea how she would begin to tell the rest of the story. She had gone over it in her mind again and again, realizing how bizarre it sounded. What was worse, she had nothing—not even a match of fingerprints to back up her story.

"And you just happen to have a key?"

"Yes," Gwen said. It was easier to just answer Racine's questions. Especially right now while the dizziness and nausea took roller-coaster turns through her body.

"So you came in," Racine said, hands on her hips, foot still tapping. Her voice kept calm even as it remained somewhat abrasive, but Gwen thought it was due to impatience rather than anger. "She wasn't here, so you went on into the kitchen and checked the trash bin?"

Gwen looked up at her and dragged her fingers through her hair, starting to feel her own frustration. "I looked around. When we got to the kitchen, Harvey went to the cabinet door and started pawing at it."

"And what about that? Do you always bring your dog with you?"

Gwen reached over and gave him a pat. He had stayed by her side the entire time, finally lying down when he realized they weren't leaving.

"He's not my dog. I'm watching him for a friend." Suddenly it occurred to her that just because she knew Julia Racine, it didn't mean Racine knew her. Gwen added, "He's Maggie's dog. Maggie O'Dell."

"Agent Maggie O'Dell?"

"Yes, she had to leave for Nebraska this morning. Maggie often leaves Harvey with me when she's out of town."

Racine turned her attention to Harvey, and Gwen could see

her softening a bit. Up until now the detective had ignored Harvey. Now she bent down to scratch behind his ears.

"I don't know why I didn't recognize you, buddy," Racine said in a tone Gwen hadn't heard her use before, a kind and gentle tone. "We spent about eight hours in my car yesterday, didn't we, kiddo? I should have recognized you."

When Racine stood, she glanced around as if to make sure none of her crew had witnessed the exchange. Her change of attitude toward Harvey, however, didn't extend to Gwen. The detective was all business again.

"The victim didn't have a roommate. Did she mention a boyfriend?"

"Yes. She said she was seeing someone new."

"Did she mention his name?"

"No."

"Do you know if she was seeing him this weekend?"

"She had plans with him on Saturday evening." She almost wished Racine would ask more difficult questions.

"Do you know how she met him? Was it over the Internet?"

"She never told me how they met." It was the truth. She couldn't tell Racine that Dena had met her new beau at work, at her office, because that would only be speculating. Maybe it wasn't even Rubin Nash. After all, the fingerprints hadn't matched up.

"Funny she wouldn't tell you more about this new boyfriend," Racine said, crossing her arms, "especially since she felt close enough to give you a key to her place."

Gwen avoided the detective's eyes. Would she be able to tell that Gwen knew very little about her assistant? Instead of responding, she focused on the crime lab technician in the kitchen. He had been removing the garbage from the trash bin piece by piece and now stood staring at the bin, perhaps contemplating how to remove Dena's head without destroying any other evidence.

"She was supposed to go to a nightclub last night with one

of her friends," Gwen finally offered. Was it possible the killer wasn't even one of her patients?

"Do you know which one?"

"She may have told me, but I don't remember. She said she was going to check out the new one."

"And I don't suppose you know the name of the friend she was going with?"

"No, I don't."

The technician reached both of his gloved hands into the trash bin, and Gwen began to feel clammy and light-headed all over again. But she couldn't take her eyes away. She was mesmerized. She knew she should look away. Up until now her mind had fooled her into believing Dena had been murdered and stuffed into her own trash bin. But she knew that wasn't true. She knew it was only Dena's decapitated head. Just like the others. She knew that and still she gasped when she saw the technician lift the plastic bag out, a plastic bag big enough only for a head.

She felt Racine's hand on her shoulder, but she didn't look up at the detective. Her eyes stayed with the plastic bag the entire time it took for the technician to remove it and place it into a small black body bag. Did they have special ones for heads? she couldn't help wondering.

Still not looking up at Racine, Gwen said, "Dena always hated taking out the garbage at the office." It was an absolutely ridiculous thing to say.

CHAPTER 44

Omaha, Nebraska

Gibson pulled out the shoe box from under his bed. He turned up the volume on his boom box to sing along with his favorite track of this CD, *Stray Cats Strutting*. He was trying to keep his mind on something, anything other than the game that was getting ready to begin in the next half hour.

He had the house to himself. After dinner his mom had gone off to her poetry class. His annoying little brother, Tyler had escaped to one of his friend's to shoot off leftover firecrackers. Though he wouldn't tattle to their mom, Gibson knew that's what Tyler was up to. He had seen him sneak a whole box of matches from the kitchen junk drawer while their mom scooped up spaghetti from the pot on the stove and onto their plates.

Yep, whole house to himself, all the peace and quiet he normally would beg for, but tonight he wished he had something, anything, to distract him. He was hoping the music and his collection might do just that.

He set the box on his desk, next to his computer, trying to ignore the computer screen and still catching himself glancing at it again and again as if expecting it to flash with an instant message any minute. Maybe he expected to get caught for talking to Timmy about the game. Caught and punished. Admitting he had seen Monsignor O'Sullivan's dead body felt like he was also admitting the guilt that came along with it. He was guilty. He shouldn't just be caught, he should be punished. And yet, the computer screen remained the same.

He started taking each item out of the box, carefully setting them one by one on the desk. Then he took out the can of Brasso metal polish, the soft cloth and box of Q-tips he used to clean them. It wasn't quite as elaborate as Sister Kate's collection, but hey, he had to start somewhere.

So far he owned three medallions, two coins and one eight-inch silver crucifix. The message from the guy on eBay that he had bought the crucifix from said it had been adhered to a knight's shield during the Crusades, that he had drawings and sketches that showed similar ones and that this one had the black welding spots on the back.

Gibson wasn't sure he believed him, but he got the medallion for less than he expected to pay, and even if it wasn't from a knight's shield, it was pretty cool. It was definitely old. He spent almost three days cleaning the tarnish from all the intricate grooves. If he didn't know it was a crucifix, Gibson would have guessed it was a dagger of some kind. Maybe he'd take it in to show Sister Kate. Yeah, maybe he'd take his entire small collection in to show her. He liked that idea.

He looked around his room, trying to remember where he had thrown his backpack. He dragged it with him everywhere, lacing it onto the handles of his bike or throwing it over his shoulder. It was a reflex action, like putting on one of his baseball caps. But he hardly ever looked in it, stuffing things in the side pockets like his keys and spare change. It probably needed to be cleaned out. He found it by the door to his closet where he had also kicked off his tennis shoes. And yeah, the backpack was bulging. He'd never fit his collection in there even if he put it all in a smaller box.

He threw the backpack on his bed, unzipped the main compartment as well as all the side pockets. He started digging everything out, separating the trash and shaking his head at the stupid stuff he couldn't believe he still had in there. The bulge in the main compartment was something he didn't recognize. Definitely something he didn't own. He didn't know where it'd come from. Who the hell put it in his backpack?

Gibson pulled out a brown leather portfolio, tossed it onto his bed and stared at it. How did the frickin' thing get into his backpack?

CHAPTER 45

Omaha, Nebraska

Maggie didn't get to her hotel room until almost midnight. She had to hand it to Cunningham, the junior suite at the Embassy Suites was more than the standard comfort level that she was used to on the road. It was also only a few blocks from the police station at the edge of a downtown area Pakula had called the Old Market. It was a quaint area with cobblestone streets and old brick warehouses remodeled into shops and restaurants that included hundreds of tiny, glittering white lights outlining the shop awnings and flat rooftops.

She had just replaced her street clothes with her nightshirt, made herself comfortable in the middle of the king-size bed and started to devour her room service when her cell phone rang. She swiped barbecue sauce from her lips as she lunged for her jacket. She had called Gwen earlier, leaving only a message when she kept getting Gwen's answering service. Maybe she was finally returning her call.

"Maggie O'Dell," she answered after swallowing a mouthful of food.

"Maggie, sorry to bother you so late." It was Adam Bonzado. "Julia told me you were out of town and probably a couple of time zones behind us. I hope I'm not waking you."

"Actually Nebraska is only one time zone behind you. But no, you're not waking me. I just got in, winding down with some room service." Room service which was her first and only meal of the day and which she was starving for. She licked barbecue sauce from her fingers. "What's going on?"

"Julia will probably fill you in on everything, but I have something I thought I might fax you directly. If I fax it to Julia and she faxes it to you, we'll lose too much detail."

"Hold on a minute. Let me find the hotel's fax number." She crawled out of bed, careful not to spill her loaded tray. She had gone a bit overboard and ordered too much.

"So you're not in bed yet?" He sounded disappointed. "I was hoping I'd catch you in your skivvies."

"My what?"

"You know, your...your pj's."

She immediately felt her face flush, but she certainly couldn't let him know that. "What makes you think I wear any pajamas?"

"I...ah...excuse me?"

She laughed, thinking neither one of them was very good at flirting. She'd let him off the hook this time. Before he could say anything more, she said, "So what's the something you want to fax?"

She found the hotel's service guide and started flipping the pages, waiting for him to get back on the business track.

"I was able to clean up the tattoo. There's a lot more of it than we expected. Once I removed some of the epidermis, the colors started to pop. That's usually the way it works with tattoos."

"Instead of a fax, maybe it would be better if you e-mail a digital image of it to me. That way I can see the colors, too."

"You're right. That's a better idea."

There was an awkward silence.

"I don't think I have your e-mail address," he finally said.

She gave him an address he could use, but she didn't want to wait. "Are you able to make out what it is?"

"The very bottom of it is missing, but there's a tattoo parlor here in West Haven. When I called the guy who owns it, he recognized the design right away from my description. He faxed me the whole image. I'll e-mail that to you, too. It's a long-stem red rose intertwined around a pink-handled dagger."

"A dagger? And this is what she had tattooed on the back of her neck?"

"More on the right side of her neck toward the back."

"Is there a way to track what other tattoo parlors offer this design?"

"Good question. I'll ask," Bonzado said. "One thing the guy did tell me is that it's been a popular design for him with what he called D and D chicks."

"D and D?"

"Dungeons and Dragons. You remember that?"

"Yes, but I thought the game was sort of passé."

"Actually some of the college kids around here have started playing the game again, only it's a computerized version. I've heard some of my students talking about it, but they don't call it Dungeons and Dragons anymore. There're all sorts of versions and spin-offs, ones that they can pretty much design themselves, creating characters by using profiles of real-life people they know, people they'd like to knock off. I've heard that one of our English professors seems to be a popular target. You know, just for pretend, to blow off steam. I don't know if that helps you, but I thought it was interesting."

"One of the other victims was a Virginia Tech student," Maggie told him. "That might explain how he meets them. May even explain why they might trust him enough to go someplace private with him."

"Do you think the killer might be a student, too?"

"A student seems too young to pull off these murders. Although his rage certainly comes out of some part of him that he has no control over, as if he reverts to adolescence. But I'm thinking he has a maturity that kicks in when he needs to hide his slip-ups."

"I'll ask some of my students how they hook up to play. If it's by invitation or if anyone can join in."

"That's a good idea. Hopefully you won't find out there's a character profile for a Professor Bonzado."

"Nah, couldn't be. My students adore me. I have them all under an ancient anthropological spell. Now if only I could do the same to a certain FBI profiler."

She said good-night without a follow-up comment. Maybe he was better at this flirting thing than she was. As she clicked off her cell phone, she realized she was smiling.

CHAPTER 46

Venezuela

Father Michael Keller stared at the computer screen. With only two citronella oil lanterns lit, the computer screen reminded him of a beacon in the dark room, bringing to light answers he wasn't sure he wanted. He had been knocked off the Internet connection several times and had long ago used up his allotted time. But like an addict, he signed on again and again, impatient and frustrated with the long dial-up and many interruptions.

He rubbed his eyes, trying to make the blur go away, trying to make the emotional sting go away. Why hadn't he thought about it before? Why had he been so stupid, so naive? Why hadn't he suspected something? Instead, he wanted so badly to have a friend, someone he could trust, that he ignored glaring signs. After all, who in the world uses such an e-mail name as The Sin Eater? And here he had simply thought it clever, taking a term from an arcane Catholic legend. He'd never felt threatened because his friend, or rather this person who lured him in pretending to be his friend, had never given him reason to feel suspicious, let alone threatened. No reason at all. Until now.

He had read the articles about the two murdered priests over and over again. Monsignor O'Sullivan was someone he had met briefly while he himself was a pastor at Saint Margaret's in Platte City, Nebraska. Yet he didn't understand the connection. Why had his friend e-mailed him these articles with the warning "You may be next"? Why did he believe Keller was in danger? Did his "friend" know about the Halloween mask? Was he the one who had sent it? Was it meant to be a warning as well and not a prank he'd hoped it to be?

He had sent back an e-mail asking his so-called friend just that:

WHY DO YOU BELIEVE I MAY BE NEXT?

He hadn't received an answer until this evening. And the answer had hit him like a bullet through his heart.

I KNOW BECAUSE I EXECUTED EACH OF THEM. AND YOU'RE ON THE LIST.

The e-mail came with an attachment, the list, and yes, his name was there, just under Monsignor William O'Sullivan's.

He had to wait until the shock and betrayal finally diminished to an ache instead of the debilitating throbbing in his temple. Then he could begin his defense the only way he knew how: know thy enemy. He started with a mad search, looking up and reading anything and everything he could find on the ancient practice of sin eating, finding only bits and pieces. At one Web site, he read: "Traditionally, each village maintained its own sin eater who lived a reclusive life on the outskirts of the village."

At another Web site he found a description of the sin eater's duties: "The sin eater came after nightfall, after all had left the dead one's side. He would eat the bread left on the chest of the dead one, thus removing the sins of the dead and consuming their sins, taking them into his own soul." The early

Catholic Church called it an "illicit practice" especially when used to provide absolution to those who had "committed crimes the church considered unforgivable," crimes such as "suicide or the assassination of church officials."

So this sin eater had taken on a double role. How clever. As an assassin he was not only killing church officials, but he was also eating, or rather consuming, the sins of those he was killing for. He had become a mediator of sorts.

Father Keller wiped his sweaty face with the sleeve of his white shirt. When that wasn't enough, he yanked out the shirt-tails and pulled them up to wipe again. Yet the sweat seemed to keep pouring out of him. And the throbbing in his temples would not go away. It banged against his skull until he wanted to rip out the pain with this fingers when rubbing wasn't enough anymore.

He was exhausted. The panic had drained him. Even the tea, the wonderfully comforting tea, continued to make him nauseous. Then it hit him and he stared at the cup of steaming tea as if for the first time seeing it for the Judas cup that it might be. Was it possible? Had his friend—no, not a friend at all. Had his enemy sent him a wonderful gift of lovely teas and cookies that were actually poisoned?

He tried to remember when he had started feeling sick. Did it coincide with the receipt of the gift? Was that the plan? To poison him? Or was it simply to weaken him so that he couldn't leave, couldn't escape and would be helpless when The Sin Eater came to finish him off?

He shoved the cup away, knocking it off the rickety wooden table and watching it splatter against the wall. That was the final betrayal. His so-called friend wanted to play games. Well, he could play as well.

He pulled his chair up to the computer and typed:

YOU POISONED THE TEA.

He clicked on Send and sat back.

Usually it took hours for a response, but it was as if The Sin Eater was sitting and waiting, expecting Keller. An e-mail came back within minutes:

YES, WITH MONKSHOOD. SINCE I CAN'T BE THERE TO KILL YOU MYSELF I WANTED YOU TO DIE A SLOW AND PAINFUL DEATH.

Why? How could he? The panic started to eat away at his insides. Or was it the poison? Could it already have caused irreparable damage? Could it already be too late?

He left the e-mail site and started clicking on news links, trying to find any new information on the slain priests. There had to be something, anything, he could use. Someone had put him on a hit list. He would find out who it was. Who could possibly know? There wasn't anyone he could think of.

This Sin Eater, this assassin, had sent him things. Surely there was DNA on the envelopes. And what about all the e-mails? Maybe someone could track them. A new AP story was posted, one he hadn't seen. It must have been posted late, expecting to hit the morning wires and newscasts. He clicked it open. Before he read a single word, he stared at the accompanying photo. He should have been alarmed, but instead he was pleased that he recognized one of the investigators. Because that's when the idea came to him. And that's when Keller knew exactly what he would do. It would work. It had to work. He had no other choice.

The only question was what price would Special Agent Maggie O'Dell be willing to pay to catch this killer?

CHAPTER 47

Tuesday, July 6
Blackwater Bay Campground
South of Bagdad, Florida

Corey Lee ignored his stepdad's yelling and kept walking. He rolled his eyes at his best friend, Kevin Potter.

"Shouldn't we wait for him to catch up?" Kevin asked.

Corey shook his head. "He won't come this way. He's taking the road. It'll take forever."

Besides, Corey didn't want to wait. They were almost to the boat ramp. And it was stupid to turn back now. Corey knew this shortcut. He and Kevin had taken it the last time the troop used this campground. It was a straight shot to the ramp, which was just on the other side of these trees. Yeah, the brush was thick and the no-see-ums came at you in swarms, but wasn't that what camping was supposed to be all about?

His stepdad didn't want them taking the shortcut. It wasn't safe, or so he'd said. He thought warning them about water moccasins and alligators would stop them, instead it only made Corey and Kevin more excited to take the shortcut. Ever since the dweeb took the position as a Scout leader he thought he knew everything about the outdoors. He already thought he knew everything about everything else. But Corey had been a Boy Scout for three years. He grew up around these wetlands. He didn't need his mom's latest "special friend" telling him what to do.

He still couldn't believe she actually married this one. Which meant Corey was stuck with him hanging around the house, but it wasn't fair that he thought he could invade Corey's escapes, too. When he complained to his mom, she told him to stop "being a baby" about it. She said that Ethan wanted this to be a bonding experience between them. Corey didn't tell her that bonding with the major dweeb was the last thing he wanted to do.

"Sounds like he's following us," Kevin said.

Both of them looked over their shoulders as they kept walking. Corey could hear Ethan, but he couldn't see him. The brush was thick, but he could hear something snapping the branches and swishing through the tall grass.

"Maybe he's not such a dweeb. Maybe you should cut him a break," Kevin said, but Corey shook his head again.

"He doesn't want us showing him up. You know, proving him wrong. Geez! Something sure stinks," Corey said and then he tripped.

Before he could catch himself he was falling, knocking into Kevin and bringing him down, too. He slammed his shoulder into a tree trunk and felt his elbow scrape against the bark. Kevin went facedown. Corey could hear the marshy slosh underneath the pine needles. Immediately his jeans were soaked. And geez! It smelled bad, like rotting garbage.

Suddenly Corey jumped up, quickly forgetting any pain. He saw worms crawling up his pant legs, fat little worms. He brushed and hit at them. Kevin watched until he saw them on his arm, then Kevin was back up on his feet, too, doing a dance to get them off.

They were so frantic getting the worms off that it took them a few minutes before they looked to see what had tripped them. Corey glanced back first. It looked like a pile of debris, dirty black rags covered with mud and leaves. There was a lot of household crap left over from Hurricane Ivan that had gotten caught up in the trees and brush.

"What the hell is that?" Kevin said, grabbing Corey's arm.

"What's going on?" Ethan shoved his way through some branches. "I told you boys—" He stopped when he saw the pile that had tripped them. "Jesus Christ! Is that a dead body?"

"Is it?" Corey asked. And now he could see what was left of a face under a moving swarm of white and brown worms.

"Wow! That is so gross," Corey heard Kevin say, and they both moved in for a closer look. He had never seen a dead body before except on TV or in *Newsweek*. He wondered if they'd be able to see any of the guts.

"Get away from there, boys," Ethan told them, but then he started gagging and wretching.

Kevin looked over at Corey. This time he rolled his eyes. "You're right. He is a dweeb."

CHAPTER 48

Our Lady of Sorrow High School
Omaha, Nebraska

Nick Morrelli slammed the door of the rented Oldsmobile, taking out his anger on the car when he really wanted to smack some sense into Tony. It was bad enough that he and Jill had to stay at separate places while they were in town. She had to stay at her mother's while he stayed at Christine's. It was ridiculous. They were adults, not a couple of teenagers. What made it worse was that's how Jill liked it. She seemed to prefer spending time with her mother and her girlfriends, which Nick couldn't really complain about. He was secretly grateful that they hadn't included him in dress shopping and cake tasting. But their first full week of vacation together that was supposed to include some wedding planning had turned into mega-planning with little vacation.

Then the one night they managed to have together—this after cooking up the lame excuse that they needed to check out the downtown Embassy Suites for their out-of-town wedding guests—even that ended up being interrupted. It was getting a little frustrating, to say the least.

This morning when he rolled over to answer his cell phone

while in that nice warm, king-size bed with Jill curved up next to him only to hear Tony's frantic voice, he wanted to tell his old buddy to screw off. He wanted to remind him that he had warned him this would happen. What did he expect? He couldn't just fuck around with police detectives even if he did supposedly have God on his side.

But instead, he had agreed to meet Tony at the school in an hour, instructing him to tell the detectives to do the same while he half crawled, half fell out of the comfy hotel bed.

"Tell them that unless they have a warrant for your arrest, you shouldn't need to go down to the police station," Nick had told Tony. "They want to talk to you, then they can come to you."

He hadn't realized he was yelling until Jill had rolled over and thrown a pillow at him. At the time it didn't stop him. He had simply readjusted his cell phone between his chin and shoulder while he put on his other shoe.

Damn it!

He wished he had time to stop at Christine's and change into something other than blue jeans and Nikes. But it was more important that he get there early, beat the cops in case he still had to drill it into Tony's thick skull that he was skating on thin ice. Whatever it was Tony thought he knew and thought he had an obligation to hide, it wasn't worth being hassled by the cops. Not cops looking for a murder suspect.

"Tell them that you can't be leaving the school," Nick had continued, "especially now that the summer session has begun. You can't be running downtown whenever they have another question they forgot to ask. Tell them to come to you. Tell them if they want to ask you any more questions we'll meet at your office…in an hour."

Now as he walked up the sidewalk to Our Lady of Sorrow High School, he wondered what other questions they could possibly have for Tony. He found him alone in his second-floor office. Thank goodness. This morning Tony wore his black trousers, black shirt and white priest collar.

"Excellent," Nick told his friend, pointing to the collar.

"Anything to remind them they're fucking around with a man of the cloth. Jesus! Sorry, I didn't mean to—"

"Curse in front of a man of the cloth and then take the son of God's name in vain?" But Tony was smiling as he said it.

"What did they say about meeting here?"

"No problem. In fact, Detective Pakula said while they're here they'd like to take a look at Monsignor O'Sullivan's office. Did you see the morning news?"

"No. You woke me up. Last night Jill and I—" He stopped himself. There were some things he wouldn't share with his friend, priest or no priest. "No, I haven't seen the news for a couple of days."

"A priest was killed on Saturday night in Columbia, Missouri. The OPD's called in an FBI specialist. Sounds like they think both murders might be connected."

"You're kidding," Nick said, dropping into the old easy chair Tony kept in the corner. He wasn't sure whether to be relieved or not. If this was a serial killer, why did they still want to question Tony?

As if he could read Nick's mind, Tony shrugged. "So, see, they can't possibly suspect me. How could I have gotten to Columbia, Missouri on Saturday night? It's, like, a five-hour drive."

"Of course they don't think you're a suspect," Nick said while wondering how Tony just happened to know how long the drive was. "So, Monsignor O'Sullivan wasn't some random murder in an airport bathroom."

"Guess not," Tony said, standing by the window, watching for the cops.

"I have to ask you something." Nick waited for him to look his way. "Remember I told you yesterday that Christine said there've been allegations about Monsignor O'Sullivan? I know I told you that I understood if something was going on that you probably couldn't talk about it, but under the circumstances it really would help if you tell me what the hell you know. Had anyone accused the monsignor of…you know, acting inappropriately with any of the students?"

Tony glanced out the window. "I honestly don't know, Nick. I've been hearing some of the same stuff Christine has been hearing. Something's going on, but I'm the last person they'd let in on any of it."

"Why is that?"

"Because I told them I wouldn't keep quiet this time."

"You told Archbishop Armstrong that?"

"I told Monsignor O'Sullivan," Tony said without emotion. "I'm sure O'Sullivan told the archbishop."

Nick could tell there was more to that story, but he was glad to be getting even an edited version. Still, he decided to push his luck. "Do you think the leather portfolio was stuffed with secret documents?"

This time Tony turned to meet his eyes. "Just between you and me, not Christine, not the cops," he said and waited for Nick to nod in agreement. "It wouldn't surprise me. It wouldn't be the first time. The Vatican has diplomatic immunity. Anything under its roof can't be used or subpoenaed. Just like *anyone* under its roof can't be extradited."

"Monsignor O'Sullivan wasn't coming back?"

"No. I confronted him that morning, before he left. He ended up admitting to me that he wouldn't be returning."

"Wow!" Nick couldn't believe it. Christine was right. "So is it possible one of the monsignor's victims offed him before he could leave?"

"Or someone wanted to put an end to the whole matter once and for all."

"Wait a minute. What do you mean by that?"

But it was too late. Tony was looking out the window again.

"They're here," he said, and Nick thought he actually sounded relieved.

CHAPTER 49

Omaha, Nebraska

Maggie checked her cell phone for messages, contemplating whether or not to turn the phone off for their interview with Father Gallagher. Still no word from Gwen. She was starting to get worried. It wasn't like Gwen. Something was going on with her. It wasn't just exhaustion. It was something more and it bugged Maggie that she couldn't figure it out. No, what bugged her more was that Gwen wasn't telling her. She wondered if she should try calling her again, but Pakula was already pointing out Our Lady of Sorrow High School up ahead.

The school's campus lived up to Maggie's expectations of a small parochial high school. It was a series of old redbrick buildings in pristine condition despite being used since probably the early 1900s. The campus was located in central Omaha, but set off from busy intersections by huge maples that lined the property on one side and Memorial Park on the other.

It surprised Maggie that Detective Carmichael didn't accompany them. She had seemed to be chomping at the bit to question Father Tony Gallagher again. After all, it was her digging that created the new suspicions. When Maggie asked Pakula, he threw her a look as if it was a sore subject. Then he muttered something about needing to keep an open mind. She could tell that it didn't help matters that he had to come out here to question the priest on his turf instead of on Pakula's. Again the detective had muttered something about "that bastard attorney" Father Gallagher had watching out for him.

But as Detective Pakula pulled in to the school parking lot, Maggie's phone started ringing. From the caller ID she knew it was Racine. She had already missed two calls from the detective. This would be a third.

"Do you mind if I get this?" she asked Pakula. "I'll make it quick."

"No, go ahead."

"Maggie O'Dell."

"O'Dell, it's about time," Racine said but she sounded relieved instead of pissed, which was what Maggie had expected.

"I talked to Bonzado last night." She thought she'd beat Racine to the punch. "He filled me in on the tattoo."

"We have another victim," Racine said without preface.

Maggie leaned back against the car seat. That wasn't at all what she'd expected to hear. "It's awfully soon."

"It gets worse. The victim was your friend's assistant."

"Excuse me?"

"Dr. Patterson. The victim worked for her."

"When did this happen? Is Gwen okay? I haven't heard from her. Why didn't she call me?"

A look from Pakula told Maggie she needed to calm down. He had just shut off the ignition and now waved at the school's front door.

"I'll wait outside for you," he said.

"I was hoping she *had* talked to you," Racine was saying as Pakula left the car. "Because she didn't have much to say to me."

"She was probably upset, Racine."

"I'm sure she was, but there was something strange going on. I don't think your friend's being totally up front with me. I'm not sure what it is she's not telling us, but she's definitely holding something back."

"That doesn't sound like Gwen." But Maggie already wondered if this had anything to do with Gwen's recent demeanor. No, how could she predict something like this? That was crazy. "Is she okay?"

"I don't know her, so it's difficult for me to tell, but I'd say she's pretty upset. She was the one who found her."

"Gwen found Dena? She found her…her head?"

"In the woman's brownstone. Actually in the garbage can."

"Jesus, Racine! Why didn't you tell me that in the beginning?"

"She said Dena didn't show up for work, didn't answer any of her calls. Dr. Patterson said she went to check on her."

Maggie couldn't imagine what Gwen must be going through.

"This one is weird, O'Dell," Racine said in almost a whisper. "He's never just left them in their homes. Something doesn't feel right about it."

"Look, Racine, I have an interview I need to get to. Can I call you back later?" She checked her watch.

"Sure. I'll fill you in then."

"And Racine?"

"Yeah?"

"Would you mind checking on Gwen for me? Please see if she's okay."

"No problem. I planned to stop by her office, anyway. I'll talk to you later."

Maggie stared out the windshield, waiting for the tension to subside. Poor Gwen. But why hadn't she called? No matter how upset she was, she should have called. It wasn't like Gwen not to call.

Pakula was waiting for her, trying to pretend he didn't mind. She locked the car door behind her. When his eyes met hers with that silent question that cops asked each other without really asking, she knew he would understand. She simply said, "A case in the District. A friend of mine just found her assistant's decapitated head."

"Holy crap!" He winced, but didn't look shocked as most people might. "You need some time? We can do this later."

"No, we're here. Let's do it now."

Her phone started ringing again and she grabbed it, quickly opening it without looking at the caller ID, expecting it to be Racine, hoping it was Gwen. It was neither.

"Agent Maggie O'Dell?" asked a male voice she didn't recognize.

"Yes?" Maggie shrugged at Pakula. He waited with his hand on the school's front door.

"This is Father Michael Keller."

At first she thought it had to be a joke. She brought the phone down to glance at the caller ID. But nothing had registered. Instead it read Not Available.

"Excuse me, who did you say this is?"

"I know you remember me—Father Michael Keller. I want to make a deal with you."

Her stomach did a flip. For months after the Platte City murders she had unsuccessfully tried to track down Keller in South America. And here he was calling her as though they were old friends.

"What makes you think I would ever want to make a deal with you?"

"Because I can help you catch this priest killer."

"Really?" So their media coverage had reached all the way to Chile, if that was where he was still hiding. "What can you possibly have that would help?"

"I'll share that with you when I'm certain we have a deal. I'll even bring what I have to you."

She couldn't believe it. Keller was offering to come back to the States. After all these years. Why would he do that?

"And why exactly are you able to help?" she asked him,

keeping her voice even and calm as if she could care less that a child killer was offering to make a deal with her.

There was a long silence, and for a moment she thought she might have lost him or that he had hung up.

"Because I'm on the list."

"What list are you referring to?" So there was a list. She shouldn't have been surprised that he would have made the list. But how had the killer found him when she hadn't been able to? So it was fear that had pushed him into contacting her. She restrained her urge to smile. Of course, Keller was scared. If the killer had been able to find him, there would be nothing to stop him from being eliminated.

At the mention of a list Pakula furrowed his brow, recognizing that this was about the case and stepping forward to jump in to her rescue.

"You know what list. Unless you're further behind on solving this case than I thought."

She could detect some anger in his voice.

"I honestly don't think you have anything that could help us. Sorry, I'm not willing to make a deal." She tried not to enjoy envisioning him squirming on the other end of the phone.

"So you're not interested in who else might be on the list?"

"Excuse me?"

"I have a copy of it, of the whole list."

"How do I know you didn't just make it up?"

"How else would I know about Daniel Ellison? You forgot to mention him to the media."

Her knees threatened to buckle, even before he added, "He was on the list and he's also dead, isn't he?" He waited, as if knowing the effect it would have when it all sank in. "I'll bring everything I have to you…only you."

"What is it that you want in return for your help, Father Keller?"

"Protection. And an antidote. I think he may have already poisoned me."

CHAPTER 50

Blackwater Bay Campground
South of Bagdad, Florida

Deputy Sheriff Wendall Galt pulled his cruiser off to the side of the road. A dozen Boy Scouts stood crowded on a mound of grass in the ditch. The barbed-wire fence kept them confined to the ditch. On the other side of the fence the trees and scrub weeds were thick. Two men waved him over. They were obviously the troop leaders although one looked like a slightly overgrown boy at best.

"I thought it was a pile of rags at first," the small guy said, coming up to Wendall so close he almost bumped into him. "We've been keeping the boys right here. No need for them to see something like that. My God! It was horrible. Just horrible."

Wendall didn't say anything. Instead, he pushed up his sunglasses. He took a step back from the guy and looked over at the boys, slapping at their legs and arms, bored, but none of them wanting to leave. Despite their Scout leaders' insistence to protect them, they were anxious to see a dead body. Although Wendall doubted that's what had been found. Not that it wasn't possible. But guys like this—and Wendall looked the guy over, noticing his designer khaki shorts and polo shirt with the teeny polo player embroidered on the pocket and leather loafers when some good hiking boots would be smarter—guys like this would fill their pants if they stumbled on a half-eaten deer carcass.

"I can't believe they sent only one of you," the guy rattled on.

"Ethan, enough already," the other one said, but it didn't matter.

"No, I can't believe it. There should be officers to seal off the area. And a crime scene mobile lab. The coroner. For Christ's sake, there's a dead guy in the swamp. He didn't crawl off on his own to die there."

"You never know in these parts," Wendall said, exaggerating his drawl for effect and enjoying the guy's response, a slightly dropped jaw. People watched too damn much TV. "What makes you so sure it was a body?"

The guy slapped a hand to his forehead to avoid the setting sun in his eyes. "Are you kidding? I think I'd know a dead body when I see one."

Wendall wanted to say, "Right, sure you do," but he was already in trouble with Sheriff Poole for what was called a "disrespectful attitude." In short, he seemed to piss off people too easily.

"Let me take a look for myself," he said instead. "Where is it?" Almost on cue they all pointed toward the trees on the other side of the barbed-wire fence.

Wendall shook his head. Hell, there wasn't even a path. A little bit of scrub weed trampled down a bit. He took his time, pretending to examine the area before he attempted to climb over the fence. Two boys volunteered to lead the way and he was just about to tell them he didn't need them when the small guy with the big mouth yelled at the boys to stay put. Wendall told the boys to come on with him, and the look on the guy's face made the impulsive decision worth it. Turned out, it paid off. The two boys, Corey and Kevin, were the ones who had actually stumbled on the pile.

"I've never seen a dead person before today," Kevin was telling him, keeping close to Wendall's side and letting Corey lead the way. "Do you think somebody brought him out here and killed him? No way they could drag him in here after he was dead, right?"

Wendall didn't answer. He didn't want to stimulate the kid's imagination anymore than it already was.

"It smells really bad," Corey said over his shoulder. "Pretty soon—" and he started sniffing the air like a bloodhound "—you'll smell it. I thought it was garbage or something like that."

Wendall still believed the boys just had active imaginations. One thing you learned quickly was that if something died in the July heat in these wetlands, it didn't take long for it to stink to high heaven, whether it was a bird or a fox or an armadillo.

He followed them anyway, not paying much attention except to the no-see-ums attacking his arms and the back of his neck. Even after you slapped them, their carcasses stuck to your sweat. He hated the humidity this time of year, with his shirt constantly stuck to his back. He was thinking how good it'd feel when he returned to his cruiser and blasted the A/C. The sudden stink of rotted meat stopped him in his tracks.

"Right there," Corey told him, pointing to what looked to Wendall like a pile of dirty old rags.

He was still skeptical, thrusting a hand out for the boys to stay put while he stepped closer.

"What the hell?" He pulled off his sunglasses and squatted over the mess. Then he jumped up and back when the realization hit him. "Jesus Christ!" he yelled. His surprise turned briefly to embarrassment when he remembered the boys. He made himself squat again.

The flies were still buzzing around, but they were few compared to the maggots that swarmed so thick it was difficult to make out what was underneath. Wendall found a branch and poked at the writhing mass, knocking enough of them off to discover a face and a neck and a…that was weird. He prodded an area around the neck, clearing it until he was certain of what he was seeing.

He could be mistaken, but Wendall thought it looked like the corpse was wearing a white collar around his neck. A collar like a priest would wear.

CHAPTER 51

Our Lady of Sorrow High School
Omaha, Nebraska

Maggie couldn't go into it with Pakula. Not right now when they were here at the school and needed to do this interview. Not when her mind was racing over emotions and memories that were colliding and fogging up her better judgment. Would Cunningham explode when she told him what she had done, what she had agreed to? Or would he simply suspect that she had agreed with Keller for the sole intention of not keeping this promise? Could he read her that well that he would see through her transparent motive of simply getting him back to the States?

"Are you sure you're still up for this?" Pakula asked again.

She insisted they continue with their morning plans and promised to give him all the details later. Then she motioned for him to lead the way.

Pakula seemed to know where they needed to go, down one hallway and past another until he pointed to a staircase. "His office is on the second floor."

She tried to focus, observing and noticing everything around them almost as if challenging herself to avoid the thought of Keller boarding a United flight in the next few hours and arriving right here in Omaha. She didn't want to start calculating how many hours, how many connections it would take. How many opportunities he would have to change his mind, to realize she wouldn't possibly honor this deal. She tried to push it all out of her mind and concentrate, instead, on this small high school with shining wooden floors and elaborate stair railings and cornices over the classroom doors.

Now she noticed that most of the classrooms appeared empty, despite Pakula telling her earlier that the summer session had begun and that was why Father Tony Gallagher insisted they come to the school. In fact, they passed only one classroom with about a dozen kids. The room's decor caught Maggie's eye—ancient artifacts and medieval relics including a sword or two lined the shelves and walls.

Maggie glanced up at Pakula and saw that he had noticed, too. He shook his head and said, "The stuff they teach kids these days."

Father Tony Gallagher was standing outside the doorway to his office, waiting for them; he waved across the vast lobby between classrooms. Maggie couldn't help thinking he didn't look like a priest—a perfect smile, handsome, perhaps in his late thirties, maybe forty at the most, his dark hair peppered with gray at the temples. And although he looked athletic, she noted that he was small-framed. She tried to imagine him with a baseball cap on and if he might be mistaken for a young boy.

"Father Gallagher, we appreciate your cooperation," Pakula said as the priest led them into his office. "This is Special Agent—"

But before Pakula could get out the introduction she heard, "Maggie?"

Both she and Pakula stopped in the office doorway. Nick Morrelli rose from the easy chair in the corner.

"Maggie O'Dell, what the hell are you doing here?"

CHAPTER 52

Our Lady of Sorrow High School
Omaha, Nebraska

Nick couldn't believe it. Just when things were settling down in his life and coming together…well, other than this colossal mess with Tony. Just when Nick was finally getting his life on track, in walks Maggie O'Dell. It didn't help that she looked better than ever. He tried to remember how long ago it had been since they had seen each other. All he knew at the moment was that it was long enough ago that he shouldn't have a knot in his stomach and weak knees like some high-school kid.

"Is there a problem here?" Pakula wanted to know, looking from Nick to Maggie.

"No problem," she answered as if it were true. "Nick and I worked a case about four years ago out in Platte City." Then she turned to Tony and put out her right hand, "Father Gallagher, I'm Maggie O'Dell, with the FBI."

"Welcome to Our Lady of Sorrow High School," Tony said as he shook her hand, but he glanced over at Nick with a knowing look as if to say "so this is Maggie." And though

Tony didn't say it out loud Nick could almost feel the tips of his ears start to burn.

"Four years ago in Platte City?" Pakula was scratching his shaved head as if it would help him remember. "Ah, I remember. Gillick and Howard murdering those little boys."

Yeah, that one, Nick wanted to say, but only nodded, waiting to see if Maggie would try to correct the record. She never did believe that Eddie Gillick and Ray Howard were murderers even though both men had been convicted and were serving life sentences. Maggie believed that Father Michael Keller, a handsome young priest who everyone in the community loved and adored, had chosen the boys because he thought they were being abused by their parents. She was convinced that Keller had been on a mission to save them and grant them eternal rest. It sounded as crazy now as it did then.

"Yes, that's the case, Gillick and Howard," Maggie said, her eyes meeting Nick's.

But it wasn't just the case, he wanted to tell her. There had been more between them, much more. Or at least there could have been if she had let it. But then she had made that decision all on her own without letting him have a say.

"Nick was the county sheriff at the time," Tony added.

"Really? Maybe that's where I remembered your name from," Pakula said to Nick. "I'm usually pretty good with names. That was one helluva case." Then Nick thought the detective's eyes softened a bit. For a moment, perhaps, he was seeing Nick as a fellow lawman.

"I have four girls," Pakula continued, "but it doesn't matter when it's kids. Every parent gets the jitters when something like that happens. One of my girls was about the age of those boys. She had a paper route, too. For weeks my wife and I took turns running her route with her. It was a scary time. Wasn't there a little boy who got away?"

"Yeah," Nick said. "My nephew, Timmy Hamilton."

"Holy crap! How's he doing?"

"He's doing great," Nick told Pakula, but he was still looking to Maggie as if his answer was for her, since she hadn't even bothered to ask about Timmy. She seemed distracted, not even interested. "He's starting here at Our Lady of Sorrow in the fall as a freshman."

"That's good. That's great," Pakula said, hands in his pockets, not knowing what else to do with them.

Nick could tell Pakula was sincere, but not so good at chitchat.

"Wow! Timmy's going to be a freshman," Maggie said, shaking her head. "How's Christine?" she asked Nick.

"She's good." He shoved his hands in his jean pockets, too, following Pakula's example, suddenly uncomfortable with Maggie asking personal questions about his sister, his family, his life, even though just seconds ago he was pissed that she hadn't thought to ask about Timmy. "Why don't we get started with your questions?" he suggested to Pakula, but looked at Tony as if to say, *This is it. Let's get it over with.*

Nick offered Maggie the easy chair in the corner by the window and she slipped by him to take it without as much as a glance. He tried not to notice her scent, something fresh and exotic like coconut and lime. Probably her shampoo. He shook the thought away and retreated to the other side of the room to be close to Tony as his friend sat down behind his desk.

Pakula leaned against the doorjamb, filling it. Nick couldn't help thinking how much the detective looked like a linebacker, flexing his shoulder blades, getting ready for his first tackle of the day. All that sincere crap already left behind. In an instant they had gone from fellow cops talking about a gruesome case to adversaries ready to outwit each other. Such is life. Nick was used to it, dealt with it every day as a deputy prosecutor. This shouldn't be any different. This shouldn't be personal. And yet, he glanced at Maggie, wondering what role she'd take.

"I saw the news this morning," Tony said. "Sounds like you think Monsignor O'Sullivan's murder could be connected to the one in Columbia, Missouri."

"Possibly," Pakula told him.

"What possible connection could there be?" Nick asked.

"That's what we're hoping Father Gallagher might be able to tell us."

Nick thought that Pakula had definitely slipped back into his tough-detective role.

"I don't know what you think Tony might be able to tell you," Nick said, glancing at Tony, still wondering what Tony had omitted earlier.

"We actually have three victims, even though we only released two of them to the media. All three were stabbed to death in very public settings. Two were priests. One was an ex-priest," Pakula said, crossing his arms, watching Tony. "I can't tell you any of the details, but there are similarities. Now, if there is a connection between these three victims, we're hoping Father Gallagher might tell us what that might be. Especially since he's one of the few people who knew all three of them."

"What?" Nick shot a look at Tony. "Is that true?"

"Surely you're not saying I'm a suspect, Detective Pakula." Tony avoided Nick's question and his eyes. "If you are, I'm sure my friend and lawyer would advise me not to answer any of your questions."

"Actually, Father Gallagher, no disrespect," Maggie said from the corner, "but if you do need an attorney, Mr. Morrelli can't represent you as long as he's still a deputy prosecutor for the state of Massachusetts."

"Is that right?" Pakula asked while Nick stood speechless, staring at his friend.

And then it occurred to Nick exactly why Maggie had come to this so-called interview. She was here to observe Tony. Was she already calculating whether or not he matched her profile? Did they really believe Tony could murder someone?

He looked over at Tony who was now sitting on the corner of his desk, appearing cool and calm and unfazed by Pakula's questions. And despite confiding to Nick earlier that he had told Monsignor O'Sullivan he wouldn't keep quiet this time if the allegations were true—despite that warning, here he was remaining quiet and evasive. And Nick couldn't figure out why in the world he would do that.

CHAPTER 53

Reagan National Airport
Washington, D.C.

He was fidgety today, more so than usual. His eyes darted around the crowded airport as he waited for his flight to start boarding. He had another hour to wait, if the digital bulletin board was correct. Why did he feel as if he was constantly waiting?

He readjusted his laptop computer, stretching his legs before settling down again. His wireless connection allowed him Internet access anywhere. It was the best investment he had made. He continued to surf for news articles, anything and everything about the murdered priests, two of them over the holiday weekend. The first had been over the Memorial weekend.

Was that how it worked? Did it have to be a holiday weekend? If that was the case, the next holiday was…what? Labor Day? That was September. He couldn't wait until September. He wouldn't wait. He had waited long enough, more than fourteen years.

His foot tapped out his nervous energy. He was annoyed by his restlessness. It hadn't stopped. Why wouldn't it stop?

There had been no reprieve like there usually was right after one of his outbursts. At least, there used to be a reprieve for a month or two. The rage would retreat for a time. Oh sure, he knew it was just beneath the surface, but still he felt that it was manageable.

He thought he had learned how to channel his anger into other activities. And that's what he had done with the game. Playing it, coming up with the characters and taking out his rage in a make-believe scenario had actually worked...or at least it had worked for a while. He couldn't remember how long it had been since he had moved beyond the game. Sometimes he had trouble remembering what was real and what was imaginary. Only his rage seemed real.

All he knew now was that it had been only a couple of days, and the twitch, the throbbing, the restlessness had not gone away. It was with him constantly. He just wanted it to go away. And he knew exactly what it would take to make that happen.

On his laptop he clicked over to weather.com. It was raining in Boston, eighty-four degrees and ninety-five percent humidity. He had already decided he'd take the subway when he got there, as he always did when he was a kid. He had only one bag, an oversize computer case, large enough for everything he would need along with a change of clothing. He had confirmed everything, planned out every single detail. By nine o'clock this evening it would be all over with and he would be catching another flight home. And the twitching, the throbbing, the restlessness would be gone.

CHAPTER 54

Washington, D.C.

Gwen Patterson stood at her office window staring out at the Potomac River. Harvey lay next to her desk. Every move she made alerted him, his head up, those watchful brown eyes searching her out, checking on her. Maggie usually complained about his overprotective behavior, but Gwen continued to find it rather endearing and comforting. She wasn't sure how she would have managed any of this without him.

She had canceled all of her appointments for the day and had already hired a temp who would be here at eight o'clock tomorrow morning when she could resume her business and get on with her life. Tomorrow everything would be back to normal.

Nothing would ever be normal again. Why did she bother trying to fool herself?

A knock at her office door startled her.

"Sorry," Julia Racine said, staying in the doorway, apologetic enough that Gwen realized she must still look as bad as she felt. "No one was out front." She stated the obvious as her excuse.

"I decided to close for business today," Gwen said without

leaving her perch at the window. "It seemed the least I could do, considering my office assistant was recently decapitated." She knew her morbid sense of humor was simply a coping mechanism. She wasn't sure if Racine would see it that way.

"I talked to Maggie earlier. She asked me to check on you."

"Did she? I didn't realize that was a service the District police department provided." Morbid sense of humor followed by flippant remarks. Was she losing it? Surely she should be able to tell. She was a medical professional, after all.

"Also, I had a few more questions," Racine said, inching her way farther into the office, but keeping her distance.

"Of course you have more questions."

"You mind?"

"Would it matter if I did?"

"I could certainly come back later," Racine told her, still patient, to the point that Gwen might have to call it polite as well. And Gwen wondered what else Maggie may have told the young detective to eke out such patience. Or was this simply some new interrogation tactic Racine was testing out on her?

"Now or later, nothing will have changed." She turned from the window and came into the room, continuing to stand, but waved at a chair, inviting Racine to sit.

Racine took time to pat Harvey, giving him a rub behind the ears before she chose the chair next to him. By now he recognized Racine and had started to identify her as one of the good guys. Gwen wasn't convinced that that was such a good idea. But maybe she should trust Harvey's instincts. The dog hadn't been wrong yet.

"There's something you're not telling me," Racine said, but it didn't look as if she was going to try to force it out of Gwen. She sat back, and instead of waiting for some explanation or confirmation she went on. "At first I thought maybe it was something about your assistant. Maybe something you were afraid would damage her good name, her reputation. You know, embarrass her family." Racine paused and Gwen could feel the detective studying her, perhaps searching to see if she had struck a chord or gotten anywhere close to the truth. "Finding her in her own home was very different from all the others. It didn't feel right."

Gwen leaned against her desk, suddenly very tired again. "Dena wasn't like the others," she said in a matter-of-fact tone.

"No," Racine agreed with a knowing calm. "With Dena he knew he could leave her in her home because he knew someone would come looking for her. With the other three victims we had to wait until he told us where to find them. I kept thinking that was the big difference, and yet, it wasn't really all that different."

Another pause, as if Racine was testing her. Gwen crossed her arms and held the young detective's stare without flinching as Racine continued. "The owner of a construction company told us where we could find the first victim. Funny, I called him this morning and asked how he had found her, but he said he hadn't. He told me that a woman had called and tipped him off. Ironically a woman and her dog found the second victim in the park while out walking."

Racine glanced down at Harvey. "But she declined to come in and file a report. Then last week when we found Libby Hopper on the banks of the Potomac it was because a woman had called in the exact location, but she used a stolen cell phone and we couldn't trace it. Dena Wayne was left in her own home. I thought that seemed totally out of character for this killer until I realized that it was actually a woman…a woman and her dog who had, again, found the victim."

Racine sat quietly now, holding Gwen's eyes as if she could see the truth within them and didn't need anything more to corroborate her wild theory.

"Sounds like you think you have it all figured out," Gwen finally said without any sort of admission. "Too bad things aren't ever as simple as they seem."

"No, they usually aren't."

"His instructions also came with subtle threats." Gwen said it in such a whispered tone she hardly recognized her own voice.

"I wondered if it might be something like that. You were afraid he'd hurt you." Racine nodded but her eyes never left Gwen's.

"No. Not me. Always someone else. Someone close to me. It would have been easier if it were me." Gwen had been threatened before. She considered taking those risks just part of the job. "I thought I might be able to outwit him," she added.

"But in the meantime he was making you an accessory to his murders."

"Yes, I suppose he was," Gwen said. "But not anymore."

CHAPTER 55

Omaha, Nebraska

Maggie excused herself from Father Gallagher's office, explaining that she had some phone calls she needed to make. Cunningham was at the top of her list. She desperately wanted to hear how Gwen was and besides, she needed a break from the testosterone battle between Pakula and Nick. She had heard enough of Father Gallagher's clever evasiveness to know their interview would provide little new information. But she wondered why the priest didn't realize that every time he answered one of Pakula's questions with a question it only stretched out the process?

It seemed obvious that Father Gallagher was hiding something, but she doubted that he could be the killer. He had a solid alibi for Saturday evening. The entire parish of Our Lady of Sorrow could vouch for him. He couldn't have officiated at the seven o'clock mass in Omaha, Nebraska, and still made it to Columbia, Missouri, to drive a knife into Father Gerald Kincaid's chest at nine-thirty.

However, in her own mind Maggie didn't rule him out completely. Father Tony Gallagher, in spite of his holy vows, could very well fit her profile. This killer could have convinced himself that he was doing something that needed to be done for the greater good. If it was confirmed that each of the three victims had, in fact, been accused of abusing young boys—or as in Keller's case, their murder—then this killer would feel he was performing a service, administering justice to those who had previously escaped punishment. He might rationalize the killings in his mind as a necessary evil to prevent more evil perpetrated against other children. He could even consider himself a crusader, protecting the vulnerable and helpless victims and avenging those already hurt or murdered. Who better to justify avenging evil than a Catholic priest? After all, the Catholic Church had a long history of crusading against evil.

She decided to put off calling Cunningham for now. She'd call him after she talked to Detective Pakula. She could use his support. Instead, she tried Gwen's office number and her cell, only to get voice-messaging services. Racine wasn't answering her phone, either. She wished Tully was back from vacation. She needed someone to make sure Gwen was okay.

She passed the classroom with the historical artifacts that she and Pakula had noticed earlier. The class must have taken a break. The room looked empty. Maggie backtracked and stood in the doorway. Several antique daggers caught her eye. They were laid out on the counter, resting on special black cloths. The metal sparkled in the streaks of sunlight. She wandered closer, standing over them, examining without touching. Two of them were much longer than regular knives, their hilts wide and narrow. The handles had elaborate carvings, some worn down and impossible to distinguish as decorative or symbolic. All had been meticulously polished and cleaned.

"You can pick them up if you like."

The voice startled Maggie, but she didn't turn around. Instead, she simply glanced over her shoulder. The woman wore khakis and a white T-shirt with bright pink and aqua-colored fish and funky lettering that read Pensacola Seafood Festival.

"This one looks like a sixteenth- or seventeenth-century European stiletto," Maggie said, pointing to the sleekest one, a thin blade about nine inches long with a hilt that curved down at the ends. Several years ago she had helped raid the basement of a serial killer who collected and used stilettos from different eras. It was a history lesson that stayed with her.

"Very good," the woman said, rewarding her with a radiant smile. Now closer, she noticed gentle lines at the edges of the woman's mouth, revealing that she was a bit older than Maggie's first impression. She figured the woman was around her own age, early to middle thirties.

"The stilettos," she continued, "were actually modeled after these." She picked up the dagger and handed it to Maggie. "This one's a bit earlier. I've been told it's from a fourteenth-century knight. It was used as a companion piece for close-contact battle."

"Close-contact battle?"

"Probably to slit his opponent's throat."

"Ah," Maggie said, and she tried to hold it with the reverence it seemed to deserve.

"I'm Sister Kate Rosetti."

"Maggie O'Dell."

"Are you with the detective questioning Father Tony?"

"Yes, but I'm with the FBI." She searched Sister Kate's eyes to see if that made a difference. Would she be like Father Gallagher and become defensive, careful with her words, or anxious to be rid of Maggie? The nun picked up another one of the daggers, but seemed only anxious to show it to her.

"This is one of my favorites," she said, turning it in the manner of a formal presentation, so that Maggie could see the intricate skull-like carving at the very top of the handle. "It's called a talisman or a wizard's knife. It has the flying serpent wrapped around the handle, but also the Celtic knotwork engraved on the blade."

"Actually it's very beautiful." It didn't seem to be the correct word to call such an item beautiful. However, it was difficult to ignore the craftsmanship, if not artistry, that went into each piece. "What inspired you to start collecting me-dieval…weapons?" Maggie looked around the counters and shelves. The glass cabinets on the wall contained different historical artifacts, but at first glance it occurred to her that most of them were, indeed, weapons of some sort.

"That's interesting," Sister Kate said, pausing for a moment. "You know, most people ask me where I found them or how I can afford such a collection. They seem more interested in the acquisition." She said this while suddenly looking at Maggie, studying her as if seeing her for the first time. "They rarely ask what inspired me." She smiled again and seemed pleased with the question, but her eyes left Maggie's to take in the surrounding shelves as she began to explain. "My grandfather used to read me wonderful tales of knights in shining armor. My parents let me spend a summer with him on his farm in Michigan."

Her gaze returned to Maggie. "I was eleven," she said. "It was right after…a particularly difficult year. I guess my parents wanted me to get away. They wanted me to be safe. I'm not too sure they would have been happy had they discovered our summer reading material. But it was exactly what I needed, knights in shining armor coming to the rescue. It was quite…comforting."

Now there was something different in her smile. Maggie thought it was softer, perhaps more genuine, but not with the radiance of before. This was a knowing smile shared with someone who had experienced a similar tragedy. What exactly was it that this woman thought they shared? Maggie had only just met her.

"How easy is it to find one of these?" Maggie asked, remembering the medical examiner's speculation that a dagger had been used to killed Monsignor O'Sullivan.

"Very." Sister Kate didn't hesitate, nor did she seem surprised at the question. "I've bought several daggers as well as swords on the Internet and eBay. Imitations are popular right now. You have to be careful and know what you're look-ing at. Whether they're imitation or authentic they're all con-sidered artifacts, so they're not treated with the same security as a regular weapon. Even when I travel with them for pres-entations I simply put them inside my suitcase and check it."

"You said the imitations are popular right now. Why is that?"

"I think it's mostly kids buying them. Many of them sim-ply can't afford the real thing. From what I understand, there are several Internet games that are based on knights and the Crusades, medieval stuff. They seem to be quite popular. In fact, one of my students brought in his collection today to show me. His seems to be authentic, though. He's done a good job bartering for the items."

She pointed to a wooden box left open on her desk. Maggie glanced inside, noticing immediately the silver crucifix that looked like a dagger. She remembered what Bonzado had said about his students playing Internet games, particularly ones that resembled Dungeons and Dragons, creating characters and playing them out on the screen, taking it as far as getting tat-toos with roses and daggers. Now Sister Kate was telling her these games were popular enough that kids were buying and collecting imitation daggers. The man who discovered Mon-signor O'Sullivan's body in the airport bathroom thought he ran into the killer on his way out, a young boy with a baseball cap. Was it possible the killer was a young boy, a teenager, perhaps? If she was correct about the killer playing the role of avenger he could very well have been a victim of one of the priests.

"Are you in town for long?" Sister Kate asked, interrupt-ing Maggie's thoughts.

Maggie wanted to say she'd be in Omaha until the next dead priest turned up somewhere else. "I never know how long I'll be in one city," she said instead.

"I travel quite a bit, too, making presentations, attending workshops. I know how boring it can be having room service in your hotel or going to a restaurant to eat alone. If you get bored, let me know."

"Thanks, I appreciate that." She was surprised by the invitation and this time she found herself assessing Sister Kate's motive. Maggie wondered if her profession made her so skeptical that she suspected everyone's motives, including a friendly invitation to dinner. She glanced around the classroom again. But then, feeling the need to prove herself wrong, she found herself asking, "Are you free tomorrow evening?"

"Yes, certainly. Where are you staying?"

"The Embassy Suites on Tenth Street."

"Oh, there are so many wonderful restaurants in the Market. There's a little place a block up from you on Eleventh— M's Pub. Why don't I meet you there around seven?"

Sister Kate's students started coming back into the room.

"I'll see you tomorrow," Maggie told her.

She took her time leaving, watching the students amble in aimlessly like teenagers with little ambition beyond their next task. She wondered if she and Pakula may have been looking in all the wrong places for this killer. Maybe they weren't seeing what was right in front of them.

As a profiler she was taught to find the similarities and use them for a foundation. But from experience she'd learned never to underestimate who could kill. She noticed a couple of boys with baseball caps. One removed his and tossed it onto the desk, revealing shaggy, dirty-blond hair growing longer over his ears. He and his friend were her height, maybe a little taller, both with slight builds.

The medical examiner had reported that it would take little strength to shove a knife, a sharp dagger, up into the monsignor's chest, piercing his heart. It was possible that a teenage boy could have done it.

CHAPTER 56

Washington, D.C.

Gwen ran her fingers through her hair, resisting the urge to grab at it and pull.

"Tell me again how this little game worked?"

Just when Gwen thought Racine couldn't get any angrier, her tone turned up a notch and so did the sarcasm.

"It wasn't a game," Gwen explained, trying to keep her calm despite the cockroaches invading her insides. It had to be all the caffeine that was ripping away at her stomach, two days' worth of caffeine and no food. Maybe that's why she felt so light-headed.

"He thought it was a game," Racine almost hissed at her. "Believe me, this psycho thought it was a game, no matter what you think."

The detective paced back and forth in front of the sofa where Gwen sat. How many times had Rubin Nash sat in her office, in this very spot, and ranted about "having himself yet another pretty, little coed?" Gwen thought it was all about sexual conquests, asserting himself and his manhood. The mov-

ies made it out to be a sexual odyssey from boyhood to manhood when an older woman seduced a young boy. But if the
woman purposely emasculated him, as in Nash's case, the
damage could be irreparable. Should Gwen have seen the
signs for his violent behavior? Should she have figured out
months ago that he could and would kill?

Racine stopped every once in a while to look over the notes,
the map, the earrings, everything that Gwen had received. She
had scattered them on her desktop, each piece encapsulated
in its own Ziploc bag, labeled like crime scene evidence. Everything except the last manila envelope and the water glass,
failing to explain her unsuccessful attempt at matching Nash's
prints.

"None of this proves your patient is the killer," Racine said.
"Maybe we'll be lucky and pull a print off something he sent
you. But I'm guessing he'd be more careful than that." She
turned to look at Gwen. "When do you see him again?"

"We recently moved his weekly sessions to Saturday mornings to accommodate his travel schedule."

"He travels?"

"Yes, I believe he sells computer software. He's mentioned
that his sales region extends as far north as Boston, I think,
and as far south as the northern part of Florida."

"By car or by plane?"

"Excuse me?"

"When he travels for his job," Racine said, slowing down
her words as if addressing a child. "Does he drive or fly?"

"I have no idea." Gwen frowned, trying to remember if he
had mentioned it. "Why would it matter?" she finally asked.

"We've never found the torsos," Racine said, expecting it
to be all that was necessary for Gwen to understand. Her face
must have showed her confusion, because Racine continued.
"If he drives, it might explain how or if he dumps the torsos
somewhere else."

"Was the rest of Dena's body…was she left anywhere else
in the brownstone?" Gwen asked.

She thought she saw Racine soften, as if the reminder of what Gwen had been through in the last twenty-four hours had brought a fleeting moment of compassion, and even her answer came in a quiet, almost apologetic voice when she said, "No. We haven't found anymore of her."

Gwen rubbed her hands over her face again, this time digging the heels of her palms into her eyes, hoping to get rid of the image. She'd never be rid of it.

"The notes, the messages," Racine started in at her again, "all of them have been delivered to your office?"

"Yes. Either dropped in the mail slot in the lobby after hours or delivered to the main desk downstairs. One of the earrings was left on Saturday in a manila envelope. Dena said she found the envelope on the reception desk after Rubin Nash's appointment." Gwen paused. "Do you think he expected me to recognize it as hers?"

"If he did, he may have wanted to taunt you with it," Racine said and Gwen could feel the detective's eyes on her as if expecting some reaction. "You know, to show you how close he could get. If you're right about him being Dena's new boyfriend, that could explain how he got the key to her brownstone and knew where she lived. Although there's no evidence that he killed her there."

Then Racine hesitated, but she was still watching Gwen, studying her. "If you had recognized the earring, would you have done anything about it? Would you have called the cops?" The harsh tone returned, cold and unsympathetic.

If Racine thought she could possibly make Gwen feel any more responsible for Dena's death, she was wrong. Gwen wasn't sure she'd ever be able to forgive herself for Dena's death.

CHAPTER 57

Omaha, Nebraska

Tommy Pakula had had enough. He felt Morrelli's attention
had followed O'Dell out the door after she'd left Father Gallagher's office. The two may have worked a case years ago,
but it seemed obvious to Pakula that Morrelli still held some
kind of a grudge. Pakula finally told both men that he'd be in
touch, thanked them for their time and left.

He found O'Dell coming out of a classroom and raised his
eyebrows at her, surprised that she would be so transparent in
her snooping.

"Learn anything?" he asked.

"Maybe. Are you finished with Father Gallagher?"

"Yeah, I've had enough of those two clowns. I should have
unleashed Carmichael on them." They started down the steps,
and he let her lead the way. "I can tell you one thing, Morrelli sure isn't finished with you. Is he going to be a problem?"

"I get the feeling he thinks there's some unfinished personal
business between us," she said with no emotion, perhaps a bit
of amusement if anything.

"Is there?"

"If you're asking if it'll get in the way of working this case, I won't let it." Her tone was serious now.

"No, actually I wanted to make sure the asshole's not gonna be hassling you. If he gives you any problems you've got my cell-phone number. You give me a call. I'll take care of it."

She stopped at the bottom of the stairs and looked up at him. "Are you trying to protect me, Detective Pakula?"

He stopped in his tracks, too, and wanted to cringe. Was she going to bust his chops about how just because she was a woman she didn't need his protection? Jesus!

"It's been a while since I've had someone want to play big brother with me," O'Dell told him, but she was smiling now. "That's kinda nice." And before he could respond she was on her way again, leaving him as she headed out the school's front door.

Back in the car, she filled him in about her conversation with Sister Kate Rosetti, the lesson in daggers and their popularity because of medieval crusader-type games on the Internet. She also shared her new theory, that maybe the killer could be a teenage boy who had been abused by a priest. He listened without interrupting, hearing her out.

"You're forgetting one thing," he finally said. "How does a fifteen- or even sixteen- or seventeen-year-old have the time or opportunity to get from Minneapolis to Omaha to Columbia, Missouri, on his own?"

"Each of the murders happened over holiday weekends. Look, I don't have this figured out. All I'm saying is that we need to consider it."

"That the killer could be a teenager?"

"Or two. Maybe they got the idea from playing one of these games."

"You think a kid—even two kids—could actually plan something like this and pull it off and in a public place? Not only that, but he could keep his cool enough to stab a Catholic priest and just walk away? You're asking me to consider all that?"

"Sounds too incredible, huh?"

"Yeah, it does."

"Okay. Try this, though. No one ever considered that two teenagers could build and plant two twenty-pound propane bombs and place them in a school cafeteria, rigged to explode and kill up to five hundred of their schoolmates. And no one considered that if and when those bombs failed to detonate, the teenagers would then arm themselves with two sawed-off shotguns, a 9 mm semiautomatic carbine rifle and a 9 mm Tec-9 semiautomatic pistol and then proceed to very calmly, very calculatingly shoot and kill twelve students and one teacher."

"I'd like to believe Eric Harris and Dylan Klebold were extreme exceptions," Pakula said, not enjoying the fact that he could be so wrong. When she put it that way, it certainly did sound like a possibility. "But you told me that the murders looked like the work of an assassin."

"Which is what some of these Internet games allow for, right? I mean, in a way, don't they allow the players to become executioners or assassins?"

"I don't know enough about the games. Look, I suppose it's possible. Anything's possible. To tell you the truth I was beginning to think it might be more than one person, but a kid…I just can't wrap my brain around that one."

"One thing I've learned, Detective Pakula, in almost ten years of chasing killers is never to underestimate who is capable of murder."

"You mean like four years ago in Platte City?" It had taken Pakula a while to remember the details of the case, but when he did he also remembered the rumors. "Didn't you make a statement someplace that you thought the wrong men were being convicted? If I remember correctly, the FBI profiler in that case—you—believed a young Catholic priest was responsible."

"I still do believe that," she said, looking out her side window at the little shops and restaurants in Dundee along Underwood Avenue.

"Why didn't you pursue it?"

"I did." This time she shot him a look and he caught a glimpse of her anger before she could control it and go back to studying the cityscape outside her window. "Everyone in Platte City, including Sheriff Nick Morrelli seemed content to believe they had the killer, or rather, killers. Timmy Hamilton escaped and was rescued. I suppose everyone thought it was a nice wrap-up."

"But if the kid got away couldn't he identify the guy?"

"No, Timmy said the man always wore a Halloween mask, a Richard Nixon Halloween mask. I certainly could understand that people wanted to put the case behind them. They thought they had the killers in custody and why wouldn't they think that? The kidnappings and murders stopped."

"Makes sense," Pakula agreed.

"Yes, but what no one seemed to notice or care about was that Father Michael Keller had suddenly disappeared. He left the country. Not even the Omaha Archdiocese knew why or where he had gone. They claimed there was no reassignment. It wasn't like he had taken a leave of absence. He just disappeared."

She paused and Pakula glanced at her. She stared out the windshield now, but seemed to be somewhere else, her hands in her lap, her fingers nagging at a loose thread on her jacket. She continued as if she needed to explain, "I tracked him for a while as best I could even though I had absolutely no jurisdiction to do so. He wasn't implicated in the case in any way and he had left the country. All I had to go on were rumors. He fit the description of an American-speaking priest who suddenly showed up at a small parish in a poor village outside of Chiuchin, Chile. No sooner did I think I'd found him and he was gone again, on to some other little village."

"How could he do that without the Catholic Church keeping track of him? What did he do, just show up and pretend to be the new priest?"

"From what I could find out, yes, I think that's exactly

what he was doing, probably what he's still doing. Many of these poor villages haven't had a priest for years. The people have to travel miles just to take part in a mass. Can you imagine a priest just coming into their village? They might not question it at all. They'd simply be glad to have him. They'd probably do anything and everything in order to keep him. Maybe even keep his presence secret."

"Unfortunately, it wouldn't be the first time the bad guy got away." Pakula flexed his shoulders. He'd wondered if he'd overdone it with the punching bag this morning.

"Maybe he hasn't gotten away, after all."

"Whadya mean?"

"That's who called me right before we went into the school," Maggie said.

"Holy crap! You've got to be kidding." Then he remembered. "You said something about the list. He's on it?"

"Yes," she said, only now she was smiling.

"What the hell did he want?"

"Protection. And medical attention. He thinks the killer poisoned him."

Pakula couldn't believe it. "Why the hell does he think we'd protect him?"

"For one thing, he can tell us who else is on the list."

"He has the list?"

"That's what he says."

"And you believe him?"

Maggie nodded. "He says Daniel Ellison is on it."

Pakula stared at her until he realized they were approaching a stop sign. Keeping his eyes on the road, he said, "You already made a deal with this guy, didn't you?" It wasn't really a question.

"We should probably talk to Chief Ramsey about this," she said calmly.

Pakula felt the sweat trickling down his back. He turned up the air-conditioning and flipped one of the vents to blast him in the face.

"We'll have to do that later," he told her. "We only have about a half hour before we meet with that snoopy reporter." And he needed to keep focused. Actually what he needed was a break. This case kept getting more and more bizarre. "How 'bout some lunch? Whadya think about splitting a pie at LaCasa's. Best pizza around."

"Italian sausage?"

"Only if we get to have Romano cheese."

"Deal," she said.

"Oh crap!" Pakula said, slapping his forehead. It hit him like a flash of lightning. "Hamilton? The kid. Morrelli's nephew is Timmy Hamilton. And you asked him how his sister, Christine, was?"

"That's right. What is it?"

"It just occurred to me and I don't suppose it's a coincidence—the snoopy reporter from the *Omaha World Herald* is Christine Hamilton."

CHAPTER 58

Our Lady of Sorrow High School
Omaha, Nebraska

Gibson waited outside Sister Kate's classroom for Timmy. He'd told Gibson that he was almost certain he recognized the woman who had been talking to Sister Kate earlier. He kept saying she was an FBI agent he knew. Yeah right, Gibson had wanted to say, but didn't. He liked Timmy. And he liked having a friend.

Yesterday they discovered that they lived only about three blocks away from each other, so Gibson invited him to come over again and play some computer games. Now he wondered what was taking Timmy so long. Maybe he ran into the FBI lady. He had gone off to use the school's ancient pay phone to ask his mom's permission about going over to Gibson's, which blew Gibson away. He couldn't believe Timmy didn't have a cell phone. Gibson thought he was the only teenager alive who didn't have one.

He was actually feeling pretty good today. Sister Kate had taken more of an interest in his collection than he expected. She even praised him, telling him she was impressed that he had been able to find and barter such exquisite authentic pieces. She had actually called them exquisite. And she said she was impressed. Sister Kate was impressed with him and his collection. Yeah, it was a pretty good day. One of his best in a long time, probably since he helped her with her cataloging project.

Maybe he'd show Timmy the portfolio he found in his backpack. He was hoping that having Timmy there with him might give him the courage to go through the damn thing. He had carefully placed it in the back of his closet after he opened it and found Monsignor O'Sullivan's name on one of the papers. He didn't want to be reminded of the dead priest let alone go through some stupid papers about him.

He slung his backpack over his shoulder and leaned against the wall. Maybe Timmy had to get change from the office. The pay phone still took quarters. Probably not many like it left. Truly ancient. He smiled and thought Sister Kate should ask for it if and when the school ever replaced it.

"You, over there. What are you doing?"

Gibson straightened up and pushed away from the wall. It was the tall, hawk-nosed guy from Monsignor O'Sullivan's office yesterday. And he was coming at Gibson, pointing a finger at him as if lasering him to the spot. It worked. Gibson couldn't move, couldn't even breathe.

"What are you still doing here? Isn't class over?"

"I…uh…" Gibson tried to answer but his tongue stuck to the roof of his mouth.

"I saw you yesterday, right? You were snooping around Monsignor O'Sullivan's office."

The guy towered over him, looking down his nose, the finger still pointing, only now poking Gibson in the chest.

"Why are you still here?"

"I'm…uh, I'm waiting…"

"You're meeting someone?" The guy looked around. "Maybe you're meeting someone to make an exchange?"

"Huh?"

"Is this what you do after everyone's gone? You make a few deals?"

The finger pokes emphasized "gone" and "deals." Gibson didn't know what the guy was talking about. His heart was beating so hard he felt sure it would explode with one more poke.

"What do you have in the backpack? Are there drugs in there? Is that what you're waiting around for? To make a few deals? Open it up."

Gibson held it even tighter. He knew they could do random searches, but this guy was scary. All Gibson wanted to do was find an opportunity to run.

"Do as I say."

Gibson tried not to look him in the eyes, almost afraid they carried some sort of evil power. He should try to look at him, stare him down, make him think he wasn't afraid, but he couldn't do it. He *was* afraid.

"Give me the bag," he said and reached for it. That's when Gibson bolted to the left and tried to run. The guy held one of the backpack's straps and he jerked Gibson with such strength it almost knocked him off his feet.

"What's going on over there?" Gibson heard Father Tony's voice, but he couldn't see beyond the black frame of his captor.

"Everything's under control," the guy said in a voice that came nowhere near the tone he had just been using. It was almost soft and reassuring. And the tugging grip on his backpack loosened a bit.

Gibson yanked completely free, twisting around the guy, missing a swipe of his clawing hand by inches. He ran down the steps. He didn't bother to answer when Father Tony called out to ask if he was okay. Like who would Father Tony believe anyway? Gibson or the Darth Vader of Our Lady of Sorrow?

Gibson ran, hitting the bottom of the stairs, pushing open the lobby doors. He kept running, past the sidewalk, past the parking lot, not looking back.

CHAPTER 59

Saint Francis Center
Omaha, Nebraska

Maggie spotted Christine Hamilton, who waved at her and Pakula. Christine marched across the large room, weaving in between the long tables, each with a dozen or so volunteers on phones. When she finally reached them she gave Maggie a hug.

"Hi, Christine. It's been a long time."

"You look great," she said, and to Pakula she offered her outstretched hand. "I'm Christine Hamilton. You must be Detective Pakula. Thanks for agreeing to meet here."

"Detective Sassco assured me this was a fact-finding mission. No hidden agenda. No media tricks."

"Believe me, Detective, I'm not the one with a hidden agenda. If anything, I'm the one trying to figure out what's going on. Pretty much like you are."

Maggie glanced at Pakula to see if he believed her, then back at Christine to see if she was being straight with them. Maggie couldn't help remembering the last time, the case in Platte City when Christine, then a rookie reporter, had used anything and everything she could to make headlines. Her son's kidnapping had straightened out her professional ethics. Of course it had. But the real question was, for how long?

"Let's see what you've got for us," Pakula said, nodding in the direction from where she had come, giving her the okay.

"I don't know if you're familiar with the center," Christine asked as she started leading them slowly through the maze of tables. She had to speak louder to be heard over the ringing of phones and the buzz from the surrounding conversations. "The Saint Francis Center started as a women and children's shelter about twenty years ago. It's grown to include this abuse hotline and also in back there's a food pantry."

Maggie surveyed the room as they cut through, noticing that many of the volunteers were simply being quiet, apparently listening to the callers. Others used soft voices barely above a whisper. She realized the nature of the calls allowed them to set up the facility with as many phones and volunteers as there was space.

"We have a room back here," Christine told them, pointing to a doorway in the far corner.

The room surprised Maggie. It looked like someone's cozy living room with a sofa and matching chairs, glass-topped coffee table and floor-to-ceiling bookcases lining the back wall. A service butler in the corner was stocked with refreshments, and the aroma of fresh-brewed coffee filled the room. When they entered, there was a woman pouring herself a cup, and a young man loaded a plate with miniature sandwiches and pieces of fruit. Both stopped and turned to be introduced.

"Wow! I guess we didn't need to have lunch," Pakula said.

Apparently it didn't faze him that Christine had invited guests, but Maggie wondered what the reporter was up to.

"Agent O'Dell, Detective Pakula, this is Brenda Donovan and her son, Mark."

There were friendly but guarded hellos all the way around with no handshakes and little eye contact. As they filled their small plates or napkins and coffee cups and settled around the glass-topped table, Maggie stayed back to observe the woman and her son. Brenda Donovan wore blue polyester slacks and a knit T-shirt with a colorful patchwork teddy bear on the front. Her white sandals were scuffed. Her hands looked scuffed too, the tint of redness possibly from handling too many chemicals or having them in water for long periods of time. Her fingernails were cut short just like her hair for easy and no-frills care. Maggie got the impression that Brenda had worked hard all her life, earning her the wrinkles around her eyes and the gray hair that had begun to take over what at one time must have been a beautiful caramel brown.

The hard ruggedness did not extend to Mark Donovan. Instead, the young man—who Maggie guessed was perhaps not quite twenty—looked soft and wide around the middle, the physique of a couch potato. His close-cropped hair was still damp as if they had pulled him from the shower only minutes ago. His puffy eyes suggested little sleep. But his appetite seemed healthy. He had overloaded the small plate until grapes and slices of hard salami hung over the edges. If this was some kind of confessional tell-all, which Maggie suspected, then Christine must have anticipated that food would bolster their confidence.

She caught Pakula's eye and nodded at his own full plate.

"I have a hard time saying no to free food." And he left her to take a place in one of the easy chairs across from the sofa, where the Donovans had taken refuge, side by side.

Maggie popped the top of a Diet Pepsi and gave the other refreshments one last look, not noticing that Christine had returned beside her.

"I heard you saw Nick this morning," she said in a low voice, keeping her back to the group across the room.

"I didn't realize he was back in Omaha. Has he given up on Boston?" Maggie asked, not letting it slip that she knew for a fact that up until last month he was still employed as a deputy prosecutor for Suffolk County. It was just one of the perks of being an FBI agent and having access to information she often didn't ask for.

"No, he's still in Boston," Christine said as she helped herself to one of the cans of soda, but unlike Maggie filled a glass with ice. Then suddenly she blurted out, "I don't know if you realize how badly you broke my little brother's heart."

"Excuse me?"

She stared at Christine, stunned and trying to decide if she was joking. It wasn't that long ago, a year maybe, that Maggie had called Nick's apartment. A woman had answered, offering to take a message and explaining that Nick was in the shower. Maggie still remembered the sting, but accepted that he had decided to move on and not wait for her.

"Sorry, I probably shouldn't even be telling you." Christine sounded sincere. "I know he'd kill me if he knew I'd said anything, but he was pretty hurt when you dumped him." Then she smiled just a little. "I don't think he's ever been dumped before."

"Dumped?" Maggie tried to keep her voice down, though she could see Pakula's head jerk in their direction. "He dumped me."

"That's not the way he tells it," Christine said, but another smile told Maggie that perhaps Christine knew better. "I suppose we should join the others."

She didn't want to think about Nick Morrelli. This morning's surprise meeting had actually gone well for her. She hadn't found herself regretting or longing for or…anything. She hadn't really felt anything. And that was despite what Pakula had interpreted as some grudge that Nick seemed to be holding, which now made sense if he believed she had dumped him. Of course, her mind had been a million miles away, focusing on Keller and his arrival. Learning that she had been wrong about Nick and that he didn't even know why she had avoided his phone calls or why she'd allowed them to drift away shouldn't make a difference after this long.

Before Maggie could consider whether or not it mattered,

Christine leaned over and added in an almost conciliatory tone, "Don't worry. He'll get over it. He'd better. He's getting married in a month."

CHAPTER 60

Saint Francis Center
Omaha, Nebraska

Tommy Pakula swallowed one of the miniature sandwiches and just as quickly popped another into his mouth, gulping down the rest of his coffee before the second sandwich had cleared his throat. It was a nervous habit for him to snarf down food whenever he felt control slipping from his grip, and he was feeling it with this case, big-time.

"Not bad," he said, referring to the food and nodding at Brenda Donovan who continued to stare at him over the mug of coffee she was sipping. Her son didn't seem to notice that anyone else was in the room. At least he hadn't acknowledged anyone else after the muttered hello during the intros. Now he stuffed food into his mouth without looking up.

Christine Hamilton offered the other easy chair to O'Dell, then pulled up a hardback chair to the edge of the small little circle so that she could sit between the law enforcement officials and the Donovans. Pakula had already guessed they were the victims.

He had to give Hamilton credit. She didn't just want to make her statement, she wanted to drive it home with a tug at the heartstrings or perhaps with something she hoped would shock them. What she didn't realize was that Pakula had seen and heard it all, the worst of the worst, from a newborn crack baby left floating in the toilet of a Gas 'n Shop to a domestic dispute where a husband had used a nail gun to crucify his wife to their living-room wall.

"Every time I've talked to Detective Sassco," Hamilton began, "he's insisted I back up the allegations I was making, despite my journalistic right to conceal my sources. Mark and his mother are very brave to be here today, but they wanted me to reiterate that this in no way implies they are willing to file an official police report."

Pakula watched Mark the entire time. The young man hadn't looked up from his food yet. He stopped once but only to take a sip of his Coke. Suddenly Pakula realized Hamilton was staring at him, waiting for his agreement to the terms.

"That's fine." He nodded at Hamilton then glanced at O'Dell, but she seemed to be somewhere else, probably trying to figure out what to do with Keller.

"Brenda," Hamilton said, "would you like to begin?"

"When my husband first passed away…" The woman set her coffee mug down and began wringing her hands. She had been staring at Pakula since he'd walked into the room but now her eyes were everywhere but on him. "Well, when he died it was hard on Mark. They were so close the two of them. Monsignor O'Sullivan, although he was only Father O'Sullivan back then, asked if he could come over for dinner, spend some time with Mark. He said he was worried about him. I was always raised to believe that there was no better way to grace your home, your family, than for the parish priest to come to dinner. You have to understand. Well, you probably can't understand," she said, shaking her head.

"No, I do," Pakula said. "I'm Catholic."

"So am I," O'Dell said.

The woman looked from him to O'Dell and back to him like she was seeing them for the first time. Pakula wondered if knowing they were both Catholic would help her trust them or simply strengthen her distrust.

"When Mark finally told me what Father O'Sullivan did to him whenever he volunteered to tuck Mark in bed after dinner…well, I'm ashamed to admit, I didn't believe him. He was ten. Boys make up all kinds of stories at that age."

"But I wasn't making it up," Mark interrupted.

Pakula noticed that all of them jerked their heads to look at him, surprised to realize that he was even listening.

"I know, I know," Brenda Donovan said, bobbing her head. "But that's what Father O'Sullivan told me when I finally got up enough courage to tell him why he couldn't come to dinner anymore. He told me that if I believed my son's lies then I couldn't come to his house for dinner anymore, either." She looked up at them again, searching their faces for understanding. Evidently she saw their confusion because she tried to explain. "You know, his house being the church and dinner being Holy Communion. I was devastated. I didn't know that a priest could punish you like that. So I went to Archbishop Armstrong."

Pakula waited, watching Brenda Donovan shake her head as if she still couldn't believe it. He glanced at O'Dell who was now not only paying attention but sitting forward in her chair.

"Tell us what the archbishop had to say, Brenda," Hamilton said.

"Father O'Sullivan must have warned him that I'd be calling. The archbishop asked me why I would want to ruin a good priest's reputation with such lies. Then he held my hands and asked me to pray along with him. He said we'd join hands and pray for him. It wasn't until we were halfway through our prayer that I realized the 'him' we were praying for was not my son, but Father O'Sullivan. That was the day I left the Catholic Church. I haven't been back since."

There was an uncomfortable silence but Pakula sat through it. He had learned a long time ago that when people confided something gut-wrenching, they didn't necessarily want someone telling them it'd be okay. They knew it would never be okay. They just wanted someone to listen.

"Mark wasn't the only boy," Hamilton finally said. "I've found seven others who are now thirteen to twenty-five years old. Two the archdiocese paid over a hundred thousand dollars each. One told me his father forfeited a payoff when Armstrong promised he'd send O'Sullivan away for treatment. O'Sullivan was gone for two months."

Pakula rubbed his jaw. He wasn't surprised. He had heard about the various scandals all over the country, but had to admit he hadn't paid much attention. He remembered being grateful that the Omaha Archdiocese seemed to have escaped it. Once, he and Clare had gotten into an argument about it when he suggested that he didn't understand why the boys didn't fight back. Why they waited until years later when they were adults and the statute of limitations had long expired. At the time he couldn't help wondering if many of the cases were simply about money. Okay, so a priest put his hand down some kid's pants, he's definitely a sicko, but is it traumatic enough to equal a couple million dollars? Clare had told him that he had no idea what those boys had gone through.

"I'm sorry both of you had to go through that, Mrs. Donovan," Pakula told her. "I just wish you had gone to the police instead of the archbishop."

"I know, I know," she said.

"Who the fuck do you think the police would have believed?" Mark asked. This time his outburst made his mother jump.

"I've got to ask you something, Mark," Pakula said. "And I don't want you to think that I'm being insensitive to what's happened to you, whatever it was, but why didn't you tell him to stop it?"

"I was ten years old." Mark's voice was suddenly low and calm, the anger evidently pushed back somewhere. "This priest who I've been taught is like God comes into my bedroom and kneels at my bedside."

He looked around the group as if making sure they were listening. Pakula noticed all of them were literally at the edge of their seats.

"He told me that God and my dad were watching us from heaven. Then he asked me to close my eyes and pray the Our Father with him, so I did. We wouldn't get halfway through the prayer and I'd feel his hand under my covers. He'd dig into my pajama bottoms, grab hold of me and start jerking at me. Sometimes so hard it hurt. I remember once opening my eyes and that's when I saw that he was still on his knees but I could see his fly was open and in his other hand he had hold of his own penis, too, and was jerking it just as hard as he was jerking me."

Mark stopped and looked Pakula in the eye. When he spoke this time he sounded like a small boy, "He told me my dad and God were watching us. I kept telling myself they wouldn't let this happen to me if it wasn't okay." Then as if that wasn't enough of an explanation he added, "I was only ten years old."

CHAPTER 61

Blessed Sacrament Church Rectory
Boston, Massachusetts

Father Paul Conley rang the small bell on his desk a second time. Where was that woman? He craned his neck, trying to see beyond the doorway without leaving his chair. He had purposely positioned his desk in the rectory's den so that he could see into the living room with a view of the kitchen—though only a slice—if he slid his chair clear to the right. But Anna Sanchez was nowhere in sight.

He contemplated ringing for her again. The woman was getting too old. He had tried to tell the church council that he needed someone younger with more energy. Someone who could not only handle the housecleaning and the cooking but also make sure there was a pot of fresh coffee available in the afternoons. Was that too much to ask?

He tipped his coffee mug, an exaggerated gesture, to double-check. Yes, it was empty. He twisted in the chair again but still refused to get up. He grabbed the bell and this time gave it an angry shake. Was it too much to ask for someone who could at least hear, for heaven's sake?

"Mrs. Sanchez?" He decided to yell in case she had chosen to ignore the bell.

Ever since he had complained to the church council about the old woman she had gotten slower and more selective in what she heard. It was probably just his imagination, still he couldn't help wondering whether one of those loudmouthed council members had blabbed to her. Most likely it was Mrs. MacPherson. The woman couldn't keep anything to herself even if the good Lord asked her directly.

"Mrs. Sanchez, what about some coffee?"

He let out a heavy sigh and pushed up out of his comfortable leather office chair, shoving it back with as much noise as he could muster. He grabbed the coffee mug and brought it with him, stomping out of the den. In the living room he stopped long enough to glance around. Where was that woman? He marched into the kitchen, expecting to see her at the sink or coming up from the laundry room.

Instead, he was startled, clutching his free hand to his chest.

"What in the world?"

At the small kitchen table sat a young man he didn't know, sipping a cup of coffee.

"Hello, Father Paul," the stranger said with a smile, then took a long slurp of coffee. "There's plenty more." He waved at the Mr. Coffee on the counter. "Mrs. Sanchez must have just made some. It tastes very fresh."

"Who are you? Did Mrs. Sanchez let you in?" Again, he started looking around the room for the woman, past the doorways and out in the backyard.

"I must admit, I'm disappointed you don't recognize me, Father Paul. Although I guess it has been over fourteen years."

"Wait a minute, are you the gardener?" He recognized the hatchet from the garden shed left by the back door alongside a black case. "Did she forget to pay you?" He pushed up his glasses, hoping a better look at the young man would reveal who he was. He had to be one of the workers. She wouldn't let just anyone in.

"Nope, not a gardener. Although I did help myself to a few tools from the shed in back. Sure is quiet back there." He sipped more coffee.

"I'm sure she's around here somewhere if you need to be paid." The priest walked over to the doorway to the laundry room and yelled, "Mrs. Sanchez, are you down there?"

"I grew up in this neighborhood," the young man said. "I was an altar boy. I'm hurt you don't remember me, Father Paul."

"Really?" Father Conley came back to study him once more, but still he couldn't place him. Besides, the man certainly didn't look or sound upset. "I've been here for twenty years," he told him. "A lot of boys have served mass with me. Surely you can't expect me to remember every single one of them?"

Now the stranger shoved his coffee cup aside and brought out a plastic bag, unrolling it on the table. Father Conley thought it looked like one of those large transparent bags that dry cleaners used when they returned your freshly cleaned garments. Ah, perhaps that was what he had come for. He must be the dry cleaner, picking up the vestments. But why come to the rectory and not the church? It didn't make sense.

"I suppose it is difficult to remember everyone," the young man said, pushing away from the table and standing up with the plastic bag now unfolded, and twisted tightly around both hands, his fingers balling up around its corners until they were fists. "But I would hope you'd remember the ones you fucked, Father Paul."

Suddenly Father Conley found himself caught in a veil of plastic, stretched over his face, cutting off his breath. He fought, clawing at the hands that continued to wrap the plastic taut around his entire head, until he could feel the knot at the base of his neck. Desperate for air, he struggled, kicking and flaying his arms, trying to dig the plastic out of his face, but the layers were many and the fight was quickly being strangled out of him.

Still, he twisted and turned, thrashing about, banging into counters and knocking pots and pans to the floor, only they seemed to no longer make a sound. He slipped to his knees but still continued to pluck at the plastic, now much of it inhaled, sticking in his mouth and down his throat as he gasped like a fish out of water.

There was no more air, no more fight left in him. He fell to the floor and the last thing Father Paul Conley saw was Mrs. Sanchez's dead eyes staring out at him from under the butcher-block table in the far corner.

CHAPTER 62

Omaha, Nebraska

Maggie was completely exhausted by the time she got back to her hotel. She and Pakula barely said a word to each other on the drive from the Saint Francis Center to the Embassy Suites. Pakula told her he'd talk to Chief Ramsey about Father Michael Keller and that the chief and Assistant Director Cunningham could discuss how to handle it. Maggie felt relieved until she remembered that she'd still have to be the one to meet with Keller. He had told her he wouldn't relinquish any information to anyone but her.

She knew he didn't mean it as a favor or a professional courtesy. He had to know she had been tracking him, asking questions, creating suspicion, making it impossible for him to stay in one place for long. This was his way to mock her, to put her in her place.

While listening to Mark Donovan it had suddenly occurred to her that she wasn't all that different from this priest killer. Keller had committed horrendous crimes. No one could look at those dead little boys and not agree. And yet, he had eluded justice and it gnawed at her. Evil against children was the most difficult to stomach, the most difficult to stand back and watch the evil perpetrator escape and possibly continue. It wasn't only unlawful, it was immoral to allow that evil to continue, to go unchecked, unpunished. At times, she found herself not just wanting Keller to pay for his crimes, she wanted him gone forever so he could never hurt another innocent boy. Wasn't that exactly what this killer was doing? Carrying out a type of justice for those priests who had managed to escape punishment, stopping them before they had a chance to hurt another boy. The only difference between the two of them was that Maggie had a badge.

The comparison didn't sit well with her. What law enforcement official enjoyed thinking of herself as a hired killer? She had even lingered in the hotel lobby, considering a stop at the lounge. It wasn't that long ago that exhaustion would never have won out over her urge for Scotch. There used to be nothing better than two or three Scotches to ease the challenges of her profession.

However, as soon as she walked into her hotel room she flipped open her cell phone. She no longer bothered to check for messages. She knew Gwen wouldn't call. Instead, she simply dialed and was surprised when Gwen answered on the third ring.

"Gwen, are you okay?" Maggie asked.

"Why does everyone keep asking me that?"

"Well, excuse me, but I haven't been able to ask you that because you haven't bothered to return any of my phone calls. I've been worried sick about you."

Silence. Maggie berated herself. Here she finally gets in touch with her friend and does the exact thing Gwen wanted to avoid by not returning her calls.

"I'm sorry, Gwen. I've just been really worried."

"I think Racine may be trying to figure out whether or not to arrest me."

"Arrest you? What in the world for?"

"You haven't talked to her today?"

"Early this morning," Maggie said, taking a seat on the edge of the bed. "What's going on?"

"It's complicated." Gwen sounded so tired.

"Tell me anyway."

Maggie listened without interrupting as Gwen told her about Rubin Nash and how she suspected that he might be the D.C. killer, but wasn't sure. She told her about the notes, a map, some earrings, even a cell phone that the killer had left for her, always at her office building. That was why she believed it had to be one of her patients, someone who could come and go and not be noticed. Gwen even admitted that when Racine called in Maggie to profile the case, Gwen thought she might be able to guide Maggie to the killer without endangering anyone close to her.

Maggie listened and wished she was there offering something more, something warmer than an "okay" or "go on." Gwen stopped and Maggie thought she was finished until Gwen said so softly she could barely hear her, "I should have told you. I should have told you from the very beginning."

"You thought you were doing the right thing," Maggie told her. "How many times have I done that?"

"But you've never gotten anyone killed in the process."

"That's not true. How could you forget Albert Stucky?" Maggie still cringed at the sound of his name. Stucky had been pure evil. He had played a deadly game of cat and mouse with her that included killing women Maggie came in contact with. By the time he was finished, he had killed four women—four ordinary innocent women whose only mistake was meeting Maggie.

Gwen promised to call in the morning, thanking Maggie. She flipped her phone shut and set it onto the nightstand. It felt a little strange. Usually Gwen was the one comforting her, getting her out of hot water and calming her down. They had started out with Gwen as her mentor, her teacher, and went on to become best friends. This time Gwen had hoped Maggie could save her.

Maggie kicked off her shoes, took off her jacket and hung it on the back of the desk chair. She unbuckled her shoulder holster and laid it next to her cell phone. It was the only reason she continued to wear a jacket in the July heat. People talked differently to a woman with a gun strapped to her side. Sometimes it was advantageous, but most of the time it was annoying.

She keyed open the minibar, suddenly too thirsty and too tired to search for a vending machine. She started to grab a bottle of water when she saw the miniature bottle of Chivas. She sat back on her feet, staring at it, and suddenly her thirst wasn't quite as great as before. She plucked the miniature bottle out of the fridge, immediately noticing how tiny it felt between her fingers. The bottle was so small it could hardly be worth it. Yet she set it and the bottled water on the small table in the corner and decided if she had the Chivas on the rocks it would be okay.

She grabbed the ice bucket, made sure she had her room's key card and left in stocking feet to search for the ice machine, realizing that only seconds earlier she had been too tired to even search for a vending machine. Amazing what a phone call from a child-murdering priest, a confession from an abuse victim and a reminder of Albert Stucky could do for the sight of a bottle of Chivas. And what an appropriate combination.

She found the ice machine at the other end of the hallway and started filling the bucket, when she heard someone walk by the small alcove but then stop and come back.

She turned to find Nick Morrelli in a T-shirt, khaki shorts and bare feet, a newspaper tucked under his arm and a hotel key card in his hand.

"Of all the hotels in this city, they had to put you in this one."

CHAPTER 63

The Embassy Suites
Omaha, Nebraska

Nick knew he should apologize. He had felt it even during their earlier meeting, that he was out of line, acting defensive…well, this morning he needed to act defensive on Tony's behalf, but now…now it was ridiculous.

"I'm not the one suspecting your friend," she said. Nick thought she looked exhausted, her eyes searching around. Was she hoping for an escape route? "A friendly piece of advice, tell him to stop being so evasive and answer the OPD's questions. He's only hurting himself by making them believe he has something to hide."

Nick leaned against the wall, a bit exhausted himself, and crossed his arms over his chest, the newspaper still tucked. "I've told him," he said, letting down his guard and allowing his frustration to show. "I've told him exactly that. He won't listen to me, either."

For the first time her eyes met his and for a brief moment he was reminded of that time four years ago when they were working the Platte City case. Why was it that whenever he slipped and showed her he wasn't quite in control, she seemed to connect with him most?

"Do you think he has something to hide?"

"I don't know, but I've known Tony Gallagher since we were both five years old. He can be stubborn and he can talk his way out of just about anything. But I know he couldn't kill someone."

"Even if he thought it was the right thing?"

"What do you mean?"

Nick waited while Maggie set the ice bucket at her stocking feet and leaned against the wall, crossing her arms to mirror him. He noticed that she had shed her jacket and wore only a white knit blouse still tucked into the waistband of her suit trousers. She looked good, better than ever. Despite looking exhausted at the moment, Nick sensed there was something about her that seemed…content. Had she finally put the demons of her past behind her?

"I'm convinced," she said, "that this killer thinks he's doing the right thing. Maybe even that he's doing the work of the Lord."

A chill slid down Nick's back, enough of a chill to make him admit that maybe he was wrong. He had been thinking about what Tony had said earlier—off the record, friend to friend—about his confrontation with Monsignor O'Sullivan. Tony said he had told him—no, he had warned him—that if the allegations were true, he wouldn't sit back and be quiet. But what did that mean?

Before Nick could say anything another guest came down the hall, ice bucket in hand, and Maggie moved out of the alcove's doorway. The woman smiled at the two of them, and they made small talk about the weather while she filled her ice bucket. Then she walked between them again with another smile. Nick wondered if she thought she was interrupting a lovers' spat. She took her time walking down the hall, and when she turned the corner he realized both he and Maggie were listening for the woman's hotel-room door to open and shut.

"Not the best place to have a serious conversation," he said with a smile and wanted to offer that they continue it in his suite, but a gentleman waited for the woman to make that offer. Maybe he was hoping she would offer. What would he do then?

He had the suite to himself tonight. Jill was going to be out late with her mother and maid of honor doing something or other. She'd be spending the night at her mom's. And why was he even worrying about this? Was he that much of an idiot? It was ridiculous. He was ridiculous.

"I need to go. I have some phone calls to make," she finally said, picking up the ice bucket, but not making a move to leave.

"Yeah, me too," he lied.

"Well, good night." And she started down the hall.

"Good night."

He tried not to watch her and didn't want to follow, but then he realized she was going in the same direction he needed to go. God had a weird sense of humor, he thought as he watched her unlock and enter a suite only two doors down and across the hall from his.

CHAPTER 64

Omaha, Nebraska

Gibson told his mom he wasn't feeling good. No, it wasn't any big hairy deal, an upset stomach, maybe a touch of the flu or something. No, she didn't need to call the doctor, but he didn't want any dinner.

He really did feel sick to his stomach, but it wasn't from the flu. It was that Darth Vader guy almost poking him into the wall. Now he wanted to stay in his room and not be bothered. He wondered if he could stay home for a few days. He wasn't so sure he even wanted to go to Explorers tomorrow. His mom wouldn't notice. She left for work before him and came home after him. If he could keep Tyler's big fat mouth shut it wouldn't be a problem. He'd need to think of a bribe. Usually Tyler's silence could be bought. It was just a matter of figuring out what lame thing he was into this week.

He sat in front of his computer, wondering if surfing the Net might help. He hadn't played the game since...since Monsignor O'Sullivan and the airport. How many days ago was that? He clicked the computer on and waited for Windows to boot up. In the meantime he grabbed his backpack from the floor and started going through it. There had to be a candy bar or granola bar or something inside. He dug his hand to the bottom and started feeling around so he wouldn't need to dump everything out. His fingers found the seam of a wrapper—success! He pulled out a Snickers bar and noticed an e-mail flashing, waiting at the corner of his computer screen.

He and Timmy had exchanged e-mail addresses. He was probably wondering why Gibson didn't wait for him this afternoon. He clicked on his e-mail and sure enough there were two from Timmy, one with the subject line that read:

WHAT HAPPENED TO YOU?

There was also an e-mail from The Sin Eater, and Gibson's stomach started to churn again. The subject line read: CAUTION!!!! He clicked it open before it managed to paralyze him. It looked like a list of instructions. At the top in caps and bold letters it read:

YOU'RE SAFE AS LONG AS YOU HAVE THE LEATHER PORTFOLIO. DON'T WORRY. I WON'T LET ANYONE HURT YOU.

Downstairs the front doorbell rang. He ignored it. His mom hadn't gone to her evening class yet.

The portfolio. How the hell did The Sin Eater know about it? Gibson left the computer and rummaged through the back of his closet until he found it. When he first discovered it stashed inside his backpack, he had opened it enough to find Monsignor O'Sullivan's name on the top paper. He should have known it was something important, something from that afternoon. That's how The Sin Eater knew he was at the airport. He was there, too. Did he see who put the portfolio into his backpack? Or did The Sin Eater put it there? If it was Monsignor O'Sullivan's and The Sin Eater took it from him, then did he see who murdered him?

Gibson stopped and sat on the edge of his bed. How stupid was he? The game. He had submitted Monsignor O'Sullivan's name as a character to be eliminated. The Sin Eater was supposedly the only one who knew and recorded the name. The Sin Eater had to have killed Monsignor O'Sullivan. Or was it all just a coincidence that both Gibson and The Sin Eater were there at the airport and happened to see the priest dead?

He could hear his mom calling for him from the bottom of the stairs. Why didn't she come up? Could he ignore her? No, 'cause then she would come up.

Gibson made himself get up off the bed and go to his door. "What?"

"Come down for a few minutes, sweetie. There's someone here who would like to talk to you."

Was it Timmy?

"Give me a couple of minutes. I need to close down something on my computer." He shut his door with a bit of slam, then very slowly and quietly opened it so he could tiptoe out far enough to see who it might be. He could hear his mom's voice, now a worried whisper. "I'm sure you must be wrong, Brother Sebastian." And the rest was muddled up the stairwell, but Gibson thought she said something about drugs.

Now he could see a slice of who she was talking to, who Brother Sebastian was. He had his back to the staircase, but Gibson recognized him anyway. It was the Darth Vader guy.

He could barely control his panic as he tried to get back to his room quietly. He closed and locked the door and then his eyes raced around his room. He had to get out. He shut down his laptop, snapping off cables and wrapping the power cord around it then shoving it into his backpack. He pulled off the gadget he had duct-taped to the underside of his headboard, worked it open and took out the folded-up cash he had hidden. It went into the backpack's side pocket. He grabbed the portfolio and slipped it in last.

He slid open the window and could immediately feel the blast of warm, sticky night air hit him in the face. He double-checked to make sure no one was out on the sidewalk. The sun had just started going down behind the trees but only the fanatics would be out walking on a night like this.

It had been over a year since he had used this exit, which required sliding down onto the porch roof and then jumping off into the grass. He hadn't needed to sneak out because his mom was hardly ever home. He hoped they couldn't see him when he dropped off the porch. He'd have to go more toward the left and then use the back alley. And damn, he'd have to leave behind his bike. It was on the porch.

He pulled on the backpack and readjusted the straps so it'd stay tight on his back. He couldn't risk smashing his laptop. He had no idea where he would go or when he could come back.

Gibson took one last look around his room, the one place he had felt safe. Then he left.

CHAPTER 65

Omaha, Nebraska

Tommy Pakula came in the back door, catching Clare at the kitchen sink. Before he could find a place to put down the two pizza boxes, he stopped and kissed the back of her neck, getting a satisfactory stroke of his cheek in return.

"You taste good," he said. "Maybe we don't need the pizzas."

"The girls are starved." She turned and smiled at him, but there was something sad in her smile. Something was wrong.

"What's happened?"

When she put a finger to his lips to hush him, he knew it wasn't good.

"Angie's pretty upset," she told him, keeping her voice low and her eyes watching out over the counter that separated the kitchen from the dining room.

"Is she hurt?"

"No, no. It's nothing like that. She received a letter from Creighton today. She'll show it to you later. We should eat first, okay? Let her tell you about it in her own way. Don't push her."

"What kind of a letter?" But he already knew and there was a lump gathering in the pit of his stomach.

"They're rescinding her scholarship. Something about insufficient funds that they've only now become aware of."

"Insufficient funds. That's bullshit."

"Tommy." This time she placed a finger against her own lips.

He obeyed and kept his voice down, but the anger was still there. "You know what this is."

"We don't know that for certain."

His cell phone interrupted them and he wanted to rip it off his belt and throw it across the room, but he was expecting a call from Chief Ramsey.

"I've got to get this," he told her and she nodded, taking the pizza boxes to the dining room where he saw the table was already set. "Pakula," he grunted into the phone.

"I got your message," Chief Ramsey said without a greeting. "I'm talking to Cunningham in an hour. Do you have any idea what this Father Michael Keller has for us?"

"He said he had the list of the priests being offed. Supposedly he thinks he has something else that could lead us to the killer, but he wouldn't spell it out to O'Dell until he knew he had a deal and until he was here in the States."

"She thinks he's on the level?"

"She thinks he's scared. He's on the list."

Ramsey was quiet and Pakula waited it out, watching Clare put ice in their glasses and pour the tea. There was something about the way she moved that had a calming effect on him.

"The shit is starting to hit the fan," Ramsey finally said, and it wasn't at all what Pakula had expected him to say. "My wife found out today that her grant for the hospital got canceled. She says it's a coincidence. I don't think so."

Pakula turned his back to Clare and the dining room and walked across the kitchen as far out of her hearing as possible. "My daughter's scholarship just got pulled. Insufficient funds."

"Jesus! You're kidding." There was a pause. "Well, we both knew this could happen."

"Yep, we did." Pakula kept it to himself that he didn't think the asshole would be able to do stuff like this or at least not this quickly. "He'll be shitting bullets if he hears what I found out this afternoon."

"What's that?"

"Seems the monsignor had a thing for little boys after all, and the archbishop knew all about it."

"Figures," Chief Ramsey said.

"Look, about this Keller guy making a deal with O'Dell. You think your buddy Cunningham is gonna have a hernia?"

"Not when I tell him we have five dead priests."

"Five?"

"Deputy Sheriff down in Santa Rosa County, Florida, just found one in the wetlands," Chief Ramsey explained. "May have been there for over a week. I'll have a copy of the autopsy report in the morning."

"And the fifth?"

"North Boston." This time Ramsey paused and Pakula could hear him shuffling papers. "Information's still coming in. Details are sketchy. If I understand correctly, it happened earlier today. This one's freaky, Pakula, and I can't help wondering if the killer is not only escalating but that he's starting to lose it."

"How freaky?"

"The victim was a Father Paul Conley at Blessed Sacrament. His head was found on the altar."

CHAPTER 66

Omaha, Nebraska

Gibson had managed to get a dark corner booth in Goldberg's Bar and Grill on Fiftieth and Dodge Streets. He didn't think he had an appetite, but he had ordered a cheeseburger and fries so that the waitress wouldn't mind him taking up a whole booth. Then it smelled so good that he started taking nibbles, and before he realized it he had it devoured, probably eating out of nervous energy more than hunger.

When he called his mom from the restaurant's pay phone she sounded hysterical, not because he had slipped out on her but because Brother Sebastian had convinced her Gibson was on drugs. He couldn't believe it and told her so. How could she believe some stranger over him? He tried his best to reassure her that he wasn't taking or selling drugs.

He couldn't tell her about the portfolio even though he was pretty sure that's what Brother Sebastian wanted from him. Instead, he told her Sebastian was a bad guy and she needed to stay away from him. But that's when she laughed, a nervous, slightly hysterical laugh. "Now you sound paranoid,

Gibson. Isn't that something that happens when you take drugs?"

"Mom, I'm not taking drugs. You gotta believe me."

But then he did lie and told her he'd be staying with a friend for a few nights. Truth was, he hadn't asked Timmy yet. It didn't make her happy that he wasn't coming right home, but she didn't argue with him. She wanted the friend's name and phone number, and when he told her he didn't know the number she insisted he call as soon as he got there. If she was this worried and suspicious from some made-up story that he might be using drugs, what would she be like if she knew he had gotten a priest killed?

He brought the mangled phone book from the pay phone back to his table. If he couldn't find Timmy's phone number or Timmy's mom wouldn't let him spend the night, Gibson wasn't sure what he'd do. There wasn't anyone else he could call. No one he could trust. No one, except maybe Sister Kate. She had sort of saved him once before though he really didn't like thinking about that day. He couldn't remember if it was the fourth or fifth time Monsignor O'Sullivan had called him into his office. Everything was such a blur every time he left. But one time Gibson stumbled into the hallway and ran right into Sister Kate. He was so embarrassed because his fly was still down. Geez! He could still feel the burn up his neck.

But she was cool about the whole thing. Asked if he was okay and when Gibson only nodded, she told him to go upstairs to her classroom and hang out for a while. She even told him to get a Pepsi for himself from her minifridge, from her private stash. He barely got to the top of the stairs when he heard her below, stomping down the hall to the monsignor's office. Gibson waited there, half leaning over the rail, listening, but he didn't hear Sister Kate knock, just a slam of the door and then muffled voices. It sounded like they were arguing.

He didn't realize until weeks later that Monsignor O'Sullivan didn't call him into his office after that day. Gibson was so relieved it took him a while to realize that Sister Kate must have said something. And then, of course, he was embarrassed that Sister Kate might know. But she never said anything to him, never treated him differently after that. Gibson hadn't thought about that day for a long time. He didn't like thinking about it. Brother Sebastian made him feel afraid and weak just like Monsignor O'Sullivan always had. He didn't like that much either.

There was no Kate Rosetti listed in the phone book, so Gibson searched the H's for any Hamiltons within three or four blocks of his own address. There was a Christine Hamilton on Cass Street just a block north of Goldberg's. That had to be Timmy's mom. He memorized the number.

He had no idea what time it was. Goldberg's didn't have a clock anywhere. It had to be late. Was it too late to call Timmy? Would his mom be so pissed she wouldn't let him come to the phone?

Gibson pulled out his wad of bills and under the table peeled off enough to pay his bill with enough for a tip, too. He folded it with the ticket and anchored it down with the ketchup bottle like he remembered his dad used to do. Then he grabbed his backpack, sliding it on arm by arm so that it sat tight against his back, more securely. He left the safety of his booth and found the cubbyhole in the far corner where the pay phone was. He sat, took a deep breath then dialed the number, hoping and praying that Timmy would answer.

No such luck.

"Hello?" a woman said.

"Um, is Timmy there?"

There was a long pause and the cheeseburger twisted a knot in his stomach.

"It's pretty late. Can I tell him who's calling?"

"Yeah, it's his friend Gibson…Gibson McCutty from the Explorers' Program."

"Hold on, Gibson." She repeated his name like she knew

him. He wasn't sure if that was a good thing or a bad thing. He wondered what Timmy might have told her about him.

It didn't take long for Timmy to come to the phone. "Hey, Gibson. Where'd you go this afternoon?"

"Yeah, I'm sorry about that. There was this Darth Vader guy at the school. I'll tell you all about it later. Right now I kinda need some help. Do you think it would be okay with your mom if I stayed overnight at your house?"

"Hold on." He could hear Timmy yell out, "Hey, Mom, can Gibson spend the night?"

Gibson couldn't hear Timmy's mom and he cringed, waiting.

"She said sure, but when you get here, she said she'll need to call your mom to tell her where you are. Sorry," Timmy said as if that ultimatum would be a letdown or a deal breaker.

"I'm at Goldberg's. Can you give me directions?"

"Hold on," Timmy said, and then to his mom who must have been asking him something, he said, "He's at Goldberg's." There was a long pause while Timmy listened to her.

Geez! Was she changing her mind? Was she telling Timmy to forget about it? Where would he go then?

"Hey, Gibson, my mom wants to know if you have any extra cash could you bring a couple orders of potato wedges and deep-fried mushrooms? She'll pay you back when you get here."

Gibson held back the sigh of relief and simply said, "Sure."

CHAPTER 67

Washington, D.C.

It was almost midnight by the time he made it back home. Thankfully his flight had been on time. Even the cab ride from the airport had gone smoothly. Yet the thumping in his chest had not subsided one little bit. His heart banged and crashed against his rib cage until he swore he could feel bruises. Every muscle ached and screamed. Exhaustion seeped into his pores.

He turned on the TV and powered up his computer while he flipped channels, watching for any news from Boston. He pulled off his sweat-drenched polo shirt and tossed it in the corner, still disappointed that he had to throw out his Boston Red Sox T-shirt and his old Nikes. It was a good thing he had brought a change of clothes. He hadn't been able to bring along enough plastic to contain the mess. And his frenzy was such this time that he hadn't even realized how much blood had splattered on him and the walls of the gardening shed while he hacked Father Paul's body to pieces. Pieces that fit quite nicely into three garbage bags. Sometimes the frenzy became almost a blackout, like he had no control over his mind or body. He could watch himself, looking down, suspended from a far corner of the ceiling, but only able to watch, not participate, not stop.

Later the calm returned, a calm after the storm instead of before. He had used the outside shower stall alongside the shed to wash himself, relishing the quiet of the afternoon and the secrecy that the six-foot wooden privacy fence, the huge oaks and flowering hedges provided. Despite the sticky, hot July air it reminded him of being in the Garden of Eden and finally he could wash away his guilt, his hatred, his sins. So why did the throbbing continue?

He stopped flipping channels, catching a glimpse of the old church on a Fox News Alert. He left the sound turned off, reading the crawl at the bottom of the screen. They showed Blessed Sacrament Church and the rectory while the crawl told that Father Paul Conley had been the victim of a brutal murder. They mentioned Mrs. Sanchez and the regret tugged at his innards. It still bothered him that he'd had to kill her. But the old woman had been in the way. He couldn't help that.

There was no mention of the display he had left on the altar, using Father Conley's key to enter the quiet locked church from the back. No mention that most of the priest was still missing. And he smiled. He had left the bags three blocks away in the back alley of Joe's Seafood Grill and Bar where the week's garbage had already piled up in smelly heaps falling out of the Dumpster. He'd tossed Father Paul Conley up on top of the heap, one bag at a time. It seemed an appropriate place for him.

Yes, despite the constant banging in his chest he felt quite good, satisfied.

He shut off the TV and turned to go to bed when he noticed an instant message flashing at the upper corner of his computer screen. It winked at him almost as if it knew his secret. He stared at it, a new wave of panic threatening to unleash itself. Without sitting, he clicked on the icon. It was from The

Sin Eater and its one-line message had him looking over his shoulder and double-checking the locks on his door. The message read:

WHAT THE HELL DID YOU DO?

CHAPTER 68

Wednesday, July 7
District Police Department
Washington, D.C.

Gwen Patterson waited in the metal folding chair Racine had offered her beside the detective's cluttered desk. Racine had disappeared for what felt like hours, but was in fact only a few minutes. She wasn't sure why Racine insisted she come down to the police station. Maybe she did intend to arrest her. Whatever the purpose, Gwen was quite certain Racine enjoyed making her sit and wait here in the middle of the noise and chaos of her world instead of what Racine would probably consider the cushy soft comfort of Gwen's office, what she believed was Gwen's world.

"He has a list of assault charges," Racine suddenly said, coming from behind Gwen, startling her so much that she jumped. Racine didn't seem to notice. She slapped a file folder on her desk, or rather one of the piles on her desk, then sat on the only corner clear of clutter. "No convictions. The good news is that we have his fingerprints on file, so we didn't need to use your water glass, especially since it was obtained without his consent or knowledge. The bad news is they aren't matching up to any prints on the stuff you handed over to us. Is that what he's seeing you for? His little habit of beating the shit out of women in the guise of having sex?"

Gwen tried not to look surprised. Was she surprised? It came with the territory for someone like Rubin Nash. Men who were abusers had often been abused as children. Nor should it surprise her that he wouldn't tell her. So he didn't want her to know that his conquests were brutal. When did they turn fatal? Should she have seen those signs?

"I didn't know he had charges filed against him," she said and evidently sounded more guarded than she meant to, because Racine was frowning at her, disappointed or angry again. It was hard to tell which. With Racine both seemed to automatically go together.

"Is this part of that patient/doctor confidentiality crap?"

"There's a fine line." Gwen took yet another stab at trying to explain it to the detective. "Yes, why he's seeing me is confidential. He's not even a suspect yet. But our professional code of ethics also makes allowances for the need to warn."

Racine rolled her eyes at her and let out a deep sigh.

"I can't tell you why he's seeing me," Gwen offered calmly, slowly. "However, if you were to ask my professional opinion as to whether I believe he had perhaps a resentment toward women I could tell you, yes, I believe he does."

This time Racine looked at her, tilting her head as if studying Gwen. She could almost see the sarcastic wiseass fade into the background while the puzzle-solver came to the surface.

"Okay, so in your opinion," Racine said carefully, like someone testing the rules of a new game, "this type of…resentment, would it become such a problem that it might extend to others?"

"Others? You mean like people he knows—friends or family members?" Gwen was growing impatient even with her own game. "Dena wasn't someone he had randomly chosen. I don't mean to be rude, Detective Racine, but why am I here? These are things we've already gone over and your questions certainly could have been answered on the phone." If Racine was going to file charges against her, Gwen would rather she just do it and not beat around the bush.

"I invited you here because I've been waiting on some new information." Racine glanced over her shoulder then above Gwen's head, looking for someone.

"New information? Oh, Jesus! Has there been another one?"

"Not sure. This one might not be connected, although there are similarities. It was in the Boston area and it was—oh, here it comes," she interrupted herself, standing to meet the uniformed officer who came from behind Gwen to give Racine a set of papers. "Here it is, or at least what details they have so far."

Racine shuffled the pages. Without looking up, she said, "O'Dell told me you've done consultation with the FBI to help them come up with criminal profiles."

"That's right, although it's been a few years since I've worked a case."

"We have a killer," Racine continued, glancing at Gwen then back to the papers, flipping and scanning, "who seems to kill and dismember in an uncontrollable rage. But he has the intelligence and wherewithal to compose himself after the murder enough not only to clean up, but to dispose of the body and strategically place the victim's head."

"I know the basics of this case, Detective Racine." What was it Racine wanted from her? Did she expect her to pick up where Maggie left off in coming up with a profile? She had a profile. She had, quite possibly, the name of the killer. What more did she want?

"He's chosen women randomly with the exception of Dena Wayne. Libby Hopper was a college student. One of the other victims was young, too, or so we think. She had a tattoo that seems to be connected to a computer game. The computer game is really popular with kids. So as far as we know, all of them were young women. Rubin Nash has a history of brutally assaulting young women."

"Is there a question for me, Detective?" Gwen's patience

started to unravel. The emotional roller coaster of the last few days threatened to push her over the edge. "What do you want to know?"

"I need to know if Rubin Nash might move on to someone other than young women he's picked up in nightclubs. Is Rubin Nash capable of this?"

And she tossed a color copy onto the desk in front of Gwen. It was a crime scene photo, a dark macabre set that looked like something from a horror movie, a decapitated head in the middle of a church altar with candles lit on both sides.

"That's all that's left of Father Paul Conley."

CHAPTER 69

Omaha Police Department
Omaha, Nebraska

Maggie stared out of the conference-room window. She hadn't slept well despite the comfy king-size bed. Maybe it was the anticipation of meeting Father Keller face-to-face again after four years. Of course, it could have been the thought of Nick Morrelli sleeping somewhere down the hall from her in the same hotel. She kept thinking she certainly would have slept much better had she given in and drunk the Chivas. But no amount of Scotch would make seeing Keller any easier. Or at least that's what she told herself as Detective Pakula handed her yet another set of reports. These were from Santa Rosa County, Florida. They had the conference-room table filled with reports, maps, autopsy photos and evidence bags.

"There's actually a Bagdad, Florida?" she asked, starting to scan and flip through the papers while she paced the length of the room.

"Just outside of Pensacola. It's spelled without the 'h' though. This campground is on Blackwater Bay. I'll show you the area in a minute." Pakula was unfolding a map, making room for it on the bulletin board next to the map of the Midwest region that already had the first three murders marked with bright-colored stickpins, a red one in Omaha, blue in Columbia and yellow in Minneapolis.

"Where's the fifth?" she asked, craning over the scattered reports. "You said there was one in Boston yesterday?"

"Carmichael will bring it in as soon as Boston PD sends it."

"He's escalating. Three of them in five days," she said. She was antsy, unable to sit still. Thank goodness Pakula didn't mind her pacing. When it got to this stage it was almost as if she could feel the killer's frenzy or panic or whatever it was propelling him to hurry.

"You think that's proof of escalation, wait until you see the Boston one." He noticed her checking her watch and added, "Kasab and a uniformed officer are meeting Keller at the airport." He checked his own watch. "They should be here in about an hour if his flight's on time."

An hour. In approximately one hour she would be staring into the eyes of a child killer and promising him protection from being killed.

She tried to concentrate on the new Florida case. The body had already been identified as seventy-three-year-old Father Rudolph Lawrence, known to friends and parishioners as Father Rudy. A recent photo sent along with the report showed a short, stocky, white-haired, almost elfish-looking man at a party, with a colorful banner behind him that read: Happy Retirement, Father Rudy! She placed that copy next to the one of his corpse at the crime scene. What was left of the face had bloated beyond recognition. There was a tuft of white hair— that and the white roman collar stood out in the otherwise mangled and dirty mess that looked more like a pile of rags than a body.

The medical examiner had estimated no less than a week. Other tests were needed for a more accurate time of death. Maggie remembered Adam Bonzado telling her that in a matter of a week maggots could consume a body down to the bone in a moist, hot environment. The Florida panhandle in July seemed to fit that environment, but the corpse had been partially hidden with debris and dirt thrown on top, which would have slowed down the process.

Maggie stood in front of the map Pakula had just finished tacking up. "Why try to hide him when he's already in the middle of what looks like several acres of thick woods."

"Wetlands," Pakula said. "They call them wetlands and you're right—it is thick with trees, scrub grass and some kind of vining crap, not to mention the mosquitoes and the no-see-ums."

"You sound like a fan of the area."

"Oh, I love it. Sugar-white beaches and emerald green water. But a lot of places inland aren't developed. A lot of it is owned by the government. I can't think what they call it," Pakula said. "Oh, I know, historic preservation. It's along the gulf coast where the early explorers landed. In fact, Pensacola would have had the oldest settlement if it hadn't been washed away by a hurricane."

"Do you usually learn this much about your crime scenes?" Maggie asked, smiling.

"No, I've got friends who live down there. I've already been in contact with them. Since they're Catholics I'm hoping they might be able to dig up some dirt for me on this Father Rudolph."

"Father Rudy," she corrected him.

"Yeah, right."

"The single stab wound to the chest is consistent with our guy, but this is definitely not a public area."

"Actually, it is." It was Pakula's turn to correct her. "It's part of a public campground. Friends claim the old priest lived about a mile away. He took walks down to the boat ramp, using, of course, the road that runs alongside this wetland area."

"Okay, so it's a public area, but why not slice him on the road and leave him in the ditch? The killer would have had to coax him into the trees and then kill him or kill him on the road and drag him into the trees. Why bother? He's left all the other bodies out in the open. He seemed to have gone to great lengths to hide this one."

"I don't know. You're the profiler, you tell me." Pakula shrugged and smiled.

"This one feels different," she said, stopping at the table's edge to glance over the other reports.

"Wait until you see the Boston one."

"You already said that."

"Yeah, well, it's pretty freaky," Pakula said just as Carmichael came waltzing in.

"You've got to be talking about this one," Carmichael said, dropping the copies in the middle of the table. "This guy's either lost it or else this isn't our guy."

Maggie and Pakula came up on either side of Carmichael to take a look. Maggie grabbed the top page, staring at the first crime scene photo with yet another decapitated head sitting on a church altar. Maggie couldn't believe it. This one resembled the D.C. killer more than their priest killer.

"Boston detective I talked to said the killer practically ripped the head off," Carmichael told them

"I hate to tell both of you this," Maggie said and Pakula and Carmichael stopped to look at her. "I think we've got more than one killer."

CHAPTER 70

Omaha Police Department
Omaha, Nebraska

Tommy Pakula couldn't believe what he was hearing. "What the hell do you mean we've got more than one killer?"

"I was working on a serial killer case back in D.C. before I came out here. All the victims have been decapitated," O'Dell started to explain.

"But they've been all women so far, haven't they?" Pakula remembered seeing bits and pieces on TV.

"Yes, as far as we know."

"And in the D.C. area. Not Boston."

"Look," O'Dell said, "I'm not sure about this, but I don't think a killer who hides a victim in the Florida wetlands would turn around a week later and decapitate another, displaying that victim's head on a church altar."

"Isn't it possible he's starting to lose it?" Carmichael asked, taking several steps back as if to get out from between Pakula and O'Dell.

"Anything's possible," O'Dell said, but she didn't sound as

if she meant it. "I'm just saying there's usually a pattern with this type of killer even when he starts to accelerate."

"But yesterday you told me never to underestimate who's capable of murder." Pakula was losing his patience. Today they seemed even farther away from finding a suspect. Now O'Dell was telling him she couldn't even come up with a profile.

"And yesterday you told me you weren't convinced one killer could pull off all these murders. That was when we had three instead of five," she reminded him.

"You're right," Pakula said, holding up his hands in mock surrender. "Okay, I'll play along. Let's say there're two killers. Makes sense that one might be taking the Midwest and another takes the East and Southeast. But how are they working together?"

Pakula shoved his hands in his pockets and leaned against the wall as O'Dell started to pace again. He sensed a nervous energy to her today that was a bit unsettling. Was it that she had no answers or could it be her anticipation in making this deal with Keller? Either way, he hoped that by hunkering down and not moving around he might be able to calm her down. Carmichael wasn't any help. She was pacing along the length of the room on the other side.

"They might have something set up over the Internet," O'Dell offered.

"Next you're gonna tell me it's a couple of teenagers playing Dungeons and Dragons over the Internet."

"You're kidding, right?" Carmichael said, stopping in her tracks and looking from Pakula to O'Dell.

"Agent O'Dell has a theory that the killer…or killers could be teenagers who have been abused by priests. Correct me if I'm not getting this quite right," he said to O'Dell, unable to contain the sarcasm and to his own surprise a little bit of anger. "That they could be taking things into their own hands, spurred on by one of those Internet crusader games that are popular right now."

When Carmichael didn't laugh or roll her eyes Pakula knew

he was in trouble. He was the odd man out. He knew it before she even opened her mouth.

"Could be why this Boston one doesn't follow any pattern," Carmichael suggested, adding her own spin. "Teenagers are unpredictable anyway. I imagine that's true when you're dealing with teenage killers, right? A kid might not be able to keep it all together."

There was a knock at the conference-room door and a uniformed officer poked his head in. "Kasab's ready for you. Said to tell you they're at the Embassy Suites. Your special guest refused to come down to the police station."

"Thanks, Bernie," Pakula told him. When he glanced at O'Dell he had to do a double take. All the color had drained from her face and she was staring at him.

"You have Keller at the same hotel I'm staying at?" O'Dell was incredulous.

"Not my idea. Chief Ramsey and Assistant Director Cunningham set this up. I was told to treat him as a guest of the Omaha Police Department."

"And how do you treat a guest of the Omaha Police Department?" O'Dell wanted to know.

"Not sure," Pakula said, scratching his jaw. "We've never had one before. But I would think the first rule is to make him nice and comfy so he tells us lots of stuff. And since it sounds like your Father Michael Keller doesn't trust us, we should start by accommodating his request to meet on neutral territory. Suppose he's afraid we might consider arresting him?"

"I'd like to do more than arrest him," O'Dell muttered, surprising both Pakula and Carmichael.

"We should get going." Pakula grabbed his jacket off the back of a chair but threw it over his arm. It had already been eighty degrees this morning when he came in. He hated to see what it was by now. "We certainly don't want to keep our special guest waiting. I hope to hell he has something we can use."

"I just can't believe Cunningham put him in my hotel."

"Probably the chief's doing," Pakula told her. "They give the police department a pretty decent discount."

The look O'Dell shot him said exactly what she thought of their discount.

CHAPTER 71

Omaha, Nebraska

After Timmy's mom left for work Gibson had convinced Timmy they couldn't go to Explorers. Actually it didn't take much convincing when he told him about Brother Sebastian grabbing him at school and then coming to his frickin' house. They sat in the living room in front of the TV with their bowls of cereal. They left it on the *Ellen DeGeneres Show,* hoping it'd make them laugh, but even the audience dancing segment didn't get either of them going.

"How do you suppose he found me?"

"The school," Timmy said. "I bet he asked Father Tony or Sister Kate."

"It had to be Father Tony. Sister Kate would never give him my address. I know she wouldn't."

"So what's in the leather thing? How do you know that's what he wants?"

Gibson hesitated, taking another mouthful of cereal and pretending that's what was keeping him from answering

Timmy's questions. He needed to trust someone and Timmy already knew about the game.

"I think there're all sorts of papers about Monsignor O'Sullivan."

"Papers?"

"Yeah, you know, like reports of some kind. Complaints."

"Did you file a report against the guy?" Timmy asked.

Gibson looked at him, wiping his bangs out of his eyes, his fingers lingering over his forehead in search of pimples.

"No," he finally said. "Did you file one against your guy?"

"No," Timmy answered, sticking his index fingernail between his teeth, his own nervous habit. Gibson could see there weren't many fingernails left to chew on, most of them down to the quick. "Nobody believed me, except my mom. And they wouldn't even listen to her because two other guys had already been arrested."

"Two other guys?" Gibson asked. They hadn't shared any details with each other. Gibson figured Timmy would be as embarrassed as he was to talk about it. Now he realized that Timmy might have had a worse thing happen to him. "Did the two guys do anything to you?"

"I really don't know for sure. The guy who kidnapped me always wore a Halloween mask. It was one of those dead presidents. So I never saw his face."

"You were kidnapped?"

Timmy stopped chewing his fingernail and crossed his arms over his chest.

"Yeah. I try not to think about it much."

"Sorry." Gibson didn't know what else to say.

"No, it's okay. I used to have nightmares. It was weird though, 'cause it wasn't about being taken, you know. It was like I was always trying to see behind the mask or pull it off. Like I needed to see who it was for sure."

"How come you think it was a priest?"

"Little things. Probably stupid things. The cops told me they weren't proof." Now Timmy pulled his feet up under him, almost curling into a ball. "Father Keller used to always trade baseball cards with us altar boys, and the masked guy brought me some. Other stuff, too. Like his tennis shoes. Father Keller always wore the cleanest, brightest tennis shoes I think I ever saw. And the masked guy did, too."

"How about the guys they arrested?"

"One never wore tennis shoes. The other wore really dirty ones."

Gibson smiled. "Not exactly CSI stuff, huh?"

"No, I guess not." Timmy smiled, too, finally uncurling himself, maybe feeling safe again. He reached for his cereal bowl. "But Father Keller's someplace down in South America, so I guess I don't have anything to worry about. I just thought putting his name into the game would help me sort of eliminate him in my mind, you know? Stop the dreams from happening and it sorta did. I haven't had one in a long time."

Gibson nodded like he understood, but it hadn't really worked that way for him. He hadn't had a nightmare until Monsignor O'Sullivan was dead.

Then Timmy added, "Do you think we should tell somebody about the leather thing?"

"I think it's called a portfolio. Who would we tell that would believe us? They wouldn't even believe you and your mom." Gibson had already tried to think who he could tell and hadn't come up with anyone. He had thought about Sister Kate, but he didn't want to get her in trouble, too. He got the feeling that anyone who knew about this portfolio might be in trouble.

"Yeah, you're right," Timmy said and slurped down the milk from his bowl, putting it back on the coffee table. There was a silence while the two boys seemed to think about it then Timmy continued, "My mom says there've been other priests killed. Do you think they were part of the game? Maybe names other players submitted when they were invited to play?"

This time Gibson shrugged. He set his cereal bowl down

next to Timmy's one on the coffee table. He sat back into the soft couch.

"I think every time we played the game and the Holy Man was terminated…" Gibson paused, watching Timmy's face "…I think maybe a real priest might have been offed."

"But who's doing it?" Timmy asked and Gibson couldn't help noticing that Timmy didn't seem shocked or even surprised by his theory.

"The Sin Eater had to be at the airport when Monsignor O'Sullivan was killed. Otherwise how did he know I was there? He knows about the portfolio. He could've been the one who put it in my backpack." It felt good to Gibson to finally be saying it all out loud, instead of going over it again and again in his mind.

"And The Sin Eater's the only one who knows all the names."

They stared at each other. Gibson still couldn't believe this was real. It was supposed to be a game. It was supposed to be a way for them to take out their anger and frustration, to help them feel in control and free. It was supposed to be a way to deal with the stuff that they had gone through, the abuse or inappropriate touching or whatever the hell they wanted or needed to call it. The Sin Eater was the master of the game.

"The Sin Eater's last message said that as long as I had the portfolio I was safe and that he wouldn't let anything happen to me," Gibson told Timmy.

"Do you believe him?"

Gibson had to think about this before he answered. The game had made him feel in control, strong. Each time he signed on he felt like he had friends in the other players and their characters. He couldn't think of a single thing about the game that was meant to hurt him or take advantage of him or make him feel stupid.

"Yeah, I think I do," he finally said.

"Do you think The Sin Eater's someone we know?" Timmy asked.

"No, I don't think so. I would have recognized him at the airport."

"Maybe he wore a disguise," Timmy suggested, inserting another fingernail between his teeth.

"I guess that's possible. There were an awful lot of people."

"Can I ask you something?" Timmy sat forward in his chair, hands now in his lap.

"Sure, I guess so."

"Why were you there?"

"Whadya mean?"

"Why were you at the airport on Friday?"

Gibson felt his face get hot and he avoided Timmy's eyes, looking at the TV as if suddenly interested in Ellen's next guest though he didn't have a clue who the guy was. He knew he shouldn't be embarrassed. At least not with Timmy who certainly knew where he was coming from. Geez, Timmy had been through even worse...

Finally he said, "I went by the school that morning to see if Sister Kate needed any help setting up for the Explorers' Program, but she wasn't there. When I went by Monsignor O'Sullivan's office he and Father Tony were sort of arguing. They didn't see me. I've gotten really good at sneaking by 'cause I don't like running into the monsignor." He paused and Timmy nodded.

"I overheard him tell Father Tony he was leaving, flying to Rome that afternoon and not coming back. I know it probably sounds pretty lame, but I wanted to make sure he really was leaving. So I checked on the Internet what flights there were and went to the airport. I wanted to see him get on that plane. Only he went to the bathroom and he didn't come out."

Gibson didn't like remembering the blood. It looked so red on that bathroom floor. He could even remember the smell. And that look on the monsignor's face. He shook his head, trying to get the image out.

"I wanted him to leave. I wanted him gone." He heard his voice crack with anger and he glanced away again. "I didn't mean for him to get killed," he added, wiping at the threat of a tear with the back of his hand.

Now he looked at Timmy and dared to meet his eyes. He had shared this much. Why not go ahead and get it all out? "But you know what? I'm not sorry he's dead. He was a real bastard."

That's when they heard the front door of the duplex unlock and click open. Gibson jumped and so did Timmy. They waited, both twisting around to try and see into the entrance-way. Was it Timmy's mom? Would she be pissed they skipped Explorers? Gibson knew his mom would be, except she wouldn't say she was pissed. She'd say she was disappointed in him. That was worse.

A man came around the corner and Gibson jerked back. He wasn't sure if they should run. His eyes darted between Timmy and the man. Timmy looked surprised and so did the man, which made Gibson push himself back into the sofa. He cringed, ready for an attack when it looked like the guy's surprise was shifting to anger. Yeah, the guy was definitely angry.

"What the hell's going on here?"

CHAPTER 72

Omaha, Nebraska

Nick hadn't meant to scare Timmy and his friend. He was just in a lousy mood. He hadn't slept much last night. And then instead of checking out of the hotel he found himself asking if the suite was available for another night. What the hell was wrong with him? Was he seriously trying to screw up his engagement?

"Don't you have your Explorers' thing today?" he asked when it looked like both boys were too guilty to offer an explanation on their own.

"Um...we, uh..." Timmy gave it his best shot, glancing over at his friend, expecting help. Nick didn't think his friend would be capable of offering any help. The kid looked like he was about ready to jump out of his skin.

"Your mom doesn't know you skipped, huh?"

Timmy finally gave up and nodded. "We have a good reason."

"Yeah, I'm sure you do and you'll need it when you tell her."

"You're gonna make me tell her? Ah, come on, Uncle Nick."

"Hey, I don't make the rules in this house. So who's your friend?"

"Sorry. Gibson, this is my uncle Nick." Timmy waved his hand between the two of them as if that made the introduction official and complete. "So where've you been the last couple of nights? I thought you were staying here."

"I had a suite at the Embassy Suites."

"The one down in the Market?"

"Yep."

"Sweet. Does it have one of those minibars in the room with the five-dollar M&Ms and six-dollar Cokes?"

"Yeah, it does. So, Gibson, are you in the Explorers' Program, too?" Nick was beginning to wonder if the kid talked.

"Yes, sir."

Nick wanted to laugh. Instead, he smiled and shook his head. "You can call me Nick, okay?"

"Okay."

"So what's the deal? You two skipped just to sit around the house eating cereal and watching talk shows? Doesn't sound very exciting."

He glanced from one to the other, watching them exchange guilty looks that seemed to include a scuffed-up backpack. They were hiding something. Didn't much matter what it was. Christine would be royally pissed when she found out Timmy was wasting her five hundred dollars, sitting around the house chewing the fat with his friend instead gobbling up all that explorer trivia.

Before either one answered there was a knock at the front door. Both boys scrunched down in their seats. Nick shook his head at them. Something was definitely up. This wasn't just about skipping school.

"Don't run out on me," he whispered, pointing a finger at the two of them. Then he went back down the hall to the foyer. Kids! It was probably a delivery person and they're practically pissing their pants for nothing.

It wasn't a delivery person. The tall man with white skin, a hooked nose and black narrow-set eyes stared at Nick, probably surprised to find a man answering Christine's door.

"Can I help you?" Nick asked, trying to place the guy. He knew he had seen him before but where?

"Is this the Hamilton residence?"

"Are they expecting you?" Nick asked instead. And then he remembered. It was the guy from Our Lady of Sorrow. The one rummaging through the monsignor's office. The one Christine had had a verbal sparring match with. She couldn't possibly be expecting him and she would never have invited him to her home.

"I'm Brother Sebastian from Our Lady of Sorrow," he told Nick while his eyes tried to get a look beyond and behind Nick. He got the impression the man didn't like having to explain himself, but he continued, "Timmy Hamilton and Gibson McCutty didn't show up for class this morning."

Nick waited, but that seemed to be all Brother Sebastian thought was necessary. As if that accusation deserved some sort of explanation from Nick.

"Wow," Nick said. "And the school sent you to check on them? I didn't realize schools did that." There was something fishy about this guy, and Nick was definitely starting to piss him off.

"Mrs. McCutty told me her son spent the night here. Is he here?" He kept his tone clipped and even, but Nick could sense the underlying anger.

"McCutty," Nick repeated like it required some thought. "I don't recognize that name." Tony wasn't the only one good at evading a question without lying. He supposed priests and prosecutors weren't all that different, twisting the truth to suit their needs.

"So the boys aren't here?"

"I don't see them? Do you?"

Brother Sebastian raised an eyebrow, the black eyes staring at him, but Nick didn't flinch.

"Very well then," he finally said then turned on his heels and left.

Nick stayed in the doorway, waiting for him to glance over

his shoulder to see that he was watching. Yes, there was the glance and Nick waved, smiling despite Brother Sebastian's scowl. Whoever this asshole was, he hadn't come here to make sure Timmy and Gibson were okay. In fact, now Nick realized Brother Sebastian probably had something to do with the boys not going to their Explorers' class. Of course, it had to be something like that. What red-blooded teenage boy wouldn't want to go to a class where a pretty teacher taught them about swords and daggers?

Brother Sebastian climbed into a shiny black Lincoln Town Car, and Nick waited until he drove away. Then he closed and locked the door. When he came back into the living room both boys were staring at the entrance as if they had just escaped a firing squad.

"That was sweet, Uncle Nick," Timmy told him. "You were awesome."

Before they could go into any kind of victory dance, Nick gave them a look that wiped the smile off Timmy's face and made Gibson slide back into the couch.

"What the hell did you boys do?"

CHAPTER 73

Omaha, Nebraska

Father Michael Keller wished his vision would return to normal. He had almost changed his mind in Chicago during a two-hour layover. Not because of fear or regret, but because his insides felt as though they would explode. He spent most of those two hours in the bathroom, vomiting until there was nothing left but the urge. As soon as his insides had settled down, his eyesight had started playing tricks on him.

It was the worst when he first arrived in Omaha, making him see double and triple. There had been one uniformed officer and a detective to meet him and suddenly there seemed to be three uniformed officers and then almost a dozen. He had walked through the airport with them, trying to ignore the feeling of walking through a fun house with mirrors alongside, distorting, elongating and multiplying images all around him. That was when he told them he wanted to go to his hotel. That if they wanted to get the information from him they'd need to come to his hotel room. And what a hotel room it was, bigger than his shack, with a sitting area and a counter with minifridge and microwave.

He'd been in the rain forest for too long. He reveled in everything, from the tiny shampoo bottles and the bright white cotton towels to the king-size bed and carpeting so soft it felt like walking on feathers. He hadn't realized how much he missed, how much he had sacrificed. Like air-conditioning! He'd forgotten how glorious air-conditioning felt except that it had given him such a chill during the ride from the airport that when the hotel desk clerk asked if there was anything they could bring to his room for him he immediately asked for some hot tea. Yes, some hot tea would ease his frayed nerves and settle his stomach. Some tea that wasn't laced with monkshood, that would restore the comforting memory of his mother and not let him dwell on the poison.

The young detective asked if everything was to his liking, if there was anything else he needed. He told him the others would be coming soon. Just as a hotel person brought in a tray with all the makings for his hot tea, the detective left in search of the meeting room they were to use downstairs off the lobby.

Keller stood back and admired the contents on the tray: a porcelain carafe of hot water, a delicate bone-china teacup and saucer, a matching plate with an assortment of teas in colorful packages, a small stainless-steel pitcher with milk and a small dish with miniature sugar cubes. If that wasn't enough of a treat, they had included a small basket, and he peeked under the linen napkin to find a treasure of biscuits and muffins still warm.

He rubbed his hands together, content, sitting and staring at the surprise feast. Finally, he chose a package of tea and poured a cup, relishing the aroma. Yes, this would make it all better. He could feel a warmth start to fill him even with the first sip.

He had been wrong to think he should have to do without these simple pleasures. It had been almost four years, four long years of punishment he didn't deserve. He had tried to make his time as productive as possible. But there were so many who needed him. So many who were miserable and starving, neglected and abused. At times it was overwhelming. He knew he couldn't be expected to save them all. But Arturo was different, special. Those sad, dark eyes were like a window into his own childhood, a constant reminder of what it was like to have no one who cared. He had been lucky to have his mother, though only for twelve short years. But Arturo had no one except those who knew only how to punish and abuse him. No, he could never have left without saving Arturo. It was the least he could do.

A knock at the door rudely interrupted him. He wished he could ignore it. Perhaps it was simply the hotel person, coming back for the tray. Did they come back this quickly? Or it could be someone else checking to make sure he was comfortable.

He opened the door just a crack. The detective had already returned.

"We're ready for you," he said, and suddenly all the therapeutic magic of the tea seemed to dissipate.

CHAPTER 74

Washington, D.C.

He called in sick. Two days in a row. His boss wasn't happy. Yesterday wasn't much of a problem. Today meant canceling an account meeting in Saint Louis, which meant canceling a flight, maybe not getting back the full refund on the ticket. The cheap bastard would buy wing seats if he got a good enough discount. Last week's trip to Florida he had even been on standby. Standby, for God's sake. Was that any way to run a business? He didn't care if he got fired. Right now he didn't care about anything except the banging in his chest that had rapidly moved to include the back of his head. He worried that soon his entire body would become one throbbing ache.

He had ignored the blinking e-mail icon in the corner of his computer screen, but he knew he couldn't ignore it forever. He felt it watching him, could feel it through the walls like some laser beam following him from room to room. It was ridiculous. Of course, The Sin Eater couldn't see him, certainly couldn't watch him. So how did he know?

He paced in front of the computer. Calling in sick wasn't

really a lie. He did feel sick, nauseated and feverish. When he glanced at himself in the mirror this morning he hardly recognized his image. His hair looked like it had thinned overnight and there seemed to be a sickly yellow tinge to his skin. His bloodshot eyes were swollen from little sleep. How could he sleep when Mrs. Sanchez kept waking him up, staring at him from the dark corner of his bedroom?

The nightmare had been so real he had forced himself to stay awake. If only she hadn't been there at the rectory. How could he know she'd be there in the middle of the afternoon? The others were different, whores waiting to have the evil slit out of them. But Mrs. Sanchez…she shouldn't have gotten in his way. It wasn't his fault. But how did The Sin Eater know?

He stared at the computer screen from across the small room. When he was invited to play the game he had to submit a name and he did: Father Paul Conley. Terminating him in a make-believe computer game hadn't been enough. He wanted him dead. He wanted to control Father Paul Conley's last breath and he had.

He had to think about this. If The Sin Eater had heard or seen the news that the priest had really been murdered, would he automatically know it was him? The Sin Eater could go back to the original list, see who submitted Father Paul's name and then know the priest's killer. Would he feel the need to punish him? Would he turn him in to the police?

It didn't matter. He had been especially careful, very careful…except for the fucking coffee mug. Jesus! He couldn't believe he had forgotten it. Everything else he had wiped down or thrown into the garbage bags. Everything except the most obvious fucking thing. By the time he remembered, it was too late to go back. But it didn't matter. He didn't care. It was over and done, and Father Paul Conley couldn't, wouldn't, be able to hurt anyone else.

Pumped with a fresh wave of adrenaline he marched across the room to the computer and clicked on the e-mail waiting for him. He could handle whatever it was. There was only one e-mail message, and it was from The Sin Eater:

YOU BROKE THE RULES.

CHAPTER 75

Embassy Suites
Omaha, Nebraska

Maggie rubbed her shoulders, trying to get rid of the chill. The room was freezing and she couldn't shake that old saying from her mind, "When hell freezes over…" It seemed appropriate since she never believed she would be making a deal with the devil. Technically, Assistant Director Cunningham had taken care of the details, but she was the one who had to sit across the table from Keller.

"Isn't it awfully cold in here?" she asked Pakula, who sipped his fifth coffee of the day.

"Actually I was just thinking it feels good."

He was no help. Maggie gave in and poured herself a cup of hot tea from the service butler in the corner. The Embassy Suites's concierge had prepared a room for them with little notice, doing an impressive job that included an assortment of afternoon refreshments. She couldn't help thinking Pakula would be pleased—more free food. However, the detective seemed content with only coffee. She had recognized his feeding frenzy as a nervous habit, which would mean that he wasn't at all anxious this afternoon. How could he not be? Was she the only one who realized the significance of this meeting?

"Chief Ramsey must know someone important," Maggie said, lifting the stainless-steel lid off a plate of fruits and cheeses and trying to calm her nerves by pretending they were here for an ordinary interview. She glanced over her shoulder at Pakula. "No doughnuts though."

"Very funny."

The look he shot back made her smile, and she realized she missed her partner, Special Agent R. J. Tully. Not an easy realization, since she prided herself in being a sort of lone warrior. But Tully had a way of calming her in situations like this and it usually included his corny sense of humor.

There was little time to take refuge in humor. Suddenly the meeting-room door opened and Detective Kasab came in, holding the door for Father Michael Keller as he entered, as if he deserved such a courtesy.

Maggie was stunned. She hardly recognized Keller. He looked much older. His skin was tanned but leathery, his dark hair prematurely peppered with gray. If she remembered correctly he was younger than her. His escape to South America had weathered him and converted his smooth, handsome, boyish looks to that of a haggard older man.

He carried a cardboard box gently in his hands, as though the contents would shatter with the slightest jerk or slip. And when he glanced around the room, slowly examining it, his eyes brushed her aside. Was he checking for back doors, maybe an escape? Did he expect to be tricked?

Pakula introduced himself, and like Kasab, was cordial and polite, treating Keller like some visiting dignitary. When Pakula made a motion to introduce Maggie she stepped forward, preempting him.

"No need for introductions," she said. "Father Keller and I are old friends. Isn't that right?" She looked Keller in the eyes, but didn't offer her hand as Pakula had. Instead, she set her cup of tea at the end of the table and took a seat.

"I'd like to believe that we certainly are not enemies, Agent O'Dell," he said with that same smooth, deep voice she remembered so well. "Do you mind if I call you Maggie?"

"Yes, I do."

"Excuse me?"

"Yes, I do mind." She sipped her tea while the three men stood silently and stared at her in the same way they'd stare at someone who stood up in the middle of a wedding ceremony and said, "I object."

She could already feel the tension crawl into the room like fog over a cold lake. So she'd be the party pooper, the curmudgeon, the spoiler of this ever-so-cordial gentlemen's agreement. She didn't care. As far as she was concerned Keller was no gentleman and certainly couldn't be trusted. She only wished the hot tea would dull the chill that had settled deep inside her. She opened a small notebook and started tapping her pen, ready to begin.

"I'll be in the lobby if you need anything," Kasab said to Pakula, finally breaking the silence. Pakula gave him a nod and Kasab left, closing the door behind him.

Maggie didn't take her eyes off Keller, almost daring him to see if he could lie his way past her.

Pakula cleared his throat and shot her a look. They had known each other only a few days and she could already read his warning. He was telling her to cool it. Then he picked up his coffee mug and wandered over to the service butler for a refill.

"Can I get you some coffee, Father Keller?"

Maggie wanted to tell him to stop being so damn polite.

Keller pointed at her cup and said to Pakula, "May I have a cup of hot tea instead?"

"Oh sure. Do you take anything in it?"

"Do you have any of those little sugar cubes?"

Pakula poked around the service butler, lifting lids. "Doesn't look like it."

"Plain is fine, then."

Maggie wanted to yell this wasn't a frickin' tea party. Jesus!

Finally the three of them settled around the long table—Maggie at the head so she purposely didn't have to sit across from Keller—Pakula to her right and Keller to her left with his box and his cup of hot tea.

It had been Keller's request that he meet only with Maggie. At least Ramsey and Cunningham had the good sense to insist Detective Pakula be here at the meeting. Though Maggie couldn't help wondering if Cunningham had insisted on it because he was concerned for her safety or if it was Keller's safety he had considered.

Maggie watched Keller taking in everything about him. His eyes were bloodshot, his cheeks a bit sunken. She was pleased to see beads of sweat on his upper lip. He wore khaki pants and a plain white cotton shirt, a sleeveless white T-shirt visible underneath. Other than wet circles forming under his arms, his clothes looked crisp and clean and freshly pressed. Although on closer inspection she could see that the shirt's collar had become a bit threadbare.

She paid particular attention to his hands. Despite his haggard appearance his hands had been well taken care of—smooth and without a single callus or unsightly cuticle, short but clean and neatly trimmed fingernails, straight long fingers. He seemed to use them with careful deliberation, almost with a reverence, everything they did was ceremonial. Even the way he picked up the teacup, slowly and delicately, bringing it to his lips as if it were a chalice. It reminded her how he had used those hands to consecrate the butchering of little boys and even try to turn that into a gruesome ritual.

He sat straight-backed and calm except that his eyes betrayed him as they continued to dart around the room. Again, she wondered if Keller was worried about them tricking him. Why shouldn't he worry? Surely he didn't think she wouldn't at least try to trap him, now that she finally had him right where she wanted him—sitting in a room with a police detective alongside her? After all, that was exactly what she had in mind.

"What's in the box?" she asked. Not able to resist an opening taunt, she added, "A fillet knife? Maybe some boy's underpants?"

He was good. Not even a flinch as he met her eyes and said, "The person you're looking for has been e-mailing me and sending me things. I've brought as many of the items as possible in the hopes that you might be able to get his fingerprints."

"If he's been sending stuff," Pakula said, "how have you been getting it? Postal service? Special delivery?"

"Postal service. All but one of them. No return addresses even on the postal service ones."

"He's been sending you things?" Maggie said. "How did he find you?"

Keller shrugged. "Probably through the church."

"Actually, the church officials told me they had no record of your whereabouts," Maggie challenged. "In fact, they said you hadn't been issued a reassignment."

"The church is very protective of her priests. Perhaps you've noticed that with this case." When he answered this time he looked to Pakula.

"Are you saying they've had your address the entire time?"

"They've known how to get in touch with me."

Maggie couldn't determine whether it was a lie or not. After what she had learned about the Catholic Church this week, she almost found herself believing him.

"How about the other one?" Pakula asked.

"I'm sorry, the other one?"

"You said the postal service brought all but one. How did you get the other?"

"One of the village boys—Arturo delivered it. He said an old man had given it to him." He reached for the teacup again.

"Any chance the kid got into it before he handed it off to you?" Pakula asked.

"No, absolutely not," he said, setting the cup down, and immediately Maggie saw why. There was a slight tremor to his fingers now. "Arturo was one of my best altar boys. He was a good boy. He would never have done something like that."

Maggie's stomach did a sudden flip. Keller had referred to the boy in the past tense. "Was? What do you mean, was?"

Keller's eyes met hers then darted off to the left. In that brief moment she thought she could see him backpedal, shifting gears. Had she caught him or was it the effect of the poison? He looked past her and to Pakula when he answered, "He used to be an altar boy for me. He's not anymore."

Pakula seemed to ignore the entire exchange.

"I highly doubt we're gonna get this guy's fingerprints no matter how much crap you've got in that box," he told Keller.

"I agree with Detective Pakula," Maggie said. "I doubt there's anything you have that will help us."

Keller pulled the box to him, suddenly protective of it, keeping it on the table but now wrapping both arms around it. "I don't think he was careful, because I don't think he believed I'd live long enough to hand this over to the authorities. And if you aren't able to match his prints, there's always the trail of e-mails. I have the list."

"Why do you suppose you're on the list, Father Keller?" Maggie asked.

"I have no idea."

"Really? No idea at all?"

She waited, giving him a second chance. He shifted ever so slightly in his chair and leaned his elbows on the table. There were a few blinks of his eyes but nothing excessive. Maggie had known killers who had convinced themselves that they had done nothing wrong, so effectively, so completely, that it became difficult to detect the lies even with a polygraph test. She believed Keller had done the same. Four years ago she had come to the conclusion that he had been on a mission. He had appointed himself a sort of savior of abused boys. Unlike The Sin Eater who Maggie suspected avenged, and thus rescued boys by executing their abuser, Father Keller simply rescued boys by murdering them, ending their alleged abuse and getting them out of their misery.

Keller must have realized they wouldn't go on until he answered. He finally said, "I have no idea why I'm on the list."

"Now, you see, that's curious to me," Maggie started to explain, keeping a calm, even tone though, she'd admit, a bit sarcastic. Surely sarcasm could be forgiven when what she really wanted to do was reach across the table, grab him by the collar and tell him he knew damn well why he was on the list. She continued, "We already know that the other priests have been accused of hurting little boys in one way or another. In fact, we believe the accusers may have somehow submitted the priests' names to be on the list. What about you, Father Keller? Who might have submitted your name? Who would want you eliminated?"

She tried to stare him down, but he didn't blink when he repeated, "I'm sure my name was submitted by mistake."

"A mistake?" She couldn't believe it. Did he really believe they would buy this crap? She looked to Pakula, hoping to see similar disbelief and frustration. Nothing. He was definitely the better poker player.

"What e-mail name does this guy use?" Pakula took over without missing a beat.

"The Sin Eater."

"Does that mean anything to you?" Pakula wanted to know.

"Not personally. I've done some research. The sin eater was a prominent figure in medieval times. Villagers would leave food items, usually bread, on the chest of their deceased loved one. After everyone was gone the sin eater would come in, eat the bread and ritualistically take the sins of the dead person into his own soul, thereby absolving the dead person of his or her sins."

"Bread?" Pakula shook his head and glanced over at Maggie. "We found goddamn bread crumbs on Monsignor O'Sullivan, and in Columbia they found some in Kincaid's shirt pocket. This is freaky crap."

"But wait a minute," Maggie said. "This killer is eliminating abusers. Why would he want to absolve the abusers of their sins?"

"I believe," Keller said, taking a quick swipe at his sweaty upper lip, "this person may feel he's absolving the sins of the person he's killing for, instead of the priest he's killed." He said it with almost an admiration for The Sin Eater, the same person who was attempting to kill him. He looked at Maggie and added, "Does that fit your profile, Agent O'Dell?"

She held his gaze without flinching. That actually made sense. The Sin Eater believed he was not only killing for the boys, but taking on their sins of submitting and wanting their abusers dead.

"Yes, actually it does fit my profile," Maggie told him. "I think you're right." Keller blinked hard at her as if he didn't hear correctly. Even Pakula did a double take. "Maybe he is rescuing abused boys from their tormentors by killing their tormentors." She paused. "Unlike you, Father Keller, who thinks he's rescuing abused little boys by killing the boys."

Both men stared at her, silenced for a second time by her bravado. Keller plucked at a piece of packing tape on his box. The room had gone so silent she could hear the scraping, pinching and pulling of his long nervous fingers.

"Is that what you did with Arturo, Father Keller?" she asked. "Did you rescue him before you left Venezuela?"

"Agent O'Dell," Pakula said, his warning calm but she could hear the impatience. "I think it's best we remember why we're here today. We're trying to stop a killer."

"Exactly," Maggie said and she looked at Keller. That's exactly what she was trying to do, stop a killer who should have been stopped four years ago. But she sat back, instead, and laced her fingers together in front of her on the table, preventing them from balling up into fists and slamming them into Keller's smug, sweaty face.

"Why don't you tell us what you have for us, Father Keller," Pakula told the priest, but now Maggie could feel him watching her out of the corner of his eyes.

"I've included copies of our e-mails," Keller continued, but now kept looking at Maggie, as if expecting her to interrupt. "I know there's a way you can trace Internet e-mail."

"Possibly," Pakula told him. "It would be better if we had your computer."

"Oh, I've brought my laptop. It's in my hotel room."

"I would guess," Pakula said, "that he's used some standard measures to prevent anyone from finding him. I doubt we'll be able to track his e-mail."

"But the FBI has all sorts of things they can do now since 9/11, right?" Father Keller asked. Now Maggie thought she could hear a tinge of frustration in his voice.

"What else do you have?" Pakula pressed on, glancing at Maggie. Finally he was showing some doubt and dissatisfaction. She sat quietly.

"I have a copy of the list," Keller said and gave the top of the box a tap. "Father Paul Conley was on it."

"What about Father Rudolph Lawrence?" Pakula asked.

"Lawrence? No, I didn't see that name."

"Are you sure?"

"When you discover your own name on a list of people to be eliminated you tend to know who else is on the list."

"How many are on the list?" Pakula wanted to know.

"Including myself, five."

Pakula let out a long breath. His eyes met Maggie's before he reached up to swipe his hand over his shaved head.

"The deal was to turn over everything that I believe might help you capture this person. It's to my benefit that he be caught. However, before I do that," Keller said, but by now there was a definite, although subtle, quiver to his strong deep voice, "there's something else I need."

Of course there was, Maggie thought. What good timing. She wanted to tell him to forget it. They weren't even sure any of his information would help. But she could see Pakula sit forward and shift in his chair. She knew he wanted to see what was in the box and if there were actually any fingerprints.

"What else?" Pakula asked, glancing at Maggie but not waiting for her okay.

"As I mentioned to Agent O'Dell, I believe I've been poisoned. I have reason to believe it's something called monkshood."

Maggie wanted to laugh at the irony but instead muttered, "How appropriate."

Both men ignored her.

"I believe The Sin Eater sent me tea laced with monkshood. That's how he thought he would eliminate me."

"But you found out?" Pakula said. "How?"

"He told me. He seemed rather proud of his cleverness." Keller wiped at beads of sweat now on his forehead despite the room's still being freezing cold. Maggie thought his pupils were dilated and one of his hands had dropped to his lap where it fisted up as if he might be in pain.

"What do you want from us?" Pakula asked.

"I think it's called digitalis. It's used in heart medication. It's supposed to be an antidote to treat monkshood poisoning. I need it. You bring it to my hotel room and I'll hand over the box and my laptop."

He pushed back strands of hair sticking to his forehead and now he stood. She saw him wince; perhaps that simple movement was painful. Maggie tried to remember what the symptoms were for monkshood poisoning but couldn't be sure of anything other than it had been used mostly during the Middle Ages. It certainly wasn't a modern-day poison of choice.

Pakula stood, too, but looked at Maggie, waiting for her response, letting her finalize what had initially been her deal.

She remained seated. "Why in the world do you think you can trust us," she asked Keller, "when I've made it quite obvious that I think you're a cold-blooded killer?"

Although he appeared to be in some discomfort—she could see him using his left hand against the table to steady himself—his voice didn't waver when he met her eyes and said, "Because you gave me your word, Agent O'Dell. And I happen to know that means something to you."

CHAPTER 76

The Embassy Suites
Omaha, Nebraska

Pakula had finished his call to Chief Ramsey, then checked his voice messages to see if any were urgent. Kasab had taken Keller back to his room before the priest ended up having some sort of attack or before O'Dell ended up strangling him. She still looked like she wanted to. Pakula thought it looked more like Keller had malaria than been poisoned, but Keller seemed pretty certain what was wrong with him.

"Chief Ramsey's wife is an internist over at the Med Center. He's having her get whatever the hell Keller said he needed." He wondered if O'Dell heard him. She was pacing again, back and forth across the room.

"That boy, Arturo," she said. "Keller murdered him before he left. He hasn't stopped."

Pakula let out a long sigh. She didn't look like she cared if he believed her or not. He knew what she was probably thinking. He didn't know Keller the way she did. He was meeting him for the first time, seeing him only as he was today, sick, sweating and trembling. However, Pakula could still remember details of that case four years ago. He'd never seen the killer's handiwork—the raw carvings sliced into the chests of those poor innocent little boys—but anything with kids was hard to stomach. He could understand it driving O'Dell crazy if she believed Keller was the killer, and especially if she believed he hadn't stopped.

"Look, O'Dell," Pakula said. "You might be right about Keller killing those boys outside of Platte City. Maybe you're right about this Arturo kid, but we have nothing on Keller. You're gonna have to let it go." He wasn't pissed at her. He hoped she could hear sympathy more than impatience in his voice. "You're no help to me in catching this killer if you don't let it go."

She was quiet and continued pacing. Then out of the blue she said, "Monkshood," and let out a laugh.

"Excuse me?"

"The Sin Eater certainly has a sense of humor."

"Careful," Pakula joked. "You sound like you're starting to admire him." He needed to get her mind on the killer and off Father Keller.

"Wouldn't you agree that the evilest of evil are those who intentionally harm children?" Her question sounded like a challenge.

"Without a doubt," he answered without hesitation.

"And what about the ones who not only intentionally do harm but use a child's respect and reverence for authority, like for a priest, in order to keep doing it again and again? Come on, Detective Pakula, you and I both know pedophiles well enough to know that Mark Donovan's experience with Monsignor O'Sullivan was not an isolated case."

"Agreed." He crossed his arms over his chest, suspecting that she was going somewhere with this, and that he didn't necessarily want to go along.

"How many pedophiles do you know who've been rehabilitated?"

"I know what you're getting at, Agent O'Dell."

"I don't know of any, but I can tell you about the little girl who was sexually assaulted and buried alive by a pedophile who had just been released from prison. In fact, I can tell you about dozens of cases." He watched her pause to run her fingers through her hair, her frustration clear. But her mind was off Keller and so he'd allow her the soapbox.

"You know as well as I do," she continued without any prompting, "that with pedophiles the violence usually accelerates, instead of stops. And yet in the last fifteen years the Catholic Church reassigned approximately fifteen hundred priests after allegations of sexual abuse. That is, of course, with the exception of a short vacation for some of them to a magical treatment center. My guess," she said, rubbing her shoulders as if she still hadn't gotten rid of her earlier chill, "is The Sin Eater is someone who simply got tired of seeing it happen over and over again without anyone else doing something about it. And yes, I suppose unlike any other killer I've profiled, I have to admit, I can almost sympathize with this one."

He was afraid that was exactly where she was going. "Is that your new profile?" he asked, smiling just enough, hopefully, to get her to relax and let the intensity go. "Yesterday you were telling me it was two killers, teenage boys who had been abused and were playing some game."

"It could be," she said, considering this as she began pacing again. "Kids sometimes have a basic, clear-cut view of justice."

"Father Paul Conley's head on the altar isn't my idea of any kind of justice."

She stopped for a minute and he wondered if she was reminding herself of the magnitude of these murders, or if she was simply envisioning Father Keller's head in Conley's place.

"I don't believe the man who killed Monsignor O'Sullivan killed Father Paul Conley," she said.

"Which follows your theory of two killers." Pakula still wasn't sold on the idea that teenage boys could pull these murders off. But he was beginning to think she was right about two killers. All the more reason they needed anything and everything Father Keller had brought with him.

"Why do you suppose Father Rudy down in Florida wasn't on the list?" she asked. But before he could answer she continued, "That may mean Keller's list is bogus. The murderer gives Keller a list knowing he'll hand it off to the authorities. Of course, he's going to include those who have already been killed to give the list some credibility. But why isn't Father Rudy on the list?"

She was back at the service butler, pouring more hot water over another tea bag. She was getting as bad with the hot tea as he was with the coffee. That was just great—both of them pumped with caffeine. Then she was back to her pacing, although a bit slower with the full mug.

He got up from the table and stretched his arms and back. He spent too many hours these days sitting. Maybe pacing would do him some good, but he only got as far as the service butler. No sense in all that free food going to waste. He'd be banging at his punching bag for an extra thirty minutes, but he sampled several of the little cubes of cheese.

"Maybe Father Rudy was a mistake." He popped a couple of grapes into his mouth. Then he remembered his voice messages. "Hold on. I forgot, I have a message from my friend down in Pensacola." He pulled out his cell phone and flipped it open, punching through the missed calls. When he got to the 850 area code one, he hit Play and listened.

"Hey, Tommy. Gotta make this short. Actually there's not much to tell. I finally found someone who didn't mind telling me that Father Rudy was a real pervert. But Tommy, it wasn't little boys he liked. There was at least one eleven-year-old girl. Call me tonight if you wanna talk."

Pakula folded up his phone and stared at it. Without realizing it, he had wandered over to the easy chairs in the corner and now dropped into one. He had treated this case like any other, disgusted anytime kids were involved. But for some reason it suddenly struck him. His youngest daughter, his baby, Madeline, had just turned eleven last month and for a brief moment he thought about her trusting a man, a priest, and that man, a priest, taking advantage of her respect and reverence for him just as O'Dell had outlined in her earlier sermon. Suddenly he could taste the bile backed up in his throat, and he felt an incredible urge to hit something.

He looked up to find O'Dell had stopped pacing and was standing in front of him, staring, waiting.

"What is it?" Her frustration was gone and now there was concern because he hadn't been able to hide his disgust. She must have read it on his face, in his grimace.

"It's nothing for sure," he told her. "Just rumors. More of the same, except Father Rudy preferred eleven-year-old girls."

He watched O'Dell close her eyes and take a deep breath, needing to compose herself. And he wondered if she ever got the urge to hit something, too.

"So Father Rudy had reason to be on the list," she finally said and Pakula nodded. "Then why wasn't he on it?"

CHAPTER 77

Washington, D.C.

From her office window, Gwen Patterson watched the rush-hour traffic below. Detective Julia Racine had left Gwen's nerves frayed and her mind preoccupied. Yet, somehow she had managed to get through the day of appointments, and she had managed to do so despite all the interruptions from her temp. The poor girl had jammed the copier, broken Gwen's brand-new gourmet coffeemaker and hung up on everyone she thought she was putting on hold, including a United States senator with an urgent question for Gwen. His impatience, however, seemed to override his urgency. He never called back. She was glad she had left poor Harvey back at her brownstone. He would have been a nervous wreck trying to keep track of all the chaos in the office today.

"Is there anything else, Ms. Patterson? I mean, Dr. Patterson?" the girl asked from the doorway.

Gwen took a good look at the girl…the young woman, Gwen corrected herself. Normally Gwen would have shaken her head at the eyebrow piercing and too short and too tight knit top. She had always tried to instill, or perhaps drill was more appropriate, into her assistants that their appearance became a reflection of her and her practice. They influenced her patients' first impressions of this office. They were the gateway to her business. All of that seemed insignificant at the moment. Her gateway had allowed a killer to pass back and forth, getting and taking advice that evidently had encouraged him to continue to kill. It certainly hadn't stopped him.

"No, there's nothing else, Amanda. Let's call it a day."

"I'm so sorry about your coffeemaker. I'll buy you a new one."

"Don't worry about it," Gwen told her, knowing poor Amanda didn't realize it would take her almost a whole week's salary to replace it. "Go home. Get some rest. We'll try it all over again tomorrow."

"Thanks, Dr. Patterson." It was the first smile Gwen had gotten out of her all day.

Amanda would probably go home and complain to her roommate or her boyfriend, maybe her mother or a girlfriend. And suddenly Gwen realized what luxury it must be to have someone like that to release the day's trials and tribulations to. And who did she have? Only Harvey and even he was on loan. She decided she'd call Maggie tonight. For a person who made her living convincing her patients that confession is actually good for the soul and the mind, she sure didn't practice what she preached. Maybe it was about time that she started.

Gwen decided she'd also take her own advice about going home and getting some rest. She slid her laptop and some folders into her leather briefcase just as the phone began to ring. She was tempted to let the voice-messaging service pick it up, but at the last minute grabbed the receiver.

"This is Dr. Patterson."

"Hey, Doc, it's Julia Racine."

So much for rest, and Gwen leaned against her desk, expecting to need the extra support.

"What can I do for you, Detective Racine?" she asked instead of saying what she wanted to say—What the hell do you want now?

"The Boston guys found some prints they think the killer left on a coffee mug. I just thought you'd like to know the prints don't match up. They're not Rubin Nash's."

"Am I supposed to be relieved?" All it meant was that Nash hadn't traveled to Boston to cut the head off some priest. She had already guessed that the two cases weren't related. "That only means he hasn't switched from killing young women to killing priests."

"I'm not too sure about that," Racine said and Gwen could barely hear her with what sounded like traffic noise in the background. The detective must be en route somewhere. "The rest of it is very much like our guy. Father Conley was strangled just like the other victims and the killer used a hatchet to chop and rip off his head. Sounds like he even dismembered him in the garden shed behind the rectory."

Gwen didn't want these details. She couldn't hear them without visions of Dena being mutilated piece by piece. She wanted to tell Racine to stop, to save it for Maggie or Tully or anyone else. She didn't want to do this anymore. After Rubin Nash her criminal-profiling days would be over.

"Those are details," Racine continued, "that we haven't released to the media, so it's not likely we have a copycat."

"Why are you telling me all this, Detective Racine?"

"Because I have nothing. And unless you can tell me something more about Rubin Nash, I can't even bring him in for questioning."

Gwen resisted the urge to hang up. She released a heavy sigh, hoping to release her frustration.

"I've told you everything I can think of," she told Racine. "The notes, the things he's left me, aren't any of them proof enough?"

"They would be if we could find his fingerprints on any of it."

"But I noticed myself that there are fingerprints. There's even a smudge of one on the map of the park."

"They're not his." Racine was shouting now, but not out of anger. It was only to make herself heard over the noise surrounding her. "Look, I've gotta go, Doc. If you think of anything, anything at all, call me."

And she was gone before Gwen could respond. She was beginning to think Racine had dropped the ball. Had she really checked out the fingerprints? Was it possible Nash had used someone else as his courier? Maybe he wanted to throw them all off.

She had just finished packing her briefcase when she heard the outside door to the office open. Amanda had either forgotten something or she'd neglected to lock it on her way out. She couldn't handle one more delivery or repairman and was about to say just that when James Campion stopped in her doorway.

"Hello, Dr. Patterson," he said, sounding out of breath.

He looked awful compared to his usual neat and tidy self. His clothes were wrinkled as if he had slept in them, his hair disheveled and his eyes bloodshot and swollen.

"James? Are you all right?"

"I really need to talk to you, Dr. Patterson."

"What's happened? Are you hurt?"

"No, no. Not hurt. At least not the way you mean."

She knew she should tell him to come back in the morning, that it was after hours. But he looked so frantic, so frightened, his boyish face grimacing, and she worried morning might be too late, remembering the hesitation marks on his wrists.

"Come in and sit." She needed to calm him down, but he was pacing the length of her office, watching out the window with every pass as if expecting to see that someone had followed him. She didn't like her patients up and about. It made them too out of control.

"We can talk, James, but you need to sit down and tell me what's happened."

Finally he stopped long enough to meet her eyes and in

what sounded like a very small boy's voice he whispered, "The pounding, the banging," and he pointed to his chest and his head, "it won't stop. I think it's because I broke the rules."

CHAPTER 78

The Embassy Suites
Omaha, Nebraska

Nick actually looked forward to the evening. After some persuasion, he had gotten Christine to agree that Timmy could spend the night with him in his suite. He had even gotten Christine to call Mrs. McCutty and convince her that Gibson could spend the night, too. Of course, it hadn't been easy. At first Christine didn't like the idea.

"I can't believe you want to reward them for skipping school," she yelled at him over the phone. "You know how much I spent on that Explorers class?"

When he told her about Brother Sebastian coming to the house, looking for the two boys, she went silent.

"I don't know what's going on," Nick told her, "but you have to admit, this Sebastian guy is pretty creepy."

"He's the archbishop's henchman," Christine said. "If there's something going on it involves Archbishop Armstrong. You don't think he's trying to get at Timmy because I've been working on this article, do you?"

"Are you kidding?" Sometimes he couldn't believe how

naive his big sister could be. "You're trying to pin a cover-up on him and you don't think he might try to stop you?"

"Maybe it would be a good idea for the boys to be someplace else. I'll call Mrs. McCutty and tell her."

His powers of persuasion worked on Jill, too, though he hated to admit there was little persuading. Jill seemed more than willing to forfeit an evening with him for another opportunity to check out flower arrangements, and oh by the way, the caterer was bringing by some samples so if he wasn't going to be around she'd invite her bridesmaids over.

He was beginning to wonder if she was more excited about the getting-married part than she was about marrying him. What was it about wedding planning that seemed to turn an intelligent, sophisticated, professional woman into a magazine-flipping, mall-hunting, shop-till-you-drop addict? Even when they did manage to get together their conversation invariably turned to mini-quiches versus miniature watercress sandwiches and whether or not one groom's cake would be sufficient. Surely they had talked about other things once upon a time, though at the moment he couldn't remember a regular conversation in quite a while.

Right now he didn't want to think about any of that. He just wanted to enjoy watching Timmy and Gibson gawk at everything in the hotel as if they were traveling through some futuristic world. They had stopped at Target on the way with the intention of buying Gibson a change of clothes, especially after the kid visibly cringed at the thought of stopping at his own house. Although they had bought pretty much only the basics, their miniature shopping spree ended up being a lot of fun. He hadn't laughed that hard in a very long time. Of course, it wasn't anything quite as elaborate as Jill and her friends would consider, but the boys seemed pleased and insisted on keeping their new shades on even as they walked the lobby and hallways of the hotel.

"Can we go to Ted and Wally's for ice cream later?" Timmy wanted to know.

"I think we'd better stay in tonight and stick to room service," Nick told him. "I don't think your new friend would think to look here or in the Old Market for you, but let's not take any chances, okay?"

But Gibson and Timmy were smiling at each other about the room service and already forgetting about their fear of Brother Sebastian. Nick was glad he could make them feel safe, but in the back of his mind he kept remembering what Tony had said about Brother Sebastian, that the man would do anything for Archbishop Armstrong. Already the guy had ransacked Monsignor O'Sullivan's office, roughed up Gibson in the school hallway and lied to the boy's mother, making up a story about him selling drugs. Nick was beginning to wonder what else Brother Sebastian was capable of. Did it include murder?

Timmy and Gibson weren't telling him everything either. First Tony and now these two. They knew something but remained tight-lipped every time he asked. He'd ply them with junk food and try again later. His first priority tonight was to keep them safe from the archbishop's henchman, as Christine had called him.

Nick was so focused on looking for Brother Sebastian that he didn't notice another tall man watching from one of the sofas in the hotel lobby.

CHAPTER 79

The Embassy Suites
Omaha, Nebraska

Father Michael Keller could feel the digitalis starting to work. He knew it was probably only his imagination. There was no guarantee that the antidote would help, let alone work this quickly. But the cold sweats had stopped. His stomach had settled down and despite being empty it no longer churned. However, he wasn't too sure if his eyesight had returned to normal.

He sat in the hotel lobby enjoying the piped-in music—a commercial attempt at Pachelbel's Canon in D Minor—and taking in all the sights outside: tourists in the Old Market strolling up and down the cobblestones, cars and buses and even Olley the Trolley zooming along. He watched it all, enjoying what in his previous life had annoyed and irritated him. His eyesight seemed fine until he saw a man and two teenage boys come through the revolving hotel door, then he wondered if he was seeing things again.

Was he mistaken or did he know the man? He couldn't place him. More importantly, the boy in the bright orange T-shirt and baggie cargo shorts looked very familiar. It was possible that they had been parishioners when he was at Saint Margaret's in Platte City.

He pretended not to watch as he sipped another glorious cup of hot tea. This place was like a dream—paradise on earth. He wished he could stay forever, but now that he had handed over everything to Maggie O'Dell and Detective Pakula his mission would soon come to an end.

On the long flight here he had reaffirmed his decisions. He wasn't going back. He'd get on the flight just as he had promised Agent O'Dell. But there was no reason to punish himself any longer. With everything he had given them, surely they would find The Sin Eater. It was only a matter of time. And in the meantime he needed to find somewhere else safe. Why not a small rural parish where no one knew him? Maybe someplace outside of Chicago.

He'd tell them the archdiocese had sent him, just as he had each time in the past four years. It might take months, maybe even a year, before anyone would find out differently. And if they did, he'd simply pick up and go somewhere else. There was no reason it couldn't work just as well here.

But there was one thing that still bothered him. Maggie O'Dell's question nagged at him. "Why do you suppose you're on this list, Father Keller?"

Until she had asked that simple question he had believed he could stay and be safe and free. But that one single question made him realize that there could still be someone else out there other than Agent O'Dell and The Sin Eater who could hurt him, who could continue to make his life miserable if he didn't stop them.

He was distracted again and heard the man with the boys speaking to the desk clerk. He couldn't make out the words.

He listened. Still no recognition.

The man turned and pointed out something to the boys and called out to the one in the orange T-shirt. He called him Timmy, and then it all came back to him as if it had happened only yesterday. He remembered and immediately he knew that must have been how he had gotten on the list. His one regret was the one little boy he hadn't been able to save. Timmy Hamilton had submitted his name to The Sin Eater.

CHAPTER 80

Washington, D.C.

G**wen** tried to calm him but he went from babbling like a small boy to a raging anger that she had never seen James Campion exhibit. Over and over he told her he had broken the rules. She had no idea what rules he was talking about.

"The rules of the game," he screamed at her. "The Sin Eater must have put some sort of spell on me. Is that possible?" he wanted to know.

She had finally gotten him to sit on the sofa, though his hands and arms still flayed about. Nothing in her past experience with him would indicate a violent manner and yet she found herself checking the door, making sure she had an escape route if it became necessary. All of their previous sessions had been more than civil. He'd always been polite, gracious and respectful. She couldn't remember him raising his voice even when confessing the most heinous of events from his childhood.

His childhood.

Why had it taken this long to hit her?

James Campion had been abused and raped by a parish

priest, a man he deeply respected and trusted. Had James ever spoken of him by name?

Now her mind raced, trying to pull pieces of information from his file by memory. Where? Why couldn't she remember where he had grown up? Not here. She was certain of that. Boston? Was it Boston? Or was she simply being paranoid again, conveniently pushing puzzle pieces into empty slots?

"James, slow down. Tell me about the game. You haven't mentioned it before." She spoke softly, the same tone that had worked for so many past sessions. "You must tell me about the game before I can help you. Do you understand?"

He nodded and she tried to hold eye contact. If she could get him to remember how comfortable, how safe he had felt here before—safe enough to confess things he hadn't shared with anyone—perhaps she could get him to tell her what had happened. Out of the corner of her eye she could see his hands in his lap, wringing the hem of his shirt. His fists balled up, the skin turning white. Suddenly she wondered if maybe she didn't want to know what had happened, what he had done.

"It helped for a little while," he said, his voice calm despite the violent wringing of his shirt. She could hear him ripping it now. She held his gaze, resisting the urge to look down. "You helped for a while. You really did. But you made me talk about it too much. It wouldn't go away when you made me talk about it. Instead it just brought out more anger. And then the game wasn't enough. Our sessions weren't enough. You—" He lifted a hand away from his shirt to point a finger at her. "You weren't enough."

He stood slowly, his eyes still holding hers as if having some sort of revelation.

"It's your fault," he said, only this time it was almost a hiss. "You made me dredge it all up again. You made me talk about it and remember. You made me remember all the disgusting details all over again. You made me do it."

And suddenly Gwen knew for certain that she had been wrong. The killer leaving her notes and maps and crying out for her attention was not Rubin Nash. It was James Campion. She had made a mistake and now she was about to pay for that mistake.

CHAPTER 81

The Embassy Suites
Omaha, Nebraska

Maggie allowed Pakula to talk her into staying at the hotel, going back to her suite and as he put it, "taking a load off." He also gave her strict instructions to stay away from Father Keller, probably regretting now that they were staying in the same hotel, separated only by two floors. It was late and she was meeting Sister Kate for dinner. Otherwise she would have insisted she join him and his team to do some of the legwork. There was a lot to do. Each of the items would need to be dusted for fingerprints and the prints run through the system for matches. Both she and Pakula agreed that The Sin Eater's e-mail address would surely be a dead end, but he'd have their computer whiz back in the crime-analysis lab give it his best shot.

She hated to admit it but there was a sense of relief—though slight—in being able to watch Pakula and Kasab leave with all the so-called goodies Keller had finally handed over. She felt exhausted, drained of energy. She felt she had lost the battle. Maybe Pakula would track down The Sin Eater, but Father Keller was free to go. And Pakula was right. The mere thought of Keller possibly continuing to kill boys, and her being helpless to stop him, was driving her crazy.

Had she really believed she might be able to trip him up somehow? Get him to admit, to confess his sins? Why should he? There were two men already in prison because Keller had planted enough evidence against them to convict them. He had manipulated and tricked law enforcement, the justice system and the Catholic Church—all of them so he could remain free to continue his twisted mission of "saving little boys." And the worst part was that she had just contributed to his power. Now more than ever, because of their deal, because of his so-called help, he would feel even more powerful, more vindicated. And if he had, indeed, killed poor Arturo, then he had no intention of going back to Venezuela.

When she returned to her suite she checked her messages but there were none. Not that she expected any from Racine or Gwen, but she had hoped one of them would keep in touch just to let her know what the hell was happening with the D.C. case. Though she was convinced that Father Paul Conley's death and decapitation were connected to this case—Father Conley was on The Sin Eater's list, after all—she was also convinced the same person who killed the Boston priest had not killed the other priests. So how did the decapitations of the three—no, four—women in the D.C. area fit into The Sin Eater's scenario. Or did they? Were there two killers working together but with two different agendas?

She exchanged her trousers for jeans but decided to keep the blazer so she could wear her weapon. Once outside of the hotel, she breathed in the warm summer air, savoring the combination of scents as she wandered along the cobblestone streets of the Old Market, passing by the various shops and restaurants and horse-drawn carriages. As she walked, the smells and sounds changed from chocolate pastry to cigar smoke to garlic to sweaty horse and from horns to clippety-clop to a harmonica and guitar. Pakula had told her the brick four- and five-story buildings had once been warehouses built sometime around the 1900s next to the Missouri River and the Union Pacific Railroad for the convenience of shipping. Now tiny white lights lined the tops and the awnings. Street vendors and musicians drew small groups on the corners, giving the area a magical feeling.

She hurried in front of a horse-mounted police officer and followed a crowd across the busy intersection. Almost too quickly she found M's Pub. Sister Kate had already secured a table on the patio. She stood and waved as soon as Maggie saw her.

"Would you rather we eat inside?" she asked, still standing and ready to move if Maggie requested it.

"No, the breeze feels wonderful. This is perfect."

Maggie thought Sister Kate looked even less like a nun this evening, dressed in linen shorts, a black knit blouse and sandals. As they sat Sister Kate brushed at her black blouse, looking a bit embarrassed.

"My roommate's dog," she explained. "I love him but he ends up shedding all over me."

"Your roommate or the dog?" As soon as Maggie said it she wished she hadn't. She'd been spending too much time with male police detectives and FBI agents, but much to her surprise and relief Sister Kate burst out laughing. Maggie joined her.

They both ordered a glass of wine and Sister Kate insisted they have the scallops sautéed in garlic and capped with mozzarella cheese for an appetizer.

"If you don't mind my asking, is your roommate a nun, too?"

"Yes. Actually I have two roommates, both nuns. We share a house in the Dundee area. It's the neighborhood just a few blocks east of Our Lady of Sorrow."

"Where do your roommates teach?"

"I'm the only teacher," she said, smiling at Maggie's surprise. "We are allowed to *do* other things, have other careers, as long as they benefit and promote the order's mission." She paused as the waitress brought their wine. "Sister Loretta manages several low-income apartment complexes that our religious order owns. We call her our resident slumlord."

Maggie laughed again, relieved to feel some of the tension of the afternoon slipping away.

"And your other roommate?" Maggie asked.

"Ah, Sister Danielle creates computer programs."

"Really?"

"She's done a variety for hospital medical records departments and secure data systems for women's centers using all that complicated encrypted stuff. She's certainly taught me a lot, and she also finds incredible rates for me on airline flights. I have a presentation in Chicago this weekend and she's found a round-trip ticket for under a hundred dollars."

"Well, you've definitely given me a whole new perception about nuns."

"I imagine the same goes for FBI agents."

"Excuse me?"

"You're definitely not what I imagined an FBI agent to be like."

Maggie raised her wineglass. "Touché."

"I suppose this case has given you a whole new perception of priests as well?"

Maggie looked across the table at her, studying her in the fading sunlight. Her warm brown eyes were serious now where they had been playful just seconds before.

"It seems this priest scandal has touched every part of the country," Maggie said, trying to keep from going into her earlier tirade. "Why do you suppose it got so out of hand?"

Sister Kate sipped her wine. "I used to joke that if women were allowed to be priests it would have never have happened, at least not to the degree that it has. But at the same time I do believe some things should be taken care of from within. These priests haven't just broken man's laws, they've broken God's laws and should be held to an even higher standard. Unfortunately, in the name of protecting the church some bishops and cardinals completely forgot about protecting the children." She paused as though thinking about something or someone and then added, "The good news is that there are many more good priests than there are bad."

Maggie wondered if she was thinking of Father Tony Gallagher. Did she consider him one of the good guys? And if he was involved, if he was helping teenagers carry on some game of execution—a game of good versus evil or perhaps more appropriately evil versus a necessary evil—would Sister Kate suspect it? Would she go so far as to perhaps even protect Father Tony if he was The Sin Eater?

"Justice can certainly be elusive sometimes," Maggie said, looking for clues in the nun's eyes and seeing instead only concern.

"I'm sure you grapple with that constantly," Sister Kate said, and suddenly Maggie realized that she was being studied, too. "How do you deal with it? You seem to have a solid moral core that I'm guessing doesn't always coincide with the FBI's moral code of justice."

Yes, and today had been the perfect example, she wanted to say. Making a deal with Keller, who murdered children, in order to catch a killer, who avenged children, certainly seemed to be one of those instances.

"That's very true," Maggie admitted. "There are times when I have to do things I don't agree with. As I suppose you do, too?"

Sister Kate's smile disappeared and Maggie thought she could see a sadness in her eyes. "Yes. And there are times when it's necessary to break a rule or two."

"Perhaps bend, not break," Maggie clarified and managed to get Sister Kate to smile again.

"My grandfather used to say that sometimes the end justified the means. At the time I never understood what he meant."

"Your grandfather in Michigan? The one who instilled your love of all things medieval, including knights in shining armor coming to the rescue?"

"You have a very good memory," Sister Kate said. "He taught me so many wonderful things about justice, about life. He was one of a kind."

"You were lucky to have him."

"And what about you?"

"Excuse me?"

"Were you lucky enough to have anyone to come to your rescue?"

"I'm not sure I understand what you mean," Maggie said.

"Maybe it's a gift. Or a curse." Sister Kate shrugged as her eyes wandered away to watch the summer tourists strolling across the street. "I can sense those of us who have suffered some sort of abuse as children. There's always a tough outer shell, but for some reason I can see beyond that."

She turned back to Maggie and met her eyes. "You were abused as a child, weren't you?"

CHAPTER 82

The Embassy Suites
Omaha, Nebraska

Nick walked past the door to Maggie's suite and found himself hesitating. Ever since last night he wanted to knock. He dared himself to knock, coming close a couple of times. His hands were filled this time with junk food he had loaded up on from the hotel-lobby gift shop. So he had an excuse.

"Coward," he muttered to himself then remembered for the third or fourth time how ridiculous he was being. He hated that Maggie O'Dell still managed to push his buttons. After all this time he was so certain he was over her, that the only remaining feeling was anger. And he was still angry. But everything seemed to melt away when he looked into those dark brown eyes, everything including his knees. He was embarrassed to admit it, but no woman had ever knocked him so out of whack as Maggie O'Dell. And he hated that she seemed to be able to do that even without trying.

He knocked, instead, on the door to his own suite with his elbow since he had no free hand to knock, let alone dig out his key card.

Gibson opened the door so quickly it startled Nick, and he juggled the bags of chips and candy bars before everything became an avalanche.

"Here, let me get some of that," Gibson said, reaching out to help.

As soon as he had a free hand, Nick punched the volume down a couple notches as he passed by the TV. The room-service menu was still on the bed. All the pillows had been pulled out from under the covers and were stacked for TV-viewing comfort.

"They've got a couple of cool movies on later," Gibson said, unpacking the stash and lining it up neatly on the desk.

"Where's Timmy?" Nick asked, glancing around and noticing that the bathroom door was open.

"Didn't you meet him in the lobby?"

"No, I was down in the gift shop getting all this stuff."

Gibson looked genuinely confused. "The desk clerk called just a few minutes ago. He said that you wanted Timmy to meet you in the lobby to help carry some stuff up."

"I never asked the desk clerk to—" Suddenly Nick's stomach took a nosedive. "Did you talk to the guy or did Timmy?"

"Timmy did. He just left. I thought he was with you."

Nick could see Gibson getting worried now and he didn't want him to see the panic that was beginning to crawl up the back of his neck.

"I'm going back down to the lobby to see if I missed him, okay?"

"I'll go with you."

"No," Nick practically shouted and saw Gibson flinch. "You stay here in case he comes back. I don't want us all wandering around the hotel looking for each other."

"Okay."

"I'll be right back." He stopped himself and put a hand on Gibson's shoulder. "Hey, everything's okay. We probably just missed each other. I'll be right back."

But as soon as the door closed behind him, Nick sprinted

for the elevators. He hadn't asked any desk clerk to call for him. If Brother Sebastian was into playing games like this then Nick hated to see what else he was capable of doing. What the hell did the guy want?

CHAPTER 83

The Embassy Suites
Omaha, Nebraska

Keller knew Timmy Hamilton didn't recognize him at all. Four years of living in the rain forest had given him a weathered disguise he didn't even expect.

Keller had made the phone call to their room all the while watching Nick Morrelli fill his arms with junk from the gift shop. When Timmy got to the lobby he greeted the boy, telling him that he was working with the Omaha Police Department. It wasn't a lie. After all, he was working with the department. However, the boy seemed to misunderstand, perhaps thinking he was a plainclothes detective, especially after Keller showed him Detective Kasab's badge. The young detective really should have been more careful earlier when he left his jacket over a chair while he used the restroom in Keller's hotel room.

Besides, it was better for Timmy if he didn't know the truth. Even though the boy had betrayed him, he would make this as painless as possible. It had become a necessity, unfortunately, to take care of such things in order to survive. But

some missions were worth the collateral damage that occurred along the way.

He told Timmy that he had already talked to his uncle,
Nick Morrelli, in the gift shop, and that they agreed to meet
in a suite the police department had reserved. That his uncle
had gone back up to their room to get Timmy and his friend.

"But he had the desk clerk already call me to come down
and help him carry stuff," Timmy said, hanging back, looking a bit suspicious but clearly not wanting to upset a police
detective.

Keller shrugged as if he didn't know anything about it.
"That must have been before I talked to him." Then to pretend that he was just as confused, he added, "I wondered why
you came down to the lobby alone."

"Couldn't we just wait for my uncle down here?" Timmy
asked.

"We agreed to meet in the suite. I don't think he's coming
back down here." Again, for good measure, he added, "Do you
want to call him?"

Just the offer seemed to satisfy the boy, and he shook his head.

He led him back to his suite. At one point he even let the
boy go first, past a housekeeping cart, and he slipped Detective Kasab's badge between the piles of towels. All the while
he kept reassuring the boy that they would talk about everything once his uncle and friend arrived.

At the door to the suite when Timmy seemed to hesitate,
Keller told him that he could wait in the hall if he wanted. But
as he opened the door he added that they needed to be careful because earlier he had seen someone following them. It
was enough to draw Timmy into the room and looking over
his shoulder instead of looking or expecting any danger from
inside. It was as if Timmy had finally accepted him as an ally.

All he had ever tried to do was help Timmy. All of the boys,
he had only wanted to help them, save them from the abuse
he believed they were suffering at home. At the time, Timmy
had claimed he bruised easily, but wasn't that what they all

said to cover up for their parents? Timmy looked okay now, a bit scrawny but healthy. Although from his own experience he knew the mental scars never healed. Perhaps that was true for Timmy, too.

"You can sit down if you want," he told Timmy.

"No, that's okay. I'll wait until Uncle Nick and Gibson get here."

The boy remained standing, watching the door and fidgeting, shifting from one foot to the other. Keller hated fidgeting.

That's when the phone rang as if on perfect cue.

"Hello?" he said, making it sound like he wasn't expecting the call.

"Good evening, Mr. Keller. This is the front desk calling just as you requested."

"Yes, Timmy's here with me. Where did you say you were?" He glanced at Timmy still standing by the door. He was far enough away he would never hear the desk clerk on the other end.

"The front desk, sir," the caller repeated.

"How long will that take?"

"Excuse me? How long will what take?"

Keller ignored the poor clerk's confusion. "Well, okay. We'll wait here for you."

"I'm sorry, sir, but I have no idea what—"

He hung up on him in midsentence, finished and pleased with his side of the conversation. Then to Timmy he said, "They're going to be a few minutes late. Something your uncle has to take care of."

He needed to come up with something, anything that would relax the boy, that would stop his goddamn fidgeting.

"In the meantime, why don't you help yourself to the minibar."

That got his attention.

"Really? Are you sure?"

"Oh yeah, go ahead. Grab me a Coke, too."

That was it. Evidently sharing his minibar was like opening a whole new avenue of trust. Suddenly Timmy was grinning and down on his knees, opening the fridge and evaluating the treasure inside.

Yes, this would be easy. Almost too easy.

CHAPTER 84

Washington, D.C.

In her mind Gwen tried to assess her escape route. Her instincts told her to make a mad dash. What was she waiting for? Why did she dare try and talk sense into him? Was that even possible? The last time she had been in a room with a madman, Eric Pratt had attempted to drive a freshly sharpened lead pencil into her throat.

This was different. There was no uniformed officer right outside the door ready to come running to her rescue. R. J. Tully wouldn't be racing in to protect her either. Not this time. She'd never make it to the door let alone the hallway or the elevator without Campion overpowering her. Her only available weapon was talk. She needed to control him with her voice and her words. She glanced around the room one more time in search of anything else. No, there wasn't anything else. At least not until she settled him down. Maybe then she had a chance of catching him off guard.

James Campion's rage came in bursts then quieted almost as quickly. He stood between Gwen and the doorway, quiet now but glaring at her with a new distrust that she was attempting to dismantle. She had to convince him she was on his side, that she wasn't the enemy.

"I'm on your side, James. Father Paul Conley abused you in a way no boy should experience. He deserved to be punished," she said, stopping herself from adding that ripping his head off and placing it on his own altar may have been a bit much. She needed to win his trust. He needed to believe she understood. "He won't be able to hurt any more boys ever again."

"That's right," he said, nodding. "Playing the game and pretending to kill him wasn't enough. It didn't stop him."

"But, James, what about the others?"

"The others? The other priests?"

"No, the young women. There were four of them, weren't there? Tell me about them. Why did you hurt them?"

"Oh, you mean the whores."

"Excuse me?"

"I met them over the Internet. We talked, got to know each other. You told me that I needed to try to have normal relationships with women. Remember? You told me." He was getting anxious again.

"Yes, that's right. I did tell you that." And she had.

It had been a major concern to him that he couldn't have an ordinary relationship with a woman. She remembered their conversations. She knew his abuse had left him with an immature attitude about sex. He always seemed anxious and concerned about it but never angry. He had talked about it all so calmly. How he wanted to take it slow and get to know and trust a woman before it turned to sex. It was the sex that seemed to worry him, to almost frighten him. Of course it did. It all made sense to her now even before he started to explain.

"We would talk on the Internet. It was comfortable, enjoyable." Campion's eyes were somewhere else as if remembering. This was good. Get his mind on something else so she would be able to catch him off guard.

"You could get to know each other," Gwen encouraged him, "without the pressure of going out on a date."

"That's right. It was nice," he said, almost like a teenage boy. "We would talk about computer games and movies and stuff in the news. But then they would want to meet me." His forehead creased with worry and his jaw became so taut she could see he was clenching his teeth. "That would have been okay, too, except that they always wanted to…go somewhere. To be alone with me. And by alone they always meant…you know," and he looked to her for help.

"They wanted to be more intimate with you?"

"They wanted sex," he hissed at her and his whole face seemed to turn a shade darker.

What was wrong with her? She was making him angry again, when she needed to keep him calm. She needed to make him believe she was on his side. That she agreed with him. He needed to consider her an ally. And yet there was one question that could not go unanswered.

"What about Dena?"

"Who?" He looked at her as though she had awakened him.

"Dena Wayne. My assistant?" Could she still pretend to be on his side if he called Dena a whore?

"I thought she'd be different. She was actually nice to me. I liked her a lot. We went out and had fun. We talked. But then, no matter how much I thought I wanted it… I kept seeing *his* face. Every goddamn time. I couldn't do it without seeing him and smelling him and feeling him. I wanted to rip off his head. I wanted to take my bare hands and rip his fucking head off. And I did. Each time I killed one of them I was really killing him. But then I realized…" His eyes met hers. They could go from angry and mad to calm and pathetic so quickly. "I left you her earring ahead of time. I thought you'd stop me."

"I…I didn't recognize it," Gwen said and her insides felt as if liquid ice had just been injected into her. He had meant for it to be a call to stop him and she hadn't even recognized the earring as Dena's.

Campion didn't seem to hear her and continued, "The notes and even a map—I sent you all of it. I thought you'd help me. But you didn't. You couldn't help me."

She had backed up against her desk and her hands reached behind her, feeling, searching for anything to use as a weapon since it was becoming obvious that her words, that her voice was not enough. But she had just slid anything and everything into her leather briefcase moments before he arrived. It sat on the chair next to the desk.

"I can help you, James," she lied, not having a clue what to even offer. "We can go over everything." She reached for her briefcase as if there was something in it that could help.

"No, goddamn it!"

His voice slammed her back against her desk again as if he had struck her with his fist, and Gwen pulled the briefcase to her chest like a shield, wrapping her arms around it tightly. It was closed, damn it. The locks snapped shut, making it impossible for her to just slip a hand inside.

"No, you can't," he said. "But I can." He pulled out a small revolver from his pocket. He held it out and pointed it directly at her.

Her heart hammered at her rib cage. Almost instantly, her breathing came in labored gasps. And her palms were slick with sweat.

"James, where did you get a gun?" It hadn't been more than a whisper and still it had been an effort. It was too late to worry about showing fear. But how could he have a gun? None of his victims had been shot. Racine had said strangled. But then how would they know for sure? All the torsos were missing. "James, put the gun down." If she said please would it matter? If she screamed would anyone hear her?

"This feels good," Campion said, waving it around. "This…this can help. I bought it a few days ago. I wanted to use this with Father Paul, but I couldn't figure out a way to get it on the plane." He was smiling now. And calm. Way too calm. His hand didn't shake in the least as he held it stretched out in front of him. "It feels so good. Better than any of our sessions. Makes me feel strong. Yes, I wanted to see the fear in his eyes. But I got something better. I got to hear his last breath. His very last breath as I strangled the life out of that bastard."

Then he stopped and looked as if he was listening for something. Gwen listened, too, hoping it had been the elevator. Maybe it was someone in the hall. She couldn't hear a thing over the pounding of her heart in her ears.

He tilted his head, still listening, and then he smiled again. "The banging. It's gone."

Of course it was gone she wanted to tell him. It was inside her now.

"You shouldn't have made me dredge up all those memories, Dr. Patterson," he said, shaking his head.

She couldn't believe it. He was really going to do this. She couldn't swallow and it hurt to breathe. Her knees threatened to go out from under her. If she fell would he shoot her where she lay? Even his eyes—though they stayed on hers—they had gone somewhere far away. Should she make a run for it? What did she have to lose? Getting shot in the back or between the eyes, what did it matter?

"You didn't fix it," Campion said and Gwen couldn't help thinking how much he sounded like an executioner, *her* executioner. "I gave you all those chances and you couldn't help."

"James, you don't want to do this," she said, but, again, he didn't seem to hear her.

"I forgive you," he told her and then he pulled the trigger.

The pain seemed to blossom, spreading throughout her body. She didn't even remember falling, but from the floor she saw James Campion put the gun in his mouth and fire one more shot. That was the last thing Gwen Patterson saw before everything went black.

CHAPTER 85

M's Pub
Omaha, Nebraska

Maggie had never believed that confession was good for the soul. As far as she was concerned, nothing much came from it, other than wasted time that could be better spent elsewhere. There was no such thing as closure. Everyone had past baggage they carried around, some just a little heavier than others. She had never talked about her mother's drunken binges with anyone other than Gwen. What good did it do to relive those miserable times? Without effort she could easily conjure up the hot, sour smell of whiskey breath from her mother's boyfriends trying to slam her small, twelve-year-old frame into the corner for a kiss or a "quick rub," as one had put it.

Instead of sharing the gruesome details, she simply told Sister Kate, "Let's just say my mother's suitors were not always the most polite of gentlemen."

Sister Kate nodded as if she understood the entire situation from that brief statement. "How old were you?"

"Twelve, thirteen. By the time I was fourteen she finally

made them get hotel rooms. Of course, that wasn't until one of her men friends suggested a threesome."

"Ah, I see," Sister Kate said, but without alarm or surprise. "Which left you all alone?"

"It felt like a blessing at the time," Maggie confided. She didn't need all her years of studying psychology to self-diagnose that being alone as a child and associating it with freedom from harm had certainly overlapped into her adult life.

"Did you ever think," Sister Kate said, "that might be one of the reasons you joined the FBI?"

"What exactly do you mean?" Maggie had no intention of this turning into a shrink session.

"Maybe it's a way for you to be that knight in shining armor who comes to the rescue—the one who never came to your rescue as a child."

Maggie took a sip of her wine when she really wanted a gulp. She was beginning to realize this conversation would take more than one glass of wine unless she could turn it around soon.

"So what about you?" she asked. "You said your grandfather had rescued you from what I believe you said was a particularly difficult situation?"

"I suppose it wasn't all that different from your situation. It was the year I turned eleven. He was a friend who my parents trusted and respected—*revered,* actually, is a better word. They'd invite him one Sunday every month for dinner." As she told Maggie her eyes began to wander across the street again. "My mother always fixed pot roast, with potatoes and those little carrots, because it was his favorite. And after dinner he'd volunteer to take me upstairs to my room, read me a bedtime story and tuck me in even though I told all of them that I was too old for such things. And so once a month for three months he raped me in my own bed."

She looked back at Maggie, checking to see if she still had her attention. Maggie simply stared at her, unable to speak.

"My parents didn't believe me at first," Sister Kate continued. "But there're some things…details, proof that an eleven-year-old girl can't make up." She reached for her wineglass and took a sip. "To this day I still can't look at a pot roast," she said, smiling.

"That's one thing that always amazes me," Maggie said. "The different ways in which each of us deals with the evil we've experienced. Most serial killers have been abused at some point during their childhood. They end up butchering innocent people, usually at random, sometimes using their abuse as an excuse or a justification. But you turned around and gave your life to the church."

"And you the FBI," Sister Kate followed up. "I guess we both wanted to be knights in shining armor."

CHAPTER 86

The Embassy Suites
Omaha, Nebraska

Nick tried not to panic. It wouldn't do any good to panic. And yet, he couldn't stop thinking that it was happening all over again just like four years ago.

No, that wasn't right, that wasn't fair. Timmy was older now. And he wouldn't go with just anyone. But what if someone had grabbed him? Brother Sebastian was a lot taller and bigger than Timmy. Why hadn't he taught the boy some self-defense stuff? Yeah right, how could he? How could he teach Timmy anything from thirteen hundred miles away in Boston. Nick shook his head. It wouldn't help to beat himself up with guilt.

He had asked the desk clerk, on the off chance that someone from the hotel had called his suite. No such luck. The clerk had been there since three and hadn't taken any outside calls for a Nick Morrelli. Although the clerk thought he remembered putting through a room-to-room call to a Morrelli. That didn't make sense. Something wasn't adding up.

He checked everywhere—the swimming pool, the fitness

center, the terrace, even the restaurant and lounge. He felt like a parent looking for his toddler and asking everyone he saw.

He walked each floor's hallway and asked housekeepers coming in and out of rooms. Those who spoke no English just shrugged. Those who spoke English also shrugged.

Finally after what felt like several hours but was, in fact, not even one hour, he returned to the suite.

"Did he call?" he asked Gibson as soon as he came in the door.

"No. You didn't see him?" Gibson sat on the edge of one bed, rocking back and forth.

"Nobody's seen him. And I've been all over this place."

Nick started pacing but stopped at the window and looked out over the Old Market. He was the adult. He was supposed to keep them both calm but all Nick could think about was four years ago when Timmy had been kidnapped by a madman and they had almost lost him for good. Where the hell could he be? Should he call Christine? No. It was too soon to call Christine. He had to be around here. He couldn't have just disappeared into thin air.

"Do you think he would have gone over to the Old Market?" Nick asked. "You know, just to pick something up or out of curiosity?"

Gibson shrugged and Nick looked out at the small shops across the street, checking out anyone wearing orange or red.

"Mr. Morrelli," Gibson said and Nick didn't know what to tell the kid. He let out a sigh before he turned around to look at him, expecting him to have questions.

"I think there's something I'd better show you," Gibson said and pulled out of his backpack what looked like a leather portfolio.

CHAPTER 87

The Embassy Suites
Omaha, Nebraska

Maggie had barely returned to her suite when there was a knock at the door. It was Nick Morrelli, only this time his hair was tousled and his eyes had a wild, almost panicked look. He had a teenage boy with him, standing back out of the way, but Maggie knew he wasn't Timmy.

"I'm sorry to bother you, Maggie, but I really need your help." Nick couldn't seem to stand still, walking back and forth outside her door and constantly glancing down the hallway. The boy seemed to repeat Nick's actions though he stood still, shifting his weight from one foot to the other, perhaps prepared to run if necessary.

"What's wrong? Did something happen?"

"I don't know what to do. Timmy's disappeared."

"What do you mean disappeared?"

"Before...when I was down in the gift shop...some guy...I'm not sure who. He called our suite. Gibson says the guy told Timmy—"

"Wait a minute," she interrupted. "Timmy was here with you at the hotel?"

"Yeah. I asked him and Gibson to spend the night. But when I was getting junk food in the gift shop some guy called. Gibson said he claimed he was the desk clerk and told Timmy I needed him to meet me in the lobby."

Maggie immediately thought of Keller as Nick continued his explanation.

"But you see, earlier today there was this guy—" He stopped, looked both ways again and leaned closer, lowering his voice. "A guy from the archdiocese office, a Brother Sebastian looking for Timmy and Gibson. I think he may have taken Timmy somewhere."

"The archdiocese office? Why would someone from the archdiocese take Timmy?" Nick wasn't making any sense.

"The boys have something the archbishop might want," he whispered.

She looked at the boy, Gibson, and he met her eyes briefly before he looked away and stared at his scuffed tennis shoes.

"It's a very long story," Nick told her, glancing back at Gibson. "I'm not sure I understand it all. They've been playing some sort of Internet game where they had to submit the name of a priest." He shook his head and rubbed his eyes. "It all sounds crazy."

"It's not crazy," she said with a sinking feeling. "And Timmy submitted Father Michael Keller's name."

Nick stopped and stared at her. Gibson did, too. "How did you know?"

"I don't have time to explain. He's here," she told them and closed the door to her suite, joining them in the hallway.

"Who's here?"

"Keller." She wanted to kick herself because she was the one who'd kept forcing Keller to think about who may have submitted his name. How could she be so stupid?

"Why the hell is Father Keller back in Omaha?" He sounded angry but Maggie recognized it as panic.

"You need to call Detective Pakula," she told him as she tucked her hand inside her jacket, readjusting her shoulder holster. Gibson's eyes grew wide when he saw the gun. Nick didn't move. "Go back to your room, Nick, and call Detective Pakula."

"You think he has Timmy, don't you?"

It didn't help matters to lie to him. "Yes, I do."

"And you know exactly what room he's in?"

This time she hesitated before she said, "Yes, I do."

"Then let's go," and he started down the hallway.

"You're not a law enforcement officer anymore, Nick," she said to his back and didn't follow.

"But I'm his uncle. And you're wasting time."

"No, you're wasting time by arguing with me."

"Gibson can call Pakula, right, buddy? You don't mind, do you?" Nick put his hand on the boy's shoulder as if only now realizing that he had someone else to worry about besides Timmy.

"You're not coming with me, Nick. And the longer you argue with me the longer Timmy is with Keller."

"Damn it, Maggie." He turned and slammed the same hand that had been on Gibson's shoulder against the hallway wall. At the end of the hall a woman opened her hotel-room door, peeked out and shut the door. "Okay," he finally said. "You win."

She left them there, walking away quickly and not glancing back. She expected footsteps and was relieved when she heard a door open and close. But she knew Nick might try to follow her. She turned the corner to the elevators but ducked into the stairwell instead, gently closing the door behind her. She wouldn't be able to get back onto any of the floors and need to go all the way down to the lobby, but at least Nick wouldn't be able to race to the elevator and watch at which floor it let her off.

She'd go down to the lobby and take a different elevator to the fourth floor. And hopefully when she got to Keller's room it wouldn't be too late.

CHAPTER 88

The Embassy Suites
Omaha, Nebraska

Father Michael Keller listened to Timmy talk about the Explorers' Summer Program he was taking. He had gone into great detail describing the swords and ceremonial cups and musical instruments his new teacher had on display in her classroom. He told Timmy what he knew about the Crusades and the early Catholic Church's attempt to spread Christianity even if it meant slaughtering thousands.

They talked about the Black Plague and the Knights Templar. They drank three-dollar Cokes from the minibar until there were none left and they devoured a can of Pringles, several candy bars and a jar of Gummi Bears.

Keller wasn't sure how much time had passed. It didn't matter. The digitalis had relieved him of most of his symptoms, though he still felt a bit feverish. The throbbing hadn't begun. The boy had begun to trust him. He had made a phone call to his own room's voice-messaging service, and while Timmy believed Keller was talking to his uncle Nick, he actually talked over the menu telling him how to access his voice mail. As long as Timmy believed he was in contact with his uncle he didn't seem to question the delay.

A loud knock on the door startled both of them.

Keller thought it might be someone from the hotel, perhaps bringing the extra towels he had requested when he knew he'd be inviting Timmy back to his suite, when he knew there would be a bit of a mess to clean up. He checked the peephole but no one was there. He started to open the door, when it swung open, slamming into his nose and knocking him back against the wall.

He couldn't see through the blur and grabbed his nose, his hand filling with blood. The sting spiderwebbed across his face. Someone shoved him into the wall and he felt the gun muzzle against his temple just as he heard the door slam shut.

"Don't move, you bastard," came a woman's voice he quickly identified. "I'd like nothing better than to blow your brains all over this room."

"Hello, Agent O'Dell." He tried to sound calm but the blood was trickling down his throat now. He hated tasting his own blood. It started to panic him, reminding him too much of his stepfather.

"Hey, what's going on?" He heard Timmy yell from the other side of the room.

"Stay over there, Timmy," she said. "Do you remember me? Maggie O'Dell."

"Yeah, I remember. I saw you at school the other day."

"You need to stay over there, Timmy," she repeated and tightened her grip on Keller's arm. Only then did the pain make him realize she had twisted his left arm up against his back.

"You can relax, Agent O'Dell," he said, hating the catch in his voice telegraphing his fear. Now that his vision was no longer blurred, he noticed the blood running between his fingers and down his arm. The sight of his own blood made him nauseous and a bit light-headed.

"Like hell I will," she hissed in his ear and the muzzle pressed farther into his skull.

"But Agent O'Dell," Timmy said, "I don't understand. He's with the Omaha police."

"Is that what he told you?"

"The boy misunderstood," Keller tried to explain, despite his arm being yanked even higher up his back. He could feel the texture of the cheap wallpaper scrape against his cheek, and again, a memory flooded back to him of his stepfather shoving him against another wall, all those years ago. It made him angry. But it also scared him. "I only said that I was working with the Omaha Police Department." He spit out blood but more trickled down his throat and the taste almost made him gag.

"Did he hurt you, Timmy?"

"Hurt me?"

"Are you okay?"

"I didn't hurt the boy."

"Shut up! I'm not asking you." O'Dell shoved the gun muzzle so hard against his temple he could taste metal, or was it his blood that now tasted like metal?

"Timmy, did he hurt you?"

"I'm okay. We just talked and stuff."

"You what?"

Her surprise at this made Keller smile, despite the pain shooting up between his eyes. He was sure she had broken his nose.

"We talked. About knights and the Crusades and stuff. We just talked."

Keller wished he could see O'Dell's face. She had probably hoped to catch him doing something worthy of her shooting him between the eyes. So that when the others showed up — because, of course, the fearless Margaret O'Dell had not waited for backup once again—she'd have to tell them that it was necessary. That she had to shoot him, had to unload every single one of her bullets into his chest or else he'd hurt the poor boy.

"Timmy, you still don't recognize him, do you?"

There was silence and now he could hear her breathing. She was breathing too hard to be in control.

"It's Father Keller," she said.

And she yanked him away from the wall for Timmy to see his face. The boy now looked at him like he was some monster. Keller saw him stepping back even farther into the room before she smashed his face into the wall again. This time he heard the gun make some weird click when she pressed it into his temple.

"What are you doing, Agent O'Dell?"

"What I should have done back in that tunnel. You remember that dark hole under the cemetery? The one where you shoved your fillet knife into my side."

"You're wrong. You don't know what you're talking about. I think you should—"

"Maybe if I had, little boys like Arturo would still be alive. How many others have there been, Keller?"

"You can't do this. You're an FBI agent." He didn't recognize his own voice, a high-pitched whine, almost a cry.

"And my job as an FBI agent is to hunt down and destroy evil."

Was she possessed? He wanted to turn and look at her, but he was afraid the slightest move and she might use it as an excuse to pull the trigger. His stomach ached. His face throbbed and he tried to keep from sobbing or the blood running down his throat would choke him.

Someone banged on the door and his heart skipped a beat. O'Dell, however, didn't seem to flinch. Her hold remained steady.

"Police," someone called from the other side of the door. "Open up."

Keller held his breath. O'Dell didn't move. Not an inch. It felt like the muzzle was making a hole in the side of his head.

"O'Dell?" the voice called. "It's Pakula. Are you okay?"

Silence except for her heavy breathing and an annoying whining sound. Oh God, the whine was coming from deep inside his throat.

"O'Dell? Are you in there? Are you okay?"

"I'm fine," she finally said and adjusted her hold on his arm.

"I'm coming in."

There was a pause and then Keller saw the door begin opening slowly. He lifted his face away from the wall only to have it shoved back, this time knocking the side of his head. But he could see Detective Pakula's alarm before the detective was able to disguise it.

"Whadya doing, O'Dell?"

"What I should have done four years ago."

"Come on, O'Dell." He saw Pakula look around them. "It looks like the kid is okay."

"But he wouldn't have been if I hadn't gotten here."

"You okay, son?" Pakula called out to Timmy.

"Yeah." But Keller noticed the boy's voice wasn't very convincing, weak and small.

"I didn't do anything to him. We just talked." Keller tried to defend himself.

"If he's done something, we'll take care of him," Detective Pakula told her, but she still didn't ease up. "Come on, O'Dell."

Keller could see that the detective was close enough to reach out and touch her, take the gun away. Why didn't he? He could stop her. He needed to stop her.

"Timmy," she said without flinching. "Go with Detective Pakula."

Keller didn't hear the boy move.

This time she yelled, "Now!" And he heard Timmy rush out, squeezing past them.

"I didn't hurt him," Keller pleaded. He knew exactly why she was making the boy leave. She didn't want him to see what she was going to do. She didn't want him to have nightmares.

"O'Dell," Detective Pakula said, checking to make sure the boy was safe in the hallway. Keller could see the detective was becoming anxious. "Come on. You don't want to do this."

Keller started whining again, sobs with chokes. Then all of a sudden he was free.

O'Dell pulled the gun away. She dropped his arm. He stayed pressed against the wall, not trusting her. He didn't move until she pushed past Detective Pakula. And even then he shut his eyes and concentrated on breathing. He thought he heard the door close. And when he opened his eyes again, he was alone.

Keller locked the door's dead bolt and made his way to the bathroom. He was shocked by the bloody, sweaty face that looked back at him. His nose wasn't broken, despite all the blood. He pulled off his sweat-drenched clothes and washed himself, rinsing his mouth and then standing under the showerhead, letting the warm water run over his pain. By the time he slid into a fresh pair of boxers he was feeling better. He had already begun to wipe the episode from his mind.

He wandered back to the bed where his suitcase lay, where he had left it earlier, ready for his evening before his unexpected visitor. He opened the suitcase and found his wooden box on top. He lifted the lid off the box and pushed aside the newspaper articles, the small tin of oil and the vial of ether. He ran his fingers over Arturo's small underpants and then lifted several more pairs until he saw the fillet knife safely tucked underneath. With a heavy sigh he covered it again and closed the lid of the wooden box.

CHAPTER 89

The Embassy Suites
Omaha, Nebraska

Maggie stared at the glow-in-the-dark alarm clock—three o'clock in the morning. She pulled the covers up and turned onto her other side. She should give up. She should have known she would never be able to sleep. She was too keyed up despite the anticlimactic end to the evening. She flopped onto her back and stared at the ceiling. Timmy was safe. Nick was happy and grateful. Christine had a Pulitzer Prize-winning story. And Father Michael Keller was free.

She had hoped that Timmy's adding Keller's name to the list meant the boy had remembered something new, anything that would connect Keller to his kidnapping four years ago. But what Timmy remembered were only small details. They were enough to solidify her and Christine's belief that Keller was, indeed, Timmy's kidnapper four years ago, but not enough to arrest Keller as a suspect then or now. And tonight even Timmy said that he may have misunderstood Keller when he told him he was working with the Omaha Police Department. Although the boy insisted Keller had shown him a police badge, it wasn't enough for Pakula to rally for a search warrant.

So in a couple of days she would have no choice but to live up to her end of the bargain and allow Keller to leave, allow him to crawl back into the rain forest somewhere in South America. The problem was she remained convinced, now more than ever, that he was still killing little boys, and no matter what Detective Pakula said, she knew he would have killed Timmy had she not intervened.

Only now did Maggie realize how grateful she should be to Pakula, not for talking her down from blowing away Keller—she still almost wished he hadn't intervened—but later for handling it like it wasn't worth discussing. After they had left Timmy with Christine, Nick and Gibson, Pakula walked her back to her suite. She had expected a lecture or at least a scolding. Instead, he told her that if he believed as strongly as she did that Keller was still killing little boys, someone may have had to pull him off the bastard, too. Then he reminded her that they still didn't have anything to go on. That even Timmy's description about the night's events didn't indicate that Keller had committed any crimes. Timmy had gone with him willingly and despite whatever story Keller may have made up, he hadn't harmed the boy.

Pakula seemed more interested in Brother Sebastian's threats and his possible role—if any—in the computer game the boys had been playing. Maggie could understand if Pakula was thinking Brother Sebastian might be The Sin Eater. Although according to Timmy and Gibson, the master of their game—The Sin Eater—had been trying to protect them, not hurt them. Even their invitations to play the game had come after they had been surfing the Net, checking out Web sites and chatrooms that might help them if they were being abused by a priest. The invitation promised help. All they had to do was submit the name of their abuser. They believed the name was submitted to become a character in the game, a character that they could pretend to execute. They never ever dreamed that someone would actually execute the real priests.

Maggie had left several messages for Racine and Gwen. She was anxious to test out her theory and needed to know if Gwen's patient could possibly be playing the game, too. It seemed a bit far-fetched, but Father Paul Conley's death didn't fit The Sin Eater's M.O. Maggie wondered if the D.C. killer could have taken the game into his own hands. It was possible that if he was playing the game and had read about or heard about the other priests being killed, he may have decided to execute his own submitted priest. Whatever the connection, there was definitely one. Maggie didn't believe in coincidences.

She rolled over onto her stomach, burying her face in the pillow with an irritated sigh. And there was Nick Morrelli. He had hugged her when she brought back Timmy. She didn't want to remember how good his arms felt around her. Besides, he was getting married in a month.

Her cell phone startled her, and she practically jumped out of bed. She stumbled trying to find her way in the dim light from the bathroom. When she stayed in hotels she always kept the bathroom light on and the door half closed to provide a night-light. Finally she found the phone where she had left it in her jacket pocket.

"Maggie O'Dell."

"O'Dell, it's Racine."

"Do you have any idea what time it is?" Actually Maggie was glad to have the detective finally getting back to her.

"Look, O'Dell, I'm not great at delivering bad news, so give me a break. Okay?"

"What happened? Is Gwen all right?" Racine didn't answer. She was quiet, too quiet. It was Gwen. Maggie found the edge of the bed with her left hand, dropping down onto it, feeling the lead weight in the pit of her stomach.

"She's not all right," Racine finally said in a soft conciliatory voice. "One of her patients shot her last night."

"Oh my God."

"Then he shot himself."

Seconds then minutes ticked by as Maggie tried to breathe and stop shaking. Suddenly she was freezing cold again.

"She's still in surgery," Racine said and for a moment Maggie thought she hadn't heard her correctly.

"She's alive?"

"She's very lucky. Her briefcase slowed the bullet down. Otherwise it might have gone through her heart."

"Is she going to be okay?"

"Yes, I think so. She's lost a lot of blood, but the doctors sound pretty positive."

Maggie wiped at her tears and took a deep breath.

"This patient," Racine continued, "his name was James Campion. We're pretty sure he killed that priest up in Boston. And probably the four women here in D.C. We're checking more prints to confirm. Which means the doc was right. It was one of her patients. She just guessed wrong as to which one."

But Maggie couldn't listen, couldn't concentrate on anything else other than Gwen.

"Hey, Racine," Maggie said, relieved enough to lie back on the bed. "You're right. You aren't very good at delivering bad news. You scared the crap out of me."

"I think I'll consider us even, O'Dell, because your friend scared the fuck out of me."

CHAPTER 90

Friday, July 9
Omaha Archdiocese Office

Tommy Pakula knew he was enjoying this just a little too much. He sat in the same hardback chair across from Archbishop Armstrong's desk and he was waiting for him, again. But this time he didn't mind. He was finally putting to rest another chapter of the toughest case in his career. Oh sure, there was more to figure out, but it was looking like James Campion may have been their priest killer. In the last several weeks his job had taken him to Saint Louis and Tallahassee, Florida. From Saint Louis he could have easily driven to Columbia and Omaha. And Pensacola was only about a three- or four-hour drive from Tallahassee.

Maybe he wanted it to be Campion so badly that he was willing to overlook Minneapolis. He had Carmichael checking to see if there could be a connection between Campion and Brother Sebastian. If the two men might know each other. He hadn't ruled out O'Dell's hunch that there may have been two killers working together. Sebastian could easily have

taken care of Monsignor O'Sullivan in Omaha and Daniel Ellison in Minneapolis while Campion killed the other three.

Something still nagged at him, though. Agent O'Dell
agreed that James Campion could have been the killer after
discovering that Father Paul Conley had raped Campion as a
young altar boy. That, according to O'Dell, would explain his
rage during that murder. Unfortunately with Campion gone
there were some things they might never know.

In the back of his mind he still didn't let Father Tony Gallagher off the hook. Nor had Carmichael. She had reminded
him again before he left the station that Father Tony's past
experience as a victims' rights advocate fit O'Dell's profile
of The Sin Eater, a tragic hero killing and taking on the sins
of the boys that the system may have failed to previously win
justice for. Carmichael also pointed out that Father Tony
would have had access to lists of victims as well as lists of
the abusing priests.

The side door opened, interrupting his analysis. The archbishop strolled in, nodding at him as he took his place behind
the desk.

"Mr. Pakula," he said, still substituting mister for detective,
"I understand you have some important information on Monsignor O'Sullivan's case. Is it possible you already have a suspect?"

"Possibly." Pakula sat back. The uncomfortable chair made
his back ache but he didn't mind. He glanced at his watch.
"We're picking up one of our suspects right about now for
questioning." And he imagined Kasab and Carmichael es-
corting Brother Sebastian to the station.

"I'm glad to hear that," the archbishop said, folding his
hands together on the desk's surface and sitting forward in his
ridiculously large throne. "Perhaps we can finally put all of
this behind us."

"Well, I'm not too sure it'll be any time soon."

"Of course not," Archbishop Armstrong agreed. "I realize
these things take some time with all the details and a trial. I

was simply speaking rhetorically about all of us having some closure."

"I'm sure there're quite a few people who'd be glad to hear that you're anxious and willing to provide some much-needed closure."

"Excuse me?"

Pakula reached down to his feet, alongside the chair leg, and brought up the leather portfolio, tossing it on top of the archbishop's pristine desktop.

"We finally found this," Pakula told him and watched all the color leave the man's face.

"Well, my goodness. Is that—"

"Monsignor O'Sullivan's leather portfolio stashed full of interesting reports and memos and letters and therapists' analyses. Quite interesting stuff. I can see why you wanted him to deliver it personally to the Vatican for safe storage. Yeah, it would be against the law to destroy all these, but since the Vatican has diplomatic immunity it would have made sense to just go ahead and store them over there. Isn't that right, Archbishop?"

"I have no idea what you think you found, Mr. Pakula," he told him, sitting forward again and regaining his composure much too quickly. "I would think you should know by now that it would be better to close this case once and for all, especially now that poor Monsignor O'Sullivan isn't here to defend himself."

"You're right about that." Pakula stood, ready to leave and the archbishop looked surprised, glancing back at the portfolio as if ready to snatch it if Pakula insisted on taking it back. "There's not much we can do in the poor monsignor's case. Unfortunately it won't come to an end very soon. You'll never guess who ended up with this old portfolio and handed it in to me." He waited for the archbishop to squirm just a little before he said, "Of all the people to get their hands on it, wouldn't you know it'd be a reporter."

And there it was—the look, the dropped jaw, the wide eyes.

That was the look Pakula had been waiting for. He turned to leave, now satisfied, but stopped and glanced back.

"Oh and by the way, I thought you might be interested to know that Creighton University called, apologizing that a huge mistake had been made regarding my daughter's scholarship. Seems a letter went out without their approval." He shook his head and said, "Wonder how that could have happened."

He didn't need an answer nor did he expect one. He had gotten more than he had come for. He left the archbishop with the coveted leather portfolio stashed with copies of incriminating documents. All of the originals were currently on their way to the Douglas County prosecutor's office.

CHAPTER 91

The Omaha World Herald
Downtown Omaha

Nick Morrelli watched his sister boss around the newspaper's top photographer and the petite blonde who wrote the front-page headlines. When she headed back in his direction he caught her smiling. She was definitely in her element, or as Timmy and Gibson would say, her zone.

"I can't believe you don't write your own headlines," he said to her, feigning disgust.

"I've told you that before," she said, swatting him on the arm. "You just don't remember anything I tell you."

"Maybe I'll listen better after you win the Pulitzer."

"Yeah, right," she said, but he could see her smile again. She liked that idea even if she knew it was a stretch.

"What time are we picking up the guys for lunch?"

She checked her watch. "They get out of Explorers early today. Let me finish up one more thing, then we can leave." She pulled several pages out of a folder and started scratching notes in the margins.

"Maybe we shouldn't be rewarding them with things like lunch."

She glanced up and smiled but continued writing. She didn't think he was serious.

"I'm not joking," Nick said and this time he waited for her eyes and for her full attention. "The other night scared the hell out of me. It was like four years ago all over again."

"But he's okay. And I really can't think of the what-ifs."

"I've been thinking maybe I should try to spend more time with him. You know, be there more often for him."

"Yeah, right." She laughed and went back to her notes. "I don't think Jill will appreciate you flying from Boston to Omaha all the time just to see Timmy."

"If I were to stick around here I wouldn't need to fly."

"Jill's not going to move back here, Nicky. I know your Jill Campbell. She might be having a lot of fun with her old girlfriends but that's wedding-preparation fun. Afterward she's going to be ready to get back to her life and her life is being a high-powered attorney in Boston at Foster, Campbell and whoever that other bigwig lawyer is."

"McDermont," Nick said, filling in the blank.

Suddenly she looked up at him as if it only now hit her. "Oh geez, are you calling off the wedding?"

"I didn't say that."

"But that's what you're thinking?"

"I didn't say that, either."

"Is it because of Maggie?"

"Christine, all I said—" and he put up his hands in mock surrender "—was that maybe I should spend more time with my only nephew."

But now she was smiling at him. No, not smiling, grinning.

"Well, since you've definitely convinced me that it won't matter one way or another whether I tell you this or not, I'm gonna go ahead and tell you." She stood and leaned in close to him, glancing around the noisy newsroom even though no one had been paying attention to their conversation.

And then Christine said to him as though they were back in grade school, "Maggie told me that she didn't dump you. As a matter of fact, little brother, this whole time you've been mooning and feeling sorry for yourself, Maggie O'Dell has been thinking you were the one who dumped her."

Nick felt as if she had dropped a ton of bricks on him.

"Not that it matters who dumped who, right?" she added.

CHAPTER 92

Eppley Airport
Omaha, Nebraska

Cunningham had told Maggie that she didn't need to be there to see Keller off, but she insisted. If she had to keep her end of the bargain and let him go, she wanted to make certain Father Michael Keller got on his plane and left for South America and this time never came back. She considered flying with him to Chicago just to make sure he made his connecting flight. There was a two-hour layover and she didn't trust him. What would stop him, she asked her boss, from just walking away, taking a cab from O'Hare and sneaking off to blend into rural North America instead of South America?

That wasn't her concern, Cunningham had told her. She was to see Keller made his flight. That was it. End of her deal. End of her obligation. He made it sound so easy.

Keller had refused to even get in the same vehicle she was in and accepted the alternative, a ride in an Omaha squad car with a police officer Pakula had assigned for the task. Keller seemed pleased with the escort. And she wished she could slap that smug look off his face. The thought of letting him go made her insides feel like liquid fire. And yet, she stood back and watched him walk down the terminal's ramp to get in line for the security check.

She had done her job. That was it. She didn't need to rub her own nose in it by standing around watching. She had other things to attend to, like Gwen. When she talked to her this morning her friend sounded in good spirits but very weak and vulnerable. She seemed overly concerned about Harvey though Julia Racine appeared to be taking good care of him. Gwen said she was okay about what had happened, but Maggie knew better. She wanted to see for herself and would be leaving for home tomorrow despite the fact that not all the pieces of this case's puzzle fit to her liking.

She turned to leave the terminal and almost bumped into Sister Kate Rosetti.

"Maggie, hi. Are you leaving for home?"

"Tomorrow. Where are you off to?" Maggie almost didn't recognize her. She wore blue jeans, another bright-colored T-shirt that read Pensacola Seafood Festival and tennis shoes. She carried a duffel bag over her shoulder and her short hair was flat today as if she hadn't had time to style it after getting out of the shower. She had to wait for an answer. They were right under a loudspeaker and it blared out instructions about not leaving luggage unattended.

"I have a presentation in Chicago this weekend," Sister Kate finally said when it was all clear.

"That's right. You mentioned it at dinner."

"One more job and that's it."

"You won't miss it?" Maggie asked.

"No, I won't," she said. Then, smiling and placing her hand over her heart like she was preparing for some Girl Scout pledge, she added, "On my grandfather's honor, this is my last job."

"After all your trips, at least you've learned to travel light."

"I wish. I have all my samples in my checked luggage. I don't like to chance getting asked a lot of questions going through security with a couple of thirteenth-century daggers." She laughed and Maggie joined her.

Again the loudspeaker interrupted them: "United flight 1270 for Denver at Gate 29 and United flight 1690 for Chicago at Gate 14 are now boarding."

"That's me. I'd better go." But she didn't move. "It was really a pleasure meeting you, Maggie."

"I enjoyed it, too, and I now know more about daggers than I ever wanted to know."

"You take care of yourself," Sister Kate said, her voice somber and not as jovial as just minutes before. She gave Maggie a one-armed hug to avoid knocking her with her duffel bag.

"You, too."

Maggie watched her show her ID and continue down the terminal ramp to the security checkpoint which had cleared a bit and wasn't as busy. She glanced over her shoulder one last time to wave and Maggie waved back. As Sister Kate continued down the ramp she pulled out a baseball cap from her duffel bag and slung it on. Maggie smiled. She couldn't help thinking that in her blue jeans, T-shirt, tennis shoes and a baseball cap she looked like one of her teenage students. And then it hit Maggie that from the back Sister Kate Rosetti looked so much like a teenage boy.

It came to Maggie in waves. All of it, everything in bits and pieces that by themselves didn't mean anything but all together... The daggers went with her everywhere she traveled. She remembered Sister Kate telling them she had a presentation in Saint Louis the same weekend Father Kincaid had been killed in Columbia. She remembered Pakula's map and the colored pins. Columbia wasn't far from Saint Louis. How difficult would it be to stab Monsignor O'Sullivan here in the men's bathroom at Omaha's Eppley Airport? Then walk right next door into the women's bathroom, clean up, change clothes and place the dagger—the murder weapon—into the luggage she would check. It sounded too simple.

Maggie leaned against a nearby wall, getting out of the passengers' way but needing the extra support if her knees failed to hold her up. Her mind continued to reel. Who better to be the advocate for abused boys than a woman, a nun who may have had to stand by and know about the abuse? Maybe she had even caught Monsignor O'Sullivan with one of the boys at the school.

She remembered Sister Kate's own story of abuse. The man was someone her parents trusted—no, she said revered. Could he have been a priest? That's when Maggie remembered the T-shirt. Sister Kate was from Pensacola, Florida. Was it possible she was the eleven-year-old girl Father Rudy had raped? Is that why he hadn't been on the list? It made sense now. She'd taken care of him for herself. For her own peace of mind. There was no need for him to be on the list.

But what about James Campion? Pakula was hoping to blame him for all the priests' murders. Maggie had never been certain that James Campion was The Sin Eater. It made more sense that Campion was simply playing the Internet game and impatient that The Sin Eater hadn't killed his priest yet. Gwen had told her that Campion kept raging about some game and breaking the rules.

Maggie ran her fingers through her hair. She hadn't gotten much sleep in the last several nights. She wasn't thinking straight. And yet it all seemed crystal clear. She remembered Sister Kate brushing her roommate's dog hair off her blouse the other night at dinner. Monsignor O'Sullivan had dog hair on the back of his polo shirt, possibly a transfer of debris from the killer. Her other roommate just happened to be a computer whiz who had taught Sister Kate to design some of her own programs and possibly an incredible Internet game. She had probably also learned enough from her roommate to know what was necessary to make it impossible for the Omaha Police Department and the FBI to track down a simple e-mail address that belonged to The Sin Eater.

It seemed too fantastic. But it all seemed to fit.

The loudspeaker announced the last boarding call for United 1690 to Chicago. That's when it suddenly occurred to Maggie. United 1690 to Chicago was the flight Father Michael Keller was taking.

Oh, Jesus!

Is that what Sister Kate meant by "one last job"? He was scheduled to have a two-hour layover in Chicago before his connecting flight to Venezuela. Sister Kate's presentation was in Chicago so she'd be getting her checked luggage, the luggage with her choice of daggers.

Maggie glanced at her watch and went searching for and found the nearest departure board. Fifteen minutes left. She had her badge and her weapon and her cell phone. She could stop the flight. It would be messy but she could do it.

Then she stopped. She tried to calm herself. She remembered last night, how badly she wanted to pull the trigger. She reminded herself how Keller's eyes darted off to the left when she confronted him about using past tense when he talked about Arturo. If her instincts were right, he had never stopped killing little boys, nor would he just because she'd smacked him around a little. And deep down, her gut kept telling her he had no intention of returning to South America.

Sister Kate had told her this was her last job and Maggie thought she meant her last presentation. Now she knew the nun was talking about her last hit. But she had said this was the last. No, she had promised on her grandfather's honor.

Maggie glanced at her watch again. Ten minutes. She could still stop the flight. She stood there, leaning against the wall and staring down the ramp, watching passengers come and go. Finally she pushed away from the wall. She hesitated as she looked down the terminal ramp to the boarding gates. Then Maggie O'Dell turned and walked in the other direction.

CHAPTER 93

Aboard United Flight 1690

Father Michael Keller waited patiently for the elderly woman to move out of the aisle. He had decided to go to the restroom at the last minute and now was one of the last passengers to board the airplane. He worried that the digitalis might not have been strong enough and that he would suffer a relapse. He dreaded another excruciating long flight like before, although this one would be much shorter.

He regretted coming so close to taking care of Timmy and having to abort that mission. His nose was still sore and a bit swollen, another reminder that he needed to be more careful in the future.

Finally the elderly woman took her seat and he could move forward. He searched the seat numbers at the top: seven, eight, nine, ten…here he was in 11B, a middle seat. He kept telling himself it was just to Chicago. A short hour-long flight. And thankfully it looked as if he was between two small-framed women and not a massive buffalo of a man like on the flight here.

He shoved his carry-on into the overhead bin.

"Excuse me, I'm in 11B," he told the woman on the aisle.

"Oh sure," she said, batting her long blond hair out of her eyes before unbuckling her seat belt. She jumped up to move out into the aisle and let him in.

"Thank you."

They both sat down and he had barely buckled his seat belt when the woman on his other side turned from the window.

"Is Chicago your final destination?" she asked.

"Yes." He answered without hesitating, no longer feeling the need to lie. "And you?"

She nodded.

"Business or pleasure?" Keller added.

"Strictly business. By the way, my name's Kate Rosetti," she said.